"**I**T'S even money that the same SS brass who saw Lutz will see us."

"Correct," said Benutti. "But that's only the start of the battle. We're going to be grilled like trout. The going-over we got in Salzburg will seem like Sunday at the zoo by comparison, and we still have to find out where Lutz went after Rome."

Caradoc was shaking his head. "You make it sound like a picnic. If we put one foot out of place, we'll all be found floating face down in the Tiber."

"Yeah, you're right. You know, I'm beginning to wonder why I'm here, though maybe a line I remember from a movie sums it up."

" 'It is a far, far better thing that I do than I have ever done?' " suggested O'Keefe.

"No. More on the lines of 'Here's another fine mess you've got me into, Stanley.' "

The
FLYING
PORCUPINE

Richard Haligon

POPULAR LIBRARY · NEW YORK

THE FLYING PORCUPINE

Published by Popular Library, CBS Educational and Professional Publishing, a division of CBS Inc., by arrangement with Futura Publications Limited

ISBN: 0-445-04715-1

Printed in the United States of America

First Popular Library printing: June 1982

10 9 8 7 6 5 4 3 2 1

For Colin and Judy Maitland

ACKNOWLEDGEMENTS

I am most grateful to the following for the help they provided. Any errors of fact are my own, as are the opinions expressed. Mr T.C. Charman and the Imperial War Museum; Mr R. Wilkie; Mr P. Fordham for his advice on gold; Squadron Leader F.E. 'Jackson' Dymond and Mr D.M. Greenwood of the Royal Air Force Museum, Hendon.

Mr Ken Hunter, custodian of the Sunderland in the Battle of Britain Museum, very kindly let me explore that magnificent piece of aeronautical engineering at length and answered my many questions.

The description of the Sunderland on pages 189 and 190 is taken from the book *Flying Boat* by Kenneth Poolman, by kind permission of the publishers, Messrs William Kimber and Company.

AUTHOR'S NOTE

Although I have named real airfields and mentioned specific appointments such as that of Commanding Officer, the characters in this book are wholly fictitious and are not intended to depict any actual person, living or dead.

In May, 1945, the price of gold was £8.8s.(£8.40) per Troy ounce. At the time of writing it is approximately £180.00 per ounce.

Diamonds have fared only slightly less well. Although there was no official market in May, 1945, I am reliably informed that the value of good quality stones has increased by twenty times since then.

Thus, if one were fortunate enough to have £1,000 worth of each in 1945, today that small cache would be worth in excess of £41,000. To put it another way, if the cache were valued at £1,000,000 in 1945, today. . . .

But the mind boggles.

Prologue: April 24, 1942

The leading Spitfire raced across the Channel at 500 feet, the pilot's eyes restlessly combing the sky. Even if the altitude fooled German coastal radar, in a few more minutes visual observation posts would pick up the bombing fleet, and then the fun would start. After the mauling the aircraft had received in last week's raid, it might take the Luftwaffe ground controllers a while to accept that Lancasters were again heading for Germany in broad daylight, but when they did they'd act fast to get the FWs and 109s in the air.

Like the pilots of the other Spitfires, twenty-four in all, Flight Lieutenant Mike O'Keefe had not been on the April 17th mission to Augsburg in southern Germany. For that matter, neither had the crews of the dozen Lancasters the Spits were escorting. And not one man of the one hundred and eight in the flotilla would have shed a tear if he'd been excluded from this sortie, either.

There was much talk in the Messes that Air Chief-Marshal Harris's new strategy of small-scale daylight raids against precision targets was one way to give the administrators of the Widows and Orphans Fund something to do. Certainly the April 17th raid had turned into a disaster, with four of the twelve aircraft from Nos. 44 and 97 Squadrons being shot down over France and another three over the target. Of the remaining five, only one reached home unscathed.

But that time there were no fighter escorts, the brass argued. The Lancs were sitting ducks once they broke their defensive flying pattern.

So the order came through to do it again, and this time put the MAN diesel works out of action for the foreseeable future.

The operations briefing was simple to the point of brutality. The Lancasters would take off from Norfolk; the Spits, from different airfields in Kent. The two groups would rendezvous beyond Dover and head south-east, feinting for Munich. At the last possible moment the bombers would make for Augsburg and clobber the factory. The fighters would protect the bombers there and back.

That at least was the theory. In practice it was somewhat more difficult.

The round-trip to Augsburg was 1,200 miles, well within the compass of a Lanc but beyond the range of a Spitfire Mark VB even with a drop-tank. So the boffins went to their drawing-boards and fiddled with their slide rules, eventually coming up with a string of calculations that said a Spitfire could get to Augsburg and back with an enlarged pair of drop-tanks and stay in combat over the target for six minutes. Anything in excess of six mintues meant they wouldn't be coming home. The consensus among the fighter pilots was that this was fine providing the brass could somehow get word to the Luftwaffe and tell their opposite numbers in the FWs and 109s that the game had to end after 360 seconds.

There was also another drawback. A Lancaster cruised somewhere in the region of 200 mph. The Mark VB's cruising speed (where fuel was being consumed at its most economical rate) was 272 mph. On paper, therefore, the Spits would be over the target while the Lancs were still in French air space.

But the boffins had an answer for this also. Because of their greater range the Lancs would have no need to conserve fuel. They could therefore battle along at around 260 mph. The weight of the drop-tanks on the Spits would, at least on the outward trip, reduce their cruising speed to about the same.

When someone had the temerity to object that it all sounded a bit Alice-in-Wonderland he was reminded very sharply of the old adage: It's not the size of the dog in the fight that counts, but the size of the fight in the dog.

In other words, get the bloody job done and don't argue.

To Mike O'Keefe it was a familiar litany, one he'd heard regularly since the dark days of 1940.

Now aged 25, O'Keefe had joined the RAF in 1939, before

the outbreak of war. His induction course confirmed the opinion of the University Training Squadron: he was a natural flier. He accepted the verdict without question, though in his heart he knew it was not enough to have a superb eye and the reflexes of a cat. Against airborne practice targets which were not shooting back that proved little. But during the few weeks that encompassed the Battle of Britain in midsummer and autumn 1940, he proved his ability was far more than textbook.

As part of 610 Squadron, 11 Group, flying Spitfires out of Biggin Hill, like many others he was making half a dozen sorties a day when things got rough. His mentor with 610 was the legendary Sailor Malan, whose Ten Commandments for survival were posted on squadron notice boards throughout Fighter Command. As far as O'Keefe was concerned the most important was the Tenth: Go in quickly—punch hard—get out.

He shot down his first German aircraft, a Heinkel He 111 of KG 26, the famous Lion Geschwader, in August, 1940, and finished the day by disposing of a twin-engined Messerschmitt Bf 110. His Spitfire was full of holes, but all he suffered from was sweat-rash.

Before the end of the Battle he had accounted for five more enemy aircraft, received promotion to Flying Officer, and was personally decorated with the DFC by King George VI.

O'Keefe stood five feet ten in his flying boots and was considered by those who knew him well to be somewhat serious in temperament. The few girls he dated thought him handsome, his face just saved from being too good-looking by a nose broken on the football field. He had his Irish father's dark curly hair and twinkling blue eyes, and he could hold his liquor with anyone.

Both his parents were now dead, though their marriage had broken up when O'Keefe was still a baby. His father remained single, but his mother remarried and bore a son by her second husband. O'Keefe's half-brother was also in the RAF, a bomber pilot, though the two men had not seen each other for eighteen months and had little in common apart from their present jobs.

"French coast coming up."

The voice crackling in O'Keefe's headphones was that of his wingman, Flight Sergeant Jim Caradoc, a quiet-spoken Kentishman and former boxing champion. The pair had known each other since the early days in 610 Squadron and were firm friends despite the difference in rank. O'Keefe had even been persuaded to act as godfather to the younger of Caradoc's children, though he had few religious beliefs.

At the briefing for escorts before the mission, radio silence was not stipulated mandatory, as anyone with a good pair of eyes would soon see the flotilla. Even so, the Wing Commander in command of the fighters butted in sharply with, "Cut the chatter."

O'Keefe glanced across at Caradoc's aircraft, fifty yards off his starboard quarter, and gave him a thumbsup.

Estimated flying time from the French coast to Augsburg/Munich was two hours, depending upon how hard and where they were bounced. It was an area O'Keefe knew well, that part of Bavaria. The family business was light engineering, and before the old man's death in 1938 he had accompanied him on many a business trip to Munich, mostly to act as translator, for O'Keefe's German was fluent and accentless.

He had even seen the inside of the local SS Headquarters, having been arrested for saying too loudly in a bar precisely what he thought of Germany's leaders. For half an hour he was lectured in perfect English by a young and hard Obersturmfuehrer (SS lieutenant) by the name of Lutz and warned that it was unwise for a foreigner, especially a decadent Britisher, to voice such slanders in the Reich.

To avoid confusion once the fighting started, the bombers and fighters were, for the purpose of inter-aircraft communication, operating on different frequencies. Thus, no one in the Lancasters had heard the Fighter Leader reprimand Caradoc.

It was doubtful if the pilot of F Fox, one of the Lancasters in the leading box of four, would have heard anything anyway. Harry Kane, nicknamed Carver because of the lethal-looking bowie knife he habitually wore strapped to his left hip, was half asleep, his usual posture until the action got under way and one that terrified new crew members until they realized that Kane was a pilot of great skill and could be relied upon to be in full possession of his faculties the minute the first shots were fired. But doing the driving until that event took place was an Irishman by the name of Paddy Mahoney. He and Kane had completed half a tour, fifteen missions, together, but mostly they communicated in sign language. Mahoney came from Belfast and Kane from the south side of Sydney, and neither understood more than one word in ten of what the other was saying.

Had the war not come along at the right moment, Harry Kane might well have seen the inside of an Australian prison. Back home he had done everything from mining gold to breaking horses, but he had a quick temper and the physique of a heavyweight to back it up.

Now two weeks short of his twenty-sixth birthday and holding the rank of Flight Sergeant, he had worked his own passage to England in 1939, arriving in July and enlisting in the RAF immediately. His educational qualifications were the bare minimum for pilot training, but he was accepted for a flight course in Lancasters and passed out second in his group. So far he had notched up a tour and a half, winning the DFM en route.

He was still inclined to get hot under the collar if provoked and tended to overlook such niceties as saluting officers, but his ability to get a bomber to its destination and back saved him from the court martial that would have been handed out to lesser men.

Mahoney nudged him and pointed up front. He muttered something that sounded like "France".

Kane opened his eyes briefly. "I've seen it before."

Piloting the leading Lancaster, B Baker, in the second box of four, Pilot Officer Jonathan Pascoe felt a twinge of envy at the sight of the sleek and elegant Spitfires dancing around the Lancs. Like fit young athletes taunting their grandmothers, he thought.

Aged twenty-one and looking every inch eighteen, Pascoe was too young to have fought in the Battle of Britain, and was again disappointed when his flying instructor recommended a posting to Bomber Command. In his own mind he

13

was temperamentally more suited to flinging a 400 mph fighter across the heavens than trundling backwards and forwards to Germany in a Lancaster. But his instructor had seen a certain wildness in Pascoe's character and judged he would not last a week in Fighter Command. The heavy, avuncular bombers would calm him down, force him to use his obvious skills at a slower pace.

There was no way of telling which of the two was right, but at least Pascoe had survived the war up to now and was the holder of the DFC with thirty-six bombing missions on his service sheet. He was also considered, by those whose opinions were respected on the subject, to be one of the best young pilots in the European Theatre.

People who did not like him (and he was a shade too arrogant to have many friends) thought he looked more like a 19th century poet than a beribboned flier. In a way it wasn't a bad assessment, though it had less to do with his slightly overlong fair hair, slim build and grey eyes than an irritating habit of, in the middle of a conversation, staring somewhere into distant space, oblivious to his surroundings. His critics called him a romantic, though they grudgingly admitted that a combination of the warrior and the aesthete were probably essential ingredients of great airmen.

The bombing fleet ploughed on, keeping as low as the terrain would allow. Fifteen minutes over France; twenty minutes. Half an hour.

On a dozen occasions the fliers saw frenzied movement around Wehrmacht gun emplacements, but by the time the flak batteries were brought to bear the planes were out of range.

And still there was no sign of enemy air activity.

Nevertheless, when it came it would come bloody fast, and one hundred and eight hearts were now beating a little quicker.

Among the fighter pilots there were two schools of thought about stooging around at damn near sea level. There were those who didn't like it, who were firm subscribers to the equation, height equals survival. There were others, in the majority, who realized that their most dangerous antagonists in the Luftwaffe were the Messerschmitt Bf 109s, and who knew that below 12,000 feet the Spitfire was a better aircraft than Uncle Willi's brainchild.

In this second group was the Tail-end Charlie of the fighters, Flying Officer Peter van der Heyden, a tall South African of twenty-two whose fair hair and deep-blue eyes had caused the recruiting officer to remark that van der Heyden was joining the wrong air force.

Because e.t.a. Augsburg was 16:00 hours and the general direction of the attack formation south-east, for most of the outward trip the sun would be slightly west of south, swinging further west, behind the bombing fleet, as the afternoon wore on. It was from that direction that they could expect to be bounced, from height, out of the sun, in accordance with the Luftwaffe manual. Van der Heyden's job, and that of his wingman, was to act as an advance early warning system for the rest of the task force by flying a mile to starboard and a little way behind. In order for the FWs and the 109s to get at the main body of the fleet they would have to come through van der Heyden.

That at least was what the bulk of the contract said, he thought, screwing up his eyes and squinting into the tinted rear-view mirror. The small print gave a somewhat different picture. Whereas he had been flying Spits for two years and had six confirmed kills to his credit, his wingman, Johnny Packer, was virtually off the assembly line. He had joined the squadron a week ago and flown only four combat missions, during none of which had he sighted the enemy.

But van der Heyden was a realist and could understand the thinking of the brass in sending out semi-green pilots on such a mission. If they dispatched twenty-four fighter aces and the dozen best Lancaster crews in Bomber Command, the raid on Augsburg, if successful, would prove nothing more than that expert pilots could do a difficult job. But for Harris's strategy to be viable for the future it had to be shown that *any* group of fliers could produce positive results.

Van der Heyden had never served with 610 Squadron, but he was familiar with Sailor Malan's Commandments and almost without thinking obeyed one of them now.

15

"Never fly straight and level for more than thirty seconds," Malan advised, and it was rigid adherence to this principle, discipline learned in a hundred dogfights, obedience to the clock in his head, which saved van der Heyden's life.

He put his port wing down, losing a fast 200 feet, and simultaneously heard the unmistakable rattle of 20 mm cannon. The shots were wide, thudding into the ground over to his right. A split second later a 109 roared past his starboard wing, banking to the west, out of harm's way.

Packer was not so fortunate.

Even as van der Heyden yanked on the joystick to get some height, he saw lumps being torn off the novice's aeroplane, where Packer was still maintaining his original height and course.

The youngster stood no chance at all. One minute he was flying three tons of elegant aeroplane; the next, the Spit's nose had dropped and it was ploughing a deep furrow in the earth below.

The sky was suddenly full of 109s and FW 190s. Thirty or forty of them at a quick guess. There was no reason for van der Heyden to say it but he did so anyway.

"Charlie One, we've got a hell of a lot of company!"

The time was 14:52. The bombing fleet was just west of Saarbrücken.

Within seconds of the opening shots being exchanged there were aircraft scattered all over the heavens.

Luftwaffe strategy was simple and direct: ignore the fighters, go for the bombers. Whatever the target, the bombers must not reach it. When the Lancasters were dispatched, then the fighters could be dealt with.

For the RAF the problem was more complex. Their main task was to ensure that the bombers got through. Less important, if only slightly so, was to make sure that as many as possible got home, bombers and fighters alike.

And they were at a disadvantage. The Spitfires, because of fuel limitations, couldn't go charging all over the sky in search of 109s and FWs; they had to wait for the Luftwaffe to come at them, and counter-punch. It gave too much of the initiative to the other side, but that couldn't be helped.

The bombers' job was relatively easy. All they had to do was keep going, throttles wide open.

The choice of altitude was proving to be a wise one. The 109s especially were slower than the Spits and less manoeuvrable in horizontal flight, and now that the element of surprise had vanished the only advantage they possessed was numbers. Moreover, it would take a very foolhardy flier to try and get under the Lancs at 500 feet. There wasn't much margin for error at that height. It had to be straight and level or out of the sun. And every time a 109 climbed it was using precious fuel.

Still, the Spits could only attack head on and that meant breaking the defensive formation around the Lancs.

In the vanguard of the task force, O'Keefe and his wingman Caradoc banked to starboard, as though locked together, the moment they heard the unfamiliar voice shout to the Fighter Leader that they were under attack. As far as O'Keefe was concerned, it was no use saving fuel for Augsburg if he was shot down over Saarbrücken.

At first glance the Spits were outnumbered by about two to one in terms of fighters, but the Lancs had a pretty formidable array of armaments, so the odds weren't as bad as they might appear to a ground watcher.

He selected as his prey a 109 that was just completing a turn over in the west. As far as he could see only one aircraft was down as yet but it looked like a Spitfire.

Caradoc saw where O'Keefe had his nose pointed and peeled off, looking to make a kill elsewhere.

The 109 levelled off at 5,000 feet. The pilot made no attempt to dive and O'Keefe guessed he was trying to lure one of the Spits upstairs.

O'Keefe decided to play along and give the German the impression that he was about to fall for a sucker punch.

His Spitfire VB had an initial climb rate of 4,750 feet per minute, about eight times slower than a 109 with its nose down and the throttle open. However, O'Keefe suspected that the German pilot was a comparative newcomer. There was something about the other aeroplane's attitude which did not ring true. An ace—*experten,* as the Germans called them— would have been further south of west, putting the mid-afternoon sun directly over his tailfin and in his opponent's eyes. This one was too far north.

A distance of perhaps 3,000 yards via an angle of 45 degrees separated the two aeroplanes when O'Keefe pulled the stick back. There were other Spitfires milling around, some heading in the same direction as himself. There were other 109s in close proximity to the one O'Keefe had his eye on. But quickly both RAF and Luftwaffe alike sought other targets. It was as though someone had decreed—right, this is between you two.

At a combined speed in excess of 400 mph, less than thirty seconds separated the 109 and the Spitfire from a head-on collision. They arrowed towards each other as though on tramlines.

An ace, O'Keefe knew, would probably bank to port at 2,000 yards, move into the sun in the south-west, and stand on his port wing tip, thus presenting the narrowest possible target for his opponent to shoot at while setting himself up to let fly with the two 20 mm cannon and the brace of 7.92 mm machine guns which armed the 109.

But if O'Keefe was guessing correctly—and if he wasn't he could forget about fuel worries—the pilot of the 109 wasn't experienced enough to try such a manoeuvre. *Keep it simple*— that was the golden rule for novices in either air force.

By keeping his foot on the left rudder and gently edging to port, O'Keefe placed the 109 a few degrees to starboard.

After twenty seconds, and at 1,000 yards, the Messer-schmitt pilot squeezed the trigger. This was enough to con-vince O'Keefe finally that he was dealing with a beginner, though some of the cannon shells came a bit too close for comfort.

The Spitfire's altitude was now less than 2,000 feet—too low for a novice to risk going underneath, particularly at the speed the Messerschmitt was travelling. Furthermore, O'Keefe was unnerving the German by driving straight at him, leaving him very few options. He could try a tight turn—

something the 109 wasn't good at at low altitudes—to port or starboard. Port was favourite as this would take him away from the approaching Spit's guns. He could pull back on the stick and attempt a climbing turn above the Lancasters. Finally, if he had the stomach, he could keep on coming, take a chance on downing the Spitfire, and yank back on the stick at the last moment.

It was no choice at all really, but a more experienced flier would have made the best of it. As it was, the Luftwaffe novice made two mistakes. Instead of turning to port he went to starboard, and instead of keeping his turn as tight as the design of his aircraft would permit, he tried to climb to where he knew he would be safe.

This brought him straight across O'Keefe's bows, and at 400 yards, with the 109 clearly in the cross-hairs of his gunsights, O'Keefe squeezed the firing button.

A Spitfire VB was armed with two 20 mm Hispano cannon containing 120 rounds per gun, and four .303 Browning machine guns holding 350 rounds per gun. A lethal dose was reckoned to be somewhere between fifteen and twenty rounds.

O'Keefe held his burst for two seconds. Twenty-three shells struck the 109, killing the pilot instantly and fracturing the fuel tanks.

Even as he turned away, anxiously looking over his shoulder, O'Keefe knew the 109 was doomed. It exploded 200 feet above the ground, littering wreckage for several hundred yards in all directions.

From the moment van der Heyden had shouted that they were being attacked to the time the 109 met its end, the encounter had lasted two minutes.

Five minutes later the Fighter Leader found a brief moment to take stock. As far as he could tell he had lost three Spitfires for three 109s. One Spitfire was trailing smoke and heading for home, hugging the deck. The Lancasters were untouched.

There was a hell of a long way to go yet and the odds were

bound to get worse as the Germans narrowed down the probable target area. But so far, so good.

The Spitfire making for England belonged to Peter van der Heyden. He had been caught in a turn by a FW 190 and was losing oil steadily. If he didn't have to take evasive action he thought he could make it back, certainly as far as the Channel. His luck seemed to be holding. The German fighters were not interested in him. He was *hors de combat*. It was the bombers they were after.

Elsewhere in the sky Jim Caradoc had got what he thought was a probable, though he hadn't seen it go down. He'd fired a quick burst which seemed to draw blood, but the 109 raced away east and Caradoc had not felt inclined to follow. It could be a trap to lure the fighter escorts away from the bombers.

Aboard F Fox, Carver Kane was now wide awake. At the bombers' briefing the skippers had been told to hold their protective boxes as long as possible and leave the Spitfires to handle the Luftwaffe, the theory being that four Lancasters could give covering fire to each other but that a lone Lanc was an easy target. So far it seemed to be working, but there were still forty minutes to the target.

In the second box, Jonathan Pascoe was calling for a damage report on B Baker. A minute earlier a 109 had penetrated the Spitfire screen and scored a couple of hits. But after checking with each member of the crew it was ascertained that the enemy shells had hit nothing vital.

Twenty minutes from the target the flotilla had lost another Spitfire and a Lancaster from the third box. The fighter broke in two and caught fire, giving the pilot no chance, but seven 'chutes, the entire crew, were seen leaving the bomber. It was later established that all seven men landed safely, to spend the rest of the war in a POW camp.

As far as the Bombing Leader, another Wing Commander in the aircraft ahead of Carver Kane's, was concerned, the next ten minutes were critical. Survive them and there was a chance the mission would succeed, for the attacking fighters would have to be withdrawn over Augsburg in order to let the anti-aircraft batteries have a crack.

If it seems hard to credit that something the size of a

Lancaster could not be disabled by half a dozen squadrons of 109s and FWs, it has to be remembered that, apart from the Spitfire screen, the bombers, too, were fighting back with two for'ard machine guns, two dorsals, and a bank of four in the tail. Equally, it is far from easy for an aeroplane travelling at 350 mph in one direction to hit one travelling at 260 in another.

It also has to be recalled that, technically, a fighter pilot became an ace with as few as half a dozen victories, and that many pilots on all sides never came anywhere near hitting an enemy aircraft. Even the greatest listed their total number of kills in tens rather than hundreds. Thus such legendary names as Douglas Bader, Johnnie Johnson and Sailor Malan only scored 22½ (the "half" for a shared kill), 38 and 35 respectively throughout the entire period of hostilities. Bob Stanford Tuck—the Immortal Tuck—got 29 before being shot down and captured in 1942. The American Don Gentile got 23 and the Frenchman Pierre Clostermann the same number. Among the Germans, Werner Mölders scored 111 and Adolf Galland, later General of Fighters, 103, but many of these victories were achieved against an inexperienced if brave foe on the Russian Front, where it was said in the Luftwaffe that it was possible to get a dozen Ivans before breakfast and a further dozen between lunch and tea.

Thus there is nothing odd in the fact that the escorted bomber force, for the most part, got through.

For get through it did.

At 15:52, when it became apparent to the Luftwaffe ground defence controllers that the force was making a return trip to Augsburg, with the MAN diesel works again the probable target, the German fighters were ordered to break contact for fear of being hit by their own flak. They would get another crack on the way back.

At the same time the break-off instruction was flashed to the fighters, the Lancasters had been reduced to nine, the Spitfire escorts to eighteen. There was nothing for the Spits to do now except keep out of harm's way and conserve fuel for the homeward trip. It was up to the Lancasters to administer the *coup de grâce*.

Flying through an anti-aircraft barrage so thick it seemed impossible to emerge unscathed, the Bombing Leader went in first at 1,000 feet—"down the chimney" as the expression has it. His aircraft was armed with a dozen 1,000-pounders, mainly incendiary, in order to get a bit of a blaze going for the others to aim at. He laid a perfect stick north-south across the MAN plant before turning away.

Next in line was Carver Kane's F Fox. Seemingly unhappy with 1,000 feet, Kane took his aeroplane down to 750. He heard his bomb-aimer exclaim, "Jesus Christ, I can see the colour of their eyes!" before a sudden buoyancy told him that the bombs were gone.

The next two aircraft in the first box laid their bombs in a circle of fire and thick smoke which already told the Bombing Leader that something was burning down there, and then came Jonathan Pascoe.

Even as he made his run, Pascoe felt the port wing lift as an AA shell exploded just beyond lethal range. The blast pushed him far to starboard, away from the target. He shouted into the intercom: "Hold it! We'll go round again!"

One by one the bombers dropped their cargoes of death and destruction. But it was not all one-way traffic. Two Lancasters in Pascoe's box and a third in the last wave were hit by flak, and all three were last seen plunging to earth. There were some parachutes, but it was hard to tell how many.

Finally it was Pascoe's turn again.

A bomber pilot could do many things, depending upon skill, to take evasive action, but paramount on a bomb-run was holding the aircraft steady, to give his bomb-aimer a fair chance.

Pascoe kept B Baker as steady as a rock, though by this time the flak gunners had more than got the range and anti-aircraft shells were exploding all around the plane.

It seemed to take hours, but in reality it was no more than thirty seconds from the beginning of the run until Pascoe heard his bomb-aimer call, *"Bombs gone. Let's get the fuck out of here!"*

Free of their bomb loads the surviving six Lancasters raced for home, accompanied by the remaining eighteen Spitfires.

The flak barrage now over, the Luftwaffe again attacked with all its fury, manic in its determination to avenge the damage done to Augsburg.

Much later, many individual stories would be told in the Messes, tales of hair-raising escapes, narrow squeaks, feats of individual heroism, attacks by the Spitfire escorts on an enemy far superior in numbers that bordered on the lunatic.

But suffice it to say that of the twelve Lancasters and twenty-four Spitfires which set out from England earlier in the day, only four of the former aircraft and fourteen of the latter managed to land safely.

Among the bomber pilots to set down in Norfolk as, in other parts of the country, families were beginning tea, was the Bombing Leader, whose crew included two dead and one who would never fly again; the entire crew of F Fox, who swore by all they held sacred that Carver Kane had another mid-flight "sleep" over France; and Jonathan Pascoe's crew.

The only other bomber to make it, piloted by a young Canadian, was found to contain just one survivor, the dorsal gunner, when the ambulance crews prised open the hatch. Somehow the Canadian had brought his aircraft to ground a fraction of a second or two before he died of head wounds.

Mike O'Keefe got home, with another Me 109 on the scorecard and about enough fuel in his tanks to fill a gin glass.

Jim Caradoc got back—though, with his engine coughing and spluttering for the last fifty miles, he was forced to put down at Manston airfield and not Biggin Hill. O'Keefe spent a few anxious hours before he heard that Caradoc was safe.

Peter van der Heyden, the South African, was forced to ditch in the Channel, but was seen crashing by a Royal Navy minesweeper and was picked up, unharmed, after being in the water less than five minutes.

Of those who didn't make it, a total of sixty-six men, eleven were later reported killed in action. Thirty-nine of the survivors were picked up by German civilians or Wehrmacht troops and, although roughly handled, eventually sent to prison camps.

The remaining sixteen fell into the hands of the SS and

were incarcerated in the Munich SS HQ. There they were kept for forty-eight hours while the senior SS officer in the district decided what to do with them.

The details of the fate of these men were not to emerge until early 1945, when it transpired that the SS, under the guise of transferring the prisoners to a POW camp, had their truck stopped on a lonely stretch of road south of Dachau and the fliers executed.

The man who gave the order for these murders was Sturmbannfuehrer (SS major) Karl-Erich Lutz, the same officer who had once warned Mike O'Keefe to watch his tongue. Neither man could possibly have known it, but their paths were to cross again.

One

On March 7, 1945, troops of Brigadier-General William Hoge's Combat Command "B", part of the US 9th Armoured Division, crossed the Ludendorff Bridge over the Rhine at Remagen, 55 miles south of Düsseldorf, thus putting Allied soldiers on German territory for the first time in the war. Within a month, even perennial optimists like Goebbels had accepted that the writing was well and truly on the wall for the Third Reich.

The Anglo/US forces in the west had attained a line roughly parallel to the River Elbe, while in the east the Russian armies under Zhukov were gathering on the river Oder, preparing for the final assault upon Berlin. Only in Bavaria and Austria was the threat to the German defenders anything less than immediate, although anyone with rank and influence had already made preparations to save his own skin.

The SS in particular knew it could expect short shrift from

the conquering Allies, though the mandatory arrest list, dropped in leaflet form by RAF Mosquitoes, held out little hope to anyone who was not of lowly rank or a *bona fide* civilian. Those to be incarcerated on sight included: all members of the Gestapo; all members of the SS; Nazi Party officials above the rank of Bereichsleiter (major); all officers of the Waffen (Armed) and Allgemeine (Civilian) SS; all members of the Sturmabteilung (SA or Brownshirts); most police; ranks above that of lieutenant in the Wehrmacht (Army, Navy and Luftwaffe).

Many of the constituent categories would, after interrogation, be released, but officers and senior NCOs in the SS knew that the least they could expect was a hefty prison sentence. More often than not, they suspected, they would be tried as war criminals and executed; unless of course they were shot on the spot.

As far as the average GI and Tommy was concerned, shooting was far too good for the bastards. Many of them had already seen the concentration camp at Buchenwald, on the hills above the city of Weimar, home of Schiller, Liszt, Goethe, and the ill-fated Weimar Republic. Liberated by troops of General George E. Patton's command on April 11th, during its eight years of existence some 56,000 of its inmates were exterminated. Above the entrance gates were two slogans: "Right or Wrong—My Fatherland"; and "To Each His Own". Two days before the liberation, the camp commandant told his charges: "After all, I am not one of the worst." He pleaded with them to tell the Americans of his generosity, but at the same time, *pour encourager les autres*, he decided to execute forty-six political prisoners.

Still to be liberated, among many others, were the camps at Sachsenhausen and Ravensbrück, directly in line with the Russian advance; Belsen; and Dachau.

Ten miles north of Munich and built in 1933 on the site of a World War I ammunition factory, Dachau was the first of the camps to be set up by the Nazis to imprison their political enemies. Only later did it evolve into a hell of brutality and mass murder, but so vile were the deeds committed there, even greater than those at Buchenwald and Belsen, that after the war its crematorium was preserved as a shrine. A monument to its tens of thousands of dead was erected in 1960.

Even in the beginning, however, it started as it meant to go on. Part of the camp regulations, drawn up by its first commandant, Theodore Eicke, later to become head of all camps, read:

> Article 11: The following offenders, considered as agitators, will be hanged. . . . Anyone who holds inciting meetings, forms cliques, loiters around with others; who for the purpose of supplying the propaganda of the opposition with atrocity stories collects true or false information about the camp, receives such information, buries it, talks about it to others or smuggles it out of the camp. . . .

> Article 12: The following offenders will be shot on the spot or hanged. . . . Anyone attacking physically a guard or SS man, refusing to obey or work while on detail . . . or bawling, shouting, inciting or making speeches while marching or at work. . . .

It was a blueprint for murder, and the camp authorities took full advantage of it for twelve years.

At 9.30 on the evening of April 20, 1945, while elsewhere others celebrated Hitler's 56th birthday, a meeting took place in a private house several miles south of the camp between four of the men responsible for much of the misery the prisoners had suffered. It was chaired by a youthful Standartenfuehrer, or SS colonel, a hard-looking man in his mid-thirties. His blonde hair was cropped short and across his right cheek, below a pair of cold blue eyes, was an old sabre scar.

The subject under discussion was whether it was now time to go to ground, assume false identities and put into operation the plan worked out years earlier for just such a contingency. In actuality there was little to discuss. There was hard intelligence to the effect that General Patch's US 7th Army was approaching at speed and unsubstantiated but credible rumours that a few miles away in Munich a small band of German soldiers was preparing to take over the city and arrest all members of the SS in order to save their own skins when the Americans finally arrived. The meeting was more to decide when to go, rather than whether to go at all.

On the Standartenfuehrer's right at the long wooden table, Sturmbannfuehrer (SS major) Hans-Dieter Fischer was chain-smoking and nursing a huge tumbler of brandy. Now aged 30, like many members of the SS his origins were lowly, having been, prior to his enlistment, a baker's roundsman. But for the advent of the Nazis and the war he would have remained just that, and he was grateful to the SS for giving him officer status and position. Not grateful enough, however, to fight to the last for his country or to take literally the SS motto—"Loyalty is my Honour". As a man who had personally supervised hundreds of executions and in many cases pulled the trigger himself, he knew that a rope was all he could expect if he were still around when the 7th Army put in an appearance.

"I don't know what the hell we're all talking about," he grumbled, glaring at the others through bloodshot eyes. "It has to be tonight. The longer we wait, the more dangerous it becomes. If we don't fall into the American net we'll be arrested by those treacherous bastards in Munich. Either way we're dead."

"You're starting to repeat yourself, Fischer," remarked the Standartenfuehrer. "If you paid a little more attention to what we're discussing instead of trying to drink yourself into a stupor, you might recall that we are waiting to make sure the roads are clear of fifth-columnists. For that we must await the return of Oberscharfuehrer Kammler. If his report is favourable, we move out tonight as arranged. If it isn't, we stay. As you rightly point out, those traitors in Munich will arrest us in an endeavour to save their own hides. We have a long way to go and time is against us, but it's not the slightest use leaving here if the roads are blocked."

"If they're blocked today, it'll be ten times worse tomorrow," persisted Fischer.

"Perhaps—in which case we think again. In the meantime,

we'll see what Kammler has to say. He should be back soon."

"If he gets back at all." Fischer would not leave it alone. "Besides, we were originally four. No one mentioned Kammler at the beginning. Adding a fifth makes it more dangerous for all of us."

"For Christ's sake shut your whining mouth, Fischer," snarled the man opposite. "The Standartenfuehrer knows what he's doing."

"I won't be spoken to like that," stuttered Fischer, "not by a non-commissioned officer."

Hauptscharfuehrer (SS sergeant-major) Heinz Mueller leaned across the table and brandished a huge fist under Fischer's nose. "You stupid bastard, what the hell do ranks matter now? This is not 1941. If you consider me insolent you can't have me put up against a wall. It's every man for himself, from generals down. Those who get away with it will do so because of their own ingenuity, not rank."

"That's enough, Mueller," snapped the Standartenfuehrer. "Until I tell you otherwise we'll observe normal military discipline."

For a second it looked as if Mueller would turn on the Standartenfuehrer also, but he thought better of it. The colonel was nobody's fool and quite right to reprimand him. Fischer was a weakling but he was also a comrade.

In his middle thirties, Heinz Mueller was the physically hard man of the quartet, resembling, in many ways, the Deputy Chief of the SS, Ernst Kaltenbrunner, a fact that pleased him not at all. Kaltenbrunner was a giant of a man, six feet seven inches tall, with a massive lantern jaw. Mueller was a bare six feet four, but broad across the shoulders and as strong as a bull. There had been occasions, during the previous six years, when he had gained some slight advantage by being mistaken for Kaltenbrunner, but those days were over. Kaltenbrunner had a price on his head and any resemblance could only be disastrous. Still, there was nothing he could do about it until he was in a place of safety and had the money for plastic surgery. And that was going to take time.

Although dressed now, as they all were, in civilian clothes, when in uniform Mueller wore the *Ehrenwinkel*, the chevron of the Old Guard, those who had joined the SS before Hitler's accession to power in January, 1933. He was a totally dedicated and fanatical Nazi, but also a realist. This war was over; the Allies had won it. But there would come another time, perhaps another leader, and he wanted to be alive to see it.

The fourth man in the room felt much the same.

Hauptsturmfuehrer (SS captain) Josef Scheringer appeared on the surface to be the sort of individual who worked in some minor capacity in an office or factory. In different times he would be an object of ridicule or pity, the butt of jokes, someone who is sniggered at behind his back and teased by the cheekier of the office girls; a man who (the rumour would go) was hen-pecked at home, took sandwiches to work in a brown-paper wrapper, and who went out in the evening dressed in a long fawn raincoat to visit strip shows and blue-movie theatres. His pinched, narrow features, rheumy eyes peering out at the world through contact lenses, would stamp him as one of the world's losers. His age would be assessed as something over forty and the gossips would stamp him as a pervert, someone whose sexual pleasure derived from tall, blonde women dressed in thigh-length black boots and carrying whips.

The gossips would not be far wrong.

Born in Leipzig and trained as an accountant, Scheringer, now aged 38, had joined the National Socialists in the early days for one reason only: in the Party he was treated as an equal. Providing he paid his subscriptions and attended the meetings, he was as good as anyone—better than most, as most did not wear a uniform.

For a man who lacked confidence in himself and who had no great belief in his own ability, the Party was a natural haven, and to his own amazement he kept on making the right decisions. He had taken part in the abortive Beer Hall Putsch when a teenager, backed the winning team when Roehm and his SA cronies were purged on the Night of the Long Knives, and was totally overcome when rewarded with an SS commission, not normally granted, even at the lower end of the scale, to men whose looks were other than pure Aryan.

In Dachau he was Heinz Mueller's nominal boss, and his excesses with the inmates, both at that camp and in others, were legendary. He was one of those beings totally devoid of conscience and, although unsubstantiated rumour had it that he was homosexual, in actuality he was a voyeur. He had a special house well away from the main compound where privileged SS troopers and selected female prisoners copulated for his pleasure. If the women pleased him with their performance, they were allowed to live and return another day; if they did not they were executed.

Needless to say, Scheringer was high on the list of Nazis to be automatically arrested by the Allies, but he trusted the Standartenfuehrer. Like the others, he had no real choice.

The temporary silence in the room following Mueller's dressing down was broken by a sudden knock on the street door. A Luger clutched in his fist Fischer went to answer it. A few moments later he returned with Oberscharfuehrer Kammler in tow.

Dressed in field uniform, Kammler marched across to the table and clicked his heels.

"Permission to speak, Herr Standartenfuehrer?"

"Yes, yes," said the SS colonel testily. "Sit yourself down and tell us what's going on."

Kammler sat down and removed his cap. Scheringer pushed the brandy bottle and a clean glass towards him. Kammler poured a small drink and downed it in one swallow.

"There are no roadblocks, that's the first thing I can tell you. And Munich itself is as quiet as can be expected. I wouldn't like to say how long that state of affairs will last, however. More than one Wehrmacht patrol took a long look at my uniform."

"Which was why I asked you to wear it. You were not molested in any way?"

"No, sir. It seemed to me as though the Wehrmacht are waiting for something, possibly to hear how close the Americans are, before making a move."

"Which would make sense," put in Scheringer. "If they revolt too quickly and the rising is not fully supported, they could find themselves wiped out in a counter-attack by loyal

30

troops. It's my opinion that they'll wait until the Americans are a day or two's march away before striking. That way the SS will have its hands full preparing to meet the 7th Army."

"I'm inclined to agree with you, Scheringer."

The Standartenfuehrer got to his feet. "Which means we move tonight. First, however, I have to send a radio signal and wait for a reply. Perhaps you would accompany me, Kammler."

"Certainly, Herr Standartenfuehrer."

Left to themselves, the other three looked at one another. Each knew their eventual destination and what lay at the other end, and each knew that getting there was going to be one hell of a risky business. Each, too, had seen the massive radio shack with its long-range equipment on the first floor of the house. What they had never seen was the wireless in operation—not once, although it had been installed for half a dozen years to their certain knowledge. Neither did they know who was listening at the other end. That was the colonel's secret and the only part of the plan he had never revealed to any of them. If he were to be killed or incapacitated in any way, they would have to carry on as best they could.

"I still don't understand what Kammler's doing in on this," muttered Fischer.

"We needed to know what was going on further south," answered Scheringer, "see if they were arresting or executing men in SS uniforms or men whose faces are familiar. If they had been, Kammler would now be dangling from a lamp-post. It's not a risk I'd have cared to take."

"Still, an extra man. . . ."

Fischer got no further before the sound of a gunshot, followed quickly by another, was heard from upstairs. Seconds later the door to the living-room was pushed open.

"Now we are four," said Standartenfuehrer Karl-Erich Lutz, holstering the still-smoking automatic. "Happy, Fischer?"

They left before midnight, after destroying the wireless equipment and booby-trapping the front and rear doors of the house and its ground-floor windows. Mueller suggested putting a torch to the place, but Lutz vetoed the idea. Thanks to some arrangement the Wehrmacht traitors had come to with Patch's 7th Army, enemy air activity had virtually ceased in and around Munich. A new conflagration would attract too much attention too soon. Besides, it amused Lutz to dwell upon the consequences for the first American troops to search the house.

Mueller was driving the unmarked *Kubelwagen*. In the trunk were as many full jerrycans of fuel as it would hold. Sooner or later gasoline would be a problem, but by then they would doubtless have to dump the staff car anyway. It was one thing to drive it through Bavaria and, as yet, unoccupied Austria; it was quite another to take it into Italy. Apart from other considerations, partisan activity was rife on the Austro–Italian border.

Each member of the group (and the same applied to many another senior SS officer and his men who were using the route and who would continue to use it for several years) carried a set of beautifully, and officially, forged papers, together with a money belt containing the equivalent of £1,000 in gold coins, quite frequently sovereigns. For those who wanted them there were genuine Argentinian passports. These were issued as blanks by Juan Peron's ever-sympathetic government, so that all a fugitive had to do was fill in his own details and supply a photograph. The passports were then franked by tame Argentinian consuls and a new identity established, ready for the bearer to board a ship for Buenos Aires or elsewhere.

But to begin with all that was in the future. First the fugitive had to clear Bavaria and Austria and cross the border into Italy without becoming ropebait for the partisans.

Lutz and his associates followed the classic route of Austria/Italian South Tyrol/Rimini/Rome, using the *Kubelwagen* until it became dangerous to do so and afterwards being shuttled from safe house to safe house, each owned by genuine SS personnel who had worked undercover throughout the war, or by SS sympathizers, both individuals and organizations. Chief among these was the German Bishop of

Rome, whose network succeeded in spiriting away to safety many thousands of war criminals.

In detail, once south of Munich Mueller pointed the *Kubelwagen* due east and crossed into Austria at Salzburg, where they rested overnight. The following morning he drove south-east to Spittal, where they were met by a guide and advised to dump the *K-wagen*. Other transport would be provided, less obviously German. This turned out to be a cattle truck, which took them across the frontier into Italy via the Lienz–Dobbiaco road. Money changed hands at the border post, but so far not one of the four fugitives had been obliged to dip into his reserves of gold sovereigns. The SS escape line, not yet called Odessa, was working well.

Every so often, at one or another of the safe houses, they came across other Germans on the run, but for the most part, for security reasons, there was little communication.

Away from the Italian Tyrol, they were shepherded to Venice, where they were told that Communist guerrilla activity between that city and Rimini was intense; it would mean travelling by sea and at night, which in one respect worked in their favour, as it cut the distance by half.

On April 28th they learned via the grapevine that Mussolini and his mistress Clara Petacci had been caught and executed by partisans near Milan. Two days later they were told that Hitler was also dead and Berlin surrounded by the Red Army. But by this time they were in Rome.

Having been on the run for ten days, all four of them were in poor shape, although Fischer, deprived for the most part of regular transfusions of alcohol, was feeling it worse than the others. Mueller proposed privately that they ditch the drunken SS major, but Lutz would have none of it.

"We are all members of the SS, Mueller. Sturmbannfuehrer Fischer may not be the man he once was, but there will come a time when his talents can again be used by those of us who see our defeat as no more than a temporary inconvenience. The Fuehrer is dead and Germany a divided nation, but it will not always be like that. If it does not happen in our lifetime that a new Fuehrer arises, it will happen in the lifetime of our children or grandchildren. But only if we remain true to our cause and teach the coming generations what we ourselves already know. In this respect Fischer is as valuable as you or Scheringer."

They were in the drawing-room of a villa on the outskirts of Rome, a clearing house for all SS men who needed help. Once processed, the majority of the fugitives were transferred to a nearby Franciscan monastery until a passage to South America could be arranged. These officers, NCOs and enlisted men were run-of-the-mill categories, important in their way, vital to the future, but without an immediate job to do apart from saving their own necks. Lutz and his associates were different; for them, escaping the vengeful Allies was only the beginning.

Which was something that continued to puzzle their contact in the Italian capital; for the life of him, he couldn't see why they wanted to go to Tripoli in North Africa and not to a port such as Genoa and on to Argentina.

Referred to only as the Trader by anyone who did not know him personally, the contact was an Italian-speaking German who had spent the entire war pretending to be a half-witted aristocrat with no political convictions. His undercover SS rank was that of Obersturmbannfuehrer (lieutenant-colonel) and Lutz, who'd had dealings with him before, was quick to point out that he was a full colonel.

As it was impossible that their conversation could be overheard, Lutz saw no reason not to speak in German and use ranks.

"It is not for you to question my orders, Herr Obersturmbannfuehrer," he said with mounting irritability. "Your only function in this affair is to do as you are told and get us to Tripoli. How you do it is your own business."

"But it just isn't feasible," protested the Trader. "Here in central and northern Italy we have a good organization, albeit relying, to a certain extent, on sympathetic *fascisti*. Further south is an unknown quantity. It would mean smuggling you across to Sicily and then bribing a fishing vessel to take you to Tripoli. And do not forget, Herr Standartenfuehrer, that the whole of North Africa is in Allied Hands. Even if you get ashore unseen, you will be in enemy-occupied territory."

"Allow me to worry about that."

"It is also my worry. I cannot endanger the whole escape line for four men."

"You can and you will."

Lutz had listened to enough. Although in civilian clothes, he and his men were still armed.

He gestured Mueller to draw his weapon. This accomplished, he said to the Trader: "Herr Obersturmbannfuehrer, I am tired of your whining. I fully appreciate that you have had a long and dangerous war, but so have we all. The man now pointing his Luger at you has served the Reich by executing many enemies of the state. If I consider you fall into that category, I will order him to execute you. Our mission is somewhat more important than getting boatloads of lesser individuals to the safety of South America. I need to go to Tripoli. It is your job to get me there. You have ten seconds to decide whether or not you can do it. In eleven seconds you will be dead."

The Trader nodded slowly. He knew Lutz's reputation and that the threat was no idle one.

"I'll see what I can do."

Two

Also on April 30, a few hours after Hitler and Eva Braun killed themselves in the Berlin Fuehrerbunker, the 3rd, 42nd and 45th infantry divisions of the US 7th Army rolled into Munich to be opposed only by cheering Germans, waving flowers. This demonstration was less due to an affection for Uncle Sam than relief that he had got there before Uncle Joe Stalin.

The fifth column Lutz had feared, known as Freedom Action Bavaria and commanded by Hauptmann Rupprecht Gerngross, had come to nothing after an abortive attempt to arrest General Westphal, Field Marshal Kesselring's chief of staff. Nevertheless, its activities created confusion and put some army units in a state of near mutiny and ready to lay down their weapons.

General Patch's troops were more than willing to accept an easy surrender until a vanguard company overran Dachau. There they uncovered scenes of such horror that even battle-hardened veterans were sick on the spot.

Many of the inmates were, to begin with, understandably mistaken for corpses, their necks so shrunken with hunger and deprivation that they seemed scarcely capable of supporting their skulls. Evidence of mass murder was everywhere. Twenty-four open railway trucks shunted into a siding were found to be full of human bodies, but so unlike human beings were they that at first they were taken to be piles of dirty rags.

Discipline among the troops vanished, and while their officers turned a blind eye the GIs rampaged through the camp, machine-gunning the guards as they were found and dug out of their funkholes. Inmates with sufficient strength left—mainly Poles, French and Russians—joined in the slaughter, using weapons taken from SS men.

On May 7th at Reims, shortly before 3 a.m., Germany unconditionally surrendered. Two days later the capitulation document was ratified in Berlin.

During the afternoon of May 10th, in the wake of the American advance, a small detachment of RAF Intelligence arrived in Munich. It was quite common, once the Rhine was breached, for American units to have British Intelligence sections attached to them, as it was for British units to contain American observers. This way each Power could protect and debrief its own nationals liberated from POW or concentration camps. In the case of Munich/Dachau it was especially important that Air Force representatives were on the spot, as it was an ill-kept secret that the camp had contained decompression chambers, used for experiments to determine the effect of high altitude on fliers.

The RAF team comprised an officer, four NCOs and a handful of clerks. It had been allocated quarters the size of a couple of cupboards in a relatively undamaged building behind Marienplatz. As far as the senior NCO, Flight Sergeant Jim Caradoc, was concerned, it was the usual business of the Yanks grabbing the best working and sleeping accommodation and leaving the RAF the dregs. Still, they'd done ninety per cent of the fighting in this neck of the woods, and he'd have to make the most of it. Squadron Leader O'Keefe would have his guts for guitar strings if the place wasn't squared-to when he got back.

A mile away, office accommodation was the last thing on Mike O'Keefe's mind.

Although in this second week of May, 1945 it was quite against the regulations for Allied personnel, especially officers, to wander around occupied German cities like tourists, O'Keefe had no qualms about disobeying the order. True, mopping-up operations against hard-core defenders were still going on, but he'd missed most of the bullets since 1939 and there was no reason his luck should change. Besides, he wanted to see how much was left of the Munich he remembered.

There wasn't much. The city had taken a real pasting. Maybe not as bad as Berlin, Hamburg and Cologne, but it had seen its share, especially from the 12,000-pounder cookies.

He wondered how much was left of SS Headquarters.

After the Augsburg raid, O'Keefe continued to fly with 610 Squadron, being promoted to the rank of Squadron Leader and winning a bar to his DFC. His final tally of enemy aircraft destroyed before joining Coastal Command and doing a spell in Catalinas was 26.

In 1944, he transferred to Mosquitoes and acted as Pathfinder to the huge bombing fleets which were now nightly pounding hell out of Hitler's Germany.

His former wingman Caradoc stayed with 610 until shortly before D-Day, when he was reported missing, believed down in the North Sea. O'Keefe spent an entire day with Caradoc's wife until news came through that the NCO was safe, picked up by the Royal Navy.

Caradoc openly confessed that the whole business had terrified him, particularly the hours being battered by the sea. Next time, he said, he would stick with his aircraft rather than bail out.

As it happened, there never was a next time. O'Keefe pulled a few strings and convinced the RAF brass that, now the Allies were in Europe, Caradoc's experience could be far better utilized in Intelligence.

Caradoc tried to persuade his friend to join him. O'Keefe had done his share without receiving so much as a scratch, but his run of good fortune couldn't last for ever.

Neither did it. In November 1944 he caught a packet from a Bf 109 Gustav over the Ruhr. Although injured in the legs, using every ounce of skill he managed to keep the Mosquito airborne and land safely behind Allied lines.

But that was the end of his career as a combat pilot as far as this war was concerned. It was not that he was unable to fly again, far from it. After two months' hospitalization and a further month's intensive physiotherapy, he charmed the station commander of a nearby fighter base and was allowed to take up a Mark IX Spitfire. For thirty minutes he happily stooged around near the aircraft's operational ceiling and was quite convinced at the end of the session that his reflexes and flying ability were unimpaired. But it was now February, 1945, and any fool could see that the war was almost over.

During an extended sick leave he received a visit from a Group Commander Bryant, of RAF Intelligence. Someone had looked up his service sheet and discovered he spoke fluent German and knew Munich well. Under the section "any other information" was the fact that he had once been arrested by the SS. The arresting officer's name, Obersturm-fuehrer Lutz, was also given.

After a curt reminder of his oath under the Official Secrets Act, Bryant told O'Keefe what was known about the fate of the sixteen airmen following the Augsburg raid of April 24, 1942.

"We're pretty sure of our facts. Admittedly our informer is trying to save his own neck, but he has no reason to lie. Lutz, then a Sturmbannfuehrer, had the men executed.

"We want him," went on Bryant. "We want him very badly. By we I mean the RAF. He's doubtless got other crimes to his name and if someone else, the Americans or the Russians for instance, get to him first, they'll stake their own claim and we'll be at the end of the queue. We'd like you to try and find him for us, though I admit the chances of achieving that are slim."

"Why me?" asked O'Keefe. "I'm not trained in Intelligence work."

"Perhaps not, but you know Munich, you've actually met Lutz, and you were on the Augsburg raid. I'd say that outweighed any lack of experience."

"Have we any reason to believe he's still alive?"

"None. But we've got to start somewhere."

O'Keefe did not have to be asked twice. He'd lost some good friends on the Augsburg mission and the thought of them being murdered in cold blood by someone he'd met face to face turned him icy with anger.

"We're a long way from Munich yet," he reminded the Group Captain.

"Not as far as you might think, but I agree it will be a couple of months before the city falls. Still, it will give you time to familiarize yourself with Intelligence procedures. Lutz is priority, of course, but not exclusive.

"You'll head up a section attached to General Patch's 7th Army, which is likely to get to Munich before anyone else. The rest is up to you."

O'Keefe asked for and got Caradoc as his number two, and thus it was, on May 10th, that he found himself standing in front of the building that had once housed SS Headquarters.

It had survived the bombing and the shelling remarkably well. True, it was badly scarred and cardboard had replaced glass in most of the windows, but it still had a roof and seemed more or less in one piece.

An absurd thought crossed his mind as he approached the uniformed GI guarding the entrance at the top of the steps: that somewhere inside, hiding in a cellar, was Lutz.

It was ridiculous, of course. Lutz was probably dead. Even if he wasn't, the odds against him being stationed in the same city for the whole war were very long indeed. On the other hand. . . .

The GI barred his way. "You can't go in there, sir."

"Why not?"

"Temporary HQ for the divisional G-2. No one's allowed in without a pass."

"Where do I get a pass?"

"From G-2, sir."

"Who are inside, right?"

"Right, sir."

O'Keefe counted to ten.

"Look, soldier, let's start again, shall we? I'm with RAF Intelligence, attached to the 7th Army. This used to be an SS headquarters and I have a special reason for wanting to see the inside of it. Now I don't want to pull rank on you or anything like that, but I'd appreciate it if you'd find someone who can issue me with a pass or otherwise get me inside."

The GI looked doubtful. "I'm not supposed to leave my post, sir. GIs start walking off post, they put you in the bucket and throw away the key."

Short of going back to his own office and getting in touch with General Patch's command headquarters from there, O'Keefe was at a loss regarding what to do next. His problem was solved, however, by the sudden appearance of a youthful major, carrying a sheaf of papers and smoking a cigar the size of a U-boat. He took in the scene at a glance.

"What's going on here, Bronowski?"

"Man wants to get inside, Major. I keep telling him it's not possible without a pass, but he won't take no for an answer."

"Okay, leave it to me. Anything I can do for you . . . er . . . Squadron Leader?" The US Army major peered at the two and a half rings on O'Keefe's sleeve.

"There certainly is."

Without going into detail O'Keefe explained that he had

once been inside the building in 1938 and that he had a special reason for wanting to talk to whoever was handling captured Nazi paperwork.

"Guess that's me—at least, I'm one of them." The major looked at his wrist watch and then at the documents he was carrying. "I reckon these can wait a little longer. Come inside. It's not every day I meet someone who knew this place before the balloon went up. The name's Benutti, by the way. Joe Benutti. And any cracks about me fighting on the wrong side earn you the door."

O'Keefe introduced himself and followed Major Benutti along a maze of corridors he only half remembered.

Typically, although 7th Army Intelligence had not been in Munich for long, Benutti's office was already organized. His desk was a mess, littered with papers in no apparent order, but in an ante-room the coffee pot was already bubbling away, supervised by a master sergeant sporting the shortest crewcut O'Keefe had ever seen.

Benutti sat down behind a desk and indicated that O'Keefe should pull up a chair.

"Coffee?"

"I wouldn't say no to it."

Benutti grinned. "You British, always using ten words where one'll do." He called across to the master sergeant. "Hansen, our visitor says he wouldn't say no to a cup of coffee and I'll just say yes."

"Comin' right up, Major."

Now they were seated, O'Keefe had a better chance to study the G-2 major. They were about the same age, 28, although the American was an inch or two taller. His near-black hair and dark eyes, together with his name, indicated Italian ancestry, hence the crack about fighting on the wrong side. Judging by his easy smile and lack of worry lines, it could well have been assumed by a casual observer that his battle experience was limited to pushing coloured counters around a table in a war room. But his left breast was a mass of fruit salad. O'Keefe had identified the Distinguished Service Medal, the Silver Star and two Purple Hearts before Hansen came in with the coffee, sugar on the side. It was the real McCoy, though Hansen apologized about the absence of milk. The supply truck was stuck down the road apiece.

"War's hell," grunted O'Keefe.

Benutti chuckled. "So it is. We only got the water going a few hours back." He shook his head. "I guess you're finding the same problem, the civil engineering side of things. Although it's strictly speaking not the business of this department, before we get anywhere with our interrogations we've got to repair just about everything the USAAF and the RAF bombed the hell out of. Water mains, power stations, sewage disposal. You name it."

"They can go waterless, fuelless and shitless for all it matters to me," called Hansen from the ante-room.

"Hansen's prejudiced," said Benutti. "His father was German."

"Grandfather, Major. I never did like that side of the bastard family. Always on the bum."

"Nevertheless," went on Benutti, "we've got to keep 'em fed and watered, though the general feeling at division is that by the time we've got that sorted out, set up some kind of military government, any war criminal worthy of the name will be long gone. Did you see Dachau?" He grimaced at the recollection. "I couldn't believe it. How the hell can people do that to other people? It's beyond me."

"Me too," said O'Keefe. "I'm no Christian, but the first churchman to mention the word charity in my presence is going to get dumped on his arse."

"Fucking right."

Benutti sipped his coffee. "Anyway, that's not what we're here to talk about. You wanted in, so you're in. There's an entrance fee, though. What the hell was an RAF Squadron Leader doing in an SS Headquarters way back in '38?"

O'Keefe hesitated only briefly before telling Benutti the whole story, beginning with his arrest by Lutz and ending with the murder of the sixteen airmen. This was 7th Army territory and if he wanted help he had to come clean.

"Bastard," muttered Benutti finally. "I hope you catch up with him."

"It's asking a lot. He's probably dead or changed his name.

I guess I expected to find him sitting in that same office."

"Which was where?"

"Hard to remember, but I think it was out of here and turn right."

"Let's go see."

Feeling that he was wasting Major Benutti's time, O'Keefe accompanied the American along the corridor. It was all different, of course. In 1938, the floors and walls were spotless; now every passage was covered in dirt and grime.

"I think it was this one," he said eventually.

A handwritten sign on the door read: *Texas has the biggest dwarfs in the world.* Benutti pushed it open without knocking.

A very young shavetail stiffened to attention.

"Relax," said Benutti, "this isn't an inspection tour. How long have you been in residence, son?"

"Since yesterday, Major."

"Taken any depositions yet?"

"A few, sir. Until an hour ago they were damn near lining up to tell me their war stories, that about all they ever actually did was act as clerks and that they were never members of the Party."

He indicated his desk, which was in a greater state of disarray than Benutti's own.

The G-2 major nodded sympathetically. "What have you done with them all, the krauts?"

"Sent them packing, sir. They're only chasing chow vouchers. I don't want them littering up the corridors and there's only a certain number I can handle at any one time. I'll get around to my quota when the plumbing's working."

"Squadron Leader O'Keefe here is trying to track down an SS officer he met way back in the boondocks," explained Benutti. "Name of Lutz. L—U—T—Z. This used to be his office."

"Used to be is right, Major," said the shavetail, "though the way I understand it this was only one of several he used when he was in Munich."

O'Keefe thought he'd misheard. "You mean you know the name?" he demanded.

Benutti nodded that it was okay to talk.

The shavetail fumbled through the shambles on his desk before coming up with a slim folder. He flicked it open.

"Standartenfuehrer Karl-Erich Lutz. Age 34. Last seen in the Munich area on April 20th. Could have left in the company of Haupsturmfuehrer Josef Scheringer, but that's only hearsay. It seems that Lutz was a big man in the SS. We're finding it a bit difficult to pin down exactly what he did, but it seems he was some kind of camp inspector, liaising between Berlin and the camps to make sure Himmler's orders were being carried out to the letter."

"May I see that?"

The shavetail handed it over reluctantly.

O'Keefe glanced through the folder. The information just given appeared to be a *précis* of the dozen depositions the folder contained. According to a note, only three seemed important, one by a woman, two by men. Apart from that there was nothing, no more than the barest physical description which could have applied to half a million Germans—except for the scar.

There was no doubt in O'Keefe's mind that Standartenfuehrer Lutz was the man he was looking for.

"Major Benutti," he said formally, "I know this is asking a lot but I'd like to borrow this file for a while and with your permission interview the three prime attestants."

Benutti looked doubtful. The young shavetail was horrified.

"Major," he protested, "that file is US Army property. If I let it out of this office into unauthorized hands I'll be in the stockade until I'm ninety-three."

Benutti was inclined to agree until he saw the determined expression in O'Keefe's face.

"Are you in this man's army for the duration or are you planning a career?" he asked the youngster.

"My father's a two-star general, Major, and he's going to kick the shit out of me if I haven't made bird colonel by the time I'm thirty-five."

"Fine. In that case I can understand your point of view. You don't want to end up in the stockade or remain a second lieutenant for the rest of your enlistment, but the only way you'll end up with stars on your shoulder is by taking chances. If you're willing to trust Squadron Leader O'Keefe, so am I. You can book the file out to me, but just to make sure this deal is a two-way street, we'll have our own private arrangement with the Squadron Leader. He can interview who he likes, but any hard intelligence he turns up that might affect our zone of occupation he passes on to you. If it's Class A stuff, you can only benefit. If there's nothing to be found, you lose nothing. Okay?"

"That's fine with me," said O'Keefe quickly. "Anything to do with Lutz that affects your area you'll have within the hour."

"Okay," said the shavetail finally, "but I don't ever see me making general. Sign here, Major."

In the corridor Benutti said, "That was a nice double shuffle, Squadron Leader."

O'Keefe looked at him innocently. "Double shuffle?"

"You only agreed to give the kid any information on Lutz that affects our area. Now you know and I know that wherever this character is, he's a hell of a long way from Bavaria."

O'Keefe had the grace to grin.

"Not that it matters," added Benutti. "I wish you luck, but the smart money says you don't stand a snowball in hell's chance of turning him up."

"We'll see."

"I guess we will. What's your first move?"

"To go over these depositions with a toothcomb, then see the Germans who made them."

"US Intelligence isn't that bad, you know. You can bet your life that whatever's in the files is all there is to be had."

"Perhaps," said O'Keefe. "But don't forget that to your men Lutz is just another name among ten thousand. To me he's special."

"You can use my office if you want to. I can easily squeeze another desk in."

"Thanks, but no. I'd better get back to my own people."

Benutti's smile was all sympathy. "You've got guts, I'll say that for you."

"How's that?"

"You wouldn't catch me drinking British coffee if they gave me Himmler gift-wrapped."

Three

O'Keefe was back at his Marienplatz base by 5 p.m. Apart from Flight Sergeant Caradoc, the two offices allocated to the RAF Intelligence team were empty. O'Keefe had agreed that the junior NCOs and the clerks could be billeted elsewhere; he and Caradoc would sleep on camp beds, on top of the job.

"Anything happening, Jim?" asked O'Keefe.

As always, when they were alone, the pair were on first name terms.

"Not a hell of a lot. The grapevine said an RAF officer was shot by a sniper earlier and I had a peculiar feeling it was you."

"Not a chance. I'm too lucky."

"Well, somebody caught it. Christ, I thought the war was over."

"It won't be over until the last German lays down the last gun. Even then it won't be over or some of them."

O'Keefe was anxious to open the folder and go over each affidavit in detail, but first things had to come first. "Anything else?"

"Nothing that justifies our *per diem*. 7th Army Signals have hooked us in to a phone system, but nobody's bothered to call. I suppose that's one advantage of being an outfit like ours. If the RAF wants to know where we are we say we're with General Patch's G-2. And if the 7th Army wants to know why we're on their ration strength, we refer them to the RAF. By the time it's all sorted out we should be on our way home."

"Spoken like an old soldier. Put the coffee on, will you? No, make that tea."

"Are we working late?"

"It could well be. I'll let you know when I've looked through this."

Caradoc pumped up the primus and rinsed out a couple of cups. An emergency water supply had been connected earlier in the day for the buildings in this part of Munich. It didn't always work as it should and occasionally the water came out looking like cocoa, but the US medical people had okayed it as fit for consumption provided it was boiled first.

A couple of years older than O'Keefe, Caradoc was more the fighter pilot's traditional build, five feet eight inches and stocky. He wore the ribbon of the DFM and had nine enemy aircraft to his credit.

On more than one occasion O'Keefe had offered to recommend him for a commission, but the offer was always refused.

"I know my way around aeroplanes, Mike, and I know how to survive in a fighter war. But I don't know too many rugger songs or a good year for claret. Neither do I want to be so worried about the second that I'll forget how to do the first. The last thing my wife and kids need is a widow's pension."

He returned with the tea, hot and sweet the way O'Keefe liked it, and perched himself on the edge of the desk.

"What's in the folder?"

"Lutz," answered O'Keefe laconically.

Caradoc's eyes widened. "Our Lutz?"

"Ours."

Caradoc was fully familiar with their prime reason for being in Munich.

"You didn't waste much time."

"Pure accident." O'Keefe explained about his meeting with Benutti.

"Anything interesting?"

"Most of it's garbage, but there are three attestants I intend having a word with myself. You never know, we might get lucky."

"How far does our brief extend exactly?"

"If Lutz is still in Germany and we can find him, we pick him up or put a bullet through his head. I'm not fussy which, though don't quote me on that."

"And if he's not in Germany? If he's in Austria or Italy, for example?"

"Then we pass the word down the line to whoever's got the

command in that area, although I'm beginning to have second thoughts on that. Wherever he is, I'd like to get him myself—even if it's Australia."

"Group won't go much on that."

"I'll handle Group, if and when we learn which rathole Lutz is skulking in. Is there anything to drink around here?"

Caradoc walked over to a filing cabinet and pulled open a drawer. From inside he produced a full bottle of whisky and two glasses. O'Keefe blinked in astonishment.

"Where the hell did you get that?"

"Never you mind. What you don't know can't be used in evidence at my court martial."

He half filled both tumblers and pushed one across the desk.

"Where do we begin?"

"We interview the three attestants who seem to have something to say, and the sooner the better. The Americans have covered the ground once, but to them Lutz is just another name. He's a big fish to us but way down the pecking order as far as everyone else is concerned. His trail's not exactly hot but it's warm. In a week or ten days it'll be colder and a month after that he'll be gone for good."

"We'd better get on with it then. Who are the three?"

O'Keefe consulted the depositions.

"Fräulein Greta Hoegel, Obergefreiters Willi Goertz and Hans Toller. The two corporals might be as innocent as new-born lambs, but it wouldn't be the first time an SS officer thought it judicious to don the uniform of a Wehrmacht NCO. The Americans seem to have done a thorough job, but I know Lutz better than anyone in the 7th Army so I might find out something they missed."

"How did the American G-2 get on to them in the first place?"

"They walked in off the streets."

"All of them? That's a bit odd, isn't it?"

"Not if they wanted to exchange information for food or cigarettes."

"But if they had something to hide?"

"Maybe. On the other hand, it's sometimes better to make

your statement and get a clearance while everyone's disorganized. Anyway, round them up. There are no addresses on the depositions so you'd better talk to the Americans first—in person, I think, rather than by phone. See either Master Sergeant Hansen or Major Benutti. Tell them I sent you. Any problems, get them to call me here."

"Where's their Headquarters?"

O'Keefe gave him directions.

Alone, he switched on the desk lamp, refilled the whisky tumbler, and extracted from the folder the three depositions which interested him most. He decided to leave the girl's until last and deal with the other two in alphabetical order. Thus, Obergefreiter Goertz's statement was looked at first.

Because, after the war, there were so many Germans to be interrogated and so few trained personnel available to carry out the interrogations, the usual question and answer method was abandoned as being too lengthy. Instead, after a preliminary and unrecorded session, the subject was simply asked to write out in his own hand information relevant to the matter under discussion. O'Keefe skipped the opening pieces where Goertz gave his rank and regiment and stated that the following was made of his own free will. It was, of course, in German.

I first met Karl-Erich Lutz when he was a Sturmbannfuehrer, in 1944, when I was assigned to him as his driver during the time he was in Munich. This was most unusual as the SS normally wanted their own drivers—and I should like to make it clear that I was never a member of the SS. I can only suppose that Sturmbannfuehrer Lutz could not find an SS driver and asked my CO for a replacement.

He was in Munich for just one day. In the morning he asked me to drive him from SS headquarters to an apartment block near the river. I forget the exact address. I was parked outside for about an hour. Later I drove him to Schleissheim airfield, where I was dismissed.

The next and only other time I saw him was several weeks ago. I believe the date was the 18th or 19th April.

He was wearing the rank insignia of a Standartenfuehrer and walking through the city in the company of an SS Hauptsturmfuehrer whose face I did not know. Lutz did not see me, or if he did, did not recognize or acknowledge me, even though we passed within feet of each other. I did hear him say to the Hauptsturmfuehrer, however, that they could expect little assistance from the Italians.

This was the last I saw of Standartenfuehrer Lutz.

O'Keefe turned quickly to the testimony of Obergefreiter Hans Toller. This began with a statement to the effect that he had never been a member of the Nazi Party and had certainly never taken part in any atrocities. He had, however, seen the inside of Dachau, normally forbidden unless you were an inmate or a member of the SS.

... It must have been November or December 1944 when I was told by my section officer to take my truck to the railway sidings. You must understand that this was over a thousand metres from the railway station itself, and my truck was one of a fleet of six.

We were told that our eventual destination was Dachau.

(The next sentence was started several times and erased completely. Then Toller got down to it.)

This had never happened before, being asked to drive into Dachau; the camp had its own railway terminal but apparently something had rendered it temporarily out of action.

At the Munich sidings we pulled up next to cattle cars and were told to stay in our cabs, that what was happening behind us was not our concern. The trucks were surrounded by SS men, but it was impossible not to see something of what was going on via my rear-view mirrors.

I don't want to write any more on the subject. I had nothing to do with it, nothing to do with these wretches, these bags of bones who stank terribly as they were loaded into my truck.

We drove to Dachau, where we were told to pull up in convoy just inside the main gates. I heard one officer addressed as Hauptsturmfuehrer Scheringer, and an SS guard—who was in the co-driver's seat, as they were in all the trucks—remarked to me that Scheringer knew what to do with Poles and Russians. He'd better, as the tall officer next to him was Standartenfuehrer Lutz from Berlin.

I was terrified. One had heard stories of Dachau, how no one ever came out, and I was frightened that we drivers might be killed to stop us talking. But that didn't happen.

I saw Hauptsturmfuehrer Scheringer several times in Munich until the beginning of April this year, and then I did not see him again. Perhaps he ran before the Americans arrived. There were rumours to that effect circulating for weeks, that the SS were going to leave us to face the music.

Standartenfuehrer Lutz I saw several times more, the last occasion being, I believe, about 19th or 20th April. But much was happening during that period to do with Freedom Action Bavaria and few of the ordinary troops knew what was going on. However, Lutz was stationed, to the best of my knowledge, in Berlin, and he would have been a fool to return there, wouldn't he?

Would he not, thought O'Keefe, draining his glass and lighting a cigarette.

So what did he have so far? That Lutz was apparently based in Berlin, but spent some time in Munich and Dachau— which seemed to indicate that he was part of the camp inspectorate, a grim official euphemism for the department which made sure that Himmler's policy of extermination was being carried out to the letter. Second, that he had a crony by the name of Scheringer on the staff at Dachau. Third, that he was last seen on the 18th, 19th or 20th April.

The Toller statement was right. Lutz was a survivor. He would not be in Bavaria towards the war's end to carry out his duties as camp inspector like a good Nazi; he would be in

51

Bavaria because Bavaria was but a stone's throw from Austria and well away from the main Allied thrust.

With a lot of patient spadework, no doubt a complete dossier on the career of Karl-Erich Lutz could be assembled, detailing his activities, his crimes, and so on, but by the time that happened he could be anywhere.

It was not the slightest use O'Keefe proving that the man was a murderer—which he knew anyway—if the murderer could not be found.

Feeling more than somewhat depressed as the magnitude of the task suddenly struck him, he turned to the third testimony. Greta Hoegel, age 23.

My name is Greta Hoegel and I have lived in Munich all my life. My parents are dead and I have no brothers or sisters. It was my intention to study law but the war precluded that.

Throughout the conflict I worked for the German Red Cross and the *Sicherheits und Hilfdienst*—the Rescue and Repair Service.

All girls of my generation were required to join the BDM, the Youth Organization for females, and I was no different from the others.

Because of my connections with the BDM, I met Karl-Erich Lutz, then an Untersturmfuehrer, in 1937, when I was fifteen. He always behaved most correctly towards me, possibly because of my youth.

Shortly after England declared war on Germany [O'Keefe underlined that phrase; it could indicate resentment], Herr Lutz was transferred permanently to Berlin. He wrote to me when other duties would permit and on visits to Munich would come and see me in the apartment I had by the river. [O'Keefe cross-referenced this with a sentence from Goertz's statement.] It will not take much imagination to conclude that we became lovers.

As the war progressed and Herr Lutz rose in rank, his trips to Munich became less frequent. I understood the need for this. He was an important man in the Reich and his country came before his private life. Nevertheless, whatever the result of the conflict, I was given to understand that whatever happened to one of us would happen to both.

This was the third time O'Keefe had read the girl's statement, but its significance was only just sinking in.

In late February or early March of this year, shortly before the Allies crossed the Rhine at Remagen, I received a private, unheralded visit from Herr Lutz, during which he indicated that he, among others, had been chosen to undertake an important commission, one that he himself had been instrumental in originating many years before. The war was over, for now: but there would be another time and another place, perhaps another leader.

He said no more, only that he would be back in Munich within a few weeks and that I would be part of whatever the great new plans were.

I never saw him again. Via other people I understand he was seen in the city during the third week of April, but he made no further contact with me.

This is a true statement made voluntarily.

Greta Hoegel's signature and the date of the testimony followed.

O'Keefe closed the folder. "Voluntarily" was the *mot juste*. 7th Army had been in Munich for ten days, Intelligence a mere forty-eight hours. With all the problems of administration, it should have taken them months to round up a witness like Greta Hoegel.

Goertz and Toller could prove important, but Greta was the gilt on the gingerbread.

There were only two questions. Was she a scorned woman out for revenge or was she a cog in some devious plot? He wouldn't know the answer to either until he'd seen the lady herself.

Flight Sergeant Caradoc returned at 21:00 hours, looking

as if he had fought fifteen rounds with Joe Louis. The whisky bottle was half empty. O'Keefe topped up a tumbler and passed it across to the NCO.

"Well?"

"I know where they are and I know where they'll be tomorrow morning, but for the moment the Yanks have got some kind of curfew on. Step outside wearing the wrong colour uniform and you wind up dead."

O'Keefe found it difficult to curb his impatience.

"So where will they be tomorrow morning?"

"Right here, Mike. On the stroke of nine."

Four

Due to sniper activity near the river, Master Sergeant Hansen was almost two hours later delivering the three Germans. He announced his arrival by blasting the opening bars of Beethoven's Fifth Symphony on the jeep's klaxon. Caradoc went out to meet him.

Because space was at a premium and a proper interrogation impossible with people walking in and out, O'Keefe had told the rest of the RAF team to lose themselves for a few hours. Thus, the larger of the two offices was to be used as a waiting-room, with Caradoc in attendance to ensure that the Germans did not compare notes, and the smaller as the interview room.

O'Keefe had decided to see Goertz first, Toller second. He would save the girl for dessert. She was a prize, if one could talk about prizes in such a context.

Goertz proved a disappointment from the start. He was a small, colourless individual, obviously terrified that he, a humble corporal, might be accused of war crimes. Nevertheless, O'Keefe knew, having taking part in post-operation debriefings on both sides of the table, that sometimes the right questions could elicit information that had been genuinely forgotten.

In the first place he concentrated on that section of Goertz's testimony which referred to driving Lutz to the apartment block by the river. It was doubtful if the Obergefreiter knew that the girl in the anteroom lived there, but if he did and chose not to declare it voluntarily, that was something to know. A man who will commit errors of omission in one respect may well do so in another.

"Tell me about the time you drove for Standartenfuehrer Lutz in 1944."

"He was only a Sturmbannfuehrer then, Herr Major," said Goertz respectfully, using the Wehrmacht equivalent of squadron leader. "And I have nothing to add to my statement."

"But you assumed he was going to see a girl, did you not?"

"I thought it a possibility, but where SS officers were concerned it was better not to ask too many questions. I didn't see the girl—if there was a girl—and I never learned her identity."

"Were you never curious?"

"As I have just explained, Herr Major, with the SS it was better not to be. They treated the Wehrmacht like dogs."

"And yet Lutz allowed you to drive for him. An SS officer of field rank actually allowed a Wehrmacht corporal to drive him to an assignation. Wouldn't you say that was indiscreet?"

Goertz shrugged noncommittally. "I have already explained that in my statement to the Americans, Herr Major. I assumed that an SS driver was not available or that Sturmbannfuehrer Lutz did not wish to let the SS know he had a girl friend in Munich. The Major may not be aware of it, but it was not uncommon in the SS for the lower ranks to be encouraged to spy on their officers. Perhaps the girl was married to a general or perhaps she had . . . racial taints."

O'Keefe snapped the pencil he was holding. Christ, they were all the bloody same.

"You mean she might have been a Jew?"

Goertz realized he had said the wrong thing.

"I have nothing against Jews, Herr Major. My record. . . ."

"Never mind your bloody record. Others will get around to discussing that sooner or later. All I'm interested in is your relationship with Lutz. I have a feeling it's not all you profess it to be. Perhaps you're not a corporal in the Wehrmacht at all. Now that Germany is defeated a great many former SS men are turning their coats and pleading innocence."

"That isn't true, Herr Major," blustered Goertz. "It is exactly as I wrote in my statement."

The man was starting to sweat, but really there was no need. O'Keefe believed him. Goertz wouldn't have been allowed within a hundred miles of an SS training depot.

"Very well," he said. "Let's take it for the moment that I accept that part of your story and proceed to the last time you saw Lutz." O'Keefe referred to the document on his desk. "The 18th or 19th of April."

Goertz wiped his hands with a filthy handkerchief.

"That is correct, Herr Major. I regret I cannot be more accurate about the date."

"It's unimportant for the moment. What is important is that he was wearing the uniform of a Standartenfuehrer and was accompanied by an Hauptsturmfuehrer."

"Correct, Herr Major."

"But you do not know the name of the SS captain?"

"No, sir."

"I see. Tell me again what you overheard Lutz say."

Goertz frowned. "It's very hard. So much was going on at the time. There was talk of revolution—gossip, you understand—and we all knew the Allies were very close. We, the Wehrmacht, did not know whether the SS would round us all up and make us defend the city or whether they would run for it and leave us to take the blame for such places as Dachau."

"Tell me what you heard," repeated O'Keefe.

"It was very brief, something about the Italians being unreliable, about not counting on much assistance from them."

"Didn't that strike you as odd? The Italians made a separate peace with the Allies in 1943."

"It did, sir. However. . . ."

Goertz looked around the room furtively, as though expecting a dozen jackbooted figures to leap from the cupboards.

"I did not get the impression that Herr Lutz was talking about the Italian armed forces. I understood him to mean that he was planning an escape via Italy. Towards the end there were many rumours that high-ranking SS officers had an escape line already planned. They were never more than rumours, you understand, but it made sense to those of us who talked about it. And where would they go? Switzerland was out of the question. It had to be south, into Austria and then Italy."

"But how could they do that without assistance? They would need gasoline, papers. And where would they go after Italy?"

"I don't know, sir. I have given you all the information I can, which I trust will be recorded."

O'Keefe was disappointed. It was no secret in Allied Intelligence circles that ranking Nazis, military and civilian, had provided themselves with an escape hatch, though details were hard to come by. It was probably the scenic route, however—Bavaria/Austria/Genoa, from where neutral ships sailed regularly to South America.

But something in Greta Hoegel's statement made him certain that Lutz was not just out to save his own neck.

> . . . indicated that he, among others, had been chosen to undertake an important commission. . . .

None of it added up, but he would get no further with Goertz. Except for one last question.

"According to the Americans," he said, "you walked in off the street and volunteered this information concerning Lutz. Why?"

"Because we ordinary German soldiers have nothing in common with the SS. They are the war criminals, not us. And I did not tell the *Amis* only about Lutz. I gave them half a dozen statements concerning other SS officers."

"You're a pleasant little bastard, aren't you."

It was obviously a well-rehearsed answer and one the Occupying Powers would doubtless hear *ad nauseam* in the coming months. By giving a little intelligence here, a *soup-çon* there, an informer could guarantee his cigarette ration for a year.

"Flight Sergeant Caradoc," called O'Keefe in German.

Caradoc appeared in the communicating door.

"Sir?"

"Take this one into the other room and see he doesn't talk to the girl. I'll see Toller next."

O'Keefe could not get it out of his head that Toller was playing a part. He seemed apprehensive enough, more so than Goertz. He also seemed to be regretting that he had mentioned his visit to Dachau. Yet O'Keefe had the feeling there was more to the man than met the eye.

He was talking almost before being given permission to sit.

"I must repeat, Herr Major, that I had nothing to do with the atrocities which I have heard were committed at Dachau."

"You do your country's efficiency a disservice," said O'Keefe. "It wasn't only Dachau. There's Auschwitz, Bergen-Belsen, Treblinka, Ravensbrück, Sachsenhausen. . . . The list is endless."

"But I have never heard of some of those places. How could I be responsible. . . ."

"Every German is responsible. Every German adult is in some way culpable."

"How can that be? We simply did as we were told, as every soldier must."

"You knew what was happening in Dachau."

"I'd . . . heard rumours."

"More than rumours, Obergefreiter. Let me repeat what you wrote in your statement. 'I was terrified. One had heard stories of Dachau, how no one ever came out, and I was frightened that we drivers might be killed to stop us talking.' Slightly more than rumours, wouldn't you say?"

"Herr Major, I swear by all that's holy that I did no more than drive a truckload of prisoners to the camp."

"Do you know what happened to those prisoners?"

"Of course not."

"But you could hazard a guess."

"No, Herr Major."

"Can't or won't?"

"I was a driver. I have no idea what happened to the prisoners."

"Then let me tell you. The majority were doubtless killed, which means that a good case for conspiracy to murder could be made out against you."

O'Keefe was far from sure of his law here, but it sounded impressive enough. It had no effect on Toller, however. The German's jawline tightened but he said nothing.

O'Keefe changed tack. He referred to Toller's statement.

"You say here that while at the camp you heard a guard mention two officers by name—Lutz and Scheringer."

"That is correct, Herr Major. I got the impression that Scheringer was on the camp staff but that Lutz was based in Berlin."

"You only got the impression that Lutz was based in Berlin? The SS guard told you he was."

"That's what I meant to say, sir."

"Then kindly say precisely what you mean, Toller. If you force me to read between the lines I might decide to do it with a crowbar."

O'Keefe lit a cigarette and saw the German corporal lick his lips at the sight of the packet. O'Keefe put it back in his pocket.

"You last saw Scheringer in Munich at the beginning of April. Is that correct?"

"Yes, sir."

"Was he a regular visitor to the city?"

"Not regular, but I'd seen him once or twice before I actually knew who he was."

"And Lutz?"

"Several times also, but not after April 19th or 20th. Perhaps a day or two earlier, perhaps a day or two later."

"You can't be sure?"

"It's hard to remember, sir."

"Yes, I'm sure it is. I'm sure there are lots of matters you would prefer to forget."

He leaned back in his chair and wondered what it was about Toller that troubled him. The man seemed straightforward enough, just scared.

"Why did you volunteer this information about Lutz and Scheringer?" he asked.

"Because I was worried that someone else might report my presence in Dachau and misinterpret it, Herr Major."

Well, that seemed reasonable enough, the action of an innocent man as opposed to a guilty one.

O'Keefe called for Caradoc. This time he spoke in rapid English. Although Caradoc's German was excellent, he did not want Toller or Goertz to understand what he was saying.

"Give the two corporals a pad of paper apiece and get them to draw a pen portrait of the Hauptsturmfuehrer they saw with Lutz. I want to see if it's the same man." If it was, he could safely assume they were on the run together. "After that, they can go."

"And the girl?"

"I'll see her now."

"Do you want me to chaperon you?"

O'Keefe missed the look of amusement in Caradoc's eyes.

"Chaperon me? Do you think I'm likely to attack her?"

"I think it might be the other way round. You don't get the full impact until she's close up, but believe me she's really something."

"Let's have her in then. Anything would be an improvement on those two creeps."

O'Keefe had only caught a brief glimpse of Greta Hoegel when she was brought in from Hansen's jeep, but as she sat down and crossed her long legs he saw precisely what Caradoc meant.

Her hair was very blonde, in no way touched up with chemicals, and tied back with a blue ribbon which matched the colour of her eyes. She was almost as tall as Caradoc, five feet seven or eight, and beautifully slim. Cosmetics were obviously hard to come by in Germany, but from somewhere she'd dug up a pale lipstick and used it sparingly. Her dark-grey two-piece, though several years old, was of quality material and clean.

She was not at all what O'Keefe had expected and he was momentarily thrown off balance.

"If you have a cigarette I would appreciate one, Squadron

Leader," she said in perfectly good if accented English.

O'Keefe had given it to her and lit it before he was conscious of either action.

"Where did you learn to speak English?" he asked.

"At school. My grammar is good, I think, but my accent is atrocious."

"Far from it," O'Keefe found himself saying.

He pulled himself together. This was Lutz's girl friend, mistress, and possibly tarred with the same brush as her lover. She was doubtless aware that she was extremely desirable and had probably used her allure to get her own way on many occasions. Well, it wasn't going to work here.

"But I think we'll carry out the interview in German," he added. "That way there will be no misunderstanding."

"Misunderstanding, Herr Major?"

She gave him a look that caused something in his groin to tell him he'd have to concentrate doubly hard if he was to retain the advantage. He cleared his throat.

"I regret having to ask questions that might cause embarrassment, Fräulein Hoegel, but I'm afraid that's part of my job. In your statement you say that you and Lutz were lovers."

"That is correct, Herr Major. Standartenfuehrer Lutz's duties involved a great deal of travelling, but he would always visit me when in Munich."

"How often was that?"

"At the beginning of the war, once a month. Later on, not so much."

"Where was he when not in Berlin or Munich?"

"I have no idea."

"I find that hard to believe."

"That is your privilege, Herr Major, but the Standartenfuehrer spoke little of his job. You will understand that that was not his reason for visiting me," she added sweetly.

Germany one, England nil, thought O'Keefe. All right, sweetheart, if you want to play it like that.

"Did you form any opinion regarding the nature of his job?" he asked.

"None." Greta Hoegel leaned forward, ostensibly to put out

her cigarette. But the movement brought her several feet closer to O'Keefe and he caught a whiff of expensive perfume, obtained from Christ knows where.

"Our relationship was the simplest and oldest in the world," she went on. "Whenever he could he made me gifts of scent, stockings, brandy, the occasional fur. In exchange, I gave him my body. It happens every day, Herr Major, and not only in Germany."

She was winning the opening rounds of this encounter hands down and it was time he did something about it. Ignoring her feelings he asked, "What about money?"

He was gratified to see her cheeks redden.

"No, Herr Major, never money. I am not a whore."

That depends upon definition, he thought, and followed up quickly with, "But you were his mistress—men sometimes say things they shouldn't to their mistresses."

"Not Lutz."

There was something about the way she said Lutz which made O'Keefe look at her sharply. She tried to hide what her eyes were revealing, but she was just too late: it was loathing.

O'Keefe thought he was beginning to understand.

"Fräulein Hoegel," he said, "there are two parts of your statement to American Intelligence that puzzle me and a third item, not actually in the testimony, that positively amazes me. We'll deal with that first. According to Major Benutti, you were one of the first on his doorstep when they opened shop. Now why should that be? I can understand Toller and Goertz informing in return for a few cigarettes, but why you? Lutz was good to you throughout the war. He gave you perfume and stockings, possibly even paid the rent for your apartment. Surely he deserves more loyalty than you're showing."

Greta Hoegel said nothing. O'Keefe pressed on, convinced he was on the right track.

"Secondly, part of your statement reveals that, on at least one occasion, he did talk about his job. You know the part I mean, of course; it's where he says he's been chosen to undertake an important commission."

"A man's bragging. Men do boast, you know exaggerate. I don't know why I bothered to mention it."

"Don't you, Fräulein, don't you really? Then there's this last piece, and I quote: ". . . whatever the result of the conflict I was given to understand that what happened to one of us would happen to both. . . ." But it didn't, did it, Fräulein? You knew that Lutz was going to make a run for it and you confidently expected him to take you along. You waited, and he left you waiting. You made enquiries and discovered that he was seen in Munich around 19th/20th April, so you knew bloody well it wasn't a question of him having been killed or captured elsewhere. After all the promises, all the love-making, he'd done what you least expected. He'd run out on you."

"You're quite wrong, Herr Major," said the girl, but her voice wavered as she spoke.

O'Keefe kept after her. "I don't think I am, Fräulein. I think we're just beginning to understand one another. You couldn't believe it at first, I suppose. You kept on expecting him to turn up. But as the Americans got closer you realized that Herr Lutz had gone for good, that the gifts meant nothing, that you'd been used until he no longer needed or wanted you."

Behind the tough, self-assured exterior was evidently some marshmallow, for Greta Hoegel was finding it difficult not to cry.

In spite of himself, O'Keefe felt acutely embarrassed at the drubbing he'd given her. To cover his discomfort he poured two small tots of whisky into a couple of glasses and handed one to her.

She accepted it without thanks.

"He had no right," she said softly, as though talking to herself. "He knew the war was coming to an end and that for those of us left in Germany, especially the women and children, things were going to be very hard. If he hadn't promised to take me with him I wouldn't feel so bitter. But he did. I understand why now, of course. He needed the use of my apartment in case the Americans arrived sooner than expected or the FAB faction took over the city."

There was a long silence.

"Just one more question and then you can go, Fräulein," O'Keefe said eventually. "Do you know where Lutz is now or where he went?"

"No." The whisky had helped; she was recovering her composure. "No, I don't."

"In that case. . . ." O'Keefe half-rose from his chair.

Greta Hoegel remained seated. "What will happen to me?" she asked.

"Nothing," answered O'Keefe. "To the best of my knowledge it's not a crime to have been the mistress of an SS officer. No charges will be brought against you. You're free to go."

"Out there? That's not freedom, Herr Major."

O'Keefe felt like showing her Dachau.

"It's all you have, Fräulein."

"Perhaps not—not if I have something to sell."

"What something?"

"Papers. Lutz left a briefcase containing some papers in my apartment. I've looked at them but they make no sense to me. Perhaps they're of no value or perhaps he intended returning for them but was unable—or unwilling."

O'Keefe was interested, but not that much. Lutz was not the sort of individual to leave incriminating evidence lying around. Neither would Greta Hoegel sell them to anyone other than the highest bidder. But he thought he could see what she was getting at. She needed a protector.

"Is it possible to get into your apartment?" he asked.

She seemed surprised.

"Of course. There is very little bomb damage and I saw no reason to move out."

Then she understood.

"Oh, I see what you mean. No, it hasn't yet been commandeered by the Americans, but no doubt that will happen sooner or later. In the meantime, I still live there. I have water from a communal tap and electricity when it works, which isn't often."

"And you still have the papers?"

"Naturally."

"Would you be willing to let me see them?"

"Whenever you wish."

O'Keefe felt himself grow hard.

"Tonight," he said. "At nine o'clock."

He escorted her to the door which led directly into the corridor, shook her hand formally, and returned to his desk. Only when Caradoc came in did he realize he did not know where she lived.

"Well, I see you've still got your pants," grinned the NCO. "How did it go?"

"Well enough. I'm seeing her later tonight. She's got some documents Lutz left behind. Probably nothing but I'd better take a look. You've got her address, I suppose?"

"Would I let you down like that? Of course I've got her address. But while you've still got your marbles, do you want to take a look at these?"

The twenty minutes spent with Greta Hoegel had caused O'Keefe to forget the assignment he had given Caradoc.

"What are they?"

"The independent descriptions made by Toller and Goertz of the Hauptsturmfuehrer they saw with Lutz."

"And. . . ."

"Identical down to the fingernails."

O'Keefe grunted with satisfaction. Caradoc looked unhappy.

"It's a big world, Mike. Okay, so they're probably together, but they could be anywhere. They've also got three weeks start on us."

"And we've now got two descriptions instead of one."

"Which leads us precisely where? Lutz is not the only item on the agenda."

"Quite right. Why the hell is it so quiet around here? There should be telephones ringing, typewriters clacking. Where the hell is everybody?"

"You told them to get lost, remember?"

"So I did. Well, they've been lost long enough. Round 'em up, Jim."

Alone, O'Keefe lit a cigarette and allowed himself to daydream about the evening ahead. A bottle of wine or two, some soft lights. . . .

Christ, he was going soft in the skull. Where the hell

65

was he going to pick up wine in this shambles of a city?

He picked up the phone and asked to be connected to Major Joe Benutti.

Five

Strip an American naked and put him in a wilderness, hundreds of miles from civilization, and within hours he will have fixed a pitcher of dry martinis, a six-course meal, and be pacing out the length of the swimming pool. Like Harry Houdini and handcuffs, you didn't ask how it was done, you just marvelled and accepted that it was.

In a brown-paper sack the G-2 major had placed a couple of bottles of dry white wine, a bottle of brandy, a ready-cooked duck, a tin of Brazilian coffee, some fresh white bread and a packet of butter.

As gifts to go a-courtin' with, they beat the hell out of a partridge in a pear tree. O'Keefe was too astonished to do more than stammer his thanks.

"Let's call it an investigation. There might be something in the briefcase to interest us."

Benutti's generosity also extended to the loan of a jeep and a PFC driver. Leaving a vehicle unattended was asking for trouble. You could disable it by removing the rotor arm, but the kraut black marketeers would strip it "quicker than a two-dollar whore climbs out of her dress." Benutti already had one man facing a court martial for losing a full tank of gas, his battery, lights, windshield wipers, plus all the tyres and wheels. He'd left the vehicle for five minutes.

It was only a short drive from Marienplatz to Greta Hoegel's apartment in a building overlooking the River Isar, but many of the streets had yet to be cleared of debris and the going was difficult. Between them, the RAF and the USAAF had destroyed something like three-quarters of the old city and approximately one-sixth of the Bavarian capital as a whole. A third of the inhabitants had lost their homes. Greta was fortunate not to be among them. Doubtless her building would be taken over sooner or later by the Allies, to be used as an administration block or temporarily to re-house some of the homeless, but for the moment that had not happened.

The driver pulled up and switched off the ignition.

"I'll try not to keep you too long," said O'Keefe, knowing he was lying.

"Don't worry about it, Squadron Leader. In a way you're doing me a favour."

'How's that?"

"I backed a six-wheeler into a wall yesterday, with some help from a bottle of bourbon. Major Benutti was going to throw the book at me, but as long as I get you home safely, I'm in the clear."

O'Keefe felt less guilty after that.

Inside, it was much as he had expected, much like other buildings he had seen elsewhere in Germany. If it was still considered habitable, Christ knows what the rest were like.

There was broken glass on the floor and rubble everywhere. There were no carpets; they had either been stored for safe-keeping by the block's owner or they had been stolen. Above everything lingered a smell of damp and decay. Not for the first time did O'Keefe think that, in any war, civilians got the worst of it.

Greta's apartment number was 5, on the second floor. There was an elevator but it didn't work. A handwritten notice on the grille said that it was temporarily out of order. It was dated November 20, 1944.

He arrived outside number 5 a few minutes after nine. There was a bell but it seemed to be in the same condition as the elevator. Eventually he knocked.

When the door opened she almost took his breath away. She had put on a short black skirt and a fawn peasant blouse, cut low at the neck, and washed and combed out her blonde hair. She had also done something with her eyes, used mascara or eye shadow or whatever the *ersatz* equivalent was. Where earlier in the day she had looked merely beautiful, now she was sensational.

She smiled, genuinely pleased to see him.

"Good evening, Squadron Leader," she said in German.

O'Keefe returned the smile. "Good evening."

She stood to one side to allow him through.

It was a small apartment: bedroom, sitting-room, kitchen and bathroom, although, she explained, there was never any water for baths, and water for cooking and washing had to be obtained from a stand-pipe at the rear of the block between the hours of midday and 2 p.m.

The furniture was old but of superior quality, and on the table and sideboard she had placed candles, acquired from God knows where.

The windows overlooking the street had all been shattered by blast, the gaps plugged with blackout material or covered with cardboard. The electricity was off and there was no form of heating, but fortunately it was a warm evening.

"I'm sorry it's not the Ritz," she said.

He realized he was staring and apologized for it.

"It's not so very different from the great many London houses I've seen in the last few years."

"I suppose not. It makes you wonder what it was all about, doesn't it?"

To cover what was becoming an awkward moment, he held out the brown-paper sack. Her reaction when she unpacked it was like a child's at Christmas.

"I don't believe it! Is this for me? Wine, duck, brandy, bread and *real* butter! And coffee. It's not possible."

She clutched the tin of coffee to her breasts. "My God, if what I have to show you turns out to be useless, you'll take it all back."

O'Keefe grinned self-consciously.

"No, it's yours."

"But where shall we start?"

"Begin at the beginning and go right through to the end."

"Like the King of Hearts," she said delightedly. "I don't know how to thank you."

"It doesn't matter."

"But it does, Squad. . . ." She stopped. "I can't keep on calling you Squadron Leader or Herr Major."

O'Keefe told her his first name.

She tried it a couple of times. "Mike. Yes, I like that. It suits you. It's direct and unpretentious. And you know mine, of course." Her voice changed as she remembered the ostensible reason for his visit. "Greta Hoegel, former mistress of Karl-Erich Lutz. If you'd like to see the documents I have them ready."

"Later," said O'Keefe. "All this food is making me hungry. Don't forget that we're not used to living like this in the RAF either. So let's open the wine and sample the duck."

"And the bread and butter. It's so long since I tasted real butter that I shouldn't be at all surprised if it makes me ill."

"The bread and butter too, then. If you'll point me in the direction of a corkscrew I'll give the wine a chance to breathe."

She held a hand to her mouth in dismay.

"A corkscrew! Oh Christ, I don't think I have one. There used to be one but it disappeared."

O'Keefe produced a clasp-knife from his tunic pocket. One of the gadgets was a corkscrew. Greta looked at him archly.

"Now I know why you won."

Watching her tuck into the food gave O'Keefe the biggest kick he'd had in years. Her features softened by the flickering candles, every mouthful consumed was accompanied by a sigh of pleasure and every drop of wine savoured as though it were the rarest of vintages.

He hardly touched his own plate or glass. She reminded him of an Australian girl he had met in London during the cold winter of 1941. Before coming to England she had spent her whole life in some one-horse Aussie town where the temperature never dropped below the eighties. Her greatest ambition was to see and feel snow. She had read about it in books, seen photographs of it and scenes depicting it on the Christmas cards. But all she knew was that it was cold and white. The first snowfall had sent her mad with joy. She had rolled in it, eaten it, thrown it, made snowmen. He had never seen such happiness on the face of an adult.

It was that same look that Greta Hoegel wore now. It

seemed unbelievable that he had first met her less than a dozen hours earlier, and unbelievable that she could be in any way connected with Lutz. Lutz was a poisonous bastard who would one day be destroyed. Greta Hoegel seemed somehow remote from anything that could conceivably be called evil.

"More wine?" he asked.

She sighed and shook her head.

"Not another drop or I shall become giggly. And not another morsel of food or I shall become fat."

"Impossible. You're one of those people who burn energy."

"Not in the least. You should have seen me when I was a little girl, thirteen or fourteen. Round as a dumpling with a face like a sausage. It was a job to squeeze me into my uniform."

"I thought German schools didn't go in for school uniforms the way we do."

"It wasn't a school uniform."

O'Keefe shrugged. "All right. Everyone knows that youngsters were forced to join one of the Party youth organizations."

"Not forced, Mike, not in the way you mean it. Not in my case, anyway. I wanted to join and so did just about every other child I knew."

"Forget it. It's over now."

"No, it isn't. If it were you wouldn't be here, you wouldn't want to find Lutz. Something tells me it'll never be over."

"That's foolish talk. In a few years it'll be in the history books and as remote as the Napoleonic Wars. We'll be in our rocking chairs, boring our grandchildren with stories of how tough it was, and they'll wonder what the hell we're talking about."

"Do you really think that?"

"Of course."

He changed the subject. "Why don't I have a look at the papers Lutz left behind while you fix the coffee? After that we can settle back to cigarettes and brandy and perhaps find something more cheerful to talk about."

"I'll get them for you."

It was more a document case than a briefcase, flat, and

fastened with a wraparound zip. The lock, a flimsy affair at best, had been forced, presumably by Greta herself.

O'Keefe was disappointed. It obviously didn't contain much. He'd expected something far bulkier.

He waited until she had cleared the table and disappeared into the kitchen, where he heard her strike a match and light the primus. Only then did he open the case and spread the contents on the sofa beside him.

A cursory examination did little to raise his spirits. At first glance there was nothing to give him any sort of clue as to Lutz's present whereabouts. Three letters, all from the Reich Main Security Office in Berlin and all old, the last dated October, 1944; a four-page pamphlet stamped *Geheim*, Secret, but which turned out to contain nothing more revealing than the calorific and vitamin contents of various foodstuffs; a scrap of paper which had the words "Weight in kilos???" written on it; a gold propelling pencil and a pair of geometric dividers in a suede case.

He felt quite deflated. He had not expected to find a Thomas Cook itinerary showing the precise route by which Lutz (and presumably Scheringer) had fled Germany, but this lot was rubbish. Still, he was a methodical man, and as the smell of coffee drifted through from the kitchen, he examined each item in greater detail.

The three letters might well be of some value to Major Benutti as it was quite clear, in spite of the oblique phraseology, that what Lutz was being asked to do in each was give a pep talk to various camp commandants in an endeavour to get them to speed up extermination processes. The word "extermination" was never used, of course, but now that what happened in Nazi Germany during the war was becoming common knowledge, such sentences as ". . . more efficient methods of disposing of the consignments . . ." took on a sinister and macabre new meaning. If the writers of the letters—all three were signed by someone different—could be found or were already in captivity, their fates were sealed. However, that was neither here nor there for O'Keefe.

He read every sentence in the pamphlet on foodstuffs twice, looking for some hidden meaning. It was possible that the words meant more than their face value, but he doubted it. It was exactly the sort of document that the Nazis would issue to men of Lutz's rank and position, and it wasn't hard to understand why. Before being "disposed of," many inmates of the camps would have a utilitarian value as slave labour. But to do any sort of useful job they would have to be fed the viable minimum, until the law of diminishing returns began to operate. Camp commandants would have different ideas on what that viable minimum should be, hence the pamphlet.

O'Keefe made a mental note to turn it over to Benutti for analysis anyway, but he doubted if 7th Army Intelligence would find it to be anything more than it purported to be.

The scrap of paper bearing the words "Weight in kilos???" baffled him, as it had no doubt baffled Greta. It could mean anything, although the series of question marks seemed indicative that Lutz was unsure of something.

But unsure of what?

The easiest answer was that it had some connection with the pamphlet on foodstuffs—either the weight of food each inmate could consume (not really feasible as that would hardly be measured in kilos, not the way the Nazis fed their unfortunate victims) or the total tonnage needed for each camp per day/week/month.

He took the gold propelling pencil to pieces, but it appeared to have no function other than writing. As for the dividers, most officers in any army, navy or air force carried a pair somewhere in their kit in spite of frequent warnings from the brass that dividers made pinpricks in maps which as a consequence could be of immense value to the enemy. If you had the bloody map to go with them, of course.

He threw the dividers to one side in disgust just as Greta returned, carrying two cups of coffee on a wooden tray.

"No use?"

"Not that I can see, not by themselves. Lutz didn't by any chance leave a map lying around, did he?"

"No. He would frequently have maps with him when he ... visited ... me, but he never let me see them and I wasn't really interested. I assumed they had something to do with the war."

"Damn it to hell. . . ."

She sat beside him on the sofa and reached for his cigarettes. He lit one for her but declined to smoke himself.

"I'm sorry I couldn't be of more help," she said softly.

He was suddenly aware of her proximity, the heavy musk smell of her perfume, the coolness of her hand where it was touching his.

He was chasing moonbeams as far as Lutz was concerned. Sheer chance had enabled him and the SS colonel to survive a conflict which had destroyed millions of others, but it was asking too much of chance that he find Lutz. Such things didn't happen in real life. He would be on a boat to South America by now or hiding in some grim attic, waiting for a contact who might not come. He could even be dead, and of all the possibilities that had to rank as favourite.

But he and Greta Hoegel were alive. It didn't matter a damn that she had once been Lutz's mistress. He would regret it for the rest of his days if he didn't take what she was offering.

He reached for her and kissed her roughly, feeling her tongue probing his mouth. Her hand reached down and he heard her gasp at his hardness and size.

She undressed him slowly, kissing every part of his body, and allowed him to take off her blouse and caress her breasts. But she shook her head when he tried to remove her skirt.

"It's better like this," she whispered.

In any case, she was wearing nothing underneath.

She hovered above him, moving backwards and forwards, stoking him with her dampness, tantalizing him.

He took hold of her buttocks beneath the skirt and tried to drag her on to him, impale her, but she slid out of his grasp.

Moving her lips slowly downwards, kissing and nibbling and giving tiny whimpers of pleasure, she finally took him in her mouth, encompassing, deep, licking with her tongue, sending shock waves through him.

He gripped her head with both hands, clutching her blonde hair, knowing he must be hurting her but not caring, trying to make her movements match his desire. But she divined his intentions and by some stratagem kept him from coming.

When he thought he could stand it no more she raised her head and kissed him on the mouth. Brutally, he pushed her backwards until she was spreadeagled on the sofa and dragged her skirt above her waist. She opened her legs to receive him.

She whinnied with excitement as he sought her. There was no need for either her fingers or his own to guide him. She was so wet that a short thrust would put him inside her, yet he held back for a few seconds, torturing them both.

"Fuck me," she pleaded in German. "Please fuck me very hard."

She responded to every thrust, pushing at him, raking his back with her nails, clawing at him. Her breath was coming in short, sharp gasps.

"Don't hold it. Don't hold it. . . ."

There was no way he could. He heard her scream from a long way off, from some private place where only she could go, and felt her shudder with spasm after spasm after spasm as she bucked and reared and twisted.

Finally, she lay still. A minute passed. Two. Five.

"Dear Christ," she said.

He dressed while she was in the bathroom. When she returned she was wearing a towelling dressing gown and looked, he thought, about fifteen. True, she had repaired her ravaged makeup and fixed her hair, but there was less of the Teutonic maiden about her.

Balls, he told himself with disgust. She's no Guinevere and you're not Lancelot. Bring it down from the clouds. You were both hungry, that's all.

She sat beside him.

"The coffee's gone cold," she said plaintively, and chuckled. "Still, it was in a good cause."

They settled for brandy, sipping it quietly, watching the candles burn lower.

"I want to tell you something," she said eventually. "I know it might spoil it but I want to say it anyway. It was never like that with Lutz. No, listen to me," she pleaded as he tried to hush her up. "Part of me loved him and part of me needed his protection. You've no idea what it was like in Germany and I had to survive. You must understand that."

74

He did. He could no more blame her for what she'd done than he could the pilot of a Messerschmitt for trying to shoot him down.

After a few minutes passed in silence he said, "Look, I'd better be going. I've got an American driver outside who must be thinking by now he didn't get the best of the bargain."

He picked up the document case and zipped it shut, his mind elsewhere.

She walked him to the door.

"Will you come back?"

He thought about it. He wouldn't be in Munich for ever and fraternizing was frowned upon by the brass, but ... well, fuck the brass.

"For now, yes. In a few weeks. . . ."

She put her hand over his mouth.

"Don't talk about a few weeks. That's a lifetime away."

Six

The PFC was dozing when O'Keefe clambered in beside him.

"Sorry I was so long."

The GI grinned.

"Don't worry about it, Squadron Leader. In my outfit waiting around comes with the territory. Just put in a good word for me with Major Benutti, that's all I ask."

The mention of Benutti's name reminded O'Keefe that he wanted to give the Lutz documents to the G-2 major for thorough analysis. It might as well be done here and now.

"You can take me to your own headquarters first," he said. "I'd like a word with Major Benutti before turning in."

"Anything you say, Squadron Leader."

Unzipping the document case to make sure he had everything, O'Keefe was horrified to find it empty. Stupidly, he looked on the floor of the jeep, to see if the papers had fallen out. They hadn't. Which meant that Greta had palmed the stuff after letting him see it. But surely to Christ that was nonsense.

Then he remembered. He hadn't replaced a single item after examining it. He'd simply tossed each one on to the sofa and after that other events had taken over. When he was leaving he'd simply zipped up the case and walked out with it. Empty. Candlelight was all very romantic but it sure as hell didn't help the eyesight.

He cursed himself for being a bloody fool. Of course, it gave him an excuse to go back, which according to Doctor Freud was doubtless the reason he had forgotten the papers in the first place. They'd still be there tomorrow—or would they. It wouldn't be long before the military authorities concluded that Greta's apartment was too big for one woman. There were ten of thousands of homeless Germans on the streets and sooner or later some sort of order would have to be established. It might well be sooner. If he left it until tomorrow he could well find the place had been commandeered and the Lutz documents chucked out with the garbage.

"I'm sorry," he said to the driver, "but I'm afraid we're going to have to go back."

"Back, sir?"

"Yes—back. I've forgotten something."

The GI gave him an old-fashioned look, one that implied that Greta Hoegel must be some broad if he wanted second helpings five minutes after leaving the joint. But he made a U-turn and headed back anyway.

They could hear the screams and the sound of a fight half a block away, and some sixth sense told O'Keefe that it was Greta who was in trouble. He didn't have to question why a group of curious German bystanders were doing nothing except listen. Anyone who had lived under Hitler for twelve years kept well away from someone else's trouble.

The jeep screeched to a halt, tyres burning. O'Keefe left it at the run. From behind he heard the driver yell, "Do you want me to come with you?"

"No. Whistle up some help."

He took the stairs three at a time. The door to the apartment was closed, but he shattered it with a kick.

He did not have to look twice at the man who was mauling Greta in order to recognize him. They'd met earlier in the day, except that now Obergefreiter Toller was no longer the cringing individual who had said his only visit to Dachau was as a dragooned driver. This man was intent upon murder and it doubtless wouldn't be his first.

The German released Greta as O'Keefe launched himself across the room. But O'Keefe had surprise on his side and his shoulder charge sent Toller sprawling.

O'Keefe wasted no time on niceties. As an airman, hand-to-hand combat had not been in the curriculum, but he was strong and fit and had the reflexes of a mongoose. He, too, had killed before, albeit under different circumstances, and he knew that the first few seconds of any battle are the vital ones. Gain superiority then and the rest was academic.

While Toller was still on the floor, O'Keefe unleashed a fearsome kick at his head. The German saw it coming and tried to block it with his right arm, but there was so much force behind it that all he succeeded in doing was tearing the muscles of his bicep, making that arm useless.

He scrambled away across the room, half crawling, half hopping, looking for a weapon. O'Keefe went after him, using his feet.

He would have undoubtedly killed the German, who was no longer in any position to defend himself, if two huge US MPs had not dragged him off. Scared that Major Benutti would slap him in Fort Leavenworth until the Second Coming if anything happened to the Squadron Leader, O'Keefe's driver had acted in doublequick time in flagging down a mobile patrol. He now stood in the doorway, clutching the document case, relieved that his charge was still in one piece. Though the way his luck was running, the jeep would probably be in eight million pieces by the time he got back to it.

Held by the MPs, O'Keefe gradually calmed down. Greta was sobbing quietly and Toller was barely conscious, his face a mask of blood.

"Will somebody kindly tell us what the hell is going on around here?" demanded one MP. "Sir," he added, spotting O'Keefe's rank.

"If you'll let go of my arms I'll try to find out."

The MPs released him. O'Keefe went over to Greta. There were bruises and welts on her face and tears in her eyes, but now she knew she was safe she was rapidly recovering her composure.

"What happened?" asked O'Keefe.

She brushed her hair from her eyes.

"It was just after you left. There was a knock on the door. I saw you'd forgotten the papers and thought you were coming back for them. Then he burst in and started hitting me."

"Why? Who is he?"

"I don't know, I swear to God. Until this morning in your office I'd never seen him before in my life."

"Then what did he want?" demanded O'Keefe. "Why did he attack you?"

"He wanted Lutz's document case. He wanted to know where it was."

O'Keefe did not understand.

"But the documents were here. That's why I came back. They were under his nose."

Greta shook her head tearfully.

"It wasn't the documents. It was the case, the case itself. He wouldn't believe me when I told him you'd taken it."

O'Keefe's driver saw freedom and a citation looming. He stepped forward.

"I think this is what you're looking for, Squadron Leader."

O'Keefe took the case.

"Have either of you two got a razor blade?" he asked the MPs.

"No, sir. Got a knife, though."

"Never mind, I'll use my own."

Carefully, O'Keefe picked a few stitches from around the edge of the case. When he had a handhold, he pulled the two sections apart. A piece of paper about a foot square fell to the floor. No one needed telling it was a map.

He held it up towards the candle. Even in that poor light it was possible to see that it was punctured in several places, the sort of punctures that would be made by a pair of geometric dividers.

"Have you got a wireless in your vehicle?" he asked the MPs.

"Yessir."

"Then get on to Major Benutti of 7th Army Intelligence. My driver will tell you where he is. Tell him that Squadron Leader O'Keefe is bringing him a parcel."

Fearful that Toller had friends who would try the same tactics, O'Keefe took Greta along with him to Benutti's headquarters. She needed minor medical attention anyway, which Hansen said he'd see to. He also promised to take good care of her while Benutti and O'Keefe interrogated her attacker.

On closer examination the map had proved to be a disappointment. It merely covered Bavaria and Upper Austria and the pinpricks made by the dividers were in Munich and Salzburg. There was a scribbled address in the Salzburg margin, but by itself that wasn't going to be much help. Lutz would certainly not still be in Austria three weeks after disappearing. Toller was the one slim clue to his present whereabouts and Toller was going to talk if it meant breaking his fingers one by one.

In a private room with the door locked, the German at first tried to bluster it out, protesting that the girl's story about the document case was a lie. He was merely looking for something to steal when she caught him at it.

This was plainly arrant nonsense and O'Keefe was having none of it, but short of carrying out his threat of physical torture, which he doubted he could do in cold blood, there seemed no quick way of persuading Toller to tell them what he knew.

It was Benutti who came up with the answer. On the other side of the river, he said, was a temporary camp for Polish DPs. Unless Toller opted to talk within thirty seconds, he would turn him over to the senior officer and drop a quiet word that he had committed crimes against Polish nationals.

That did it. It was no secret that the Poles were cutting the balls off war criminals before executing them.

Toller's original statement turned out to be mostly fiction. He had given his correct name, but he had never served in the Wehrmacht, as an Obergefreiter or anything else. Until recently his rank was that of Unterscharfuehrer or SS sergeant, and he had worked in the orderly room at Dachau.

"Although I swear to you that I had nothing to do with the crimes that were committed there."

"That's for others to decide," said O'Keefe. "Tell us what you know and it might go better for you."

There was little chance of that, of course. Unless the German could prove beyond all doubt that his hands were bloodless, he had a date with a rope. Nevertheless, it was a straw and Toller clutched it.

"I saw Standartenfuehrer Lutz on several occasions when he came to inspect the camp and I was telling the truth when I said that the last time I saw him was April 19th or 20th. He was talking to Hauptsturmfuehrer Scheringer in one of the offices and it was apparent they didn't know they were being overheard.

"At first I thought of declaring my presence, but then I decided against it. We all knew the Allies were close by and I thought I might learn something to my advantage. In any case, after the first couple of sentences it would have been fatal to let them know I was listening. They would have had me shot instantly."

"Tell us about the conversation," said O'Keefe.

"May I have a cigarette?"

Benutti tossed him a packet and a book of matches. Toller lit up and inhaled greedily.

"There isn't much to tell," he said. "You have to realize that I was worried about being discovered and that, in any case, I could only hear snatches."

"The exact words," said O'Keefe.

Toller held his head in an effort to remember—or perhaps to take away some of the pain occasioned by O'Keefe's boot.

"Scheringer said something to the effect that they would

80

have to make their move soon, and Lutz agreed with him."

" 'What about the girl?' " asked Scheringer.

" 'To hell with the girl,' " answered Lutz. " 'She's nothing to me.' "

" 'I trust you haven't left anything incriminating lying around in her apartment.' "

"And at this," continued Toller, "Lutz suddenly became concerned. He mentioned a document case. He wasn't worried about the contents, but he'd sewn a map into the lining. Scheringer demanded to know why the hell he'd done that, but Lutz didn't reply directly. Instead he reminded Scheringer not to talk that way to a senior officer.

"Scheringer made some sort of apology but said that the document case would have to be picked up. They couldn't afford to risk it being found. Lutz vetoed this. With the Freedom Action Bavaria people about to make a move, it wouldn't be wise for an SS officer of his rank to be seen on the streets. Besides, the girl would ask all sorts of questions."

Toller ran a hand across his forehead. It came away damp and bloody.

"I could use a drink."

"This isn't a bar, friend," Benutti reminded him. "Get on with the story."

"There isn't much more to tell. Lutz said it was doubtful if anyone would discover the map and even if they did, he, Scheringer and the others would be well away by then."

O'Keefe pounced.

"Others? You mean it wasn't just Lutz and Scheringer in on it?"

"Apparently not, Herr Major, but the other names I don't know." Toller hesitated. "You must understand that many of the Dachau staff were disappearing at this time—those with some sort of rank or influence, that is. I have no way of knowing how many accompanied Lutz and Scheringer."

"Carry on," said Benutti. "What happened after that?"

"Nothing." Toller looked very worried, sure he was not going to be believed. "You have to accept my word for this. Perhaps Lutz and Scheringer realized they were saying too much or perhaps they'd said all they had to. In any case, they left the orderly room. I heard no more."

"So what did you do next?" asked O'Keefe.

"I began to think about my own survival. Goebbels had warned us in February that all members of the SS were to be hanged without trial. It was obvious that senior SS men had an escape line organized, but that they were not going to let junior ranks in on it; that we were to be left to face the Allies alone, take full responsibility for ... all ... that had happened in Dachau and elsewhere.

"Alone, I knew I stood no chance of getting away. I would need the sort of help that Lutz and Scheringer were to receive, but I couldn't ask them for it. The map was a clue, but the map was sewn into a document case at present in some girl's apartment."

"Wait a minute," said O'Keefe. "*Some* girl's apartment? What do you mean, *some* girl? You must have known it was Fräulein Hoegel or you wouldn't have attacked her earlier."

"But I didn't know it at the time, Herr Major. If I had, would I still be here now? I had no idea who Standartenfuehrer Lutz's mistress was."

O'Keefe winced at the word "mistress," for he and Lutz now shared her.

"And obviously I couldn't ask too many questions," continued Toller, "otherwise word might have got back to Lutz. I made some discreet enquiries, naturally, but to no avail. No one I spoke to knew anything about Lutz's private life in Munich.

"It began to drive me crazy. The Allies were but a few miles away. Lutz's map would guide me out but I didn't know who had it."

"Yet you found out," said Benutti. "You not only tracked down Fräulein Hoegel, you became Obergefreiter Toller instead of Unterscharfuehrer Toller."

"The change of identity wasn't difficult. Many Wehrmacht troops were killed in the last few days and it wasn't hard to find one whose uniform fitted me. Papers were unimportant. I could always say I'd lost mine, and who would suspect a Wehrmacht Obergefreiter who walked in off the streets and volunteered information about an SS colonel."

"Which I don't understand," said Benutti. "Why take that risk?"

O'Keefe had been chewing this over also and thought he had the answer.

"Toller knew a map existed in some girl's apartment but he didn't know who the girl was. If he couldn't find her, she had to come to him."

Toller nodded, eager to please.

"That is exactly right, Herr Major. I reasoned that the girl would be angry at being left behind and would seek revenge by telling American Intelligence all she knew about Lutz. If I offered information about him also, sooner or later we'd meet up, as happened this afternoon. When Goertz told me outside that you'd been questioning him about Lutz, I realized that that was why we were all there and that the girl was probably the one I was looking for. Even so, I had to follow her home to find out where she lived."

"Then why didn't you break into the apartment before I arrived?" asked O'Keefe.

"I didn't want trouble. I was hoping to do it when the girl wasn't there, but she didn't go out all day. When I saw you leave I realized I couldn't wait any longer, that time was running out."

That seemed to be the end of it. O'Keefe looked at Benutti, who shrugged his shoulders. They were no further forward. Toller didn't know which way Lutz had gone.

It was bloody disappointing.

Toller sensed that the interrogation was over. He looked from one Allied officer to the other.

"You will remember that I tried to help?"

"We'll remember," said Benutti, "though whether it stops somebody from grinding you to hamburger depends on what sort of record you've got. Innocent men don't need escape routes."

"But I have already explained that," protested Toller. "Goebbels told us that all SS men were to be hanged."

"And you believed him?"

"Of course."

"Fuck me," said Benutti with feeling.

He called for Hansen.

"Take this one away and lock him up for the night. We'll decide what to do with him tomorrow."

"Right, Major. What about Fräulein Hoegel?"

"How is she?"

"She's doing fine, Squadron Leader. She's had a mug of chocolate laced with brandy and she's sleeping like a baby."

"Let's leave her that way for the moment. If that's all right with you, Major."

"Fine. And let's drop the 'Major' bit, shall we? The name's Joe."

Hansen was in the process of closing the door when Benutti said to him, "You might see what you can do about rustling up some chocolate and brandy for the workers in this outfit."

"Coming right up."

Benutti lit a cigarette and blew a couple of smoke rings.

"Well, what's your next move?"

O'Keefe was studying the map. He held it up every which way looking for further pinpricks and examined it with a magnifying glass for pencil dots or anything else that might lead him further than Salzburg. There was nothing. For some reason best known to himself Lutz had marked out the distance between Munich and Salzburg and scribbled down an address. But that was all. The rest of the route was either in his head or on maps in his possession.

It was going to be bloody difficult to swing, but somehow he was going to persuade Group to let him and Jim Caradoc take up the chase. An hour ago he'd been willing to forget the whole thing, but an hour ago he hadn't had an address. He had to follow it up.

He'd like Benutti along too, if he could sell him the idea. The presence of an American was almost essential. They had ways of pulling strings that were impossible for anyone else, like producing cold duck and coffee in a war zone, for example.

"We go to Salzburg," he said.

Seven

Benutti turned it down.

"Not a chance. I've got a job to do here. There's no way 7th Army is going to let me run halfway round Europe and Christ knows where else looking for a couple of fugitive SS officers. Sorry, Mike, but the brass would have my balls for maracas if I even suggested it. I know you've got your reasons for wanting Lutz and I wish you luck. But you'll have to count me out."

But O'Keefe was not that easily discouraged.

"Think about it again. Your job's intelligence, right, and part of that job now the war's over is to capture and interrogate war criminals before handing them over for trial. Right?"

"Right. But once we get organized I've probably got enough raw material right here in Munich to keep me going until 1950."

"Maybe, but that's routine stuff."

Hansen returned with the brandy-laced chocolate and gave them a mug apiece.

"Keep the pot bubbling," said Benutti. "Squadron Leader O'Keefe here has something on his mind and it could take all night."

" 'Kay, Major."

"You were talking about routine stuff," prompted Benutti.

"Correct. Something a clerk can do. I'm pretty new at this job so I'm not sure of the procedure, but I imagine it works something like this:

"The Germans have precious few facilities and almost no food and water. In order to put the fetters on the black marketeers and make sure no one gets more than his fair share, you're going to have to issue some kind of ration cards."

"Something like that."

"And before a man gets his ration card he's going to have to present himself at one of your centres, where he'll be grilled. Name, address, what did you do in the war, daddy—and so on. Straightforward characters—if there are any in Germany— will be processed more or less immediately; others will be passed down the line for further interrogation. You may catch a few big fish, but I doubt it. The whales have gone; only the minnows are left. Am I making any sense?"

"Some. Keep talking."

"Remember the rumours we've heard and what Toller told us a few minutes ago—that senior Nazis have had an escape hatch organized for some time? It's only logical that they would, of course. Any German with half a brain knew that they'd lost the war after Stalingrad, certainly after D-Day. But the top dogs would be forced to stick around while Hitler was alive, otherwise they'd be strung up by their own people."

"You're not telling me anything I don't know."

"Fine. Let's see the bottom line, then."

O'Keefe sipped his chocolate. Christ, you could fuel a Spitfire with it.

"There's probably only one route out of southern Germany. It would be logistically impossible to set up hundreds of safe houses and border crossings all going in different directions. Apart from that, it wouldn't make sense. If you've put a lot of time and effort into making one route foolproof, why bother with others? You don't need them."

Benutti began to see what O'Keefe was driving at. He picked up the map and studied it closely.

"Then what you're saying is that by following this lead to Salzburg we're not just stalking Lutz and Scheringer."

"Right. The Salzburg address is only a link. From there the chain goes elsewhere—down through Austria into Italy. Christ, I don't know. But crack the Salzburg end and you're well on your way to closing down the whole line, rounding up the real criminals who are responsible for Dachau and Buchenwald and God knows how many others we haven't found yet. Shut down the line and they've nowhere to go. After that, it's simply a matter of time before we round them up. Maybe

Lutz is already out, but there must be thousands like him in Germany waiting to make a move. I don't know about you, but to me putting a cork in that bottle seems a hell of a sight more worthwhile than issuing ration cards and waiting for someone whose credentials don't check out."

In principle Benutti liked the idea. Putting the lid on an SS escape hatch wouldn't do his career and promotion prospects any harm. But there was still a great deal he wanted clarified.

"Okay," he said, "let's say I go along with it so far. What happens at Salzburg? I've had a few brushes with the SS and they're not boy scouts. We go in like gangbusters and somebody winds up carrying his head. They wave guns, we wave guns, and that's the ball game."

"No guns," said O'Keefe. "We infiltrate the line. We go to Salzburg posing as SS men on the run."

"Oh Jesus," groaned Benutti, "let me off. I've just remembered another appointment. We wouldn't get further than the door. They'll have code words, recognition signals and Christ knows what else."

"I doubt it. If you give a code word or a recognition signal to thousands of people, suddenly it's not such a big secret. All anyone will care about is whether we're the genuine article and we know enough about the organization of the SS to be able to fool them, at least for a short time. We've all seen Buchenwald and Dachau. We can establish the chain of command in either camp with a couple of phone calls. We know an SS man has his blood group tattooed under his left arm. We all speak fluent German. We've got an address and a couple of names to fling around, Lutz and Scheringer."

"And we're dealing with a bunch of guys who look upon murder as less of an offence than jumping a red light. Make one mistake and you end up floating face down in a river."

"Jesus Christ, Major, where have you been for the last few years? You've had worse odds every day since June 6th 1944. Or did you get those medals for cornflake tops?"

Benutti grinned.

"Okay, okay. But don't try to fool an old soldier, Mike. You've given me a lot of bullshit about the kudos to be earned by shutting down the line. Okay, I accept that. But before I sign the contract I'd like to get the ground rules straight. Is the object of this exercise to make the SS run for cover or is it so that you personally can stick a knife in Lutz?"

"A bit of both, though I'm not going to lie to you. Lutz is my number one target. Don't forget what his job was; he was an inspector of camps and that doesn't mean he was working for the Red Cross. If you dug long enough and hard enough you'd find the scalps he's collected weren't only Polish and Russian. Some of them will be American."

"That's dirty pool. We've not proof of that."

"Please yourself."

Benutti drained his mug of chocolate.

"Why do you want me along anyway? Okay, I speak German and could pass for a kraut, but I don't see the point."

O'Keefe decided that honesty was the best policy. He told Benutti about his theory of Americans opening doors that would otherwise remain shut, and added a second reason.

"If I go to my brass tomorrow and ask if Caradoc and I can go on what could be a wild-goose chase, they'll probably put me out to grass. But if I tell them I have the support and backing of the 7th Army Intelligence, they'll have to listen."

"Jesus, you don't pull your punches, do you?" Benutti shook his head, mostly in admiration.

"No time to. Lutz could have covered another twenty miles since we started this conversation, another fifty if he's on a clipper heading for South America. While we sit around jawing, the trail's growing colder."

"Maybe it's dead already."

"Maybe—but we won't know until we've tried it."

"You'd make a helluva brush salesman."

"Thanks, but you still haven't bought anything."

"I'm trying to think of a few more reasons why I don't show you the door and get back to a quiet life. Three of us against a whole SS network. Jesus Christ, they'd never believe it in Canarsie."

"Four of us," O'Keefe corrected him.

"*Four*? Now look here, Mike, I haven't said I'm on the team yet, but if you want Hansen as well I'm not sure I can swing it."

"Not Hansen. Greta Hoegel."

"The girl!" Benutti was aghast. "You must be out of your gourd. It's damn near impossible as it is, but taking along a woman is asking for a marble slab."

"Not at all."

Whether Benutti came or not, O'Keefe had already made up his mind about Greta.

"Look at it like this. It's almost seven years since I last saw Lutz. Apart from the fact that he will have aged, he could have grown a beard or a moustache in the last three weeks, put on or lost weight, changed his appearance in a dozen ways. We could have a photograph of him taken a month ago and I might still walk past him in the street. But Greta knows him. She'd recognize mannerisms that even Lutz doesn't know he has. Doesn't that make sense?"

"I guess it does," Benutti admitted reluctantly. "I had a girl back in the States who swore that if I were in a lineup of twenty naked men, all arranged so that our heads and torsos were hidden by a board, she'd know me at once. I never could work out whether it was because of my prick or my nobbly knees. But a woman—Jesus. She'll stand out like a hockey player in a ballet."

"No, she won't," persisted O'Keefe. "Think of the women in Ravensbrück and the other places. Some of them are due for a rope too. It stands to reason they'd want to get out."

"Yeah, but they don't carry enough clout to rate a ticket. Anyway, I've seen pictures of some of those beauties. They've got more balls than Hansen. Fräulein Hoegel doesn't fit the bill."

"Maybe not, but she's coming."

"Have you asked her?"

"Not yet."

"Then perhaps you'd better get that item off the agenda. If she turns you down it's three strikes against you and academic whether or not I agree to enlist."

They sent for Hansen to wake Greta up.

It took no great feat of rhetoric to persuade her where her immediate future lay. As O'Keefe pointed out, Germany was no place to be for the next few months. Food would be short, cigarettes and alcohol practically non-existent. She would also be losing her apartment in a day or two.

"But let's make a couple of things quite clear," he concluded, putting out of his mind their intimacy of a few hours back. "This is not going to be a picnic. It's going to be hard and dangerous. One slip and we're all dead. Secondly, my personal interest in this is Lutz. If Major Benutti comes with us, his objectives may be different. But I go where Lutz has gone and you come with me. I want you to understand that."

"I understand perfectly," said Greta with dignity. "You need me to identify Lutz and you want to be sure I will. You needn't have any fears that I'll change my mind at the last moment. Lutz left me behind, to die for all he cared, because he had no further use for me. A little while ago you stopped the man Toller killing me. I don't think I have to say any more."

O'Keefe murmured an apology.

"I'm sorry but I had to be sure you knew what I'm letting you in for."

"Of course." She smiled wistfully. "Am I to go back to my apartment?"

"No," said O'Keefe. "I don't think that would be a good idea at all. Toller was almost certainly flying solo on this one but we can't be sure."

"Fräulein Hoegel can stay here," offered Benutti. "I guess we've got more room than you have and it might save a few awkward questions on your side of the fence. Hansen will fix her up until we decide what the next move is."

After Greta had gone O'Keefe asked, "Well, what is the next move? Are you in or out?"

"Half and half. I'd like to sleep on it and then talk to my brass, put it to them more or less the way you put it to me and do some checking on Lutz for myself. Let's say we meet back here tomorrow at 16:00 hours. Though if I'm told no, then it's no."

"A lot will depend upon how persuasive you are."

"Oh, I'll have a crack at selling it to them, though Christ knows why. It must be that Irish charm."

"Let's hope some of it rubs off on Group," said O'Keefe.

* * *

Coincidentally Group headquarters was at Augsburg, fifty miles north-west of Munich, and, in spite of the congestion on the roads, by 10.30 a.m. O'Keefe was in the office of his immediate superior, Wing Commander Wendell. Wendell wanted nothing to do with what he called "this hare-brained scheme to track down runaway war criminals."

"I know the limit of your brief, O'Keefe. It's restricted to German territory. If you have information that Lutz is in Austria or points south, get in touch with the local authorities and let them handle the matter. Good God, man, we're understaffed as it is. Have you any idea how many RAF aircrew we've got to feed and house, debrief and somehow get organized?"

O'Keefe confessed he had not.

"No more have I," admitted Wendell, "but there are a hell of a lot, I can tell you that. I need every man I can get. I can't have an experienced officer and a senior NCO chasing wild geese all over Europe."

"I'm hardly experienced in Intelligence work, sir. I'm a complete new boy."

"Nevertheless, you're more use to me here than you would be pursuing war criminals. Write a report and pass all the relevant documents to this headquarters, including the map. We'll see they get into the proper hands."

O'Keefe's expression was a picture of misery and Wendell took pity on him. They had, after all, known each other a long time.

"Look, Mike, I understand your feelings. I know you were on the Augsburg raid and that some of your friends were shot by Lutz. But perhaps you're too close to this for your own good. You can't turn it into a vendetta just because you knew Lutz personally. We don't run the RAF that way. Sorry and all that, but there it is. Now if you'll excuse me I have work to do—as I'm sure you have in Munich."

Realizing that it was useless to argue in the face of such intransigence, O'Keefe left the building feeling thoroughly dejected, pondering his next move. There didn't seem to be one. He could go higher up the ladder, see if Group Captain Bryant would extend his brief, but that would take time.

Caradoc was waiting for him at the wheel of the one-tonner. One glance was enough to tell the NCO what had transpired.

"Wouldn't listen?"

"Oh, he listened all right," said O'Keefe bitterly, "and then he very politely told me to go back to being an office boy."

"It's not as bad as all that."

"It damn well is. I've known Wendell seven years and all he can do is ask me to write a report and send him the Lutz documents."

"But you can't, can you?" said Caradoc carefully.

". . . And I remember the time that same Barrie Wendell took on three 109s single-handed and got two of them . . . What do you mean, I can't?"

"Major Benutti's got them. It may be an arguable case, but strictly speaking they're now the property of 7th Army Intelligence. Now, if Benutti persuades his top brass to go for the idea of Salzburg but tells them it's no go unless he has the pair of us . . . and if a two-star general on their side talks to a Air Vice-Marshal on our side. . . ."

But O'Keefe was already out of the one-tonner.

"Thanks, Jim. Stick around while I make a couple of phone calls."

"I wasn't going anywhere," muttered Caradoc to himself, "and I'm not sure I've done either of us a favour."

Two hours later O'Keefe was back in Wing Commander Wendell's office, and Wendell was far from a happy man.

"I'm not sure how you accomplished this, Squadron Leader, and neither can I guess why you were still sitting on my doorstep when you should have been back in Munich. But for the last forty minutes I've been getting all manner of flak from upstairs regarding why I refuse to cooperate with US Army Intelligence. It seems that if I don't let you pursue your lunatic scheme I could well find myself demoted to AC2 and cleaning the latrines—that is, if I'm not in the Tower of London."

O'Keefe remained silent.

"I'm not going to ask myself what strings you pulled or whether you pulled any at all," continued Wendell, "but you now have my permission, if not my blessing, to do whatever the hell it is you want to."

"Presumably that includes Flight Sergeant Caradoc also, sir?" asked O'Keefe.

"Yes, dammit, it does include Caradoc, though why you didn't ask for a dozen WAAFs and the chorus line from the Folies Bergère as well is beyond me. Now get out."

When O'Keefe was at the door Wendell added, "I should have remembered you from 1940. At least one of those 109s belonged to you. Good luck, Mike."

A few minutes before 16:00 hours O'Keefe walked into Benutti's office. In spite of their brief phone conversation earlier in the day, O'Keefe had no idea why the American had bloody near refought the War of Independence to put pressure on Wendell.

With the coffee poured and after the news that Greta was being helped by Hansen to move her few remaining belongings to a place of safety, O'Keefe asked just that question.

"Well, in the first place," drawled Benutti, "when a pal asks for help you try to give it. And in the second place it makes every Yank feel good to start making waves with the British brass. We're ex-colonials and we haven't forgotten it. But in the third place I did that checking I spoke to you about last night. Information's a bit hard to come by, as you can imagine, but it seems that Lutz is not unknown to our OSS people. Neither is Scheringer. They've both got a hefty price on their heads."

O'Keefe was still bemused. The OSS, Office of Strategic Services, was the equivalent of the British SOE, Special Operations Executive, both cloak and dagger outfits. Once those boys got on to something, they didn't let go easily. Any plaudits, they wanted them.

"I still don't see how you swung it. The spooks don't have much time for the rest of us."

Benutti winked conspiratorially.

"Good old American know-how. After you called, I went upstairs and said that this British Squadron Leader had info on an SS escape line which he'd turn over to Special Operations unless he got some cooperation from this end. That would mean that the OSS would get to hear about it and Army Intelligence pushed out. Then I let things take their natural course."

"Very devious," said O'Keefe, admiringly.

"I'm picking it up from you and we're going to need plenty of it if we're to pull this thing off."

Benutti opened a desk drawer and took out a manila folder.

"I haven't been idle in other respects either. In there you'll find a whole wad of information on the SS in general and those bastards at Buchenwald in particular. It's far from complete but it's worth you and Caradoc studying."

O'Keefe took the folder.

"Tell me," he said, "why the change of attitude? Yesterday you thought I was out of my mind. Today you're all for it."

"Fräulein Hoegel asked me more or less the same question. I told her about Lutz and the Augsburg raid, by the way. She was curious why it seemed such a personal matter to you, and as we're all in this together . . . I hope that was okay?"

"Sure. I should have told her myself. And you still haven't answered my question. Why the change of heart?"

Benutti shrugged.

"Who the hell knows?"

"I guess it's better than sitting behind a desk."

"I guess it is. Shall we go get ourselves tattooed?"

Eight

A continent away, a young man who normally wore the uniform of a Flying Officer in the Royal Air Force dragged his eyes from the naked form of the pretty dark-haired girl dozing beside him and gazed out at the Tripoli waterfront.

Christ, it was hot, and the bloody fan was on the fritz again.

A towel around his waist, he padded out to what passed as a balcony in the second-floor apartment, rented without the knowledge of his base commander from a local Libyan businessman, and sank into a canvas chair. His watch was on the bedside table but he judged it to be late afternoon. Soon he would have to wake Hanna up and make a move.

After Augsburg Jonathan Pascoe flew six more missions over Germany before transferring out to Coastal Command, where he quickly earned the reputation of being a brilliant pilot of the giant Sunderland flying boat. Between September 1942 and February 1943 his crew set new records for sinking U-boats.

But Pascoe found he missed the excitement of bombing runs and requested a return to Lancasters. This was granted with a minimum of fuss, and shortly afterwards his squadron was posted to North Africa.

When the Axis Powers were finally kicked out of the desert in mid-1943, the squadrons of Middle East Command continued to take part in the war with air sweeps over Sicily and Italy. Later, some moved forward to support Allied ground forces once a foothold was gained on the Italian mainland, some went to the Far East, and others were left behind to keep the flag flying for Britain in North Africa. As always, British foreign policy was based upon possession being nine points of the law, and no one was particularly anxious to give up airfields until the postwar political situation stabilized.

By the end of the second week in May, 1945, however, there wasn't much left at Tripoli; remnants of No. 122 Maintenance Unit, remnants of No. 2 Fuel Transport Company, and No. 53 Embarkation Unit. Further along the coast, Benghazi had fared somewhat better. Still there were No. 5053 Airfield Construction Squadron and Nos. 4609 and 4617 Airfield Construction Flights; No. 5153 Mechanical and Electrical Squadron, No. 25 Embarkation Unit, No. 2 Bomber Group Maintenance company. Both bases had a sprinkling of Halifaxes, Lancasters and DC3s lying around, mostly used for ferrying supplies, and a few fighters which no one had yet found a home for.

For the ordinary army Tommy, whose main task was making sure that the thousands of Axis POWs still in captivity toed the line, and for ninety-five per cent of RAF personnel, ground and aircrews, avoiding a Far East posting and going home were uppermost in their mind. But for a handful of others the end of the war was the end of an era. Soon their rank and positions of privilege would disappear. Postwar Britain, for fliers, was no place to be; their skills would be at a discount; for every position available with a commercial airline there would be dozens of applicants; an ability to shoot down Messerschmitts or successfully pilot a bomber to the target and back would not be required. In a postwar world only one thing would: money.

Jonathan Pascoe thought he saw a way to make some, perhaps a lot. The key was Hanna's father.

Behind him he heard the girl stir and glanced over his shoulder. But she was merely changing position.

It was a strange relationship they had and one that did not have official sanction, or was at least frowned upon. For Hanna and her father were German.

They had lived in North Africa for years, of course, first in Benghazi and later Tripoli, where the old man and his daughter ran a small coffee shop in the European quarter. From what Pascoe could gather they had left the beauties of Hitler's Reich a year or so before the war, presumably for political reasons though that was only a guess.

During the period of Axis occupation they had not, of course, been bothered. In fact, partly due to Hanna's prettiness and youth, business had boomed. Later, when the Allies took over, again no one troubled them. They were not interned or interrogated or interfered with in any way. They were put under surveillance for a while to ensure that the old man was not sending wireless messages to the Abwehr, and after that left alone.

The same applied to many other expatriate Germans and Italians who had been in business in Libya for a number of years, sometimes a generation or two. Providing they did nothing to offend the Allies, they were left in peace.

Pascoe met her in January during a casual visit to the coffee shop and was immediately attracted to her. She was on the small side and slim as a whip, but she had a fiery temper and a stubborn will. Her dark hair was cut to the shoulder and swung loosely on either side of her face. She had green eyes and a pale, porcelain complexion in spite of her years in the sun. She spoke excellent English, as well as Italian, Arabic and some Greek, and told him she was twenty years old. She displayed a sense of humour by adding that her father was a widower, she couldn't possibly leave him alone at night, she hated fliers as a breed, and when would he, Pascoe, be taking her out?

Plotting his seduction of the girl carefully he rented the waterfront apartment, and in March, six weeks to the day after their first meeting, they went to bed together.

Pascoe was delighted to discover she was a virgin. After the tens of thousands of troops of all nationalities North Africa had played host to in six long years, it seemed impossible that any girl over the age of puberty had kept her maidenhead. But she had, and proved more than willing to be initiated into the mysteries of sex.

It has been said that no one is more carnal than a recent virgin, and Hanna proved no exception. Quite often, she exhausted him.

By April he had decided he wanted to marry her, but there were two difficulties. The first was that ex-RAF officers returning to England with German wives were not going to have the banners hung out for them. The second was money, though possibly the old man could do something about that.

Earlier in the day, when he called to pick up Hanna, she seemed as nervous as a kitten. She announced that her father wanted to talk to him. Alone.

Pascoe feared the worst, that it was shotgun and altar time, but he was way off the mark.

They spoke in English. Pascoe's German was good but not as good as the old man's English.

"I am in trouble, my young friend," he said when they were by themselves in the sitting-room behind the coffee shop. They were drinking arak and Turkish coffee. It was far too hot for either, but after a while you picked up the customs.

Pascoe thought of the near-zero state of his savings account.

"No, it's not money," smiled the old man. "I wish it were, but I'm afraid it's something quite different."

"If I can help in any way. . . ." Pascoe was genuinely fond of Hanna's father, which was almost a condition of the relationship with the daughter, who adored him.

"I'm not sure you can, but if you can't I don't know who else I can ask."

"You'd better explain. I'll do anything within my power."

"I wonder if that's true."

Pascoe considered the possibility that the old man was losing his marbles. He must be sixty if he was a day.

"Look, I can't help if I don't know what the problem is, so the sooner you tell me the better."

"Contraband," said Hanna's father. "Without going into too much detail at present I have certain items which must be smuggled into South Africa without delay. For many reasons a ship cannot be used. It has to be an aircraft. But I have no access to aircraft. Indeed, I have no access to airmen other than you."

Pascoe was dumbstruck. He must surely have misheard.

"You're involved in a smuggling racket?"

"Not a racket. In fact, never before. This is the first time."

"Then I don't understand."

"It's quite simple, Jonathan. I need an aircraft and a pilot to transport items of contraband to Cape Town."

"*Cape Town* . . . ? Christ, that's. . . ."

"Five thousand miles away. I know. But you're the only person I can turn to. If it's impossible. . . ."

"No, wait. . . ."

Pascoe studied the old man's face. There was more than anxiety registered there; there was also fear.

"You'll have to tell me more, much more before. . . ." He paused; his eyes narrowed. "Does Hanna know anything of this?"

"Yes."

Which explained her nervousness.

"You'd better tell me the whole story," said Pascoe.

"I'm not empowered to, not yet. It happened a long time ago. I made an arrangement with some people for which I was paid in advance."

"Which people? What arrangement?"

"That I can't tell you either, not unless you agree to help. All I can say is that there is a lot of money involved and possibly the forfeiture of my life and Hanna's if I fail."

"You must be joking!"

"I wish I were."

"But who are these people? Why not turn them over to the authorities? No one can make you do anything you don't want to."

"You're wrong, but if you can't or won't help, I must look for someone who can."

Pascoe's mind was racing. It didn't seem credible that the old man could be involved in something that might result in his and Hanna's deaths.

It suddenly occurred to him that he hadn't heard, in the last few minutes, any sound from the living quarters of the coffee shop. Usually Hanna sang as she worked.

"Where is Hanna?" he demanded.

"Quite safe. At the moment she is upstairs, being held as security for my good conduct. But she's free to leave when you do."

"Who's holding her? Who's got a pistol to your head?"

"I can't tell you that." The old man leaned forward and gripped Pascoe by the wrist. "But think on what I've been saying. If you can find a way to help, give a message to Hanna. You can talk to my principals later on today. If you can't help. . . ." He shrugged.

"I'll do what I can."

Pascoe left the balcony and dropped the towel as he walked over to the bed.

From Hanna Baumann he now knew a great deal more.

Although her recollections were vague, she had told him how, as a young girl, she and her father had left Germany one cold and snowy night and how they had flown to Cairo; how four German-speaking men had turned up at the coffee shop twenty-four hours ago and how her father had confessed that he had owned a wireless transceiver for years, though he swore he had only used it once.

Pascoe climbed into bed beside her and turned her on to her stomach. She gave little grunts of pleasure as he stroked the inside of her thighs, but held him away when he raised her up and tried to enter her.

"Jonathan . . . ?"

"I'll help. Tell your father I'll help."

"Oh, Jonathan. . . ."

She gripped him, squeezed lovingly, and guided him expertly inside her. He felt her tighten on him.

As he began to move on her, hands cupped around her unusually large breasts, he knew that he, too, was going to need some help. Though equally, he knew precisely where to find it.

Three hours later, sipping warm beer in a Libyan-run bar just a few hundred yards from the coffee shop, he saw the avarice in the eyes of the two men opposite and knew it was going to be okay.

Carver Kane, still a Flight Sergeant, didn't like Pascoe much, considering him too flashy as a flier, but as they'd served in the same squadron for most of the war, excluding Pascoe's months with Coastal Command, he'd learned to get along with the fair-haired Pom.

While Pascoe was flying Sunderlands Kane had completed his second tour, earning a bar to his DFM in the process, and was in the middle of a third tour when the war ended. He was considered by his contemporaries to be something of a phenomenon, as only two per cent of aircrew survived three tours. His old co-pilot, Paddy Mahoney, hadn't even completed one, being killed on his twenty-fourth mission, decapitated by a lump of shrapnel just four feet from where

Kane was sitting. The Australian didn't even get scratched.

Anyone less suited to staying behind and ferrying supplies around North Africa could scarcely be imagined, but, like God, the RAF works in mysterious ways its wonders to perform.

Since early 1945 he had dabbled in the black market. There was always someone who wanted a few spare cans of aviation gasoline or a dozen tyres, and equally there was always someone to sign the phoney manifest. But it wasn't going to make him rich and neither had he the sort of looks or background to put him in close touch with millionairesses hunting husbands.

Because he was physically very strong, not far off peak condition in spite of the gallons of beer he consumed, he never had much trouble finding a woman, either the local variety or service personnel, WAAF officers as well as the lower ranks. But not one of them had ever told him they had wealthy parents and a few thousand acres in the background, and even if they had, his part in the drama would be that of Mellors, never old man Chatterley.

Carver Kane was a realist.

So too was the third man at the table, Peter van der Heyden, now a Flight Lieutenant.

The South African's total score for enemy aircraft destroyed during the war was ten and two probables. He had also been shot down twice, the second time over Italy in January, 1945.

His leg injuries and body burns were not severe and he soon recovered physically. But an RAF psychiatrist was not so sure about his mental state and recommended that van der Heyden be grounded. He had, in any case, done his bit, and there were plenty of other youngsters anxious to have a crack at the Luftwaffe before it was all over.

He was posted first to Benghazi and then to Tripoli as Supply Officer. There he was fortunate enough to meet up with Kane who suggested, as one colonial to another, that it might be lucrative to go into business for themselves. Van der Heyden studied the odds and agreed that a postwar non-taxable pension had a lot to be said for it. But like Kane he had concluded that the odd black-market coup here and there wasn't going to put him on easy street. Perhaps nothing would, unless Pascoe's idea had something going for it.

". . . Anyway," Kane was saying, "what the hell have we got to lose by listening? I don't give a shit whether they're Germans or Martians."

Van der Heyden agreed.

"Somebody wants something smuggled into South Africa, right? Okay, I'm a South African citizen and providing it's not the size of an elephant I reckon I can wangle myself some leave down home, stick the bloody stuff in a dufflebag, and take a chance at the other end. Christ, we've been sitting here for months now, wondering what the hell we're going to do after the war. Well, I'll tell you. We're going to join the unemployment queue. Medals and war stories won't fetch the price of a pint in a hock shop, and it's only a matter of degree between selling black market tyres and gas to the wogs and holding up the Bank of England."

"You both sound as if you're trying to convince yourselves," said Pascoe. "And we're wasting time."

Although it was close on dusk, the heat in the flyblown streets was overpowering and it was with relief that they entered the coffee shop, where a slowly spinning ceiling fan was doing its best to cool the customers, mainly service personnel off duty.

Hanna's father led them through a beaded curtain and along the corridor into the sitting-room. There was no sign of Hanna but Pascoe was unconcerned. She wouldn't have been allowed out earlier if she was in danger.

"Wait here," said Baumann.

"If any of these characters is in a position to smuggle something worthwhile," said van der Heyden, looking distastefully at the worn furniture, "they're keeping it well hidden from the rest of the world."

"There's been a war on, you know," retorted Pascoe.

"I can vouch for that personally, sport," said Kane.

"As we all can," said Lutz from the doorway. "In fact, I think we can safely say we were on different sides throughout the whole of it."

Nine

In spite of the fact that Lutz was wearing second-hand civilian clothing that was stained and torn in places, none of the three fliers was in any doubt that they were in the presence of a German officer, probably of field rank. His whole bearing was military and his voice that of a man accustomed to command.

Pascoe looked at van der Heyden and Kane.

"What the hell. . . . We knew we weren't meeting the Salvation Army."

He turned to Lutz.

"Hanna said there were four of you."

"Fräulein Baumann is correct," replied Lutz in his customary faultless English. "My associates are upstairs—with the fräulein and her father. For insurance, you understand."

"Fuck that," said Pascoe.

It was important to show the German from the word go which way the land lay. Give this sort of bastard an inch and you wound up cleaning his boots.

"You can either surrender the policy here and now or this conversation goes no further."

"I really don't think I can do that," murmured Lutz.

"And I really don't think you've got much bloody option," said van der Heyden, taking his cue.

"What I have to say is for your ears alone. The girl and her father. . . ."

". . . Can stay upstairs," interrupted Pascoe. "But not under duress. Just tell your people to let them go, there's a good fellow."

After a moment, Lutz inclined his head deferentially. There should be no danger. The fliers wouldn't be here unless they wanted to listen.

From the doorway he called upstairs in German that Hanna and her father were to be released but confined to their bedrooms.

"With the doors open," said Pascoe.

"I see you speak German."

"A smattering. Pass it on."

Lutz did so.

"Excellent," said Pascoe. "Now, having wasted valuable minutes establishing the ground rules, perhaps we can get down to business. I'm Pascoe, incidentally. The gentleman with the wicked-looking knife is Flight Sergeant Kane and the one with the venal eyes Flight Lieutenant Peter van der Heyden. I didn't catch your name."

Lutz saw no reason not to tell them, adding, "Van der Heyden? A great many of your countrymen had more sympathy with our cause than that of the Allies, Flight Lieutenant."

"Which goes to show that even South Africans can back the wrong horse. The last bulletin I heard said your side lost."

"So it did, so it did. However, that's all over now."

Lutz had meant it as a question but no one responded. He tried again.

"What I'm trying to say is that I hope none of you bears a grudge. We all fought the war we had to and the Allies were victorious, but I trust that doesn't mean that every German is your sworn enemy. What I am going to propose is a simple—no, a complicated—business transaction, but we'll all be wasting our time if any of you feel that the only good German is a dead one."

"Why don't you get on with it, Herr Lutz," said Pascoe.

Being a frequent visitor to this part of the premises he knew where the booze was kept. From a cupboard he took a bottle of brandy and four glasses.

"Tell us what you're selling and what the price is and let us make up our own minds."

Lutz made a play of fixing a cigarette in his holder and lighting it, arranging his thoughts as he did so. He would have to trust these people. They had fallen into his lap as a bonus and it would be foolish not to take advantage.

"To begin with," he said, "I shall have to give you something of a history lesson, otherwise you might think there is no point in examining the problem, for problem it is. I also intend to be blunt. We are here to do business, not discuss politics or morality."

Oh Christ, thought Pascoe, he was one of those who dotted his "i's" and crossed his "t's".

"Some years before the war that many of us in Germany knew was coming," Lutz went on, "huge amounts of gold and precious stones were appropriated from Jewish families and businesses. The rightness or wrongness of that action is no longer important. Suffice it to say that it happened. The gold—which took the form of ornaments, wedding-rings and other items of jewellery—was melted down and cast into ingots each weighing 22½ kilos, around fifty pounds in your scheme of weights and measures. The stones were sold on the open market and the proceeds invested in polished diamonds. The total sum involved was tens of millions of dollars, but we are not concerned with totals here, only fractions."

Lutz drew heavily on his cigarette and filled his glass. He had, he was pleased to see, their undivided attention. It was marvellous what the mention of gold could do to a man's concentration.

"Much of the money was put into the German war chest, but some of it was kept to one side for, shall we say, future eventualities. In spite of the fact that most Germans thought we would win the coming conflict, defeat was not out of the question. Some of us—the names don't matter—came to the conclusion that it would be advantageous to have a large part of the fortune outside the Reich. Once the war started it would be impossible to transport valuables by ship or U-boat without the danger of them being lost to enemy action. Switzerland was an obvious place to store some of it, but putting all our eggs in one basket, especially a European basket, could be risky. If we lost the war, many of us would have to make a run for it or spend a number of years in Allied prison camps. We therefore decided to ship quantities of bullion and diamonds to different parts of the world. Each cache was to be the same size: one-fifth bullion, four-fifths diamonds, and each officer in command was given a different destination. Mine was Lagos, Nigeria. The precise location of the cache will remain my secret for the time being, but its value I can tell you. At 1945 prices it is approximately five million pounds sterling."

There was a long silence.

"Jesus Christ," whistled Kane, but Pascoe was unimpressed by this window dressing. Five million was the same as fifty million if it couldn't be reached.

"Now tell us the problem," he said.

"The problem," answered Lutz, "is getting from here to Lagos and from Lagos to Cape Town, picking up the cache en route. For reasons I don't wish to go into I cannot use a ship. It must be an aircraft, an amphibious aircraft at that. In Cape Town you will be paid off and you will never see us again."

"Paid off with how much?"

"One million pounds—either in bullion or diamonds or a combination of both."

"Try sticking that in your dufflebag, Peter," grinned Pascoe.

It took a moment or two to sink in, the fact that each one of them was potentially £350,000 richer. Then they adopted Pascoe's attitude; it was play money if it couldn't be done. There were scores of snags, the main one being the aircraft.

Van der Heyden had made some calculations on the back of an envelope.

"It's not possible," were his first thoughts. "From Tripoli to Lagos is around 2,000 miles and from Lagos to Cape Town another 3,000. There isn't an aircraft flying that can do that trip without refuelling at least twice. With phoney documents we might get away with it once, say in Lagos, but not a second time."

"Now hold your horses, sport," interrupted Kane. "Let's not go jumping the gun. We've managed fake documents before for gas and tyres. Let's kick it around a bit. How long have we got?" he asked Lutz.

"There's no real time limit, but obviously the sooner my associates and I are on our way, the better it will please us."

"It's moonshine, Carver," said van der Heyden. His face

was a mask of disappointment. "Forget it. You're joining the unemployment queue with the rest of us. The most we can hope for is to turn these characters in and claim the reward."

Lutz's eyes flickered with alarm until he realized the South African was joking.

Pascoe wasn't sure van der Heyden's disillusion was justified. A glimmer of an idea had occurred to him at something Lutz had said, one that could perhaps be made to work. But first of all there were other matters to be settled.

"Carver's right," he said. "We need to kick it around a bit. But before we do so I'd like to be certain this whole thing's not a confidence trick. You've given us some tale about a fortune in gold bullion and diamonds in Lagos," he said to Lutz, "but how can we be sure of that? For all we know you're just a group of Germans on the run, willing to tell any cock and bull story to get out of Libya. There might not be a cache."

"In that case you simply shoot us in Lagos."

"Unless you shoot us first. If we can somehow get an aircraft, what's to prevent you taking it over in mid-air while we're busy with the controls?"

"The fact that none of us is a pilot. If we were, we would have considered stealing an aeroplane ourselves."

"They're not exactly left lying around like pebbles, you know."

"Perhaps not, but nothing's impossible."

Right enough, thought Pascoe, but he preferred to see some more tangible evidence of good faith.

"It's customary in a business deal to see some money up front," he suggested.

Lutz extracted a bulky envelope from an inside pocket.

"In here you will find the equivalent of fifteen hundred pounds in gold sovereigns. Enough of an advance for you to consider the problem in detail, I believe."

"And non-returnable, of course."

Lutz gave him an old-fashioned look.

"Of course."

Pascoe took the envelope and passed it to van der Heyden. The South African put it away without checking the contents.

"Right," said Pascoe, "let's go."

Lutz was puzzled.

"You're leaving?"

"That's correct. We've got some thinking to do."

"But I assumed I would be included in your discussions."

"You assumed wrong. If we come up with an answer, we'll let you know."

At the entrance to the sitting-room Pascoe turned.

"Just one more item. We'll be taking Hanna with us but she'll be returning later on. I don't want any more bloody nonsense about holding her or her father for insurance reasons, have you got that? Neither are you to upset or offend either of them in any way. If I hear any complaints, not only is the deal off but I'll be back with a regiment of soldiers. Understood?"

Lutz controlled his temper with difficulty. He wasn't accustomed to being spoken to in that fashion by junior officers.

"Understood."

"Then tell your cronies to send Hanna down."

While waiting for her to appear, Pascoe spoke to Kane and van der Heyden.

"I'll meet you in the bar we just left. We've met the chief but I want to hear what Hanna has to say about the Indians, whether they're armed and so on."

"Do you think it can be done, Jonathan?" asked van der Heyden.

"I've got one idea that we can work on."

Pascoe said nothing to Hanna until they were sitting behind drinks in the waterfront apartment. Then he asked her about the four men and how her father had got mixed up with them.

"I told you all I could earlier."

"Tell me again."

"Well, their names are Lutz, Scheringer, Fischer and Mueller. Lutz is the leader and Papa says I've met him before, but I don't remember."

"Have they got guns?"

"Yes. Well, I've seen two of them with pistols."

"Just pistols?"

"I didn't see anything else."

"Okay, go on. How does your father come into it?"

"It seems he made an arrangement with Lutz before the war. Lutz paid him money to come out to North Africa and set up in business."

"Why?"

"It's hard for me to understand. Papa was given a wireless but was told not to do anything with it, never to use it, never to risk being caught with it. It was pre-set on a fixed frequency and all he had to do was listen nightly once he heard the news that the Allies had crossed the Rhine. I didn't know he was doing it, of course. He didn't tell me any of this until this morning. I think he'd almost forgotten about the arrangement with Lutz and hoped he was dead." Her large green eyes were troubled. "I don't understand any of it."

"I do. Your father's known in the trade as a sleeper agent. Lutz probably had several of them scattered about North Africa in case one or more got killed or did a bunk. He's a great man for insurance, is Lutz. If Germany had won your father would never have been called upon, but once it was obvious that the Allies had it sewn up—that's why he had to keep a listening watch once the Rhine was breached—Lutz would get in touch and tell him to expect visitors. Your father would then have to hide them and feed them until they figured out their next move. They couldn't have known about us. The important thing was to get out of Germany and to a place of safety en route to West Africa. We're icing on the cake."

Pascoe told her about Lagos and Cape Town, about the bullion and the diamonds.

"But can you do it?"

"I don't know. I think so but it's early days yet." He noticed her expression. "You'll be coming with us, of course, you and your father, because if what I have in mind works out, we won't be coming back. Besides, if anyone ever got to hear that your father had kept an illegal transmitter on the premises throughout the war, he could be shot, even now."

"But he wasn't a spy."

"A good prosecutor could make him seem like Mata Hari.

109

He was in wireless contact with Germany before the war finished and he's helping Germans now."

"So are you."

"True enough." He grinned cheerfully. "We'll just have to make sure no one finds out, won't we."

"God, why didn't he smash the bloody wireless? Why did he have to keep it at all?"

"It makes no difference. Lutz would probably have turned up out of the blue anyway and I wouldn't judge him to be the sort of man who'd take kindly to having his signals ignored. Your father was probably thinking of you."

She looked at him across the rim of her glass.

"It scares me, Jonathan. Two days ago everything was fine, and now. . . ."

"Two days ago everything wasn't fine," Pascoe corrected her. "Two days ago I was wondering how the hell to take a German-born wife back to England and how to support her. Now I stand a chance of solving both problems. Within a week or two we'll be able to go anywhere in the world and do whatever we like."

"Are you sure?"

He was far from sure but there was no point in telling her that.

"Very sure."

He drained his glass.

"Look, I must go. We've got a lot of midnight oil to burn, Kane, van der Heyden and myself. Stay here if you like."

"No, I'd better get back. You'll be in touch soon?"

"As soon as I can."

Kane and van der Heyden were drinking beer at a corner table when Pascoe arrived. A third glass was already set up and it went down without touching the sides.

"Well," he asked, "any ideas?"

"Nary a one." Van der Heyden shrugged his shoulders gloomily. "As I told Lutz, there isn't an aircraft flying that can do that trip without refuelling at least twice, once in Lagos, once somewhere downcoast. Carver and I have just

110

been discussing it. We'd probably have to hijack the bloody thing in the first place and while we might get away with phoney fuel documents in Lagos, we couldn't try the same stunt elsewhere. The balloon would be well and truly up by then."

Kane was reluctantly compelled to agree.

"It's a bastard, but there it is. We've got nothing on the base apart from a few coastal and short-haul transports, Halifaxes and some ancient Lancs. The transports and the Halifaxes are automatically eliminated because they've got nothing like the range, and the Lancs are Mark IIIs. I haven't checked the flight manual for a long time, but I know the Mark III won't get us from Lagos to Cape Town in one hop. In fact, unless it was in first-class condition it might not even make Lagos. We're scuppered before we start."

"You know," said Pascoe, "I'm starting to think that I'm the only one with any bloody flying hours in this outfit."

He put a match to a cigarette and studied the flame for a second before blowing it out.

"You weren't listening to the man, were you? He mentioned an amphibious aircraft, which I judge to be a layman's language for seaplane. I don't know why that's a stipulation but it so happens that a flying boat is about the only plane that could make the Lagos-Cape Town run without refuelling. And not any old flying boat at that. I'm talking about a Sunderland."

Van der Heyden and Kane had an immediate mental image of the huge aircraft, the military version of the old Empire class.

Nicknamed by the Luftwaffe the *Fliegender Stachelschwein,* the Flying Porcupine, because of its tremendous ability to defend itself against all-comers with a firepower battery of two .50 and twelve .303 machine guns, it certainly had the range, 2,980 miles on full tanks. There would be no problem about housing the passengers either, as the normal crew complement was thirteen, spread around the ship on two decks.

But Pascoe was out of his mind. Where the hell were they going to find a Sunderland?

"Anchored offshore at Benghazi," Pascoe answered van der Heyden. "I saw it a couple of days ago when I was coming back from a milk run."

"How do you know it wasn't on a visit? Benghazi isn't a Sunderland base."

"Maybe not, but let's take each step as it comes. Five minutes ago you didn't think it could be done. Now at least we know the hardware exists. I've flown those ships, don't forget. Assuming we can get our hands on the one at Benghazi and we can wangle a refuelling stop at Lagos, it'll do the trip easily. I'll have to check how much actual bullion is involved and its weight, but I don't think the payload will bother something that size."

"And we just ask the nice men if they'll lend it to us, do we?" asked Kane. "And what about the squadron of Mosquitoes they send after us?"

"Christ, you're a miserable bugger," moaned van der Heyden. "You were the one who said let's kick it around."

"He's right to have doubts, though," said Pascoe, "about Mosquitoes or anything else. We've got to be prepared for any eventuality, which means some long and careful planning and maybe a double portion of that derring-do we flying types are supposed to be renowned for."

"When do we begin?"

"Right here and now. Set the beers up again, Carver."

Ten

Salzburg was crawling with troops: US, British and French as well as the Red Army. Many of the latter were busy tacking up road signs in Cyrillic script. The Russians were apparently less interested in rounding up fugitive Germans than in staking a claim for this piece of real estate for when the postwar bargaining began.

Travelling down from Munich had proved easy enough for O'Keefe, Benutti, Caradoc and Greta Hoegel. They all carried US Army Intelligence credentials signed by the highest authority. If it came to the crunch, they could just about order 7th Army to invade Switzerland, though the warrants were only to be used when all else failed. It was possible that the checkpoints were being monitored by the SS and none of them wanted a bullet in the head because they'd been observed receiving undue courtesy from Allied soldiers.

In the short time available Benutti had performed minor miracles of logistics by arranging for civilian clothes with faded Weimar labels, a chemical ageing process for the blood-group tattoos, perfectly forged documents (printed on captured presses), and the equivalent of 500 dollars apiece in gold coins. The only thing that worried him was that the tattoos still looked new and he wasn't sure which women wore them. Some of the captured wardresses had, some had not; there didn't seem to be a general rule. But to be on the safe side Greta had undergone the needle also, the entire operation performed by a German doctor anxious to ingratiate himself with his new masters.

If that was the sum total of his worries, O'Keefe had told him, he was a lucky man. They had their cover stories straight enough—all ex-members of the Buchenwald staff, with enough knowledge of the camp and its overseers to be able to answer any but the most unexpected questions—but that was just the start of it. They were going in blind. They had no more than a rudimentary idea of the SS command infra-structure, no passwords, no way of verifying their fake identities. It would have to be bluff all the way. Like the man who puts his head in the lion's mouth, they would have to convince the lion that they meant it no harm.

They had to barge in and hope for the best.

The address given on Lutz's map was on the left bank of the River Salzach, near the Cathedral and just a few hundred yards from the river itself.

Benutti volunteered to do a reconnaissance.

"It'll be a real kick in the head if the shutters are up or it's now being used as a billet."

Trying not to make themselves too conspicuous for fear of being told to move on as loiterers, O'Keefe, Greta and Caradoc waited for him by the Mozart bridge. All three were gasping for a cigarette, but cigarettes were in short supply for Germans and they weren't carrying any. It was that sort of attention to detail Benutti had insisted upon. Things were going to be rough enough without making elementary mistakes.

A quarter of an hour passed.

"What the hell's keeping him?" muttered O'Keefe.

"I wouldn't worry if I were you," said Caradoc. "If you need any proof that the US Army can take care of itself, take a look around."

O'Keefe had already done so. Officers and enlisted men wearing 7th Army patches proliferated everywhere, and the actions of some of them made him feel hot under the collar. He liked most Americans as individuals, but *en masse* they could be a pain in the arse. Even lowly PFCs were swaggering around as though they were on first name terms with Patton. They made no secret of the fact that they considered themselves superior to other Allied troops, and they certainly saw themselves as the liberators of Europe. Because they were better paid than any other Allied soldier, sailor or airman, they thought that their money would get them anywhere. They conveniently forgot, of course, that their war had started two and a bit years later than everyone else's, and although there was no doubt about their courage as fighting troops, they could get on an Englishman's nerves, as one of them did a few minutes later when a jeep drew up on the far side of the road and the sergeant at the wheel called across in pidgin German that the *fräulein* had only to say the word and she could earn herself a couple of bars of chocolate.

Greta knew this game of old and walked over to the jeep, swinging her hips provocatively. She spent five minutes in smiling conversation with the sergeant and when she returned produced two packets of Luckies from the pocket of her tattered trench coat.

"What was that all about?" asked O'Keefe.

Greta raised her eyebrows.

"What do you think? That he wanted to paint my portrait? I've agreed to meet him later by the Nonnberg Convent. I don't think he'll be too disappointed when I don't turn up. For a carton of the same brand he can have the Mother Superior."

She puckered her mouth elfishly.

"It's all the rage nowadays, haven't you heard? Any German or Austrian girl can be had for a price. Some bread and butter, a couple of bottles of wine. . . . In mediaeval times it used to be called barter."

O'Keefe realized he was being teased.

"Don't do it again anyway. The next one might not be willing to wait until later. And toss those cigarettes away."

"Do I have to? I've been thinking about it. If I were running an escape line I'd think it much more suspicious if a woman with my supposed background turned up *without* some American booty."

"Get rid of them, Greta. We don't want any complications."

Pouting, she thrust them into the hands of a passing youth. He took them eagerly but rewarded her with, "Yankee whore."

O'Keefe chuckled at the expression of wounded amazement of Greta's face. Cast your bread upon the waters and the bloody seagulls eat it.

"Here comes the Major," said Caradoc.

Benutti made sure they were not under surveillance before crossing over to them. His face was flushed, as though he'd been running.

"Where the hell have you been?" demanded O'Keefe. "You were supposed to be doing a recce, not a Cook's tour of Austria."

"I've been in the house," said the American, unable to keep the excitement out of his voice. "I've actually been inside and met the local boss man. Come on, let's walk."

Crossing Mozartplatz in the direction of the Cathedral, Benutti explained why he was so long.

"It's just a house like any other house and at first I thought I'd come to the wrong place. But I banged on the door and kept on banging until somebody answered. You should have seen the guy. If he was under seven feet tall my name's von Ribbentrop. What the hell did I want? he asked me. If it was food or shelter I was out of luck. I'd just have to stand in line for the soup kitchens like the rest.

"Well, I'll tell you, he pissed me off right away, and with my assumed rank of SS Sturmbannfuehrer I proceeded to give him both barrels. What the hell had I got to lose? Either he was the guy we were looking for or he wasn't. If he wasn't I'd lost nothing, but if he was I had to make like we meant business.

"So I told him that there were four of us on the run from the Allies and that we needed to go down the line—by which time, because we were still talking in the street, he was about ready to throw a litter of pigs. Anyway, he let me in.

"Who was I? Where had I come from? Who were the others? How had I got this far? How was he to know that I was who I purported to be? Those were the sort of questions he was tossing at me, but I had him by the short and tufties. If I was some sort of agent he'd said enough already to be doing a short jig on the long rope. If I was what I said I was, he'd better start listening.

"Anyway, he decided he'd better hear me out, though I told him I wasn't saying any more until I'd got the rest of my bunch in out of the sun. Then I threw him my curve. He told me to open my mouth. I told him to go to hell. I open my mouth, I said, and he crunches my jaw and the cyanide pill with it. That really shook him, I can tell you."

This was one of the subtler touches of Benutti's preparations. SS officers and NCOs of any importance or clout carried cyanide pills, shaped like a tooth, in their mouths. If there was ever a chance that they would have to face the rope and the ignominious trial which preceded it, they could always bite on the cyanide tooth and take the easy way out. All four of them had undergone minor dental surgery before leaving Munich, but what looked like a cyanide tooth was no more than a harmless porcelain crown.

"Anyway," continued Benutti, "once having put the bastard off balance I let him look in my mouth. He seemed satisfied, but not that much. He wanted to examine my blood group too, but I told him he could stick it where the monkey put its nuts. When the rest of my group got here he could

116

examine us all to his heart's content. Prior to that, nothing doing. If I turned out to be a phoney and arrived back with eight Sherman tanks in tow, he could swallow his own fucking pill. Sorry, Fräulein. But if we turned out to be genuine and he messed us about any longer, I wouldn't give an old button for how long he continued in his present job."

They were close to the Cathedral now, close to the house. Benutti slowed the pace.

"How many helpers has he got?" asked O'Keefe.

"I don't know, but there are bound to be some in the woodwork. Neither did I see any other fugitives, but you can bet your life they have a quick turnover. You can also bet your life that they're going to put us through the mill when we get there. They'll probably separate us for some kind of preliminary interrogation, so for Christ's sake remember your cover stories. We're all out of Buchenwald. We all have a price on our heads. If this organization's run with anything like normal Nazi efficiency, we'll be on our way elsewhere by tomorrow."

"Together, I hope," said Caradoc.

"That's paramount," put in O'Keefe. "I don't give a damn what excuses they give us—wherever one of us goes, so do the rest."

"They may try it on," warned Benutti. "They may say they can't possibly get four of us out in the same parcel."

"Then we pull rank or sling a few of these gold coins at them," said O'Keefe. "Whatever happens we have to stick together."

"There's another thing," said Benutti. He hesitated. "When I mentioned that one of our party was a woman, the Jolly Green Giant's face damn near broke into a grin. It seems women are in short supply. Any woman, that is, but with one who looks like Greta. . . . Well, I don't have to spell it out."

"Shit," swore O'Keefe.

Benutti raised his shoulders.

"I don't think it's up to us."

"It isn't," said Greta calmly. "It's entirely up to me."

"Can you handle it?" asked O'Keefe.

"I think so."

"Let's hope so," said Benutti, "because right up ahead is where all the answers start."

"The passes," Caradoc reminded him. "The Intelligence credentials."

Benutti stopped in mid-stride.

"Christ, I'm losing my marbles. If they found those in a body search we'd be dead before we hit the ground. Thanks, Jim."

"Think nothing of it. I've got into this habit of breathing and I can't break it."

"But if we get rid of them," said Greta, "we'll have nothing with which to prove our identities if things go wrong."

"If things go wrong, sweetheart," muttered Benutti, "the only identification we'll be asked for is by St Peter looking through his big book. We can't ditch them here; we may be under observation from the house. Let's make it once round the block and dump them elsewhere. It's the sort of caution the Jolly Green Giant will appreciate anyway."

Five minutes later they were inside the house.

Benutti was right about the man he'd nicknamed the Jolly Green Giant. He was seven feet tall if he was an inch, with fists the size of soup plates. One of the fists, none of the newcomers was overjoyed to see, held a Luger with the safety off. The three other men in the downstairs room were similarly armed.

Benutti got straight to the point, playing the role of an SS officer to the hilt.

"You won't be needing those. If you've got any sense in your thick skulls you'll put them away."

"They'll be put away when I think it's safe to do so," said the giant. "Until then, Herr Sturmbannfuehrer, you will kindly do as you are told. You are in our hands now and the success or otherwise of your escape depends very much on what I decide to do with you. In the first place, I should like to know how you got here."

"You should know better than to ask questions like that," snapped O'Keefe. "The less you know, the safer we'll all be."

The giant looked at him coolly.

"Your rank, Herr . . . ?"

They had agreed to adopt SS ranks corresponding to their own. Thus O'Keefe and Benutti were Sturmbannfuehrers, Caradoc a Scharfuehrer.

"Sturmbannfuehrer," said O'Keefe. "And yours?"

"Hauptscharfuehrer."

"Then I suggest, Sergeant-Major," said O'Keefe sarcastically, "that you remember something of military courtesy. And that goes for all of you," he added to the other three gunmen. "The war may be over on paper, but the SS will never accept defeat and neither will it be disbanded. You are still a non-commissioned officer and I am your superior. If that situation ever changes, I'll call you 'sir'. Until then, you will show proper deference. Is that quite understood?"

O'Keefe had struck precisely the right bullying note. The giant lowered his pistol sullenly and indicated that the others should do the same.

"I apologize, Herr Sturmbannfuehrer, but you must appreciate that in our position we cannot be too careful. The Allies are all around us. We have heard rumours that they will shortly begin house-to-house searches, and it is not beyond the bounds of credibility that one day they will learn that an escape route exists and try to penetrate it.

"Further down the line the problem is not so acute, but here we are in the middle of what is still a war zone. We are not the first link in the escape chain, but we are an important one. If something happened to us, many of our comrades would be captured and executed."

"You will be rewarded for your services," said O'Keefe pompously.

"Serving the cause is reward enough, Herr Sturmbannfuehrer."

"Nevertheless, a little gold can always come in useful. And while we're about it, you'd better stop using ranks. Walls have ears. It would be helpful, however, if we knew what to call you and the others. Your first names will do."

The giant introduced himself as Kurt. The others were Sepp, Hans and Klaus.

Now that a pecking order had been firmly established, Kurt was still apologetic when he said, "There are certain formalities to be gone through, you will understand. I know you are anxious to be on your way, but the correct procedures must be observed."

"Naturally," said O'Keefe. "You wouldn't be doing your duty otherwise, a fact that would be reported in the appropriate quarters. Just tell us what the procedures are and let's get on with them."

"To begin with we must make a complete body search." Kurt glanced with a mixture of lust and anticipation at Greta. "We do not, I regret to say, receive many women here. The fräulein will have to be examined by one of us."

And no prizes for guessing which one, thought O'Keefe.

He quickly decided that a protest could be fatal. In their assumed roles a woman's modesty was the least of their worries. In any case, Greta solved the problem for him.

"I have no objection to anything that will get us out of this filthy Allied-occupied city," she said. "Kindly do what you have to and let's get it over with."

Unable to believe his luck, Kurt was a paragon of efficiency after that. Benutti drew Hans, Caradoc Klaus, and O'Keefe Sepp. Kurt kept Greta for himself, naturally.

They were all taken to separate rooms, two on the ground floor, two upstairs. O'Keefe found himself in one that overlooked the street, though the windows were boarded up. In the room was a single bed, a table and two upright chairs. Although he had no way of knowing it, he and the others were the only occupants of the house. The escape line got rid of its "customers" pretty quickly.

Sepp was bespectacled and underweight, and resembled a small-town grocer. But so did Heinrich Himmler.

He closed the door and asked O'Keefe to strip, examining each article of clothing carefully. This was ostensibly to check that none of it carried a label "Made in London", but O'Keefe suspected another reason—for the males, at least. Being circumcised did not prove beyond doubt that a man was Jewish, but not being so proved he wasn't.

O'Keefe passed the test.

Sepp asked him to lift his arm. He prodded and probed, but apparently the doctor and the ageing chemicals had done the trick. Sepp was satisfied. He told O'Keefe to dress.

When they were seated on opposite sides of the wooden table, the German said, "In spite of what was said downstairs, sir, I regret I must ask how you came to learn of this address."

O'Keefe was about to repeat that he had no intention of divulging such information when it occurred to him that this was a perfect opportunity to ascertain whether and when Lutz had passed through.

He hesitated, as though debating the matter.

"From Standartenfuehrer Lutz," he said finally. "You may not know his name but you will certainly recognize his description."

Before O'Keefe could give it Sepp butted in.

"The inspector of camps?"

O'Keefe felt his heart pound with excitement.

"He was certainly taking a chance, telling you who he was."

"He didn't, but Herr Lutz is a well-known figure in these parts."

"Not too well-known, I hope," said O'Keefe wryly.

Sepp grinned, revealing a set of blackened teeth.

"It doesn't matter now, sir. Herr Lutz and his companions are many hundreds of miles away."

O'Keefe's spirits plummeted. It was only to be expected, of course. Lutz was last seen in Munich in the middle of April. But he'd hoped for something more encouraging.

"I'm glad to hear it," he said, "though I must say you surprise me. When I last saw Herr Lutz he gave me the impression he would not be leaving for some time."

"And when would that be, sir—when you last saw him?"

O'Keefe pretended to think.

"It's difficult to remember. April 19th or 20th, I believe."

"In Augsburg?"

"No, Munich."

"You were at Dachau, then?" The question came in like a whiplash, but O'Keefe was ready for it.

"No, Buchenwald—except Buchenwald became a dangerous place to be at the beginning of April and my companions and I decided to make for Munich."

"You were all at Buchenwald?"

"Yes."

"The woman too?"

"Of course."

"What were your functions at the camp?"

O'Keefe adopted his haughty tone.

"That is one question I refuse to answer. If you don't know what happened at Buchenwald, Dachau, Sachsenhausen and the others, you're an ignorant fool and it's better you remain one."

But obviously Sepp knew a great deal about Buchenwald and began firing questions at O'Keefe with machine-gun rapidity. Who was the commandant there in April? Who was the one before that? Who were the major political prisoners? What, where, when, how?

Thanks to Benutti's briefing and his own researches, O'Keefe fielded the questions with ease, though his stomach turned somersaults of revulsion when Sepp asked him to estimate the total number of deaths during his period there.

"Who can count that high?" he answered.

Sepp nodded his approval.

O'Keefe made a few deliberate mistakes because no man could be expected to recall every detail. The ability to do so would automatically arouse suspicion.

For example, he said that Doctor Petr Zenkl, the former Lord Mayor of Prague and an inmate of Buchenwald for years, had been executed in March, whereas, to his certain knowledge, Zenkl was now safely in American hands.

Sepp was evidently aware of at least part of this story, which seemed to prove that others from Buchenwald had been down the line.

"I think you may have made a mistake on Zenkl," he murmured, "but it's something we can check and it's a useful piece of information to have. If he's dead, all well and good. If he's alive, he may one day be able to testify against some of the comrades."

"I think I'm right in saying he was executed."

"Well, it's possible. We'll see. And now, if I may, I must see your papers. The forgeries, of course, as I trust you've had the good sense to destroy anything which may reveal your true identity."

They had discussed this, the showing of their phoney papers, and concluded that they were to refuse if asked for sight of them. They were perfect as far as they knew, but perhaps too perfect. They were only being carried in case someone decided to go through their pockets one night.

"You know I can't do that," said O'Keefe. "To my certain knowledge we shall not be crossing any frontiers legally and therefore there is no reason for you to check how good the forgeries are. It's also a breach of security. You don't know my real name because that's how it should be. But if I show you my travel papers you will know my false name. If you are taken alive by the Allies you could reveal that information, and Allied Intelligence would soon be hunting the man whose name is on the documents."

Sepp accepted this without demur, rapidly becoming convinced that the man in front of him was the genuine article. But he still had a couple of nasty questions up his sleeve.

"Tell me," he said in a matter-of-fact tone of voice, "if you were in Munich on April 20th, as you must have been to see Herr Lutz, why didn't you leave immediately? The Americans were close, the FAB people were active . . . why wait? You could have been in Salzburg in a few hours, yet over three weeks have elapsed."

They had discussed this too. It was one of the weakest links in their story. No SS officer with an escape route planned would hang around.

Eventually they'd come up with some sort of answer. It wasn't foolproof, but it was the best they could do in the time available.

"We had some business to transact," said O'Keefe. "Financial business. Obviously we didn't wish to travel with empty pockets, but it all took longer than we thought. As it was, we had to leave considerable sums behind. Were it not for the girl. . . ."

Sepp interrupted him.

"Yes, I was coming to the girl."

His eyes narrowed lewdly.

"I trust she is nothing special to any of you?"

"Nothing."

"That's just as well because now she is undoubtedly something special to Kurt. However, if she has no value. . . ."

"I didn't say she had no value," said O'Keefe. "She has considerable value. She's with us because she's good cover and looks nothing like the witches one normally associates with the camps, although her appearance and her temperament have nothing in common. I could tell you some stories . . . but I digress. To repeat, the girl travels with us because she is useful. Three men of military age in civilian clothes might be picked up. But three men and a girl are rarely suspect."

"Which presumably explains why you were able to travel through enemy occupied territory and checkpoints without being arrested?"

They hadn't found an answer to this one, although again they had talked it over. Obviously it was possible to get from Munich to Salzburg because others had done it. Given a lot more time they might have cracked it, but time was at a premium.

In the end they'd agreed to fake it. The unanswerable would not be answered.

"I can't tell you how we did it for the same reason you cannot be told what my real name is, what the name on my false papers is, and many other things. You might be caught."

O'Keefe tried to sugar the pill.

"You're a brave man, Sepp, you're all brave men. While we go on, you must stay behind. But others may wish to get to Salzburg the way we did. The less you know, the better it is for everyone."

Behind his spectacles Sepp's pale eyes flashed with fanatical arrogance.

"You need have no fear that anyone in this cell will be taken alive. We all have our cyanide capsules."

"So did many others," said O'Keefe, "but only a mere

fraction have had the courage to bite them. When it comes down to it, every man thinks he can bluff his way out, and life is infinitely preferable to death."

"Without the Fuehrer, life is nothing."

Fuck me, thought O'Keefe, he means it.

"That's not true," he said. "If it were, we should all be dead."

Sepp nodded his understanding.

There was a noise on the stairs. It seemed as if at least one of the others had finished.

"A final question," said the German. "To the best of your knowledge is your photograph on any file which might now be in the hands of the Allies?"

"I suppose it must be—somewhere. But so are several million others. If we can be moved out quickly. . . ."

"You'll be moved out quickly enough. It's in our interests as well as yours. Tonight if it can be arranged. If not, tomorrow. We shall have to see."

"Presumably in the same direction as Herr Lutz and his companions."

"Why do you presume that?"

"I've known Lutz a long time. It's thanks to him that we were given this address. I'd like to meet up with him again."

"Well, perhaps you will; perhaps you won't. It very much depends upon circumstances. Shall we go downstairs?"

Caradoc and Benutti, Hans and Klaus, were already there. One glance was enough to tell O'Keefe that all had gone well.

A few moments later Greta appeared, followed by the giant Kurt. Greta's face was flushed, her hair untidy. It didn't take much to deduce that her interview had taken place in bed, although she never spoke of it.

"You will rest in there," said Kurt, pointing to a door which led to the rear of the house. "We may be able to get you out tonight, we may not. But it will be a long, uncomfortable journey, so I'd advise you to get some sleep."

Benutti could not resist a triumphant look in O'Keefe's direction. They were off and running.

Eleven

As Supply Officer at Tripoli, van der Heyden was responsible for everything that came in and went out, from nuts and bolts to airframes, and it was from this position of trust that he had been able, in the past, to "liberate" the occasional few hundred gallons of petrol or aviation gasoline and the odd truckload of tyres. If the proper paperwork couldn't be faked, the shortages were usually put down to "thieving wogs". He had a nominal superior in Squadron Leader Benson, who was supposed to authorize consignments of an unusual or sensitive nature (which generally meant they were bloody valuable), but in practice the South African was left to run the shop himself. Benson had a penchant for gin and dusky-skinned girls, and as long as van der Heyden didn't take too many chances and handed over a cut of the profits, Benson couldn't care less what he did. The bloody war was over, wasn't it?

Part of the Supply Officer's duties was to make sure that each aircraft on the base could be kept flying by holding in reserve the necessary spare parts. But as can happen in the best-run organizations, shortages sometimes occurred. It was then a question of picking up the phone and contacting other airfields, to see if a little barter could be arranged. Alternatively, a good Supply Officer would do favours for other bases when he held a surplus of whatever the requirement was, then call in those favours when he needed them most.

Van der Heyden was a good Supply Officer, but try as he might he could think of no one he knew down in Lagos, nor any favours he was owed. Yet it was essential for Pascoe and Kane to scout the route and establish whether a Sunderland could be refuelled down there. There might be all sorts of snags that didn't show up on paper.

According to the bulletin, dated May 1st, there was a squadron of Sunderlands, 270 Squadron, at Apapa, on the mainland opposite the island on which Lagos stood. The airfields in the capital itself held No. 38 Embarkation Unit and some of 298 Wing; at Ikeja was No. 1561 Met. Flight and No. 26 Squadron flying Wellingtons.

It was a damned bloody shame that it had to be Lagos, for West Africa was littered with Sunderland squadrons; at Abidjan, Bathurst, Dąkar, Fishlake and Jui.

The morning after their meeting with Lutz they put their heads together, Pascoe, Kane and van der Heyden, and quickly concluded that the only way out was to resort to that good old acronym known to the military throughout the world as "snafu"—situation normal, all fucked up. Lagos might not require several hundred gallons of coolant, but that's precisely what they were going to get.

Because the mean May temperature in Tripoli rarely dropped below the nineties, work on the base tended to begin early and finish early. Even so, the clerical Leading Aircraftman who walked whistling into the Supply Office at 08:00 hours was surprised to see van der Heyden already at his desk.

"Good morning, sir," he said cheerfully. The LAC was due for a home posting before long, but the South African officer could easily block it if he chose to. "You're up and about early."

"Flap on," said van der Heyden. "Those buggers down at Lagos are about to run out of coolant and have come whining to us for help."

"Lagos, sir?"

The LAC walked across to the huge map of Africa that was pinned to the wall.

"That's a long way for the crates we've got at our disposal. There must be a dozen airfields that are much closer."

"Which I presume Lagos has already tried," said van der Heyden testily. "Besides, I owe a favour or two down in that direction."

"Of course, sir."

LAC Cummings got what he thought was the picture.

Lagos might want coolant, but he'd lay odds there'd be a few bottles of gin going down on the same plane.

He checked the aircraft availability board.

"There's no need to bother with that," said van der Heyden. "If I send a Halifax the bloody crew will set down somewhere to refuel and spend the rest of the week getting drunk and complaining about engine trouble. I want this done in one hop, the crew back here just as quickly as they can turn round. It'll have to be a Lancaster and it will have to be a crew I can trust not to spend a fortnight savouring the delights of the Lagos brothels and the next month in the Sick Bay having penicillin rammed up their arses. Flying Officer Pascoe goes as pilot, Flight Sergeant Kane as co-pilot and engineer."

"Wireless op. and navigator, sir?"

"Forget it, Cummings. If Flying Officer Pascoe and Flight Sergeant Kane can't get themselves from here to Lagos and back without assistance, I'll begin to think they bought their medals in a junk shop. Besides, I'm not having a bloody riot on my hands by sending a wireless operator and a navigator down to West Africa in this heat."

Again, LAC Cummings thought he understood. It was no secret that van der Heyden, Kane and Pascoe were as thick as thieves. If something crooked was going on, the Supply Officer would naturally want to use his friends.

"Get on to the Flight Office and sort me out the best Mark III we've got," added van der Heyden. "And I do mean the bloody best. If it comes down somewhere in the middle of the Sahara, it's your head I'll want on a pole."

"Right away, sir."

Cummings went to pick up the telephone.

"Do it in person and quote my authority," said van der Heyden. "They'll give you all sorts of excuses if you use the phone."

The LAC turned to leave the office. Van der Heyden decided there was no harm in adding a sweetener.

"By the way, Cummings, I understand from Group that your posting is on its way through. Keep your nose clean and don't do anything to offend me and you should be saying hello to your wife and kids in next to no time."

Over a late breakfast Kane could be heard complaining loudly that it was bloody unfair to be given the Lagos run.

"I mean to say," he objected, "why should my name be pulled from the hat? As for flying second to Pascoe, Christ, that really beats all. I've got more hours in Lancs than he's got in fucking shoes."

His fellow NCOs were unsympathetic. As far as they were concerned, it was just Carver Kane's bad luck. Rather him than any of them. Tripoli might not be London or Paris or Sydney, Australia, but it was a fucking sight better than flying 2,000 miles across a continent that was mostly desert and freak up-currents.

"Look on the bright side, Carver," said one of the men at his table. "From what I've heard of West Africa you can screw a whole villageful of young girls for a few shillings."

"Yeah," said Kane laconically, "and three weeks later your dick drops off."

Over in his quarters Pascoe was drinking a leisurely cup of coffee. Ideally he would have liked to go to Benghazi himself to check on the Sunderland, but time was limited and it was important he saw what the situation was in Apapa. It should be okay, uncrowded. Only part of 270 Squadron was based there; the rest of it was upcoast in Abidjan.

On a pad in front of him he had a list of things to do when he got round to them. The most important item was underlined. *Handguns*. If Lutz and his cronies were carrying them, so too should he, Kane and van der Heyden. It was as well to be prepared for a doublecross.

Forty-five minutes later in the Supply Office, van der Heyden handed over the flight documents. As captain of the aircraft, Pascoe had already filed his flight plan.

Apart from the three of them, the office was empty. LAC Cummings and his two clerical assistants were on their break.

"Okay," said van der Heyden, "the Lanc's fully tanked up, coolant aboard, and ready to go. All you have to do is get there, dump the cargo no matter what the objections, and get back here. What are the winds like, Jonathan?"

"Okay as far as the Met. boys are concerned. Providing not too much goes against us, I should be putting down in Lagos about eight hours from take-off."

"Is the booze aboard?" asked Kane.

"It is. Two cases of gin marked glycol. Cost a bloody fortune." Van der Heyden winced at the thought. "If anybody kicks up a fuss you can make out that it's not really for them but you'll let them have a case if they'll take the bloody coolant off your hands."

"Sounds phoney to me."

"Trust in natural greed, Carver. You won't go far wrong."

"What about the liaison situation between Lagos and Apapa?" asked Pascoe. It had been worrying him that while he would be landing the Lancaster at Lagos, his real interest was in Apapa across the bay.

"We've struck lucky there," answered van der Heyden. "Now they're running down the West African bases, the same Supply Officer looks after both. He flits backwards and forwards across the bay. Name of Saunders, though I can't find out anything about him."

"He's bound to be bent," chipped in Kane. "They all are."

Van der Heyden grinned.

"And you'll recce the Sunderland?" asked Pascoe.

"Leave it to me. If it's where you said it was, I'll find a way of getting aboard and ascertaining what its plans are for the next few days. If it's not there. . . ." He shrugged. "If it's not there I guess we call the whole thing off."

"The hell we call it off," grunted Pascoe. "We make it work because the alternatives I don't want to think about. Neither should you, Peter. With a lot of luck Carver and I could be flying commercial aircraft in a couple of years. Okay, we won't be making enough to pay our bar bills and mostly we'll be in the hands of the sort of bastard who's spent the war behind a desk, building up a fat list of contacts. But you, you're grounded, and wherever you go looking for a job your service sheet is going to follow you around. The best you can hope for is a bowler hat, a rolled umbrella and pushing a pen at six quid a week. So let's have no shit about calling it off."

Van der Heyden looked uncomfortable.

"Well, when you put it like that. . . ."

"Damned right I put it like that." Pascoe tapped the DFC ribbon above his left pocket. "They gave me this for shooting down Germans and knocking out their towns and being a little luckier than the poor bastards I clobbered. At the time it didn't seem such a bad deal, but now I want more than congratulations. What's more I've earned it. So has Carver, so have you. This is the best chance we'll ever have and we go all the way even if it's in an Anson."

"Amen to that," said Kane. "Though if we're going at all we'd better make a move. It's going to be bloody near dark by the time we hit Lagos and the last thing we need is you bending the Lanc round the Control Tower."

From the veranda of the Supply Office van der Heyden watched the Lancaster taxi towards the runway. Had he been totally unaware of events and the pilot, he would have recognized one of Jonathan Pascoe's take-offs. Most fliers gave any four-engined bomber far too much gun before they were off the apron. It was as if they thought the quicker they got up to maximum revs, the better their chances of unsticking.

Not Pascoe.

He had the four Packard-built Merlins turning over sweet as a nut and with precious little more noise than a good driver would get from a Morris 10 before allowing the aircraft to drift forward at a pace that seemed to be its leisurely own. Some pilots needed their engineer to help them unstick, but van der Heyden knew Pascoe would be performing the whole operation by himself. Carver Kane might have more hours on Lancs than Jonathan had had hot dinners, more hours in the air, for that matter, but when it came down to it Pascoe could make all but the very best look like beginners with just a couple of entries in their log-books.

The Lancaster went down the tarmac straight as an arrow, no rudder work necessary to correct a swing that wouldn't happen anyway. And as always, Pascoe used every bit of available runway, almost as if he were dicing with the death

131

he had avoided for so long. Van der Heyden had flown with him and knew what it was like.

You seemed to be poodling along at 60 or 70 mph, with lots of tarmac in sight. Gradually, as the speed of the aeroplane increased, runway availability decreased. And there came a moment when you knew, beyond all possible doubt, that Pascoe could not unstick in time. The trees or the perimeter fence were too close, the undercart still down. There wasn't a snowball in hell's chance that you wouldn't clip trees or wire with your landing gear, turn a cartwheel, and fry in your own fat and a few hundred gallons of aviation fuel.

And then you were above it, whatever the obstruction. Then you were at 500 feet without knowing how you got there, how the pilot had danced seventeen tons of aircraft up into the air like a ballerina. Suddenly Pascoe was rapping out commands. Bring up the undercarriage. A few degrees less flap. Give me a heading.

Like a lot of fliers Jonathan Pascoe was trying to prove something, but Christ, it was proved the second his hands touched a control column. He was the best van der Heyden had ever seen.

The South African became aware of LAC Cummings beside him on the veranda, watching the Lanc bank to port and head south.

"Mr Pascoe," said Cummings unnecessarily.

"Mr Pascoe," agreed van der Heyden.

There were only a few like Jonathan Pascoe. Bob Stanford-Tuck, Douglas Bader, Guy Gibson, "Sailor" Malan, Leonard Cheshire, Mike O'Keefe. Whether you were Bomber or Fighter Command, there were only a few who ranked among the greats.

"I'll be away from the base for the rest of the day, Cummings," said van der Heyden, "probably overnight. Arrange a jeep for me, will you. I'll drive it myself."

"And if we need to reach you, sir?"

"I'll be in Benghazi."

It was a hell of a long drive, close on 500 miles, along the coast road from Tripoli to Benghazi, with the sun beating down all the way and the remnants of the desert war, burnt-out tanks, half-tracks, lorries, littering the landward side of the highway. An aircraft could have made the trip door to door in ninety minutes, but van der Heyden was grounded. Although he had made one or two unauthorized flights in the recent past and got away with it, this was too important to risk being caught and court-martialled. It was a bloody bore and would mean cadging a bed for the night, but there was nothing else for it. Besides, when the time came—assuming the Sunderland was where Pascoe had last seen it—the whole run would have to be made by road anyway. So in some ways this was a fact-finding expedition.

It was late afternoon when he arrived, but even from several miles away there was no mistaking the distinctive shape of the Sunderland. Moored to a Saunders-Roe pontoon five hundred yards from the jetty, it really was a beautiful sight. If the Lancaster was the king of aircraft and the Spitfire the prince, the Sunderland was certainly the queen. White and gleaming in the afternoon sun, its tail fin twice the height of a London double-decker bus, it was undoubtedly one of the most magnificent aeroplanes ever built.

There was a launch moored at the end of the jetty, an RAF Regiment guard carrying a Lee-Enfield .303 alongside it.

Van der Heyden left the jeep and sauntered up. The guard shouldered arms and slapped the stock of the rifle in a salute that would have brought tears of joy to the eyes of his drill sergeant.

Van der Heyden acknowledged the salute.

"Good afternoon," he said amiably. "I was just admiring the Sunderland. Haven't seen one for a long time."

The guard took in van der Heyden's campaign ribbons and friendly manner and decided he wasn't one of those bloody officers who were out to make trouble.

"She's a beautiful aircraft, sir."

"That she is. As a matter of fact I've never even been aboard one, though I understand the crew accommodation rivals the best London hotels. There's no chance of sneaking a look, I suppose?"

"I really couldn't say, sir. You'll have to check with the Flight Office."

Thirty minutes later van der Heyden was back on the jetty, unable to believe his good luck. In the Flight Office he'd come across Flight Lieutenant Wilberforce, the skipper of the Sunderland, who was just about to make a trip across to his aircraft to ensure all was in order for an early morning take-off.

Van der Heyden was alarmed. Take-off to where? He was quickly reassured. Now that the war was over the Sunderland was being used as a hospital ship, ferrying sick and injured servicemen due for repatriation to Malta for onward transportation to the UK. The flying boat was still carrying its red, white and blue roundels and not a red cross, because who the hell was going to be shooting at them?

Wilberforce was a caricaturist's dream: red-faced, an incipient beer-belly and a massive ginger moustache. He was also proud of his toy and van der Heyden leapt at the invitation to look it over.

Halfway across in the launch, van der Heyden learned something else that alarmed him. The Sunderland would only be at its present mooring for a further seventy-two hours, starting from 08:00 tomorrow. After that, it was needed elsewhere.

He fought back the urge to curse. Seventy-two hours was plenty of time. If Kane and Pascoe could sort out the Lagos end, they'd be ready to move in forty-eight. And the fact that the aircraft was being used as a hospital ship gave him an idea.

Only seven hundred-odd of the giant flying boats were built during the war and like most enthusiasts with a willing listener to hand, Flight Lieutenant Wilberforce was eager to show off his charge.

The first thing that struck van der Heyden was the immense size of the aircraft's interior. Over eighty-five feet long and almost thirty-three feet high, it had ample space on two decks to contain sleeping quarters for the 13-man crew, an officers' wardroom, a workshop and a galley.

"This is the Mark V," explained Wilberforce. "There's talk

134

of a Mark VI, but I doubt if they'll ever get it off the ground. It's powered by four 1200 h.p. Pratt and Whitney Twin Wasp R-1830 radials, which could bloody near take you to the moon with the wind behind you. We've got a maximum speed of 213 mph at 5,000 feet, though we can go up to pretty near 18,000 if necessary. However, this ship wasn't built for height. If you run into bad weather you've just got to sit it out. Mind you," he added with boyish delight, "it would take something like a hurricane to throw a Mark V about."

Van der Heyden wanted to know about armament.

Wilberforce told him that some Mark Vs carried fourteen guns—not for nothing had the Luftwaffe christened it the Flying Porcupine—but not this one. It had two Browning .303s in the Fraser Nash nose turret and four .303s in the FN 4B tail turret. In addition there was a single .50 Browning on each beam, port and starboard. Missing were the four pilot-operated forward-firing .303s and the brace of mid-upper machine guns.

"Not that it matters a tuppenny damn anyway," he added, "because we don't carry ammo. We might as well take the guns out and save on payload, but you know what the RAF's like. Until Moses descends from the mount with the commandments, there they stay."

"I don't suppose payload matters too much anyway, does it?" asked van der Heyden. "For the milk run to Malta it's minimum fuel and a quick turn round."

Wilberforce shook his head emphatically.

"Not on your bloody life, old boy. I tank up with everything she'll take, enough to get me to the UK if necessary. I was halfway to Malta a few months ago when they diverted me to Cyprus for reasons best known to God and the air traffic controller. I landed with about enough fuel to start a donkey engine. From that time onwards I don't take off without full tanks, which is one of the reasons I'm aboard now. It has been known for one of those erks in the Flight Office to take orders literally and fuel each aircraft with just enough to get it to its destination. I've managed to train most of them to think that Flight Lieutenant Wilberforce does not ascend into the bright blue bloody yonder unless the fuel's running down the fuselage, but there's always the odd idiot who thinks he's saving tax payer's money. Let someone court-martial me if they want to, but that's better than seeing your gauge read zero somewhere over the Med."

Which solved one problem, thought van der Heyden, as Wilberforce went off to complete his checks; there was no chance they'd come down in the middle of the Sahara.

He sat down in the for'ard hatch and thought it all over.

It was going to be difficult, bloody difficult; at first glance the snags were insurmountable. They had to make their move within seventy-two hours, preferably before dawn three days from tomorrow. They had to overpower the guard and get aboard the aircraft. Then they had to get the hell out of it.

So far, so bad, but the thing that worried him most was the lack of ammo for the guns. The Sunderland had a well-deserved reputation for being able to take care of itself—but not with empty guns. There was plenty of .50 and .303 ammunition in the armoury at Tripoli. Somehow they'd have to acquire some and damn the risk.

His thoughts were interrupted as the four Pratt and Whitneys roared into life. Then just as suddenly the aircraft was silent again.

Wilberforce came down the ladder from the flight deck.

"Well, everything seems to be in order," he said cheerfully. "Seen everything you want to see?"

"Yes, and thanks very much for the guided tour."

"Not at all. My pleasure. Bit bigger than a Spit though, isn't it?" Van der Heyden had mentioned in the Flight Office that he had flown Spitfires before being grounded.

"Just a bit. On the other hand, a Spit's a smaller target and a damned sight faster."

"Well, each to his own, I suppose, but don't think this ship's a pussy cat. I know of one pilot not a million miles from here who was attacked by six Ju 88s. He shot one down, forced another to land, and the rest of the buggers sheered off."

It was almost dark and from the launch the lights of Benghazi twinkled in front of them.

"You're not thinking of driving back to—where was it?—Tripoli tonight are you?" asked Wilberforce.

"Not if I can get myself a bunk."

"Consider it done. We'll have a spot of dinner and I'll show you the night life."

God forbid, thought van der Heyden.

"Thanks," he said. "I'll take you up on that."

Once on the jetty Wilberforce said, "By the way, you never did say what you're doing in this direction."

"Just sightseeing," said van der Heyden.

Twelve

At about the same time as Wilberforce and van der Heyden were having their first drink of the evening, Pascoe put the Lancaster down in Lagos with a gentleness that wouldn't have broken a thin-shelled egg. Considering he'd been at the controls the whole trip, it was an impressive performance. Kane had offered to do some of the donkey work, but Pascoe had turned him down flat.

"Just look after the wireless and make sure we're heading in the right direction. I'm the only one who can fly a bloody Sunderland. I'd better get used to staying awake."

The Duty Officer examined the cargo manifest with great care, checking it against his own list of expected supplies. He was a very young Pilot Officer without wings or ribbons to his name.

"There's nothing here about a consignment of coolant," he said finally, "and from what I can see we don't need any."

"Well, it's here and you've got it," said Kane belligerently. "Just sign the papers, point us in the direction of the nearest bar, and make sure the Lanc's tanked up for a quick getaway tomorrow morning. After that, you can get back to your comic book."

Pascoe nudged Kane with his elbow. Take it easy. There

was no point in upsetting anyone and there was certainly nothing to be gained by making a fuss.

"What the Flight Sergeant is trying to say," he smiled, "is that we've flown a long way with that coolant and we can't take it back without getting our arses kicked. There's obviously been a cock-up somewhere so let's sort it out. Who's your Supply Officer?"

"Flight Lieutenant Saunders, sir." The young officer felt much more at home talking to his own kind than he did to this vulgar Australian, even though the Aussie had the DFM and Bar ribbons pinned to his chest.

"Then let's get him out from wherever he's hiding," suggested Pascoe. "He can take the responsibility. Either the coolant stays or it goes. Let him decide."

"He's probably trying to drum up a bridge game at this time in the evening."

"Get him anyway," suggested Pascoe.

The youngster picked up the internal phone. Pascoe pulled Kane away from the desk.

"Now pack it in, Carver," he warned. "Don't make a bloody nuisance of yourself. What the hell's eating you anyway?"

"Pack it in yourself," snorted Kane. "It's that kind of young prig who gives the Royal Air Force a bad name. Jesus, I'll bet he's not shaving yet and the nearest he's been to a German is the back row of a cinema, watching reruns of "All Quiet on the Western Front". It's that sort of young brat that makes me want to puke."

Pascoe understood something of Kane's resentment. It had nothing to do with nerves. The "brat" was an officer for no better reason than that of speaking the King's English and, presumably, having attended the right school. Kane was an NCO, bemedalled notwithstanding, because he talked with a nasal twang and had no respect for authority. It was a very curious system, Pascoe thought, not for the first time, but one as English as marmalade and nothing was going to change it.

"Look on the positive side," he said to Kane. "In a few more days you'll have more money than that kid's going to see in the whole of his life. Use it properly and one day people like that will be doffing their caps to you."

"Yeah." Kane brightened at the thought. "Yeah, I hadn't thought of it like that."

"Flight Lieutenant Saunders is on his way across, sir."

Saunders turned out to be a foxy-faced individual in his thirties. Everything about him was a little overdone. His moustache was too neat, his hair too oily, the crease in his trousers too much of a knife-edge. It was six to four in tenners that when in London he hung around the smarter hotel bars and tried to charm middle-aged ladies into investing in racing systems.

He was also annoyed at being dug out of the Mess.

"Now what the hell's all this about?" he demanded. "Pilot Officer Taylor tells me you've turned up out of the blue bearing gifts like the bloody Magi. Well, let me tell you something: this isn't a stable, my name's not Joseph, and unless Intelligence has got the whole thing snafu'd, there's no infant about to be born. I don't need coolant. I don't need one gallon, let alone hundreds. I have nowhere to put it. If you want to know the absolute truth I have enough bloody coolant to lubricate every moving part on every aircraft north of Port Elizabeth. So you can turn your Lanc right round, still laden, and head back whence you came. Do I make myself clear?"

Pascoe coughed to smother a grin.

"I suppose I must have the wrong Flight Lieutenant Saunders, sir."

"You certainly haven't got the wrong Flight Lieutenant Saunders. To the best of my knowledge there's only one of us within a thousand miles of this godforsaken hole. In any case, who gave you my name? Who the hell do I know in Tripoli who'd send me hundreds of gallons of coolant I neither need nor requisitioned?"

"If I may have a private word with you, sir."

Pascoe eased Saunders to one side, out of earshot.

"I'm merely acting as ferry pilot on this run, sir," he said earnestly, "and quite honestly I don't know whether or not you requisitioned coolant. But I know I can't return to Tripoli with it without some awkward questions being asked—as I also know I was asked to deliver to Flight Lieutenant Saunders in person the crate of gin that's aboard the Lanc but which is not on the cargo manifest."

Saunders was not a man to look a gift horse in the mouth. Obviously there'd been a cock-up in Tripoli, because he knew no one there who owed him a crate of gin. The Saunders they were looking for was not he, but what the hell did it matter? By the time it was all sorted out the gin would be well swallowed, and that was an end to it. If the genuine Saunders turned up one day, hard luck. Fortunes of war, old boy.

Of course he could find room for a couple of hundred gallons of coolant. For a crate of free gin he'd find room for a couple of thousand.

"You should have said so in the first place, Flying Officer . . . ?"

"Pascoe, sir."

"Ah yes, Pascoe. You should have said so right at the beginning, Flying Officer Pascoe."

"That would hardly have been good politics, sir." Pascoe indicated Pilot Officer Taylor. "After all, this sort of thing could get around in no time flat."

"Quite right, absolutely right. And we don't want to corrupt the young, do we?"

"Positively not, sir. But if we can unload the cargo as quickly as possible, my Flight Sergeant and I would like to see a little of Lagos before flying back tomorrow morning. Accommodation would also be appreciated."

"Consider it done, old boy, consider it done. It might however be meet if we supervised the unloading of the high-octane stuff ourselves. The erks can take care of the coolant. And while we're about it, I know one or two places on the waterfront myself. Not quite top drawer, you understand, but safe as houses as far as the women are concerned." Saunders leaned closer and whispered conspiratorially. "I presume your Flight Sergeant is all right?"

"First rate, sir. Though being Australian he'll probably drink us both under the table."

"I doubt that, dear boy. I very much doubt that."

Three hours later Pascoe was inclined to agree. There are precious few people in the world who can outdrink an Aussie and Carver Kane was somewhere near the top of his national league. But in the club/cum brothel/cum dancehall the trio hit long before midnight, Saunders proved himself to be among the best.

As the clock ticked into the small hours, Pascoe was beginning to wonder if he would ever get an opportunity to pump Saunders about Apapa. Every time he brought the subject up, Saunders complained about shop-talk and buried his head in a glass.

Yet somehow Pascoe had to find out about facilities, security, and a host of other matters. Very soon he would be asked to land one of the biggest aeroplanes in the world across the bay and he wanted to make sure he could do it without reducing twenty-seven tons of flying boat to so much matchwood.

But it was impossible to prise Saunders away from his bottle. When he wasn't drinking he was dancing—or what passed for it in these parts. Kane wasn't being much help either; he'd struck up a conversation with a pretty Eruasian girl and the next item on the agenda seemed to be a trip upstairs.

Suddenly Pascoe had had enough. He was tired after the long flight down and they could play around like this all night and get nowhere. Saunders was venal, that much was already established. It was time to take the bull by the horns.

While Saunders was on the far side of the dance floor, demonstrating a series of complicated steps for the benefit of a Warrant Officer and his girl friend, Pascoe dragged Kane away from the prostitute.

"We've got to get that bastard out of here."

"We? I'm just beginning to enjoy myself. You get him out. I've got other things planned."

"You can forget about it, Carver. This isn't a pleasure trip."

"Don't tell me what to do." The Australian had drunk just enough to be dangerous. "Those rank tabs don't matter shit to me."

"They'd better, because if you're going to bugger around and not pull your weight, you're out of the whole deal, beginning now."

Kane half rose to his feet before thinking better of it.

"Yeah, you're right. I'd probably get a dose anyway."

Seeing a client about to evaporate, the prostitute tugged at Kane's sleeve.

"Piss off," he said, and gave her a handful of small coins.

When Saunders came back to the table he was ready for some fresh air anyway. It hit him like a brick. After a couple of dozen lurching yards he confessed he would have to sit down for a while.

"Can't take it the way I used to," he muttered. "It's this bloody climate."

Pascoe was worried he would fall asleep.

"Oh, it can't be that bad," he said airily. "A quiet enough life. You can't get many visiting brass this far south."

"True enough, but that doesn't make up for the heat. If it wasn't for the liquor I don't think any of us on the station would last a week."

Pascoe seized his opportunity.

"Well, there's always a chance we can make another few trips carrying glycol."

Saunders was suddenly alert. His eyes narrowed cunningly.

"Yes, I suppose I am owed a few favours from Tripoli."

Nothing ventured, nothing gained, thought Pascoe, and plunged in.

"Come off it, Flight Lieutenant. It was obvious from the start that you were not the Saunders we were supposed to deliver the gin to. There's been a foul-up somewhere, but we all know it's easier to take advantage of a foul-up than to try to explain the mistake. We were told to deliver a crate of gin to a Flight Lieutenant Saunders. The coolant was just cover. But what happened once can happen again. All you have to do is sign the cargo manifest and refuel us for the return trip. The trouble is, we might not be able to use a Lancaster next time. I've done about a thousand hours in flying boats and there's talk of transferring Kane and myself to Sunderlands or Catalinas, for which we'll need. . . ."

"You're talking a load of bullshit," Saunders interrupted him. The Lagos officer's head cleared with a rapidity which was truly astonishing. He might have been three-parts drunk when he left the club and there was no doubt that some time in the future he would be a candidate for Alcoholics Anonymous. But for the moment he had all his faculties.

"Bullshit," he repeated. "I don't know what the game is but nobody goes around giving away cases of gin without wanting something in return. You people are up to something. What is it—drugs, spare parts, something bigger? Diamonds, for instance?"

Pascoe looked at Kane, who nodded. He'd seen enough shady characters in his life to recognize another. Saunders was not about to blow the whistle. What he wanted was a piece of the action.

Pascoe took a deep breath. It was all or nothing.

"You're right," he said. "We are on to something. What it is I'm not about to tell you, but the next time we head down in this direction we'll be in a flying boat and probably landing at night. What we'll need from you is the facilities at Apapa. We may be here a few hours and we'll want the ship refuelled, no questions asked. We'll also need the use of a couple of 3-tonners."

"I'll need to know more. I could be putting my head in a noose."

"Sorry, I've told you all I'm going to."

Saunders thought it over. It sounded hairy, but it wouldn't be the first time and doubtless not the last he had taken part in something completely illegal.

Providing a pair of 3-ton trucks and refuelling facilities across the bay was simple, easier than Pascoe knew, though he wasn't about to say so. From tomorrow, the whole of 270 Squadron was going up to Abidjan for ten days. Apapa would be empty.

"I'll want a thousand pounds or the equivalent in US dollars," he said.

Kane was about to agree when Pascoe silenced him with a gesture. It wouldn't do to let Saunders know that so much money was so readily available.

"That's a hell of a lot of loot."

"I'm taking a hell of a lot of risk. I've got some pull over in Apapa, but arranging to have a gasoline bowser on tap costs money. So does the paperwork. Anyway, that's my price. You can take it or leave it."

"We'll take it," said Pascoe.

"Half in advance."

"Don't be bloody ridiculous. Do we look as though we carry that sort of money around with us?"

"It shouldn't be necessary anyway," put in Kane. "If we don't turn up with the money we don't get the gas. That leaves us stranded."

Saunders mulled this over.

"Okay, that sounds fair enough. No money, no fuel. I take it you'll be needing full tanks?"

"Up to the gunwales."

"You sound as though you're going a long way."

"Not really," said Pascoe hastily. "It's just that we don't want to go through the same performance elsewhere."

"Understandable. When is all this to take place?"

"Hard to tell. Two or three days, perhaps."

"You'll have to send me a signal advising the exact time and date of your arrival so that I can inform the wireless room. I'll also need your call sign."

"What are your initials and month of birth?" asked Pascoe.

"A. S.—September."

"Let's make it Able Sugar Nine, then."

Much later, in the quarters Saunders had arranged for them, Kane said, "Van der Heyden's not going to like this one bit. If Saunders wakes up with second thoughts in the morning, we'll all be spending the rest of our lives in prison."

"Don't you believe it," said Pascoe confidently. "He's not going to do anything to jeopardize a thousand quid—which we'll have to pay him in sovereigns, by the way."

"Risky."

"It can't be helped. He'll have to take it any way he gets it. Hell, he's not paying for the bloody fuel or the 3-tonners."

"Which reminds me," said Kane. "What are the trucks for? This is the first I've heard mention of them."

"Christ, Carver, you're beginning to worry me," said Pascoe. "How the hell do you expect to transport the gold from the cache to the Sunderland—in a sack?"

Van der Heyden arrived back from Benghazi a couple of hours ahead of the Lancaster, but by mid-afternoon all three were closeted in the South African's office. Quickly he told them what he had learned about the Sunderland's state of readiness and how long it would be at its present mooring. He took the deal that had been made with Saunders without batting an eyelid.

"I sometimes think," he said, "that all Supply Officers are born crooks. I haven't met one yet who didn't have his finger in some sort of pie. I wish I'd thought of it earlier. We could perhaps have arranged the whole business by wireless."

"I needed the flying experience anyway," said Pascoe. "Although you can take a Sunderland close to 18,000 feet, for maximum speed you have to stooge around at 5,000. Even then you're only getting a little over 200 m.p.h. out of her. I also wanted to make sure that there was nothing in the way I couldn't get over or round."

"And?"

"It shouldn't be too difficult. I'm going to need some help on the engineering and navigation side because these things aren't Tiger Moths, but you're both fliers so there shouldn't be any problem. It's the flight down to Cape Town that bothers me most. I'll have to hug the coastline most of the way and at our height we'll stand out like a nun in a boxing-ring."

"Which is a hitherto unthought of advantage of using a flying boat," said van der Heyden. "We don't need airfields. If necessary we can fly by night and put down somewhere during the day."

"There's another item," said Pascoe. "Cape Town is just about the limit of our range. We'll be arriving with bloody near empty tanks as it is and I still have no idea of the payload."

"I've been working on it." Van der Heyden picked up a piece of paper and read from it. "If I heard Lutz correctly, a fifth of the cache, one million pounds, is in gold. That weighs 8,000 lbs."

"Okay," said Pascoe, "we're well in. The next move is to talk to the Germans. And I mean *all* of them. We've only met Lutz up to now and I like to see what I'm up against. Let's not lose sight of the fact that we've been fighting these bastards for the last six years and I doubt if more than a handful have ever heard of the Marquis of Queensberry."

"You think there might be trouble?" asked Kane.

"It's always a possibility. There's a lot of money at stake. We should be armed, Peter."

"It's on my list. That and about ten thousand other things. Christ, it's a tight schedule. If only the Sunderland would still be there in a week."

"Well, it won't," said Pascoe, "so it's no good wishing. In just over sixty hours it will have gone for good, which means the latest we move is the day after tomorrow."

Thirteen

Within seconds of meeting Mueller, Fischer and Scheringer, the three fliers were glad they'd put handguns on the menu. A more poisonous-looking trio it would have been hard to imagine.

Van der Heyden acted as spokesman.

At first Lutz did not see why Hanna and her father should be included in the briefing, but finally he accepted the necessity of their presence.

To begin with, van der Heyden asked how many of the Germans spoke or understood English.

"They all do," answered Lutz, "but perhaps not enough to follow a complex conversation. However, that needn't bother you. Anything they do not understand I'll translate for them. You may address your remarks to me."

His tone was that of a headmaster urging a junior prefect

to get to the point, and van der Heyden was having none of it.

"We'll lose that attitude for a start. I don't know what rank you carried in the Wehrmacht, but it doesn't amount to owl shit now. Here you're less than equals because without us you stay here and rot."

"And you remain poor."

"Perhaps. But kindly remember you're in our hands. If what we have planned fails, we're all dead."

"Then you'd better tell us what you have in mind and let us judge for ourselves."

Van der Heyden explained about the Sunderland, where it was moored and how long it would be there. Leaving Flight Lieutenant Saunders' name out of it, he told the Germans that arrangements had been made for refuelling in Lagos— or rather, across the bay at Apapa.

"What about transferring the bullion from the cache to the aircraft?" asked Lutz. "The diamonds will be simple enough; great wealth in a chest a child could carry. But according to my calculations the gold weighs almost four tons."

"Three point six four tons or 8,163 lbs," said van der Heyden, referring to his notes. "A tidy weight, I agree, but we've also arranged to have two RAF 3-tonners on hand— which we shall drive ourselves, of course."

"And the Sunderland will take such a payload?"

Pascoe couldn't resist it.

"In balmier days it used to carry almost 5,000 lbs in bombs. You know, for sending U-boats to the bottom." Before Lutz could comment, he went on, "I presume the gold is in bullion boxes?"

Lutz nodded.

"Perfectly normal boxes with rope handles. Each one contains a single ingot and weighs fifty pounds."

"Couldn't be better," murmured van der Heyden. "If anyone's watching all they'll see is a group of men shifting a lot of boxes which could contain bananas. It's going to take time, however."

Lutz agreed.

"Not counting Herr Baumann and his daughter, we are seven. Some of us are stronger than others, but on average

147

we should be able to manage one box per man per trip. However, we shall have to transfer the bullion from the cache to the trucks and from the trucks to the aeroplane."

"You're missing out the intermediate step of the launch," said Pascoe.

"A launch?"

"Wait a minute," interrupted van der Heyden. "Let's take it step by step or we'll be here all night. We won't be seven but five," he told Lutz. "Neither Pascoe nor Kane will be anywhere near the cache. They must remain with the aircraft to ensure the refuelling goes off without a hitch."

"That's madness," protested Lutz. "We need every pair of hands we can get."

"No, we don't." The South African had done his homework well. "Believe me, I've spent several hours checking and rechecking my calculations, and assuming an average of five minutes per trip from the cache to the trucks, each man carrying one box, that part of the operation can be completed in two and three-quarter hours. Allowing for short rest periods, say three hours in all. Once at the launch it will be easier. We'll be able to run a fire-bucket system with each man passing a box to the man in front. The same will apply between the launch and the aircraft. Say, another four hours all told."

"Why do we need the launch?" demanded Lutz. "My experience of flying boats is limited, but the ones I've seen have frequently been moored to a pontoon adjacent to the shore or harbour."

"That isn't always the case," said Pascoe. "It isn't at Benghazi, for example, and we decided against using a flying boat berth at Apapa to keep away the curious. We'll moor a couple of hundred yards offshore. It'll take longer like that but it's safer."

"Precisely how long I haven't been able to estimate," said van der Heyden, "because I don't know how far away the cache is."

"About half an hour's drive in each direction," said Lutz.

"So, another hour in all. Let's allow two more for the odd thing that might go wrong and we're talking about a total of ten hours. Nothing has to be added for refuelling. That will be taking place concurrently. If we land at Apapa around dusk, say 7 p.m., we should be well on our way before dawn."

Lutz rapidly translated the substance of the conversation for Mueller, Fischer and Scheringer, though it seemed they'd followed most of it. When he had finished he said, "All right—so far, so good. There is however one slight problem you haven't mentioned. The cache is in Lagos, the Sunderland at Benghazi, and we are here. How do you propose to bring the units together?"

"Very simply," answered van der Heyden. "We hijack the Sunderland and get on our way."

"Really. And how do you plan to do that?"

"Walk aboard and take it over."

Lutz raised his eyebrows.

"And might not someone object?" he asked sarcastically.

"Only if we don't do it properly. And we intend doing it properly."

The Sunderland was being used as a hospital aircraft, he explained, and the best way to get aboard a hospital aircraft was to appear to be injured. The four Germans and Herr Baumann would be bandaged as walking wounded; Hanna would be dressed in the uniform of a QARANC nurse. They would have no trouble stealing a uniform. Kane had several girl friends in the nearby military hospital and it was just a question of turning up on some pretext and lifting a uniform while the owner wasn't looking.

Kane nodded to confirm this.

The next thing they needed was a vehicle. A field ambulance would be too difficult to get hold of so it would have to be a 3-tonner, signed out in the normal manner and carrying spare jerrycans of gas.

"But the trickiest bit of all," he continued, "is ammo for the Sunderland's guns, calibre .50 and .303. We should be able to get hold of some, but if we can't. . . ." He shrugged.

"It surely makes no difference," said Lutz.

Pascoe looked at him as though he suddenly sprouted wings.

"It may not make much difference to you, but it sure as hell does to us. RAF Benghazi is not going to take kindly to someone swiping one of their aeroplanes. There's always a chance we'll be pursued and I'd like to be able to defend ourselves. If we can't, we'll be forced or shot down and that's an end to it."

While accepting the logic of this, Lutz was nevertheless intrigued.

"The only people who could conceivably attack us are the RAF, am I correct?"

"Quite correct."

"And you're willing to shoot back, shoot at aircraft carrying RAF markings, shoot down your own kind?"

"Once we're airborne they won't be our own kind," said Pascoe. "We'll be on opposite sides."

He had thought carefully about this but there was no way round it. It wasn't only for himself, he reasoned; it was for Hanna and her father.

"We're beyond the pale as soon as I'm in the driving seat of the Sunderland," he went on. "If we're attacked we either fight back or we go under. Still, at the moment it's academic. It depends whether or not we can get ammunition."

"It shouldn't be too difficult," said van der Heyden. "As Supply Officer I can get more or less what I want. I'd think twice if I were coming back, but this is a one-way ticket."

How right you are, thought Lutz.

"You seem to have covered everything except for one very important item," he said. "You haven't yet said when we leave."

"Two days from now, in the afternoon. It's a long drive to Benghazi, but hopefully we shall arrive before dawn."

"Hopefully?" queried Lutz. "You're cutting it a bit fine, aren't you? If anything goes wrong with the truck or we're delayed for any other reason, the Sunderland will have gone."

"It can't be helped. There's a great deal of preparatory work to be done."

"Which we'd better get on with," said Pascoe.

At the door he added, "You two go on ahead. I'll make my own way back. I want to have a word with Hanna."

In the jeep van der Heyden said, "Drop me off at the base,

Carver. I'd like to catch Benson before he becomes incapable. I might need his signature for that ammo."

Kane was surprised.

"Drop you off? Where am I supposed to be going?"

"Don't be dense. You're about to reacquaint yourself with one of your nursing girl friends."

With Pascoe and Hanna out of the way and old man Baumann upstairs, Lutz went over the whole business again with Mueller, Fischer and Scheringer. When they had finished their discussion, Scheringer asked, "When do you propose to tell Pascoe that our destination is not Cape Town?"

"Not until Lagos."

"And the aircraft, this Sunderland—it's capable of making the journey?"

"Why do you think I told them we were going to Cape Town?" asked Lutz. "The distance from Lagos to the southern tip of Africa is almost identical to that from Lagos to our rendezvous. If the Sunderland can do the first without refuelling, it can do the second."

"And what if they raise objections?" demanded Mueller.

"There's no reason why they should. If they do, we shall have to persuade them otherwise. It works to our advantage that they want the Baumanns aboard. If they hadn't suggested it, I would have done so myself. Pascoe will fly us anywhere we wish with a gun pointed at Fräulein Baumann's skull."

"The girl I can understand," said Fischer, "but the old man's just so much excess baggage."

"But useful nevertheless. The daughter has an absurd amount of affection for him. Via him we have an extra lever on her, and via her a thumbscrew on Pascoe."

"I'm not so sure of that," muttered Mueller. "He's tough, that one. You heard what he said about shooting down pursuit aircraft."

"Of course he's tough," said Lutz. "If he were not he would be of no use to us."

"He won't be easy to get rid of—or fool."

"We'll concern ourselves with that when the time comes. For the moment, we need him, and we must do nothing to make him suspicious."

"Besides," grinned Fischer, "he's being well paid."

The four Nazis thought this a great joke.

"Considering they're going to get nothing," said Mueller, "we could have offered them half."

"Three-quarters," spluttered Scheringer.

Lutz brought them back to reality.

"You may well laugh," he said sombrely, "but consider this ... If we do not intend to share the cache with them, they may well have decided not to share it with us."

"I'd like to see them try," grunted Mueller. "That bullion is earmarked for a different purpose."

"Well said, Mueller."

Now familiar with the geography of the house, Lutz went to the cupboard and brought out the brandy and glasses. He filled each one and raised his own.

"A toast, gentlemen. To SS members everywhere. May they flourish."

Although the sun was in the process of disappearing behind the Atlas Mountains, way over to the west, it was still stiflingly hot as Hanna and Pascoe made their way along the waterfront to the apartment. Occasionally they were accosted by young boys, some barely off the breast, either begging or offering quite useless wares for sale. Both Hanna and Pascoe had been in Libya long enough to know how to handle these pint-sized hucksters. Argue with them or berate them and they took it as a sign of encouragement; ignore them and sooner or later they went away.

As Hanna's mood would not.

Inside the apartment Pascoe fixed the drinks. One day, he promised himself, he was going to have a fridge that worked and gin that did not come out of the bottle warm enough to swim in.

Hanna sat on the bed. Pascoe handed her a drink. She sipped it and pulled a face.

"I know what you mean," he said. "Still, it won't be for long. This time next week we'll be in Rio or Caracas or wherever we choose."

"You really think so?"

"Of course I do. Are you having doubts?"

"I don't know. Yes. No. Oh, I don't know. It seemed so simple at the beginning, rather like a grown-up game. Now we're talking about stealing an aeroplane, ammunition, shooting at other aeroplanes. It's not what I imagined."

"The ammo's just a precaution," Pascoe reminded her. "I doubt if we'll ever fire the guns."

"That's what murderers say."

"Murderers?"

"Yes. You know, how they only took the revolver along to frighten somebody, that they had no intention of using it. But it always goes off."

"Not always. Not this time. We'll be in and out of Apapa before anyone has a chance to blink, you'll see." Hanna was silent. She took a pull at her drink before asking, "Does the money mean that much to you?"

Pascoe clicked his tongue irritably.

"We've been over this before. You know precisely what it means to both of us, to the three of us if we include your father. Don't start having second thoughts now, for Christ's sake. It was you who asked me to help in the first place."

"I know. It's just that . . . Oh hell, it's all such a mess."

"No it isn't. It's perfectly straightforward. And if it's the ammunition you're worried about, forget it. You can forget about pursuing fighters also." He smiled and tapped himself on the chest, not totally with self-mockery. "You know what van der Heyden and Kane say about me—I can just about outfly anyone."

"Including Douglas Bader, Sailor Malan, the others you've told me about? Including your half-brother?"

Possibly Bader, possibly Malan, thought Pascoe, though about his half-brother he was not so sure. Although they had never got along and he hadn't seen him in years, Mike O'Keefe would give any flier alive a damn good run for his money.

Fourteen

Having established their credentials in Salzburg, O'Keefe and the others were whisked down the escape line with amazing rapidity the day after their interrogation. O'Keefe suspected they could have been moved out even quicker but for the fact that Kurt wanted another helping of Greta's body, but the German girl neither confirmed nor denied this. She did not, however, spend the night in the same room as the others.

In spite of the vast number of Allied troops in Austria, they had no difficulty in making it as far as Spittal, eighty miles south-east of Salzburg, by mid-afternoon of their first day on the road; and although they were not to know it, they were following the same route taken by Lutz several weeks earlier.

Travelling in the back of an open truck piled high with furniture and driven by Kurt, they had been warned to keep their mouths shut no matter who spoke to them. Kurt would handle everything—which he did with an ease which made O'Keefe despair. The SS NCO obviously had all the right papers and knew where to place his bribes. If it were as simple as this, Lutz could be several continents away by now.

They were stopped at regular intervals by Allied road-blocks, but not once were the passengers required to produce any form of identification. If the driver had the necessary travel permit, then it was okay.

On reflection a lot of it made sense. They were not alone on the road; far from it, they were part of a loose convoy of delapidated vehicles crammed with household goods and careworn people. Most were Italians, returning home after months or years spent working in German factories; some were non-Communist citizens of countries now overrun by the Red Army. It was impossible for the Allies to check everyone's documents. It would have taken weeks to process or verify a mere handful and in the meantime the traffic had to be kept flowing. The general attitude seemed to be: let's get them the hell out of our zone. The whole of Europe was in a state of chaos and the SS was taking full advantage of the fact that the easiest time to effect an escape is directly after a city's (or a country's) fall, before the occupying authorities got round to issuing identity cards. Later it would not be so easy, but for the moment the only inconvenience was travelling at altitude in an open-topped truck clad in inadequate clothing.

Kurt had warned them at the start that it might get more difficult the closer they got to the Austro–Italian frontier, where bands of partisans, mainly Communist sympathizers, were roaming at will and dispensing rough justice to anyone who seemed in the least suspect. But even this turned out to be a false alarm, and they crossed the frontier without mishap.

By nightfall on the first day they were in Dobbiaco, five miles into Italy. Whatever Kurt had under the bonnet of the truck was certainly not the original engine, for, judging by outward appearances, the vehicle stood no chance of climbing the rugged mountain roads.

O'Keefe risked a remark to Benutti, once they were clear of the border.

"I don't know who's in charge of Intelligence in this sector, but somebody should have a word with him. No one has once asked Kurt how the hell he expects to get up mountains in this heap of scrap iron."

"If we get back I'll do just that," said Benutti. "In the meantime, thank your lucky stars that you don't have to have an IQ of 160 to be a dogface. Somebody starts asking questions, we're in big trouble. We've nothing to prove who we really are so it's possible we get shot by our own side. If we start bleating, that's the end of it. Either Kurt puts a bullet in us or somebody puts one in him."

During happier times the town of Dobbiaco, at 4,000 feet saddling the divide between the valley of the Rienza and the

Danubian basin of the Drava, had played host to the international ski-ing set, those who were tired of the usual resorts. Now it was a staging-post for the 5th Army, and O'Keefe had to admire the guts of the SS NCO. He had no idea how many languages Kurt spoke or how fluent he was with them, but driving in among the Anglo-American troops took nerve. As a fighter pilot O'Keefe understood nerve, though for it to be present in an individual who was otherwise anathema seemed perverse.

During the Battle of Britain and later, O'Keefe had tackled the best the Luftwaffe could field. Although today he could not put names to his opponents, later he would know he had fought, and never been bested by, men such as Adolf Galland, Werner Mölders, Theo Osterkamp, Werner Baumbach and Helmut Wick. Never mind that they were trying to kill him, they were fearless and skilful, fighting for a cause they believed in.

Nerve, guts, character, bravery—call it what you will; they were admirable qualities in any human being. But they implied nobility. A man such as Kurt, who had participated, even vicariously, in the slaughter of millions, should be cowardly and craven, unworthy of anything but ignominious execution. Yet Kurt was risking his own life to save theirs. Instead of running as the rest of them were running, fingering their necks uneasily, Kurt stayed.

Meine Ehre heisst Treue. Loyalty is my honour, the motto of the SS. However wrong, however misguided, Kurt was living true to his oath.

The safe house in Dobbiaco was in the old quarter of the town, within sight of the castle built circa 1500 for Emperor Maximilian I. The middle-aged couple who greeted Kurt appeared anything but an integral part of an SS escape line. He had a peasant's face and was smoking something foul-smelling in a battered meerschaum; she had greying hair, wore a blue polka-dot apron, and looked as though she laughed a lot. In another time they would be put down as people who ran a tiny bed and breakfast establishment where wayfarers always received value for money. The old man would have his favourite chair by the stove and tell tales of the famous skiers he had known; she would bake homemade pastries and gossip with the neighbours.

It was perfect cover.

When Kurt had finished talking to them he said, "I am leaving now. I must be back in Salzburg by tomorrow. There is no one in the house apart from yourselves, but that is not to say that others will not arrive. If that happens, you will ask no questions nor answer any.

"Early tomorrow you will be collected and taken on the next stage of your journey. Don't ask where. The less you know, the better it is for all of us, though you may tell the comrades at the other end that we, too, are doing our job."

"What are we to say if asked how long you can continue to operate?" queried O'Keefe.

"For as long as we can. We're in no immediate danger. The Americans are fools and the Russians drunkards. But if we're forced to run we're well prepared."

"And close down the Salzburg house?"

"There are others, many others, though needless to say I do not know their locations. It's only in Italy that places of refuge become less common, which was why we gave you such a thorough interrogation in the north. If we in Salzburg are betrayed, nothing is lost save a few lives. But the loss of a single safe house in Italy could be disastrous, which is why I must repeat that you ask no questions nor answer any. *Auf wiedersehen.*"

Supper comprised black bread and thick if meatless homemade soup and was more or less a silent affair, mainly because the old woman kept popping in and out of the kitchen to see that everything was in order. They did not see the man again that evening; presumably he had gone off somewhere to arrange the following day's transport.

The meal over, the woman came in to clear the table and apologize for the fact that all four would have to sleep in the same room. It was not the most convenient of arrangements, she said with a shrug of her shoulders to Greta, but these were distressing times and doubtless the fräulein would understand. The only washing facilities were those at the kitchen sink, and the lavatory was outside. They would, however, find it clean.

Later, in a room which contained four sets of two-tiered bunks, jammed so close together that it was difficult to move without bumping into something or someone, Benutti concluded it was safe to talk providing they kept their voices down.

"I don't think they'll have anything as sophisticated as hidden microphones in this neck of the woods, but there's no way of telling how thin these walls are."

O'Keefe was depressed and confessed it.

"I still don't believe we've got this far. Christ, did you see how Kurt got us through those roadblocks? It was like buying a ticket for the theatre. I could have stood up in the back and sang the Horst Wessel and nobody would have given a damn. I tell you, this whole business is running on cylinders so well-oiled that half the war criminals in Germany could be out of the country before our people catch on."

"Not once we get to the other end," said Benutti. "When we get there, wherever the hell there is, we blow this network sky high. And I'm not forgetting Lutz, Mike. I want the lot, not just bits and pieces."

"I'm glad to hear it."

"Well, I figure it like this. If it wasn't for Lutz I'd be sitting quietly in Munich now, minding my own business, drinking Hansen's coffee with maybe a slug of bourbon in it, smoking a cigarette with my feet up. He's got a lot to answer for."

"What gets me," said Caradoc, echoing O'Keefe's sentiments, "is the efficiency of the bloody operation. They must have had it set up for years. I can understand Kurt and his bunch, but what about these people? And the people further down the line—the Italians, I mean. What the hell have they got to gain?"

"They're committed *fascisti*," said Greta. "You didn't live through it; I did. A lot of people are now saying that the Italians hate the Germans and always did, that they were forced into the war against their will. But the Rome–Berlin Axis wasn't concluded by Hitler twisting Mussolini's arm, and neither were Mussolini's Blackshirts a figment of somebody's imagination. They existed, hundreds of thousands of them, some with a greater admiration for Hitler than many Germans had. Obviously quite a number still do, although. . . ."

"Sssh," interrupted Benutti, and held up a finger.

They heard a shuffling in the corridor. A moment later the old woman called through the door, in German: "You will be leaving at 6 a.m."

"Which is our cue to get some sleep," muttered O'Keefe, when he was sure she had gone. "Next time we mightn't hear her coming."

After being awoken by the man with the meerschaum (they never saw him without it clenched between his teeth), they were driving west then south to Trento in a truck smelling of decaying vegetables. Not a word passed between them and their driver but, as with Kurt, he had no trouble with travel permits.

In Trento they were given a few hours rest in a house on the Via Francesco Barbacovi before being moved on in the small hours to Verona, where they were taken to a villa near the city centre. Its owner and their contact was a handsome-looking woman in her forties who told them to call her Contessa. Whether the title was an affectation or a cover name or whether she was a genuine aristocrat, they never found out. Neither did they much care. Although there were other fugitives in the villa and they still had to share rooms, sleeping accommodation for men and women was segregated and there was the luxury of hot water, enough for baths.

They were seldom alone now and private conversation was difficult. Neither was Greta the only woman being passed down the line, although she was by far the most attractive, a fact that Benutti was quick to see the Contessa noted. It could be useful; it might have to be because Verona stood at the crossroads between Venice and Genoa. Lutz could have gone to either. He could even have gone to Rome. In any event, it shook them all rigid that someone as evidently influential as the Contessa could run such a massive staging-post for the SS. Then again, they reasoned, if you really wanted to hide something valuable, you put it out in the open. A stolen painting went on a wall, not in an attic; a priceless collection of stamps lay on a desk; SS fugitives stayed in a grand house.

Not that any of them seemed happy with the arrangements. They were grim-faced men and women, accustomed to the furtive, the clandestine. They rarely spoke and never smiled and gradually, over a period of hours, individually and collectively, they left for the next location.

During the afternoon of their one and only day in Verona, Benutti managed to corner O'Keefe and Caradoc. Greta was elsewhere, presumably catching up on some sleep.

The American propped the door open and stood by it.

"We'd better do some fast thinking before they ship us out," he said, keeping his voice down. "Can you picture a map of Italy?"

O'Keefe and Caradoc said they could.

"Then you'll remember where Verona stands in relation to Genoa and Venice. I don't know where the Contessa plans to send us next, even if she's got a choice in the matter, but wherever it is we'd better find out if that's the direction Lutz took. Otherwise we could get funnelled off on to a branch line."

"It makes sense he came through here," O'Keefe speculated. "The SS wouldn't build up and fund a contact like this and not use it for senior officers. Afterwards—who the hell knows? Venice is closer but Genoa's more logical. From there, if this organization is half as good as we've seen so far, we could get a boat to South America. On the other hand, the Adriatic Coast south of Venice is littered with ports."

"And don't forget Rome. He could have gone straight down the main drag. If I were running this network I'd make sure I had a bunch of contacts in the capital. It would be like leaving out London or New York if the positions were reversed."

O'Keefe glanced out of the window. Verona. Jesus. How did it go? "In fair Verona where we lay our scene/From ancient grudge break to new mutiny/Where civil blood makes civil hands unclean. . . ." The bloody place hadn't changed much since the Montagues and Capulets locked horns.

"We're scuppered," he said, "unless we ask a few questions."

"And if we ask a few questions," put in Caradoc, "we get chopped."

"That depends who does the asking," said Benutti. "Maybe you two have had your minds on other things, but I've been watching the Contessa and the way she looks at Greta. If that isn't lust I see it's the nearest thing to it since Jean Harlow came out of a cake at a lumberjacks' stag night. The Contessa, gentlemen, is more interested in girls than boys."

"So?"

"So we use that juicy fact to our advantage."

"I don't like it," said O'Keefe.

"What's to like. Christ, don't go all moral on us. Where's the harm in Greta playing up to the Contessa a little? She went to bed with Kurt in Salzburg because it was part of the deal. Going to bed with the Contessa is no different. Well, maybe it's a bit different but I'm in no position to judge. Use your head, Mike. You want Lutz should be in Argentina while we're still pissing around in Italy? You're not flying Spitfires now. It's not one against one with the ground rules all nicely worked out in advance. In this war you shoot down your man even if he's dangling from a parachute. That way there's one less of the bastards to deal with and maybe we all get to rock away our retirement on the porch."

O'Keefe looked at Caradoc, but the NCO merely shrugged.

"Only Greta can ask the right questions," continued Benutti. "If we ask about Lutz or a blonde man with a scar, the Contessa will tell us to get lost. She may even decide we're security risks and slip/something in our coffee."

O'Keefe suddenly felt out of his depth. The crack about not flying Spitfires was closer to the truth than Benutti would ever know. Ridiculous though it might sound, there had been a sort of nobility in that.

He remembered someone saying in the Mess, during the battle of Britain, that to have fought in it and survived must be the greatest experience a man could have. And someone else, the Education Officer—Schoolie as everyone called him, a man with a string of decorations from World War I—had contradicted the speaker. "No," he had said. "To fight in this and *not* survive, that's the great experience. Because after this, gentlemen, your lives will be all downhill."

They'd sniggered behind their hands, the others in the Mess. They all knew that the Education Officer was a bit of an eccentric with a penchant for the works of Sophocles.

O'Keefe had had his quiet chuckle too, but now he suspected the older man was right. The days of heroism and dedication were over; what was left of this war would be fought in the gutters.

"We'll let Greta decide," he asked.

"Let Greta decide what?" asked the German girl from the doorway.

Benutti wasted no time putting his proposition. Neither did he mince his words. They had to move quickly, before the Contessa passed them down the line.

She listened in silence, her face deathly pale. When she heard what was required of her she looked at each of them in turn, seeking a reprieve. Benutti. Caradoc. Finally O'Keefe.

He held her gaze. They had made love just a few days ago, but she was nothing to him, never could be.

"I'd better make myself look a little more presentable," she said.

She was away an hour. When she returned O'Keefe thought he saw evidence of tears. But that could have been his imagination.

"Lutz went via Venice," she said, "but his destination was Rome. I've persuaded the Contessa to send us to Rome also but by a more direct route. We'll be leaving in a few hours, much though the Contessa wants me, at least, to stay."

She paused by the door.

"It's not the first time in my life I've been degraded, but it's the last. And mark me well—somebody will eventually pay for it."

"Rome," muttered Caradoc when Greta had gone. "Christ."

"Christ nothing," said Benutti. "Let's just thank whatever

we've got left we hold sacred that Lutz didn't head for Genoa. I wouldn't give us one chance in a million if he had. But Rome—Rome's different."

"It's a bigger bloody city, that's what's so different about it," said O'Keefe. "It's got about two million Italians, maybe three hundred thousand troops, and God knows who else."

"So what? Figure it this way. Rome's got to be the end of the line or pretty close to it. Otherwise, why go there? The further south they go, the less the Germans are likely to come across friendly faces."

"Maybe Lutz didn't get a choice," said O'Keefe. "We haven't been given any. We're just pointed in a direction and that's the way we go."

"Because we don't count for beans," insisted Benutti. "What are we? A couple of SS majors, an NCO and a girl. But Lutz was a full colonel with a lot of clout, and they don't grow on bushes."

"What are you suggesting?"

"I'm suggesting that Rome's the centre of the operation. If you haven't got a ship ready to hop in one of the northern ports, you get ferried to Rome where you're kept on ice until whoever's running the ball game down there decides what to do with you."

"That's a pretty wild guess."

"Then let it be a pretty wild guess. You're not going to tell me that Lutz went to Rome just because somebody told him to. That's not how I read his character. He'll have gone because he has connections down there."

"Which doesn't mean to say everyone else has."

"Maybe not," admitted Benutti, "but the escape line wasn't set up for Lutz's exclusive benefit. He carries a big stick but he's not Himmler. Rome's the clearing house, I'd stake my pension on it. Down there is where they decide who goes where, when and how."

"Which doesn't put us any closer to Lutz."

"But which does put us close to the fountainhead."

Benutti frowned as he arranged his thoughts. Christ, but he could murder a drink.

"Look, we're all travelling in civilian clothes, right? Nobody's

163

asked for any passports or code words or crap like that, right? Therefore anyone can masquerade as any rank, within certain limitations. I could call myself a major-general and no one's going to say I'm a liar. Or are they?"

"Of course they are," retorted O'Keefe. "You're too young, for a start. You're about my age at a guess and there aren't many major-generals in any fighting force under thirty. I know wartime promotion got out of hand, but start telling people you carry stars and we'll all end up in a cellar surrounded by men wielding rubber truncheons."

"Very good," applauded Benutti. "Dead right, if you'll excuse the expression. But if I were ten years older who'd know the difference?"

"The man you spoke to, I suppose." O'Keefe began to see what Benutti was driving at.

"Very good again. Which means there has to be a man to speak to, top brass, probably several. There has to be someone in Rome who decides the pecking order, who gets the first ticket on the pleasure cruise to Buenos Aires or wherever. All these bastards are trying to save their necks, the quicker the better. But some necks will be more important than others. If any bloody fool with the right age and background can walk in off the street and claim to be Kaltenbrunner's right-hand man, who judges whether or not he's telling the truth?"

O'Keefe had it now.

"Which means it's even money that the same SS brass who saw Lutz will see us."

"Correct," said Benutti. "But that's only the start of the battle. We're going to be grilled like trout. The going-over we got in Salzburg will seem like Sunday at the zoo by comparison, and we still have to find out where Lutz went after Rome."

Caradoc was shaking his head.

"You make it sound like a picnic. If we put one foot out of place we'll all be found floating face down in the Tiber."

Benutti concurred.

"Yeah, you're right. You know, I'm beginning to wonder why I'm here, though maybe a line I remember from a movie sums it up."

"'It is a far, far better thing that I do than I have ever done?'" suggested O'Keefe.

"No. More on the lines of 'Here's another fine mess you've got me into, Stanley.'"

Fifteen

More dingy houses, squalid rooms, poker-faced silent men and women whose only common denominator was the fear of retribution.

More cities, towns and villages that had suffered under bombs and artillery as Field Marshal Kesselring's forces retreated before General Mark Clark's XV Army Group; places that no longer resembled habitable communities.

More journeys in open and closed trucks—and, once, a dilapidated bus—that all smelled of past cargoes, animal and vegetable.

Bologna. Florence. A slight detour to Arezzo for a reason that was never explained. Chiusi. Orvieto.

Sometimes it seemed to be day, sometimes night, yet in all they were on the road barely twenty-four hours before reaching Rome.

They had picked up three others, all hard-looking men, in Chiusi, and conversation was impossible after that. But earlier they had discussed the strategy to be adopted upon reaching the Italian capital and decided that they would have to play it by ear. The important thing was not to get split up. O'Keefe thought it unlikely that anyone would try to separate them except perhaps for interrogation, but it was this that worried him. Even if he, Benutti and Caradoc could bluff their way through, what about Greta?

Benutti told him to forget it, that Greta was as tough as any of them.

O'Keefe wasn't so sure, but there was nothing to be done about it now. All afternoon he watched the hills of Rome grow larger in the distance; by early evening the truck had reached a villa on the outskirts of the capital, where the driver, snapping his fingers impatiently, urged them inside.

They were in an entrance hall the size of a tennis court. The floor was mosaic marble and along the walls, on plinths, were busts of various Roman dignitaries. If they were copies, they were very good ones. Wherever the war had been prior to June 4, 1944, the day the first American forces entered the city, it was a hell of a long way from here.

The driver told them to stand where they were and disappeared through a side door. A moment later he reappeared accompanied by two men, both wearing civilian clothes of good quality. One was tall and silver-haired, a man in his late thirties; the other short and plump and several years older.

It was instinct that made O'Keefe stiffen to attention, but his instinct was right and the other five men were not far behind. There was little doubt that they were in the presence of officers of field rank.

After a few words with the driver, who then left the house never to be seen again, the silver-haired officer walked slowly from one end of the rough line to the other, looking at each individual carefully but saying nothing. He nodded approvingly when facing Greta. The plump man remained in the background.

Finally the silver-haired officer appeared satisfied. When he addressed them his voice was soft, as though he had spent years talking in whispers, which was indeed the case. Neither O'Keefe nor the others knew it but they were being spoken to by the same man who had arranged the passage to Tripoli for Lutz.

"I'm not going to bid you welcome," he said, "because this is not the place nor the occasion. Neither do I wish to know your true identities, as you will not learn ours. For purposes of reference I am known as the Trader and the gentleman by the wall as the Dispatcher. Later you will be required to hand over any papers you are carrying, but for the moment all I need to know are your ranks. Begin from the right, please."

O'Keefe and Benutti were the senior officers present. One of the three strangers was an Obersturmfuehrer, a lieutenant, and the other two Oberscharfuehrers, quartermaster-sergeants. Caradoc was the most junior of the NCOs and Greta had no rank.

The Trader nodded benevolently.

"Good. I don't think you need be told that the Dispatcher and myself are senior to all of you and normal military courtesies will be observed while you are here or elsewhere. Where that 'elsewhere' is comes later and involves many factors. You will be happy to know, however, that you are not the first to pass through our hands and neither, I trust, will you be the last. You have all served the Fatherland and the late Fuehrer well or you would not be here, and you may be called upon to perform similar duties in the future. I know you will not fail us or your oath."

The last sentence was said in the same soft undertones, but there was no doubt about its implications: obey orders or pay the penalty. It had escaped no one that the plump man's *nom de guerre* was a two-edged sword. He either sent you on your way to safety or to your death.

O'Keefe was told by the Trader to accompany him, and Benutti was singled out for attention by the Dispatcher. It was as the American had foreseen; rank was getting first crack of the whip.

The others were instructed to remain where they stood.

The Trader led the way along a wide corridor and into a room that was being used as an office. It contained a desk, a chair on either side, a telephone and some filing cabinets. There was also a man with a gun, an MP 40 machine pistol if O'Keefe was any judge. Doubtless there was another guard with Benutti and the Dispatcher and probably others throughout the house. They took no chances, these buggers.

In spite of himself O'Keefe shivered. It did not go unnoticed.

"Cold, Herr Sturmbannfuehrer? On such a warm evening too."

"Just tired, sir."

"Ah yes, that applies to many of us. Please sit down."

O'Keefe waited until the Trader had taken his own seat on the far side of the desk before following suit. His back was to the door and the trooper with the MP 40 was leaning against it.

"Tell me a little about yourself, please."

O'Keefe did so, keeping to the fiction of Buchenwald. He hoped to Christ he would not be asked for a more specific biography, details of his birthplace, his parents, his date of enlistment in the SS, where he was commissioned. This man was no Sepp to be browbeaten.

But apparently the Trader was only interested in a general background. If a man had got this far, presumably he was genuine or he would have been liquidated *en route*. Still, there must be a reason for the questions. O'Keefe wished he had Benutti's experience in Intelligence. The American was no doubt finding the whole process a damned sight easier.

"And you come from Salzburg, I understand."

O'Keefe wondered how the hell he knew that until he realized that from driver to driver, right down the line, information would be passed on. The man who had driven the last forty or fifty miles would have it all at his fingertips.

"Yes, sir."

"And after Salzburg?"

O'Keefe told him.

"The girl is with your group?"

"Yes, sir."

The Trader permitted himself a smile.

"She's very beautiful. No doubt she made the acquaintance of the Contessa."

"I believe so, sir." O'Keefe decided a little cheek might help. "At least, she disappeared for a couple of hours yesterday afternoon."

"Strange lady, the Contessa," mused the Trader, making a pyramid of his hands. "I must say I never took to her myself. Then again, I suppose there's no reason why I should."

The conversation didn't seem to be leading anywhere, but O'Keefe was familiar with this interrogation technique, known as honey-and-zappit in the 7th Army. He remained on his

168

guard and was more than half-prepared when the Trader doffed his mask and aimed for the jugular.

"I don't believe you're a Sturmbannfuehrer at all," he said, his voice rising a couple of decibels. "For that matter, I don't believe you're a commissioned officer in the SS."

He leaned across the desk until he and O'Keefe were eyeball to eyeball.

"You're a jumped up bloody NCO trying it on."

"I take exception to that, sir. . . ."

"Do you, by God! In this room you don't take exception to anything I say, Corporal! You are a junior NCO, aren't you? You might as well admit it. You've heard rumours that officers are getting privileged treatment so you promote yourself. Well, it won't work. You're a bloody liar and a menace, Corporal, and we have methods of dealing with people like you. All right, Hans, take him outside and shoot him."

Some part of O'Keefe's subconscious took over at that moment. There were no rational thoughts involved. Rationale would have told him that no one was going to start shooting off MP 40s in postwar Rome without attracting a lot of attention.

Instincts learned in the hard battle for survival as a fighter pilot saved him, otherwise he might have broken into English. But even as he heard the MP 40 click into a firing position he was flinging himself backwards, moving towards the spot where he expected Hans to be, knocking over the chair in the process.

Hans was slow, much slower than he should have been for one guarding such a valuable property. Or perhaps he simply knew the rules of the game, knew that he had to take no direct action, merely go through the motions while his superior officer made the judgements.

Whatever the truth of the matter, O'Keefe had him pinned against the door and disarmed almost before the Trader had finished speaking.

With the Trader scrambling to his feet in amazement at the speed of events, O'Keefe put his finger on the trigger and pointed the machine pistol in the general direction of the desk.

To Hans he said, "You half-baked son of a syphilitic whore! If I had you under my command I'd shoot you here and now! When a man has his back to you and he's a threat, you shoot him dead without thinking about the Italian harlot you'll be fucking later! And if I were you, sir, I'd get myself a more efficient bodyguard and feed this one to the dogs."

O'Keefe counted slowly to ten, feeling better than he had done for weeks, before returning the machine pistol to the sullen and confused Hans.

"Wait outside," said the Trader.

The door closed quietly behind Hans.

"You may sit down, Herr Sturmbannfuehrer. Whatever else we discuss will be in private."

O'Keefe feigned mild indignation. The Trader was on the defensive now and this was the best chance he, O'Keefe, would ever have to get some answers.

"There was no need for that, sir. Somebody might have been killed and it could well have been you. If you'd asked me I could easily have proved my rank."

The silver-haired officer had a fast recovery rate. His voice was again its customary softness as he asked, "How? You cannot be carrying anything to prove you were an officer at Buchenwald or that you were an officer at all."

"Not in documentary form, sir, but in my head. How do you suppose my companions and I got to Salzburg in the first place?"

"By the usual methods, I presume."

"A little unusual, in our case. My brother was on the staff at Dachau. Had it not been for certain business we had to transact in Munich, we would have travelled with my brother, Hauptsturmfuehrer Scheringer, and Standartenfuehrer Lutz."

The Trader remembered the Standartenfuehrer only too well. The bloody problems he had caused. . . .

"That is no proof at all," he said. "If you recall what I said earlier, we do not exchange names here. In fact, you have violated the rule by mentioning those of Lutz and Scheringer, but I'll let that pass. You could claim to be anyone's brother. It means nothing."

Unaware that the Trader had had dealings with Lutz prior to Rome and therefore knew his name, O'Keefe kept after it.

"You would remember the Standartenfuehrer, sir. He was about as tall as you, blonde hair, and a sabre scar across his right cheek."

The Trader nodded slowly and wrongly assumed that O'Keefe's next request would be to go where Lutz and Scheringer had gone. But there would be no more of that.

"I do indeed remember him, but you can go to hell if you think I'm sending you and your group to Tripoli also."

"Tripoli!" It was out before O'Keefe could stop it.

"I see you didn't know. Evidently you were not as close to your brother as you thought."

O'Keefe was totally confused. Tripoli. Good God, why would Lutz leave Occupied Europe for Occupied North Africa? It was lunacy.

He made an effort and collected his thoughts.

"I suppose we weren't that close, sir. My brother resented the fact that I outranked him in spite of being younger. If he went to Tripoli, so be it. I have no intention of doing anything so foolish."

"You have no say in the matter, Herr Sturmbannfuehrer. You will go where we say and when we say. In the meantime, I have already spent too long with you. You will oblige me by returning to the hall and sending in the Obersturmfuehrer. Say nothing of what took place here."

"Of course not, sir."

O'Keefe got to his feet, wondering if he should throw a Hitler salute. He opted not to. The Trader didn't seem to notice.

In the entrance hall O'Keefe saw that Benutti was already back, standing in a corner with Caradoc and Greta. The Obersturmfuehrer was chatting casually to one of the NCOs. Of the other NCO there was no sign. Presumably he was already being grilled by the Dispatcher.

"You're next," said O'Keefe to the Obersturmfuehrer. "Along the corridor, third door on your right."

Trying hard to keep his pace leisurely but inside bubbling with excitement at what he had just learned, O'Keefe sauntered over to Benutti and the others. The American started to say something, but O'Keefe motioned him to silence with a wave of his hand.

"We've got to get out of here," he said.

"Out?" queried Benutti. "Christ, I know it was rough, I've just been warning these two. . . ."

"Listen to me," muttered O'Keefe. "I know where Lutz went. It's going to sound insane but he shipped out to Tripoli."

"Tripoli . . . !"

"For God's sake, keep your voice down." O'Keefe glanced over his shoulder. The remaining Oberscharfuehrer was examining a tapestry.

"But Tripoli. . . ."

"Never mind why for the moment. Let's just accept it and get the hell out. We're finished with the escape line. You can bet your last cent it doesn't have a cell in North Africa. Lutz is on his own from here."

"It doesn't make sense. . . ."

"It does to me," murmured Greta.

They looked at her.

"I've just remembered something Lutz said, oh, a long time ago. I can't recall his exact words but it was to do with quickly acquiring an African suntan if the war went badly. He was being flippant, of course, and it was such a trivial remark that it completely slipped my memory until now."

"That clinches it," said O'Keefe. "Okay, let's go before they get round to Jim and Greta."

"Go how?" asked Benutti.

"Through the bloody front door, that's how. We don't need these bastards any more."

It was sheer bad luck that as they crossed the entrance hall the Dispatcher chose to reappear, a sheet of paper in his hand, a querulous frown wrinkling his forehead. He saw what they were doing immediately.

"Where are you going?" he demanded in a high-pitched voice.

"Just keep walking," muttered O'Keefe.

"I asked you a question!"

"We need some fresh air," called Benutti.

"You will stand precisely where you are! Guards!"

The echo of his shout was still ringing around the hall when several doors on the ground floor were flung open and three or four armed men burst out. Simultaneously another pair appeared at the head of the wide staircase.

"Run for it!" yelled O'Keefe.

They should not have made it. They were a dozen yards from the front door and it was closed. By rights they should have been cut to ribbons by the machine pistols. The reason they were not was because each gunman waited for the order to open fire. The MP 40s were there to threaten, intimidate, never to be used except as a last resort. The Trader could not afford an investigation by the authorities into a shooting incident.

Fractions of a second after O'Keefe shouted, the door was wrenched open by Greta. She ran into the street, followed by Caradoc. Benutti was next and all three were twenty yards away, legs pumping like sprinters', as O'Keefe began to slam the door behind him.

It was only then that the gunmen were brought out of their trance.

"Shoot them, you damn fools!" screamed the Dispatcher. *"Kill them!"*

Half a dozen MP 40s opened up in unison, the 9mm Parabellum bullets carving huge chunks out of the woodwork and incidentally killing the Oberscharfuehrer still to be interrogated, who had neither the wit nor the time to hit the floor and who was directly in the line of fire.

But by this time the door was closed and O'Keefe already running hard.

From first to last, from when the Dispatcher walked into the entrance hall to the moment the first shots were fired, the whole business had taken under ten seconds. Another sixty and O'Keefe's group was two streets away, still going flat out.

No one followed them. Although not sure what had happened or why, the Trader's instinct for survival was working overtime and within minutes he had issued instructions to vacate the villa and move to the back-up house.

173

Neither he nor the Dispatcher were ever caught and the escape line continued its work. Today both men are living quite openly, though under assumed names, in West Germany.

If the mills of God grind slowly, they nevertheless move with meteoric speed when compared to those of any military authority anywhere.

It took an hour before O'Keefe and Benutti could get anyone to listen to them and then it was only an infantry captain, who decided that the four moth-eaten individuals standing before him were either crazy or should be referred to higher authority. Accomplishing the latter took another hour and it was close on 10 p.m. before the whole story had been told to a two-star US general.

Checking with Munich that Benutti was who he claimed to be and could vouch for the others occupied a further two hours, and it was close on midnight before beds were finally found for the quartet.

O'Keefe was all for bumming a ride to Tripoli that same night. Although they had started out three or so weeks behind Lutz, getting him across the Mediterranean could not have been easy for the Trader and there was a good chance they had closed the gap.

Benutti talked him out of moving right away. They all needed sleep. If Lutz was already in Tripoli, he was going to find it a bloody sight more difficult to move around than in Europe.

The American was also against putting a call through to Tripoli Intelligence to start the ball rolling. They'd come this far by themselves and it would be criminal if someone else got the credit for picking up Lutz. After a good night's rest he'd do his famous string-pulling act and have them on the first military flight after breakfast.

As it happened, it took him all of the following morning to hitch them a lift, and that was a morning too late.

Sixteen

In Tripoli a dozen hours earlier, while O'Keefe and his group were still between Orvieto and Rome, Carver Kane had driven a covered 3-tonner towards the main gates of the airfield. For once in his life he paid strict attention to the signs which warned all drivers that the maximum speed was 10 mph. This was no time to be picked up by a regimental cop pissed off by the heat. Beside him in the passenger seat, Pascoe stared silently ahead, lost in his own thoughts. Both men wore tropical uniform.

Perched in the back near the tailboard and also in uniform, van der Heyden was making quite sure he could be seen. The gate guard might think it unusual for the senior rank aboard to be occupying the most uncomfortable position, but that was better than the guard getting nosey and taking a look inside the truck.

Although earlier in the day, using perfectly legitimate documents signed by himself, van der Heyden had supervised the withdrawal from the armoury of 5,000 rounds of .50 ammunition and 20,000 rounds of calibre .303, he had no authorization to take them off the base. To have obtained such a warranty would have needed the signature of Squadron Leader Benson, and even Benson would have wanted to know where the hell van der Heyden proposed to go with enough cartridges to start World War III.

The Flight Sergeant in charge of the armoury had also expressed some surprise, though he wasn't going to argue with the Supply Officer, not while he had the proper paperwork.

"Point five-oh, sir? Haven't been asked for those in a coon's age."

Van der Heyden was prepared for a few raised eyebrows and had his story ready. Not many aircraft used .50. The Catalina, Liberator and Mitchell were all he could think of offhand—as well as the bloody Sunderland, of course.

He feigned disgust.

"Some sort of scheme Group's dreamed up with the Americans," he said. "There's no bloody end to it, is there."

A firm believer in the theory that the best place to hide a book is on a bookshelf, van der Heyden had Kane reverse the 3-tonner right up to the armoury in broad daylight and commandeered a fatigues party to do the loading.

"I hope you're not planning to leave that lot lying around in the open, sir," said the armourer. He was a career NCO who felt that something was wrong but did not know what. When van der Heyden had signed for the ammo, he was in the clear—but he was still unhappy. For a start, the Aussie at the wheel wore pilot's wings and you didn't often see the glamour brigade dirtying its hands on jobs usually performed by lesser mortals.

"Not a chance, Flight," van der Heyden reassured him. "I'll watch over it like a mother hen. You can do me a favour, though."

"A favour, sir?"

The NCO's eyes flickered warily.

"Yes. Don't put that chit through to headquarters until later today. The Yanks aren't due until the small hours, but I don't fancy going through this exercise in the middle of the night. I'm sure you wouldn't appreciate being woken up either."

The armourer breathed a sigh of relief. That's what was wrong. The Supply Officer was going out for a night on the town and didn't want to be disturbed by a bunch of bloody Americans turning up. He was doing tomorrow's work today and who could blame him?

"Rely on me, sir. I'll hold the chit until morning."

Which was damned nice of him, thought van der Heyden as the 3-tonner approached the main gates; and which would doubtless earn him a court martial in the near future.

Kane rapped on the communicating panel to indicate that they were close.

Apart from the ammo, van der Heyden was taking through two other items of contraband. The first was three handguns, Webley .38s, and one hundred and fifty spare rounds, enough to prevent the Germans, he thought, from pulling off a doublecross. The second item was forty gallons of gasoline, in jerrycans, for refuelling en route. He was no newcomer to taking black market gasoline off the airfield, but normally the operation was planned well in advance, the gas drawn from the fuel dumps weeks before it was needed and only transhipped to the customer when the fake paperwork was ready. In this case there had been no time.

But they had to carry enough fuel to get them to Benghazi, and van der Heyden had done his homework on the Bedford 3-tonner. The tank capacity was around thirty-two gallons and it did approximately 9 mpg. With Benghazi 500 miles away that meant almost two full tanks. It also meant, at 40 mph, about as much as the Bedford could manage flat out, a trip of twelve or thirteen hours if they wanted to arrive well before dawn.

There was no trouble at the gate. Kane had a work ticket showing his destination to be Misratah, and the sight of an officer in the passenger seat and another shouting from the back that he'd have someone's scalp for a boot brush if they were late—that was enough for the guard to wave them through. The guardroom thermometer read 107 degrees Fahrenheit and that was too bloody hot to argue.

The Bedford's time of exit was jotted down in the log books as 14:12 hours.

"Step on it, Carver," called van der Heyden, when they were clear of the base. "The bloody krauts'll think we're not coming."

That the three fliers would not turn up never crossed Lutz's mind. As the clock ticked up to 14:30 he took a last look round, to make sure they were not leaving anything behind. Hanna and her father were upstairs, Mueller was skimming through a six-month-old edition of *Picture Post,* and Fischer was at the table, polishing off the brandy.

"It's going to complicate matters," Scheringer was saying. "We're supposed to be walking wounded yet we're all dressed in civilian clothes. It's going to be difficult enough without taking along someone who is obviously too old to have fought in the war."

"We've been over this," said Lutz wearily. "If van der Heyden tells us that stealing uniforms is impractical, then we must believe him. The walking-wounded label is not intended to fool anyone for too long. It's simply a device to get us close to the Sunderland. We'll be arriving in pitch darkness, don't forget, and I doubt if anyone will take more than a passing interest in us until it's too late. If they do, we shall have to take care of them."

"And Baumann?"

"Baumann has to come with us. If he didn't, neither would the girl and possibly not Pascoe either."

"It's a risk."

"Of course it's a risk. It's all a risk until we arrive at our final destination, but we've done the hardest part. We got out of Europe."

Lutz cocked his head at the sound of a klaxon.

"And now it's time to leave North Africa. See to them, Mueller."

Upstairs Hanna had also heard the 3-tonner's horn. She made a final check on her appearance in the full-length mirror.

The nurse whose pilfered QARANC uniform she now wore was evidently slightly taller and fuller about the hips, but in the dark no one was going to notice.

She picked up the wooden medicine chest by its sling. Inside were the bandages to make Lutz and the others look more like the real thing on reaching Benghazi. Carrying it over her shoulder, she walked along the passage to her father's room. The door was open, the old man sitting on the bed.

"It's time to go, Papa."

Her voice seemed to startle him. He peered at her without really seeing her.

"It's been a great many years."

She understood. He was not being allowed to take anything with him and he knew he would never see again the place that had been his home for so long.

"A great many years," she agreed.

"You grew up here. When we first arrived you were only a little girl. I remember you complaining that you didn't like the heat."

"I remember too."

He shook his head sadly.

"You should have had a mother. I should have married again."

She put her arms around his neck.

"I've been luckier than most girls with two parents."

"We must hurry, Hanna," said Pascoe from the doorway.

"Of course. Is everything all right?"

"Yes, but we've no time to lose."

"We're coming."

It was blisteringly hot out of doors and even worse in the back of the 3-tonner, especially for the four SS men and Herr Baumann, as van der Heyden insisted they retreat to the depths of the truck. He and Hanna sat where they could be seen, either side of the tailboard, though until they were clear of the town van der Heyden asked her to keep her head inclined inwards, in case someone who used the coffee shop should recognize her and wonder why she was dressed as a nurse.

Shortly before 3 p.m. they were on the coast road and in top gear. To their left the Mediterranean shimmered in the afternoon heat haze. Ahead lay Al Khums, Misratah, Sirte on the Gulf of Sirte, As Sidar, Ajdabiyah, and Benghazi. Van der Heyden had calculated the distance from Tripoli to each town and knew precisely where they should be at any given minute, assuming an average speed of 40 mph. Still, they were cutting it bloody fine, even though he had taken the precaution of removing the governor from the Bedford in order to gain an extra few miles per hour.

It grew dark. Somewhere east of Misratah, Pascoe took over the wheel, allowing Kane to grab some rest. A little later, with 250 miles on the odometer and the gauge reading dangerously low, midway between Al Buaryat and Sirte, they pulled off the road for twenty minutes to refuel and top up the radiator.

Surprisingly, there was very little traffic going in either direction, though a few miles west of As Sidar they were forced to join a convoy of a dozen trucks travelling at under 35 mph. There was no way round without incurring the wrath of the occupants of the lead vehicle, but fortunately As Sidar proved to be the convoy's destination. Nevertheless, taking into account the refuelling stop, they were forty minutes behind schedule.

Van der Heyden called through the communication panel that he would take over, but Pascoe declined. The inactivity would drive him mad. He knew that he, more so than the others, would have to be fully alert in a few hours' time, but he was wide awake. In any case, he had a tube of Benzedrine in a side pocket.

The headlights probed the darkness. Pascoe kept his foot on the floor, coaxing the 6-cylinder engine up to 44 mph.

He could feel the adrenalin coursing through his body. It was like going on an operation. No, it was better than that because, after the first half-dozen or so, excitement disappeared and a kind of cautious wariness took over. You knew your own ability and you had more than a rough idea what to expect from the opposition. It was like a game of three-dimensional chess; there were certain moves you could make and a number of countermoves you could expect. It was simply a question of getting to the target, doing the job, and getting back.

It was said that the good ones always knew that they would survive and he had certainly never expected to be the victim of enemy flak or night fighters. Neither, to the best of his knowledge, had he ever been frightened, though he took good care to conceal this from his fellow pilots and members of his crew. No one liked flying with or alongside a man who wasn't scared before and during every mission. A man who could not feel fear had something wrong with him; either that or he was becoming overconfident.

Still, it was a fact of life and had to be faced. It wasn't false bravado or a mask; he just didn't get frightened.

Beside him Kane grunted, opened his eyes briefly, then promptly fell asleep again.

Pascoe smiled to himself.

In the back of the truck van der Heyden checked the luminous dial of his wrist watch; coming up to 2 a.m. His instincts told him that Pascoe was squeezing a few extra mph out of the Bedford and that they had probably made up the forty minutes. That being so, they were a couple of hours away, at most, from Benghazi. It was time for Fräulein Baumann to begin doing her stuff.

She was dozing when he tapped her on the knee.

"Bandages," he said.

She nodded and reached down for the first-aid box. As well as the bandages it contained a powerful flashlight. She flicked it on and directed the beam towards the front of the truck. Quite by accident it picked up Lutz first. He stared unblinkingly into the light, his face frozen to reveal whatever it was he was thinking. She thought she had never seen so much evil in one man.

"Bandages," called van der Heyden.

Because of the speed at which they were travelling and the swaying motion of the 3-tonner, it took thirty minutes to furnish each of the SS men with a head bandage and two with slings. Whether by design or otherwise, as Hanna was seeing to Lutz she felt his hands caress her body. It was done so swiftly that she had neither the time to recoil nor the confidence to protest. Nevertheless, she felt violated.

For her father she had fashioned a sort of mask which left gaps for his eyes and mouth. It would do little to disguise his true age if anyone looked closely, but it would have to suffice.

She returned to her seat by the tailboard.

"Finished," she said, unnecessarily.

Van der Heyden did not respond. He was hoping that

Pascoe would remember to pull off the road when he got close to Benghazi. The last few miles were to be driven by the South African, as only he knew precisely where the Sunderland was moored.

A further thirty minutes went by with not a sign from Pascoe that he intended relinquishing the wheel. Either they were further from Benghazi than van der Heyden had estimated or Pascoe had forgotten his orders.

Cursing beneath his breath, the South African was about to go forward to find out where they were when he felt Pascoe drop down a gear. Moments later the 3-tonner cruised to a halt.

Van der Heyden hopped over the tailboard and was astonished to see the lights from Benghazi flickering in the middle distance; five or six miles away at a guess. It was a little after 3 a.m. and he permitted himself a silent whoop of exultation. For better or for worse, the first part was over.

Kane had woken up and was rubbing his eyes.

"Jesus, are we here?"

Pascoe jumped down from the driving cab.

"All yours," he said to van der Heyden.

"Fine. Are you all right?"

"Never better. What's the next move?"

"I'm going to drive right up to the jetty. I've got to get as close as possible because of those bloody ammo boxes."

"There's bound to be a guard."

"Bound to be, but Carver can take care of him."

"Make sure he does it properly. Lutz and his crew are carrying guns, don't forget, and I don't want one of them going off in a panic."

"Leave it to me."

Pascoe clambered aboard the truck and touched Hanna's arm reassuringly.

"Okay?"

"Yes. You must be tired."

"I feel fine."

"Are we nearly there?"

"Very nearly. Not long now."

Van der Heyden slipped into first gear and rolled the

3-tonner forward. As it gathered speed he gave Kane his instructions concerning the sentry.

"Rap him over the head or punch him on the jaw, but do it quickly."

"Got it."

Fifteen minutes later van der Heyden pointed through the windscreen.

"Look."

Kane followed the direction of the South African's finger and saw the mooring lights of the Sunderland where it lay at anchor against the Saunders Roe pontoon. It was about a quarter of a mile ahead and some five hundred yards out, and although dawn was still several hours away there was enough synthetic light about to make out the shape of the flying boat. Christ, it was enormous. Ten feet wider than a Lancaster fifteen feet longer and a dozen feet taller. But figures alone did not indicate its bulk. The Lancaster was pencil-slim compared to the Sunderland.

"How far's the jetty?"

"Coming up," Van der Heyden switched the headlights to full beam. *"Shit!"* he swore.

The headlights had picked up the jetty right enough, but instead of one figure, a solitary guard, standing there, there were two. And van der Heyden knew full well who the second man was. Even in an air force where huge moustaches were the rule rather than the exception, the second man had to be Flight Lieutenant Wilberforce.

"That's the Sunderland's bloody skipper," he said, when they were close enough to make positive identification. "The bloke with the hairy lip."

"You sure?"

"Of course I'm bloody sure. He's the one who showed me over the aircraft the other day."

"Then he'll recognize you."

"One of your more penetrating observations."

They were fifty or sixty yards away now but closing at a snail's pace on the two men at the jetty. Van der Heyden deliberately kept his lights up. He could see the expression of

183

annoyance on Wilberforce's face as the Flight Lieutenant shielded his eyes from the glare.

"We won't be able to get away with the walking wounded ploy now," muttered Kane anxiously.

"It won't be necessary," said van der Heyden. "Listen, the moment we stop nip round the back and tell Jonathan and the others not to move a muscle until I say so. I'll keep Wilberforce and the guard talking. Join me as soon as you've finished with Pascoe and take your lead from me. I'll handle Wilberforce, you deal with the guard. They won't be expecting trouble so let's make it fast."

Kane reached for the holstered Webley. Van der Heyden had distributed the handguns at the refuelling stop, reasoning that it was better if the Germans knew the crew was armed.

"No shooting, Carver. We just want them unconscious, not dead."

The 3-tonner rolled to a halt. Wilberforce was already making for the driver's door when Kane leapt to the ground and raced round the back.

"What's the matter?" asked Pascoe.

"A hitch but nothing we can't cope with. Stay here until you're called for."

"Right."

Van der Heyden climbed from the driver's cab in time to hear Wilberforce complaining: ". . . more bloody sense than to come in here lit up like Blackpool bloody Tower. . . ."

Van der Heyden smiled at him.

"Sorry about that, old man. I'm not used to driving one of these wretched beasts."

Wilberforce stared at him, recognition dawning.

"Van der Heyden? What the hell are you doing here at this unearthly hour?"

Out of the corner of his eye the South African saw Kane return and stand within a couple of feet of the guard, who, in the presence of two officers, had taken half-a-dozen deferential steps backwards.

"I might ask you the same thing," said van der Heyden. The Sunderland's skipper was not carrying flying gear so it didn't look as if the departure time had been brought forward. On the other hand, his gear could already be in the launch.

"I've been warming her up," answered Wilberforce.

"At this hour?"

"At this hour because.... Look, what the devil is all this?"

Still smiling, van der Heyden moved closer to Wilberforce and smelled the booze on his breath. That explained it. They'd probably been having a farewell bash in the Mess and Wilberforce was completing the pre-flight check he should have done earlier. Then a few hours sleep before saying goodbye to Benghazi.

"Need to borrow your plane, old boy."

Wilberforce's mouth gaped open with astonishment. Van der Heyden closed it with a right uppercut that started somewhere near his knee. The jetty guard didn't get any further than moving his rifle a fraction of an inch before Kane hit him across the back of the head with the butt of the Webley. Both men went out like candles.

"They won't stay that way for long," said Kane.

"Tie 'em up. Use their belts and bootlaces and stick something in their mouths. We'll take them out to the pontoon and dump them there when we leave."

Van der Heyden ran for the 3-tonner.

"What's all the noise?" demanded Pascoe.

"A little trouble but it's all right now. Come on, we've got no time for debates. Let's get the ammo boxes aboard and get the hell out of here. By my calculations we've got another ninety minutes of darkness. I'd like to be seeing nothing but sand under the fuselage by dawn."

"Where's the Sunderland?"

Van der Heyden waved an arm.

"Out there. And you'll be happy to hear it's warmed up."

The Germans were told to remove their bandages and help with the loading of the ammo. Hanna and her father were to get aboard the launch and wait.

To Lutz Pascoe said, "When we reach the Sunderland Kane, van der Heyden and myself will be fully occupied

185

getting the plane airborne. That means you're in charge of seeing that the ammunition is transferred from the launch to the aircraft and that everyone is seated for take-off."

"What about those two?" Lutz pointed to Wilberforce and the guard, now bound and gagged.

"We'll dump them on the pontoon."

"Alive," added Pascoe.

"That's too risky. They'll have the exact time of our take-off and perhaps work out our heading."

"Not if you knock them cold again they won't, assuming they're conscious anyway."

Lutz decided it was better not to argue. The three fliers would be busy on the flight deck and wouldn't have a clue what was going on behind them. But no guns, he reminded himself. The sound of a shot would carry for miles.

Working flat out it took twenty-five minutes to stow the ammunition boxes. By the time the passengers were aboard also the launch was dangerously near the waterline. But there was nothing to be done about that.

Thirty-three minutes after arriving at the jetty, van der Heyden cast off and opened up the throttle. It took him a few seconds to get the hang of the controls and locate the searchlight. There was nothing to lose by switching it on. They couldn't work in the dark and if anyone saw it they would assume Wilberforce was still out there.

Crouched aft, Pascoe was also thinking about searchlights. He would need the Sunderland's on for take-off. She was a big ship and needed lots of ocean to unstick. He could do without having all four Pratt and Whitneys doing maximum revs and finding something in the bloody way.

It seemed to take an hour but in actuality it was only a couple of minutes before van der Heyden had the launch tied fast to the pontoon. Sixty seconds later, the for'ard port hatch was open and Pascoe aboard. Kane and van der Heyden at his heels.

On the pontoon Lutz issued his instructions in rapid German. The guard was still unconscious, but Wilberforce had recovered. His eyes bulged with incredulity and fear when he realized what language was being spoken.

"Baumann," said Lutz, "you and your daughter will go aboard next and check the galley. Be prepared to give me an estimate on the number and size of our meals for the next seventy-two hours. We may not get a chance to restock in Nigeria."

Wordlessly, Hanna and her father disappeared through the hatch.

"Mueller, Fischer," continued Lutz, "you will take the ammunition boxes as Scheringer and I pass them up to you. As soon as everything is aboard, start loading the guns. We may need them before we're airborne. Quickly now. *Schnell!*"

The pontoon was stable enough and the water motionless, but even so it was forty minutes before the last box went through the hatch.

On the flight deck Pascoe turned over the port and starboard outer engines in sequence and went through his check list. Trimming tabs set, mixture controls at Auto Rich. Propeller speed control levers fully up, fuel correct—cock settings, tank contents, booster pumps. Flaps one-third out. In the engineer's berth Kane moved the carburettor air-intake levers to Cold.

They were ready to go.

Lutz told Scheringer to get aboard and give Mueller and Fischer a hand with the guns.

"What about them?" Scheringer jerked his head at Wilberforce and the guard, whom Kane had hit harder than he knew.

"Leave them to me."

Lutz knew nothing about boats and had no idea where, if at all, the seacocks were. But the two bound men could not be allowed to live.

He checked the guard first. The man—boy if the truth were known—was still unconscious. Lutz heaved him over the side.

Wilberforce saw his turn coming. He tried to struggle to his feet, but it was hopeless. Even so, Kane had only gagged him and tied his hands. His ankles were unfettered, and as Lutz lashed out with the pistol, Wilberforce threw himself overboard.

Lutz peered anxiously into the depths. There was no movement. Neither was there any time.

The flight deck was just above the for'ard hatch. Lutz yelled at the top of his voice to move out.

In the right-hand seat van der Heyden slipped the quick-release mooring gear and switched on the searchlights. Pascoe opened up the outer engines to take-off boost. The Sunderland moved forward, straining at the leash like a dog anxious for its run. When the nose came up Pascoe gave the inner engines the gun, first port then starboard. As he reached take-off speed, he eased back on the control column. With a gentle lurch the giant aircraft left the water and climbed into the night.

A mile aft Wilberforce gained the surface. His will to live was strong and, using legs alone, he succeeded in making the pontoon. He could not remove the gag nor loosen his wrist-bindings, but somehow he kept afloat, knocking his head against the pontoon at intervals to stay conscious.

He was found three hours later, delirious but still breathing.

Seventeen

Pascoe levelled out at 5,000 feet and set a course of 320 degrees, roughly north-west. If he was showing up on Benghazi radar and being tracked and logged as a matter of routine, he wanted the operator convinced that his destination lay somewhere in Europe. For the moment no one would be interested in him; he'd simply be recorded as an unidentified aircraft. But in a few hours they'd be looking for a missing Sunderland, and the place they'd start would be the radar log.

Twenty minutes after take-off and some fifty miles out

over the Mediterranean, he descended to 400 feet and changed his heading to 214 degrees—sou'sou'west. 2,000 miles away in a straight line was Lagos.

Radar would now have lost him, though he didn't want to be stooging around in pitch darkness at that altitude for too long. It was his intention to re-cross the coast west of Sirte and climb to 5,250 feet, the height at which the Mark V could get somewhere close to its maximum speed of 213 mph. There were no mountainous obstructions in the way; he wasn't worried about hitting anything. But the desert was a peculiar place for low-level flying, particularly in something as massive as the Sunderland. Once the sun rose in half an hour's time, all kinds of weird and wonderful updraughts could be expected.

For take-off van der Heyden had occupied the co-pilot's seat and Kane the flight engineer's berth, but now that he no longer needed any help in flying the aeroplane Pascoe asked the South African to check that the passengers were okay and to take a look at the charts.

"Sure you can manage?" asked van der Heyden.

"Sure as I'll ever be. It's like riding a bike. You never forget how once you've acquired the knack. Just keep us pointing in the right direction."

"You won't be able to take us all the way to Apapa by yourself."

"True. I'll give you and Kane the five-minute driving course later. There's really nothing to it once you're up. But for the moment let's get as far inland as we can."

Christ, but he'd forgotten just how bloody big the Sunderland was, thought Pascoe. After flying Lancs, this was like being in an airborne hotel.

Many pilots and navigators, even those who had spent the war in heavy bombers, got the same impression of vast space on first boarding a Sunderland.

From nose to tail the Mark V measured 85 feet 4 inches; its wing span was 112 feet 10 inches and height almost 33 feet.

The flight deck was huge compared to that of any other aircraft flying, with plenty of leg- and head-room for the pilot, on the port side, and the co-pilot, on the starboard. Between the two seats were the throttles and mixtures controls. Behind a curtain the navigator had a large chart table, and to the left of this was the wireless operator's desk. Aft of the navigation berth sat the flight engineer, his position bounded by the main spars and the lattice small-bones of the wing. In the extreme nose was a power-driven turret, which could be slid backwards into the hull to provide an open cockpit for mooring operations. This turret was also a gun platform for two .303 calibre machine guns.

At the foot of the ladder leading from the flight deck to the lower deck there was a lavatory on the starboard side and to port a corridor, with two metal suitcases stowed in its walls and room to hang coats and oilskins. The corridor led aft to the wardroom, which had a table with folding flaps in the middle and a bunk on each side. Further aft was the galley, which contained an ice chest, a Primus stove with a small oven, a sink and a draining board. The canvas drogues sometimes used for slowing the boat in water were stored here in semi-circular bins below the portholes.

Aft of the galley the double-deck arrangement came to an end. Two compartments with two bunks in each formed a continuation of the lower deck. The first of these compartments was also the bomb room, where the bombs were loaded on racks which slid out on to the under surface of the wing on the pressing of a button by the pilot. In the case of this particular Mark V, of course there were no bombs aboard. The compartment was presently occupied by Lutz, Scheringer, Hanna and her father.

Beyond the sleeping berths, on a level with the upper deck, was a narrow bridge connecting the two midships gun platforms, where Mueller was just completing the loading of the port .50. From the bridge a catwalk led for'ard to the flight engineer's position and a ladder down to the lower deck. Aft of the ladder, above the rear knife-edge of the planing bottom, was a workshop with a bench and a vice. The marine distress signals were stowed here.

Last of all, in a hollow tunnel lined with the metal bones and ribs of the hull, another catwalk led to the rear gunner's station and his four .303 Brownings. This would be Fischer's position in the event of a firefight and he was not at all happy with it; it was a bloody lonely place to be. Mueller, port midships, and Scheringer, starboard midships, had each other for company, and Lutz had grabbed the nose turret where he could see what was happening.

Emerging from the galley van der Heyden grinned to himself at the expression on Scheringer's face. This intrepid warrior of the Third Reich was obviously not too keen on flying, though God help him if it ever got really rough.

"Is everything all right?" asked Lutz.

"Fine at the sharp end. What about down here?"

"Everything in order, I believe. Where precisely are we?"

"Precisely I couldn't tell you. But approximately we're crossing the coastline. You'll be able to see for yourself at sunrise."

"How is Pascoe faring? He's had very little sleep to the best of my knowledge."

"He'll be grabbing some later."

A look of alarm spread across Scheringer's ratlike features. In heavily accented English he asked who would by flying the aeroplane while Pascoe was resting. Van der Heyden smiled wickedly at the German's discomfort.

"We'll manage somehow. The trick is getting it up and down. Fräulein Baumann could even drive it once the difficult bits are over."

"I may take you up on that later," said Hanna. "I like to see where I'm going." She too was tired and the frenzied activity of the last few hours was beginning to take its toll. But the worst was over, she kept on reminding herself.

"Fräulein Baumann has made an inventory of the food and drink stocks," said Lutz. "It's mostly tinned meat, but there's more than enough for our purposes if we're careful. There's also some coffee, tea and dried milk."

"Then I suggest someone makes us a hot drink," said van der Heyden. "We could all use one. After that you should try to get some sleep. We've a long flight ahead and God knows when you'll get another opportunity if we run into trouble."

Baumann got to his feet.

"I'll see to the drinks," he said, waving his daughter's

protests aside. "It's the least I can do for my passage."

Nodding affably van der Heyden returned for'ard and climbed the ladder to the flight deck.

"Everything's shipshape below," he informed Pascoe. "Old man Baumann's rustling up some coffee." He shook his head in amazement. "Chirst, can you imagine it—a fully equipped kitchen and room service. You had a bloody easy war for at least part of it, Jonathan."

Pascoe grinned over his shoulder.

"You wouldn't have said that if you'd been poodling around at zero feet with a bloody great U-boat taking potshots at your belly."

"Hey," called Kane through the curtain, "take a look to port."

Pascoe and van der Heyden did so. The sun was coming up over the horizon, a huge orange globe. It was going to be a beautiful day.

Not so in Rome, however, where rain clouds loured over the Eternal City. Without reference to a clock it was impossible to tell whether it was early morning or late afternoon.

Benutti's boast that he would have them on an aircraft heading for Tripoli right after breakfast proved to be an idle one. The best offer to date was a C-47 leaving somewhere around noon. This would put them on the Libyan air base at approximately 3:30 p.m., local time.

O'Keefe could not disguise his anxiety at the delay and was all for contacting RAF Intelligence in Tripoli by wireless.

"And what the hell will we tell them?" demanded Benutti. "That we think they've got a bunch of SS fugitives running around loose? That if they see anyone wearing a swastika armband will they please arrest him? No way, Mike. They'll either think we're out on licence from the funny factory or by some miracle pick up Lutz and his merry men themselves. Let's keep it in the family for the time being."

"I still don't understand the significance of Tripoli," said Caradoc. They had been over this a dozen times and no one else did either. "Are you sure Lutz didn't drop any other hints?" he asked Greta.

The blonde German girl pulled at a cigarette. A good night's sleep, a bath and some borrowed clothing had done wonders for her physical appearance, but she seemed edgy.

"I've told you everything I remember, which I admit isn't much. All I can add is that I got the impression that Tripoli was—what did you call it?—another staging-post."

"Doesn't help," said Benutti. "We know damned well Lutz has no intention of hanging around North Africa. The trick is, where is he going from there and why there in the first place."

"We'll know that when we catch up," suggested Caradoc.

"*If* we catch up," said O'Keefe gloomily, staring out at the rain.

Pascoe was asleep on the starboard bunk in the wardroom. Once on course he had handed over the controls to van der Heyden with orders to keep the Sunderland at between 5,000 and 6,000 feet and an air speed of around 180. Providing all went well, that should put them over Lagos at dusk, the time Flight Lieutenant Saunders was expecting their wireless signal.

The South African estimated that, after four and a half hours in the air, they were somewhere south of Ghat in French West Africa. So far he had seen neither tail nor whisker of any other aircraft, military or civilian, but to be on the safe side he had instructed the Germans to man their gun platforms. There might be nothing below them but the vast expanse of the Sahara, but equally they could be showing as a blip on somebody's radar screen. It was as well to be ready. By now the balloon would have gone up back in Benghazi.

The C-47 Dakota took off from Rome at 11:48. Conditions were not brilliant up front, they were informed, but their pilot saw no reason why they should not be in Tripoli on time.

Three-quarters of an hour earlier, O'Keefe had finally lost patience with Benutti, the USAAF and the weather, and insisted on radioing ahead. He told Tripoli nothing more than to expect company, but that would at least mean the officer commanding the Intelligence unit would not have sloped off to the Mess.

He and Benutti had also taken the precaution of refurnishing each of the quartet with fresh documents, one set signed by the American authorities, one set by the British. The security classification of the papers was such that any of the four could demand co-operation right up to the top, no questions asked. They could just about reopen hostilities if the mood took them.

A mile below the Sunderland a sandstorm was raging. From his position in the for'ard gun turret Lutz studied it with unconcealed fascination. It resembled a coffee stain or a Rorschach ink-blot, a dirty mark soiling the whiteness of the desert. Although he knew it must be moving at speed and that anyone caught in the middle would be feeling the full impact of its fury, from where he sat it appeared benign and stationary.

A dozen feet behind him, Carver Kane was also keeping a wary eye on the phenomenon. Standing his watch in the right-hand seat of the dual-controlled aircraft, as far as he could tell the storm's apogee was 2,000 feet. He wondered if he should wake Pascoe, but eventually decided against it. The sun would be setting in a couple of hours and Pascoe needed all the rest he could get.

The pilot of the C-47 was a shade optimistic in his e.t.a. He had the transport on the tarmac at 3:40, ten minutes behind schedule.

Coming from a cold, wet and dirty day in Rome, the afternoon Libyan heat hit O'Keefe and the others like a clenched fist. Benutti muttered jokingly that his brain didn't know what to expect next, whether it was to be a bowl of chili or a cold drink in a tall glass.

O'Keefe's wireless messages had worked the oracle. There was a jeep waiting for them at the unloading bay. At the wheel was the Intelligence Officer, a Flight Lieutenant who looked as if he'd been up all night. He examined their credentials and said he had orders to take them directly to the base commander, Group Captain Holland.

On the way across Caradoc nudged O'Keefe.

"I'd say there was a flap on."

O'Keefe had spotted it also. There were too many armed guards around and the general atmosphere was charged with a sense of urgency. An outsider would have noticed nothing unusual; but to two men brought up on airfields the whole place appeared to be expecting a bomb or a royal visit.

"Has something happened?" O'Keefe asked the IO.

"You're damned right something's happened."

"Sir," O'Keefe reminded him.

"Sir," the IO added. "But the CO wants to tell you himself."

It took Group Captain Holland a while to get round to it. Immaculate in full summer rig and seemingly straight out of the shower, he viewed the civilian clothes of the newcomers with distaste. He was even less impressed when Benutti opened his mouth and revealed his country of origin, but the body blow was when Greta was introduced. He forgot his manners completely.

"A German?" It was as though he had been told that the Archbishop of Canterbury was addicted to cunnilingus.

O'Keefe brought him down to earth by pointing out that Greta, too, carried an Intelligence pass and that they were all to be afforded every facility and no delays.

Holland cleared his throat.

"Quite right, Squadron Leader, although I'm not sure how our domestic troubles affect you."

"Perhaps you'll allow me to be the judge of that, sir."

Holland searched the ceiling for inspiration. Perhaps these people could help. If they couldn't, he could say goodbye to his career.

"Yesterday afternoon," he began, "my Supply Officer, one

195

other officer and an NCO, all aircrew, left the base without authorization. Prior to doing so the Supply Officer withdrew from the armoury 20,000 rounds of .303 ammunition and 5,000 rounds of calibre .50. He also commandeered a Bedford 3-tonner, which turned up this morning in Benghazi."

There was a few seconds' silence. Holland shook his head. He knew he was wide awake but his words were those of a nightmare.

"Sir?" prompted O'Keefe.

Holland took a grip of himself.

"During the small hours a Sunderland flying boat went missing from its mooring in Benghazi and an RAF Regiment guard and the legitimate pilot of the Sunderland were assaulted, tied up, and left to drown. The unfortunate guard is dead, but Flight Lieutenant Wilberforce survived. He is in poor shape, of course, but he managed to tell the IO at Benghazi that it was my Supply Officer and my other personnel who hijacked—I can't believe it!—his aircraft, taking aboard the stolen ammunition. They were not alone. They were accompanied by six others, five men and a woman, some of whom spoke German."

Benutti slapped his palms together.

"That's it, the big apple. It's them. It has to be. Were there any descriptions of the men who spoke German, Group Captain?"

"And any indication which way the Sunderland headed," put in O'Keefe.

"I know very little more than I have told you," said Holland, "though I understand an unidentified aircraft was logged by Benghazi radar heading north-west at about the time the Sunderland disappeared."

"North-west?" Benutti didn't believe it. "That's not possible. North-west would take them back to Europe."

"Them, Major?" queried Holland. "Are you saying you know these people?"

"We're not sure, sir," interrupted O'Keefe. "They could be members of the SS we've tracked from Austria."

"Could be nothing," snapped Benutti. "It's Lutz, you know it is."

"And the woman? No one's mentioned a woman up to now."

"Someone they picked up en route, maybe a contact. Who cares. That's Lutz, Mike, I can feel it in my bones. But why north-west? And why go all the way to Benghazi when this airfield's littered with planes?"

"I can answer the first if not the second," said O'Keefe. "The pilot knew he'd be logged by radar as a stray. To confuse the issue he headed first of all in the last direction he was going to take. I'll bet he disappeared off the radar screen pretty damned fast."

O'Keefe looked at Holland for confirmation.

"I believe something of the sort did happen."

"It's an old dodge," went on O'Keefe. "Stay on the screen to show a false direction then dive below the radar net and double back. Under normal circumstances it might have worked. What Lutz—if it is Lutz—didn't know is that we were right behind him. And *we* know he's not going back to Europe. But a Sunderland—why a bloody Sunderland? You're right, Joe. If Lutz has somehow persuaded three RAF aircrew to join him, why didn't they take a plane from here?"

"An armed Sunderland at that," interjected the Group Captain. "It seems this appalling crime was planned well in advance."

"We'll know more when we've spoken to this—what was his name?—Flight Lieutenant Wilberforce," said Benutti. "I'm afraid we're going to have to ask you for transport to Benghazi, Group Captain."

Holland didn't bother to debate the point. These people seemed to know what they were doing. He picked up the telephone.

"I'll arrange it."

While the base commander was talking to the Duty Officer, Benutti asked O'Keefe, "Okay, you and Jim are the flying types—why a Sunderland?"

"Only two reasons I can think of. I did a tour in Catalinas during the war and a flying boat's no place to be if you want to get somewhere in a hurry. But a Sunderland has two advantages that I can see. One: it can land on water. Two: it has a massive range. It can do around three thousand miles on full tanks."

Benutti groaned in despair.

"Christ, they could be anywhere. Okay, which is it: water or range?"

"I don't know. Perhaps Wilberforce can tell us. What's the matter, Jim?" O'Keefe saw Caradoc frowning.

"Maybe nothing, but I wouldn't have expected someone with flying-boat experience to be here. What did we see on the way over—Lancasters, Halifaxes, a few short-haul transports. What's someone who can fly a Sunderland doing on a land base?"

Group Captain Holland put down the telephone.

"There's a Lancaster on stand-by," he said. "It can leave any time you're ready. Benghazi's ninety minutes away. And I think I can answer your question, Flight Sergeant. One of my missing officers has about a thousand hours in Sunderlands. My Supply Officer, Flight Lieutenant van der Heyden, was grounded. The NCO, Flight Sergeant Kane, was and is a bomber pilot. But Flying Officer Pascoe ... Are you all right, Squadron Leader?"

O'Keefe had got to his feet.

"Who did you say, sir?"

"I said Flying Officer Pascoe has a thousand hours in Sunderlands. . . ."

"Would that be Flying Officer Jonathan Pascoe?"

"It would. But how. . . ."

"If you'll excuse me, sir. . . ."

White as a sheet, O'Keefe turned on his heel and left the office.

"This entire airfield has turned into an asylum," said Holland, totally bewildered. "Now what in God's name was that all about?"

Caradoc enlightened him. "Flying Officer Pascoe is Squadron Leader O'Keefe's half-brother, sir. . . ."

Fully rested, Pascoe was again at the controls. For the past ten minutes he had been locked on to the Apapa radio beacon, but really it was unnecessary. Although it was dark the weather was fine and up front he had a visual on the lights from Lagos. All he needed now was the flare path of Apapa.

Kane was in the co-pilot's seat and van der Heyden at the wireless table, ready to call Apapa tower. If Saunders wanted to earn his £1,000, they should be waiting for his signal.

"Let's hope to Christ no one this far south's looking for a missing Sunderland," muttered Kane.

"Amen to that," said Pascoe. "Okay, Peter, give it a whirl."

Van der Heyden pressed the transmit switch.

"Able Sugar Nine, Able Sugar Nine. Apapa tower, this is Able Sugar Nine requesting clearance to land. Over."

There was a hiss of static and a faint voice behind it.

"For God's sake put the bloody thing on net, Peter."

"Able Sugar Nine, Able Sugar Nine. Apapa tower, this is Able Sugar Nine."

"Apapa tower to Able Sugar Nine—wait one. Over."

"Is that Saunders?" asked van der Heyden.

"It doesn't matter. Someone's expecting us. Ask them where the hell their flare path is."

"Apapa tower, this is Able Sugar Nine. We're strangers around here and we could use some help. We do not, repeat do not, see your flare path. Over."

"Roger, Able Sugar Nine. Sorry about that but a couple of Wellingtons have just landed at Ikeja and we try not to confuse them."

"Just tell them to light the bugger," said Pascoe.

"Apapa tower. . . ." began van der Heyden—but suddenly, three miles ahead, the path lit up like a Christmas tree. About 2,000 yards long and 100 wide, it was off their starboard beam and running east-west.

"Got it," said Pascoe.

"Able Sugar Nine, this is Apapa tower. Heading 270 is good. Wind zero knots. Over."

"Tell them we're okay now," said Pascoe.

"Thank you, Apapa tower. We'll manage now. See you on the ground."

"1,200 feet, Jonathan," said Kane.

"Fine. Keep calling it."

Pascoe put the Sunderland into a shallow starboard bank and lined up on heading 270, due west.

"800 . . . 700 . . . I don't know about you, Jonathan, but if this were a Lanc I'd say you were high."

"If this were a Lanc I would be. Just watch my altitude."

"500 . . . 400 . . . 350 . . . You're still high, Jonathan."

"Not a chance."

"Those lights are coming up bloody fast," said van der Heyden.

"Have a little faith. . . ."

"150 . . . 100 feet, Jonathan. . . ."

"Here we go. . . ."

Eighteen

Though dazed by the revelation that his half-brother was piloting the Sunderland, during the short flight to Benghazi O'Keefe took a grip of himself. Speculation was futile. Why Jonathan had acted as he did would have to wait. For the moment he owed the others some form of explanation—especially Benutti. The American had made no accusations but there must be a suspicion in his mind that he was being dragged into some sort of conspiracy. Which was not the case, as Jim Caradoc could attest. Though even Caradoc did not know the whole story, and it was time to remedy that.

"You don't have to tell us anything you don't want to," said Benutti.

"Thanks, but it's no big secret. My mother divorced my father in 1919, when I was two. It was the usual story of a wartime marriage that didn't work out. I stayed with my mother until I went to boarding school. My father was just starting his engineering business and apparently had precious little time for anything, or anyone, else.

"My mother remarried in 1920 and Jonathan was born in 1921. My step-father wanted to adopt me, but my own father was having none of that. Thus, Jonathan grew up with the surname of Pascoe and I kept my own name of O'Keefe.

"I suppose you could say we never really got along, Jonathan and myself. We didn't dislike each other, it wasn't as strong as that, but the older I got the more I missed my natural father, this peculiar Irishman who would turn up out of nowhere from time to time and bring me presents or take me to the zoo."

O'Keefe ran a hand through his hair. It made him feel uncomfortable, talking like this.

"When I was in my middle teens I used to see a lot more of him than I did of my mother, step-father and half-brother. He used to visit me regularly in school and I spent many of my vacations with him. He never married again, incidentally.

"After he died, I saw my mother a bit more often, though less once I joined the RAF and war was declared. Her health wasn't too good and it didn't help matters when my step-father died also. She was worried about the war, worried that I was flying, and terrified that Jonathan would want to follow suit as soon as he was old enough. She asked me to use my influence to see that that didn't happen. Well, I had no influence, of course, but Jonathan was always convinced that somehow I had put a block on him joining Fighter Command. He wanted to fly Spitfires and he thought I'd manoeuvred him into Lancasters and Sunderlands, though where he got the idea it was safer in Bomber Command and Coastal Command I have no idea. He is, by the way, a first-class pilot, one of the best.

"Until late 1941 we kept up some sort of correspondence but then my mother—our mother—was killed in an air raid. After that, we didn't bother any longer. I knew he was somewhere in North Africa, but that was all."

The Lancaster droned on. Finally it was Benutti who broke the silence.

"Sorry," he said. "For what I was beginning to think, I mean. But you've got to admit it's a helluva coincidence."

"It's been a war full of coincidences of one kind or another."

"I can't argue with that."

Benutti was chomping on an unlit stogie. He took it from his mouth and examined it for a second before asking, "I suppose I'm the one who has to say this, but are you sure you want to go on?"

"Of course I am. Why the hell shouldn't I? It could be a mistake. Jonathan could have been forced into this against his will."

"And if that's not the case?"

"We still go on. It's Lutz I want. Jonathan is incidental."

Benutti wasn't so sure.

"What if we catch up and get into a firefight—will Pascoe be incidental then?"

O'Keefe hesitated.

"It's a fair question," went on Benutti. "I don't want to sound melodramatic, but it's not just your life at stake here. We're all in this together. If we run into trouble and you don't pull the trigger at the right time because your mind's elsewhere, that could cancel all our subscriptions."

"I don't know the answer to that one," said O'Keefe carefully, "and I won't until I'm faced with it."

Benutti appeared satisfied, but there were one or two other things bothering him.

"Is it likely that Pascoe knows who Lutz is, knows what happened to the captured fliers after the Augsburg raid?"

O'Keefe said he doubted it.

"There's no reason why he should. I only found out myself in February and I don't think it's general knowledge."

"These things have a habit of getting around."

Benutti finally decided that the stogie was beyond saving and ground it underfoot.

"What I'm trying to establish is whether Pascoe knows all about Lutz and doesn't give a damn one way or the other."

"Now wait a minute," O'Keefe protested angrily. "Let's not start handing down the verdict until we've had the trial. I said Jonathan and I didn't get along, not that he was a strait-jacket case."

"I'm just looking at the facts," murmured Benutti.

"Facts my foot! You're jumping to conclusions."

"Not me." Benutti counted on his fingers. "Fact one is that your half-brother took part in the theft of a 3-tonner and 25,000 rounds of ammo. I haven't heard anyone say he was doing it under duress. According to Group Captain Holland Pascoe is the only one who can fly a Sunderland and a Sunderland's missing. That's fact number two. Number three is that he and his buddies have killed one man and tried to kill another. Fact four is the evasive action the flying boat took after getting airborne. That doesn't sound to me like the action of a man with a gun to head."

O'Keefe looked at Caradoc and Greta Hoegel for support. He found none. Well, maybe he wasn't thinking straight, maybe Benutti was right, but. . . .

"I'll believe Jonathan is a thief and a killer when I have irrefutable proof," he said coldly. "Is there anything else you want to say?"

"Just this. Up to now we've been tracking Lutz on the ground. Now he's airborne. That means we have to flash our credentials and commandeer a plane in Benghazi. I asked you a minute ago what happens if we get involved in a firefight. You said you didn't know and I accept that. But if we do catch up and you decide you can pull the trigger, are you quite sure you can outfly Pascoe?"

O'Keefe didn't answer. He hadn't flown a combat mission in months, and when it came right down to it he wasn't sure just how good Jonathan was. But one thing he did know: an armed Sunderland was a terrifying opponent.

If Flight Lieutenant Saunders wondered about the six civilians, including a girl, who had disembarked from the flying boat an hour earlier, he was keeping his curiosity to himself, thought Pascoe. There was no indication, either, that any word of a hijacked Sunderland had travelled this far. No reason why it should have done, of course. It would be impractical if not impossible for Benghazi to alert every RAF station within refuelling range, especially as the radar log would show a course of 320 degrees. By the time Benghazi tumbled the subterfuge, the aircraft would be in Cape Town.

203

As good as his word, Saunders had carried out his side of the bargain to the letter, providing two 3-tonners and a gasoline bowser. The trucks should be close to the cache by now, and the Sunderland's thirsty tanks were already a quarter full. In return, Saunders had in his pocket the equivalent of £500 in gold sovereigns. He had expressed no surprise at the manner of payment, merely remarking that it suited his purpose to have gold as opposed to paper currency.

It all seemed too bloody simple to Pascoe and Kane, but so had driving off the airfield in Tripoli and hijacking the Sunderland. With a little nerve and the right contacts nothing was impossible.

At the wheel of the leading 3-tonner, van der Heyden was also thinking that everything was going absurdly well. Beside him, motionless, sat Lutz, his eyes missing nothing. In the back of this vehicle were Hanna, her father and Scheringer. Mueller was driving the second truck, accompanied by Fischer.

"How much further?" asked van der Heyden.

"Not far."

"We're going to look bloody sick if the warehouse has been taken over by the British."

Now that they were actually in Lagos, Lutz had seen no reason not to tell the South African the location of the cache.

"It's derelict, I've already told you."

"Or rebuilt then."

"That would not be possible. Arrangements were made many years ago via a dummy Swiss corporation to ensure that it stayed a ruin. Had anything happened to change that, I'd have been informed."

"It still seems a crazy chance to take, hiding the loot in a British colony."

"In 1938 we rather hoped it would not be a British colony for long," remarked Lutz drily.

Beyond the Lewis Street market the SS colonel told van der Heyden to slow down and take the second turning on the right.

"Nearly there," he said quietly. "About ten more minutes."

While Benutti was checking in with the Benghazi Flight Office, O'Keefe went across to see the IO. He first of all asked, and was told, how the Sunderland was armed: a bank of four .303s in the tail and two in the nose; a .50 Browning in each beam. Eight guns in all.

He then asked what other flying boats were on the base and was informed that there were two Catalina PBY-5As. One was conventionally armed with a single .303 in the nose and ventral positions, and a .50 in each blister, port and starboard. The other one had had the ventral gun removed and had been further modified by replacing the nose .303 with a .50, rigged and sighted so that it could be fired by the pilot.

O'Keefe left it at that for the time being. It was pointless getting either Catalina warmed up if there was no way of ascertaining where the Sunderland had gone.

Flight Lieutenant Wilberforce was sitting up, but the MO warned them that he was still weak and mustn't be tired. Neither could he be allowed four visitors; two was the maximum. Caradoc and Greta were sent to get something to eat.

O'Keefe first of all apologized to the moustached RAF officer for the need to question him before he was fully recovered. There was, however, a certain amount of urgency in the matter.

"That's all right, sir. I don't feel so bad now, more bloody angry than anything else."

Wilberforce took O'Keefe and Benutti through the whole story, beginning with van der Heyden's solo visit a few days earlier.

"Nothing peculiar about that," he said. "I'm used to giving the five-bob tour. The Sunderland's such a beautiful ship and not many people have seen one close up. We only built seven hundred-odd, you know."

"I know," said O'Keefe.

"Did van der Heyden give any indication, say anything at

all, about a possible destination before he slugged you?" asked Benutti.

"No, sir. When the IO here told me you were coming and the sort of questions you were likely to ask, including that one, I gave it a lot of thought. Nothing came through the fog, I'm sorry to say. You've got to remember that that bloody South African caught me on the chin when I wasn't looking. I don't know how long I was out, but I was quite groggy when I came to. We'd also been having something of a farewell bash in the Mess. I was probably somewhere on the wrong side of total sobriety, otherwise I might have seen the punch coming."

"Wait a minute," interrupted O'Keefe. "Let's take this stage by stage or we might miss something. Tell us what happened when the 3-tonner turned up."

"Before I do that, sir, can you tell me what it's all about?" asked Wilberforce. "I've been kept pretty much in the dark and I'd like to know who tried to kill me and why. A few more seconds and I'd be on a slab like that poor bloody guard."

"It's an Intelligence matter, I'm afraid," said O'Keefe cautiously, "but you can have the bare bones. The Germans, at least some of them, are SS personnel on the run. Major Benutti and I have tracked them from Austria. We're not sure where our own people fit in as yet. They could have been operating under duress."

"No, sir." Wilberforce shook his head emphatically. "From what I could see they were most cooperative. The Germans weren't forcing anyone to do anything."

O'Keefe's spirits took a nose dive. So Jonathan was in it of his own free will.

Benutti changed tack.

"Tell us what happened from the moment you saw the 3-tonner."

"Well, it was coming towards me with its lights full beam and I thought it was some erk who didn't know any better. Van der Heyden was doing the driving and you could have knocked me down with a NAAFI custard when he said something to the effect that he was going to borrow the Sunderland. Then he clobbered me. I didn't recover consciousness until we were about to tie up at the pontoon. My hands were bound and someone had stuck a handkerchief in my mouth, but my feet were free."

"And you could see and hear?" asked Benutti.

"Oh yes, sir. It was probably a reflex action, but the first thing I did was count the strength of the opposition. There were three in RAF uniform, van der Heyden and two others. I couldn't make out their faces or their ranks from where they'd dumped me, though I understand from the IO that you know who they were."

O'Keefe ignored the implied question. It was better Wilberforce remained in the dark.

"Go on," he said.

"Well, the three RAF boys went aboard through the for'ard hatch and one of the Germans began issuing orders to the others."

"You speak German?" asked Benutti.

"Schoolboy stuff, sir, but enough to pick up a few words here and there, especially the names. The girl was addressed as Fräulein Baumann and the oldest of the men was her father. Three of the others were called Mueller, Fischer and Scheringer."

Benutti glanced at O'Keefe.

"And the other man," said the American, "the one who was giving all the orders—did you hear his name mentioned?"

"No, sir, but I can give you a rough description. Tall, light-coloured hair, and a scar here."

"You're sure of that?" asked Benutti.

"Quite sure, sir. He's the bastard who tried to kill me. I'm not likely to forget his face in a hurry."

If there had been any doubts before there were none now. It was Lutz.

"And the attack took place while the three RAF people were aboard?" asked O'Keefe.

"Yes, sir. Whoever was in the driving seat had already turned over the port and starboard outers. He seemed to know what he was doing."

Well, that was something, thought O'Keefe. If Jonathan was on the flight deck he could have had nothing to do with the murder of the guard and the attempted murder of

Wilberforce. He might be a thief but he wasn't a killer.

"Carry on," he said to Wilberforce.

The Flight Lieutenant looked at him blankly.

"I'm afraid that's it, sir. From the moment I was in the water I was fighting for my life. I don't recall anything else. I don't even remember the Sunderland taking off."

"Think hard," urged Benutti. "It's very important and you're our only hope. While Lutz—that's the name of the guy with the scar, incidentally—was issuing orders, didn't he give any clue which way they'd be going? I mean, you've given us a few names and that's fine, but Lutz must have said something else."

"As I explained, sir, my German's of the schoolboy variety. The girl and her father were simply told to get aboard. Two of the other men—Mueller and Fischer, I believe—were told to load the guns. That's about all I can tell you, except. . . ." He puckered his brow in a frown.

"Yes?" said Benutti.

"There was some reference to provisions and . . . No, I can't remember. I'm sorry."

"We're fucked," said Benutti, when he and O'Keefe were outside. "He might remember in a week's time, but in a week Lutz could be in Australia."

"Not without refuelling a few times he couldn't."

"So he refuels a few times."

"A Sunderland's not an Austin 10, you know. It needs more than half a dozen gallons to get it from A to B."

O'Keefe stopped so suddenly that Benutti had walked another five paces before he realized he was by himself.

"That's it!" said O'Keefe.

"That's what?"

"The bloody Sunderland will have to refuel somewhere if it's to go any distance and you can't just bung it down anywhere and ask the nice RAF men to kindly fill her up. That sort of thing would have to be arranged in advance—well in advance. Someone would have had to make contact with another base."

Benutti was not impressed.

"You're forgetting that it was full to the gunwales when it

took off. What did you tell me, that it can do 3,000 miles on full tanks?"

"Sure, but what lies within 3,000 miles that would be any use to Lutz?"

"About one-eighth of the world in any direction."

"No, not in any direction. We've already agreed that the north-west course was a fake. I think we can assume that anywhere else in Europe is out too. They've just come from there; they wouldn't be going back."

"Keep talking," said Benutti.

"It's obvious. Where outside Europe would a bunch of Nazi fugitives have friends?"

"South America?"

"Precisely—South America. I'll have to check on a chart, of course, but I'm pretty sure that anywhere in South America is way beyond the range of a Sunderland flying from Tripoli."

"So where does that get us?"

"It gets us to the point where they have to make their refuelling arrangements. We know Lutz hasn't been in North Africa very long, say a week at the most. It shouldn't be hard to check."

"Check what, for Chrissake?" snapped Benutti. "You're the flying type and you're talking Navajo to me. I'm a simple soldier who doesn't even know the length of 42nd Street."

"We check their logs for the last week," said O'Keefe. "We check the flight logs of my half-brother, van der Heyden and Kane. If they've made any trips to any base that would put the Sunderland, with refuelled tanks, within striking distance of South America, that's where they've gone."

"Jesus, I think you've cracked it," muttered Benutti. "And it's even easier than you think. If I remember correctly, Holland said van der Heyden was grounded. Now he may be a very clever guy, this South African, but I don't see him risking a court martial by flying without proper authorization, not when he's got two pilots at his disposal."

Twenty minutes later O'Keefe was talking by wireless to LAC Cummings. No, Cummings was quite certain Flight Lieutenant van der Heyden had made no illicit flights recently. As for Flying Officer Pascoe and Flight Sergeant Kane, they had only done local hops, mainly around North Africa. Except for one occasion earlier in the week when they had ferried some coolant to Lagos.

O'Keefe and Benutti practically ran back to Flight Lieutenant Wilberforce's sick bed.

"That's it, sir," said the moustached officer. "Lutz mentioned something about Nigeria."

"Got the bastards," whooped Benutti.

The warehouse stood by itself, flanked either side by a stretch of open ground. The nearest building was sixty or seventy yards away. But it wasn't this that caused van der Heyden's heart to pound with alarm. What did was the fact that the warehouse had evidently suffered considerable fire damage in its distant past. It appeared to have four walls and a roof, but all openings, including the massive double doors, were battened with lengths of timber.

Lutz came close to smiling when he read the South African's thoughts.

"Yes, it was quite a fire. It happened during my last visit here in 1938, about twenty minutes after I left, as a matter of fact. The whole place went up in a sheet of flame. There was no one in it at the time, of course; at least, no one who could be found. Fortunately for the Swiss corporation which owns the premises, the firefighters were on the spot within minutes. One might almost think they'd been briefed to wait in the wings. They couldn't do much about the contents, but they managed to save the building."

Van der Heyden was completely baffled.

"Let me get this straight. You made your cache then set the bloody place on fire. That's lunacy."

"Not in the least. It makes perfect sense. No one would think of looking for a fortune in gold and diamonds in such a ruin, am I right?"

"You're dead right."

"My reasoning also when I originated the scheme. Of course I stayed behind for a week or so until the ashes were cold and then removed the worst of the debris with bulldozers.

But as the Swiss representative of the owners I had to tell the local authorities that we were unable to rebuild for the moment. All we could do was seal off the premises and make sure they were safe."

"And the cache is inside?"

"Let's go and see."

"How?"

"By removing the battens from the doors. They're mostly for show. It shouldn't take long."

Using tools from the 3-tonners it took fifteen minutes. Headlights full on, van der Heyden was told to drive to the far wall. Mueller followed in the second 3-tonner. When both trucks were inside and the engines off, the warehouse doors were closed again.

The air was foul and from several corners there came the squealing of rats. In the back of the lead truck Hanna shivered.

"What's happening?" she asked, when van der Heyden poked his head over the tailboard.

"I'm damned if I know, but you and your father had better stay here for the moment."

"Don't think I'm going to move. I hate rats."

"We could have stayed with the aircraft," said Baumann.

"I don't think Lutz trusts Jonathan not to take off."

"Without the gold?"

Van der Heyden watched Lutz start at the wall and pace out forty steps. He looked up at the roof as if checking something, then took another forty steps to his right.

"About here," he muttered, and ordered Mueller to bring the flashlight.

On his hands and knees Lutz scrabbled among seven years' accumulated filth. After a few minutes' search he said, "Ah," and grunted with satisfaction. "Perhaps you'd like to give me a hand, van der Heyden."

Van der Heyden walked across and knelt beside the SS colonel. His fingers touched a metal ring.

"Pull," commanded Lutz, "but stop when I tell you."

Together van der Heyden and Lutz heaved at the ring.

211

Slowly a trapdoor opened. When it was at an angle of 45 degrees Lutz called a halt.

He fumbled around by the hinges and yanked at something. Bringing his hand into the light he showed van der Heyden a length of wire.

"A small device to neutralize the curious. If anyone had got here before us they would have been annihilated as soon as the trap reached the vertical. Mueller, the flashlight."

Mueller handed it over. Lutz shone it downwards, revealing a flight of steps descending twenty feet to a wide cellar beyond.

"Follow me, van der Heyden."

"What happens when you're tanked up?" Saunders asked Pascoe.

"You dismiss the bowser and we wait with the launch."

"For how long?"

"Why do you want to know?"

"Because I don't want a bloody great Sunderland on my hands at daybreak, that's why I want to know."

"You won't have. We'll be well on our way to Cape Town by then."

Pascoe bit his lip in annoyance; there was no reason to tell Saunders any more than he needed to know.

"You can forget I said that, incidentally."

"I'm not likely to repeat it, am I?"

"You'd better not."

Kane fingered the bowie knife at his hip.

"You might as well live to spend your money."

Van der Heyden held his breath as Lutz swept the torch from one end of the wall to the other. Stacked in neat rows, covered in dust and dirt but otherwise undamaged, were one hundred and fifty, one hundred and sixty wooden boxes, a rope handle at either end. It now became clear why each box weighed only fifty pounds, contained a solitary ingot; trying to drag or lift anything heavier up a flight of steps that steep would take a week.

"Perhaps you'd like to see what you've been risking your neck for," said Lutz.

Without waiting for a reply the German reached for a box on the extreme left of the top row. Unlike the others, this one had a black cross stencilled on its side. The lid was nailed down but there was a crowbar, rusting with age, on the floor. Taking hold of it while van der Heyden held the flashlight, Lutz prised off the lid.

"Shine the lamp."

Van der Heyden was way ahead of the German, the torch beam already picking up the contents of the box. They blazed with a fire which hurt his eyes. He shivered with avarice.

"Handpicked blue and white diamonds," said Lutz in a matter of fact tone. "Average weight between ten and twelve carats. Total value some £4,000,000 as near as I can estimate."

"Christ," muttered van der Heyden.

"Give me some light here, please."

Lutz already had the crowbar under the lid of a second box. In a moment it was off. Compared to the brilliant iridescence of the diamonds, the sight of the single ingot, stamped with the eagle of the Reich, was almost an anticlimax. But like men of any race or time when first shown gold in quantity, van der Heyden could not take his eyes off the bar. It was worth in excess of £6,000—more than he could earn in ten years.

It took him a moment to realize that Lutz was speaking.

". . . *Judengeld,* of course—gold taken from Jewish enemies of the State before the war, melted down and recast. Some people called it *Blutgeld*—blood gold—and say it's cursed. I trust you do not subscribe to such superstitious nonsense."

"You can't spend superstition."

"A very practical attitude. The diamonds were purchased on the open market, as I believe I explained in Tripoli. I myself prefer gold, but the transportation problems were too great. If this cache were entirely in gold it would weigh almost eighteen tons."

"What you have here weighs over three and a half," said van der Heyden. "Stacking it couldn't have been easy."

"I had help of course," said Lutz. "Where was it now? Ah yes. Shine the torch in that direction, van der Heyden, towards the far end."

Van der Heyden did as he was told and nearly dropped the flashlight in horror as the first thing the beam picked out was a grinning skull still attached to the skeleton of its torso. Nearby was another.

"My assistants," said Lutz easily. "Needless to say they had to die once their usefulness was at an end."

Van der Heyden didn't need it spelled out. What could happen once could happen again unless he, Kane and Pascoe watched their backs.

Nineteen

After checking with the Benghazi IO that there was a flying-boat base at Apapa, it was Benutti who suggested raising them on the wireless and O'Keefe who objected, though later he was to think the American major had double-bluffed him superbly.

"It's the end of the line for Lutz and his buddies," enthused Benutti. "They'll be dancing a jig at the end of a rope before they can sing the first verse of the Horst Wessel."

"So will Jonathan," O'Keefe reminded him.

"How do you figure that? You heard what Wilberforce said. Pascoe was already at the controls when Lutz killed the guard. He's out of it. He might have to spend a few years in a military lock-up, but that's all."

"You're not familiar with English law," said O'Keefe. "I don't know what it's like in the States, but we've got something which says that if two or more people go out to commit a felony and murder is the result, then they're all guilty of that murder regardless of who pulled the trigger. Jonathan may still not be aware that the guard's dead, but a court won't be interested. He'll hang with the others."

"Now wait a minute." Benutti caught hold of O'Keefe's sleeve. "Are you suggesting we let them make a run for it?"

"Perhaps."

"Perhaps nothing. You said it yourself, with full tanks a Sunderland can reach South America."

"I should at least give Jonathan a chance to talk to me personally. And me to him. He's not a killer whatever a Court might say."

"You're playing judge and jury, Mike."

"He's my half-brother, for Christ's sake. His mother was my mother. What the hell d'you think I'm going to feel the morning they hang him?"

Benutti shook his head doubtfully.

"I'm not sure I can go along with this or that I understand what you're saying. We let Pascoe go, we let Lutz go too. I'd have thought that's the last thing you wanted."

"It is. Bear with me," pleaded O'Keefe. "Let's both take a look at a map before we make any hasty decisions."

Ten minutes later, with a chart of the South Atlantic spread out before them and away from inquisitive ears, O'Keefe was making notes on a pad.

"Look," he said, "assuming we're right about Apapa, only the north-east tip of Brazil is within range of the Sunderland, even tanked up to the gunwales."

"Brazil fought on our side," Benutti pointed out.

"True, but it was touch and go which camp they joined until 1942 and it has a massive German population, some of whom are bound to be Nazi sympathizers."

"Okay, I'll buy it."

O'Keefe referred to his notes.

"We know the time of take-off from Benghazi and from that we can calculate their e.t.a. at Apapa. They probably landed in the last hour or so. It'll take a while to refuel, so they're still on the water. They won't be airborne for a couple of hours or more."

"And we're two thousand miles away."

"But we know where they're heading."

"We *assume* we know where they're heading. They could go in another direction entirely and we've used up a hell of a lot of assumptions. Apart from which north-east Brazil is a big place."

"Not so big," said O'Keefe. "They can only make that stretch of coastline between Natal and Recife."

Benutti peered at the chart.

"Which seems to me to be two hundred miles long."

"And the Sunderland's a big ship. There's no place to hide it."

"Spell it out to me, Mike."

O'Keefe thought about it. He was convinced he was right. The Sunderland had been chosen not for its range *or* its ability to land on water, but for both.

"First of all we radio Apapa as you suggested, check that the Sunderland's actually there. No more than that. We just want to know we're not on a wild-goose chase. Next, we get the hell out of here as quick as Christ'll let us. If the Sunderland's still in Apapa when we arrive, so much the better. If not, we set off after it."

"In what?" asked Benutti.

"In a Catalina. They've got two PBY-5As here and I've flown them before."

"A flying boat? Why don't we see if they've got something faster?"

"Because we may not get to Apapa until after Jonathan's gone, and if they've got a flying boat we need a flying boat. They may have hijacked the Sunderland just for its range, but I doubt it."

"Another of your assumptions? All right, tell me about this Catalina. Is it as good as the Sunderland?"

"Nowhere near it."

O'Keefe explained that the PBY-5A had only two Pratt and Whitneys compared to the Sunderland's four; that it was 30 mph slower going flat out and that its range was around 2,400 miles.

"Which puts us out of gas smack in the middle of the Atlantic, right?"

"Wrong," said O'Keefe. "Take another look at the chart. That pinprick in the centre is Ascension Island and on Ascension Island the US Air Force has a base. It's about 1,500 miles from Lagos and the same distance from north-east Brazil. That's where we refuel."

"What's this other little pinprick down here?"

"That's St Helena, way off course. It hasn't got an airfield either."

Benutti scratched his nose thoughtfully.

"Let's see if I've got this straight. We fly down to Apapa in a Catalina. If Lutz is still there, we make our move then. If the Sunderland's been and gone, we take off after it, heading for Brazil, where we call in the troops. Unless we catch up in the meantime."

"Something like that."

"It's wild, Mike," said Benutti after a moment's consideration. "The whole scheme's wilder'n a cat with a firecracker tied round its cock."

"It's better than the alternative. If the authorities get to Jonathan before I do, he's dead."

"And if you get there first?"

"I don't know."

"But you'll presumably give him the benefit of the doubt and let him head for the hills."

"Perhaps."

Benutti mulled it over.

"Well, I can't say I blame you. I'd probably do the same in your position."

"Then you go along with it?"

"I guess so."

"Thanks, Joe."

"Save the thanks. If they all get away with it I'll tell the brass you had a gun in my back. I'd also like to make one stipulation."

"Name it."

"When we radio Apapa we ask them to plot the Sunderland on radar if it leaves before we get there. I'm still not convinced about Brazil and it wouldn't do my ulcer a lot of good if we took off in the wrong direction."

"Agreed. We don't tell them why, though. We just quote our authority and order them to get it done."

"Okay."

"Anything else?" asked O'Keefe, seeing the American hesitate.

"One thing. You've told me that the Catalina's got fewer engines than the Sunderland, that it's slower, and that it's got less range. You didn't mention comparative fire power."

"The Sunderland's got eight Brownings. A bank of four .303s in the tail, two in the nose, and a .50 on either side. The Catalina I propose commandeering has a single .50 up front and one each in the port and starboard blisters."

"In other words we're outgunned almost three to one."

"Yes."

"Jesus Christ," said Benutti.

Leaving the American to radio Apapa, O'Keefe sought out Greta and Caradoc, finding them both in the Sergeants Mess, where the German girl was attracting a good deal of attention. As quickly and as briefly as he could, he explained what was happening.

"No questions," he said finally. "They can come later when we're in less of a hurry."

It had already occurred to him that they no longer needed Greta to identify Lutz. They were not looking for the SS colonel now; they were looking for a flying boat. Where it was, that's where Lutz would be.

Greta objected vehemently when he put it to her.

"I refuse to stay behind. I've come this far, I'll go all the way."

"It could be dangerous," warned O'Keefe.

"And what was Dobbiaco, Trento, Verona, Rome? If I'm left here I'll be arrested, interned or repatriated. I have no money nor anyone to vouch for me."

"That can all be arranged."

"While you're alive, yes. But what happens if you're killed?"

O'Keefe didn't bother to point out that if he were killed while she was aboard the Catalina, more than likely she would be dead too. In some ways he was glad she wanted to see it through.

He told her to go to the general canteen and get them to make up a dozen flasks of hot drinks and as many sandwiches as they could muster. Whatever happened, they would be airborne for some time.

"If you get any objections, show them your credentials or get in touch with me through the Intelligence Officer."

"What are we going to do?" asked Caradoc, when Greta had gone.

"We're going to ask, very politely, if we can please have a loan of one of their Catalinas."

In the meantime, transferring the bullion boxes from the cellar to the 3-tonners was under way.

Fifty lbs may not sound too much, and isn't much, when dealing with only one or two units, but in this instance there were one hundred and sixty-two boxes to be manhandled up twenty feet of stairway.

Lutz quickly decided that Baumann was too old to be much use and his daughter, naturally, could not be expected to lift anything so heavy. Nevertheless, he was unwilling to leave them both unattended up top. They were a long way from home and there was nowhere to go, but Lutz had survived the war because he took no chances. The Baumanns were therefore brought down to the cellar.

Hanna saw the two skeletons immediately and stifled a scream of terror with the back of her hand.

"The dead can't hurt you, Fräulein," said Lutz. "It's only the living you have to be wary of."

After some trial and error it was concluded that the easiest method of getting the boxes to ground level was to use the breakdown ropes from the 3-tonners. Mueller and Fischer were positioned at the top of the steps, Lutz and van der Heyden at the bottom. Each box was dragged to the foot of the stairway and a rope attached to its handle. Once up the steps Scheringer took the rope and pulled the box to the nearest truck, while Mueller and Fischer let down the second rope. Later, when the entire cache had been removed, they would all help to load the trucks.

But it was going to be bloody hard work.

When the Sunderland was refuelled and the gauges checked out to Pascoe's satisfaction, Saunders dismissed the gasoline bowser. Pascoe then settled down to get some rest. The others would not be back for quite a few hours.

Kane stayed awake, drinking coffee and playing cards with Saunders in the galley. The Australian could have used some shut-eye too, but he wanted to make sure that Saunders did not take it into his head to decamp and to hell with the other half of his £1,000. The Supply Officer had been showing signs of nerves ever since he realized the Sunderland's guns were loaded.

The Duty Officer in Benghazi was impressed with O'Keefe's credentials but unwilling to release one of his precious Catalinas until he received the go-ahead from above, especially as O'Keefe wanted the aircraft's three Brownings armed.

"That could take a while," he warned.

O'Keefe threatened a junior officer for the first time in his life. The PBY-5A could do around 180 mph flat out and cruise somewhere in the region of 160. From Benghazi to Lagos was 2,000 miles, which meant thirteen hours in the air, assuming no snags.

"It had better not. If you've got a fraction of the sense you were born with you'll get the armourers cracking while you're talking to the CO. If you're not back here in twenty minutes and I'm not unsticking a quarter of an hour after that, you'll find yourself scrubbing the latrines for the remainder of your tour."

While the Duty Officer was on the telephone Greta came in. She was carrying two canvas holdalls bulging with sandwiches in greaseproof wrappers, and Thermos flasks filled with hot coffee and Bovril. A few minutes later Benutti appeared, grinning from ear to ear.

"It landed a couple of hours ago," he said. "Call sign Able Sugar Nine, and it's still on the deck. At least it hasn't asked for take-off clearance. Does Able Sugar Nine mean anything? I'd hate to fly down to West Africa and find we're chasing the wrong bloody Sunderland."

"It's probably a code worked out between Lutz and whoever's helping them down there," said O'Keefe. "But it's ours all right. The flying time fits exactly."

"Then what are we waiting for?"

"We're waiting for these bastards here to get off their arses and tell us we can have one of their bloody planes."

"Not any more," said Caradoc. "Here comes the boy wonder."

It was just after 19:30 hours when O'Keefe received permission from the tower to take off. Three minutes later the Catalina was airborne. E.t.a. Apapa, 08:00.

Loading and stacking the boxes in the 3-tonners took much longer than any of them had anticipated, and it was close on 2 a.m. before they were back at Apapa. Sunrise for this part of the world was a few minutes before 06:00, and van der Heyden knew they hadn't a snowball's chance in hell of being airborne by then. But there was nothing to be done about it.

Towards 4 a.m., with almost 1,300 air miles behind them, O'Keefe handed the controls to Caradoc for the second time and went aft to grab something to eat. With any luck he would also get a couple of hours' sleep. Caradoc was a good pilot and a quick learner. He could certainly keep the aircraft on course and in an emergency could probably put it down safely.

Benutti was curled up in a ball, dead to the world, but Greta was wide awake, staring out into the darkness through the port gun blister.

"Everything all right?" asked O'Keefe in German, knowing she was more comfortable in her own language.

"Yes. How about you? You must be tired."

"A little, but nothing a cup of coffee and a sandwich won't cure."

Greta passed them over. Briefly her hands touched his.

"Thanks," he said.

"It's I who should be thanking you. For one horrible moment I thought you were going to leave me in Benghazi."

"You may yet wish I did."

"I don't think so. We've been together for so long, the four of us, that it wouldn't seem right to split up. I keep asking myself if it's not all a dream. Have I really been to Rome and Tripoli and am I really, now, several miles in the air heading for West Africa."

"You have and you are. You can take a look in the log if you want proof."

Greta chuckled throatily. It was one of the most attractive sounds O'Keefe had ever heard. There hadn't been too much laughter on this trip.

"Always the practical man, aren't you. An Italian or a Hungarian would have said that he knew we'd been to Rome because without me it would just have been another city."

O'Keefe grinned at her.

"Okay, without you Rome would have been just another city."

"But you don't mean it."

"How do you know?"

"Because I know you."

"That's a mighty sweeping statement and probably untrue. Still, the bigger the lie. . . ." He stopped.

"I remember that one too. It was one of Goebbels' dicta. The bigger the lie the more likely people are to believe it."

"That's not what I meant."

"Of course it's what you meant. I keep forgetting I'm a German and that one day I'll have to go back."

"The one doesn't necessarily follow the other."

O'Keefe leaned forward and touched Greta's shoulder.

"Look, when it's all over I'll see what I can do about keeping you out of Germany. I may even be able to get you a permit to stay in England."

"And then?"

"And then what?"

"Nothing," said Greta. "Nothing at all."

Without exception everyone worked until they thought they would drop. Even Hanna and her father were dragooned into doing what little they could. But it was still a few minutes after 07:30 before the last of the bullion boxes was stowed to Pascoe's satisfaction.

Saunders had watched the whole operation with growing fear. He had guessed correctly what was in the boxes and had overheard conversations in German. Whoever these people were they were not run of the mill smugglers. But he was in too deep to back out. He had accepted the second half of his payment and all he wanted now was to see the last of Able Sugar Nine.

Back on dry land he heaved a sigh of relief. Take-off clearance had been given and they should soon be on their way. What the hell was the hold-up?

There was no way Saunders could know it, but on the flight deck Lutz had just delivered his bombshell.

"What the hell d'you mean, we're not going to Cape Town?" demanded Pascoe.

"Precisely what I say," answered Lutz. "After take-off I want you to fly a heading of 240."

"*You* want *me*. . . . Who gave you command of this aircraft all of a sudden?"

Van der Heyden was examining a chart.

"240 takes us to Recife in north-east Brazil. Is that where we're going, Lutz, Brazil?"

"That's where we're not going," said Pascoe. "This ship's bound for Cape Town."

"I'm afraid not," murmured Lutz. He called down the ladder to Mueller. "Do you have Fräulein Baumann with you?"

Mueller said he did.

"He's also got a pistol to her head," Lutz advised Pascoe, "which he'll use if I tell him to. I'd like to debate the matter and have your willing co-operation, but we haven't got time. The heading is 240. Believe me, this is not a whim."

Van der Heyden had been making a few calculations. Brazil was on—just. Providing they didn't run into foul weather or adverse winds, they could make Recife with about enough fuel left in the tanks to fill a couple of cigarette lighters.

"What's the difference?" he said to Pascoe. "We're probably better off in Brazil than we would be in South Africa."

"I don't like last-minute changes of plan," said Pascoe, "and I particularly don't like being kept in the dark."

"Basic security," said Lutz. "What you don't know you can't reveal. And we're wasting time."

Pascoe thought about it. Van der Heyden was right. Brazil was a hell of a lot safer than South Africa.

"All right," he said, "240 it is. But you can tell Mueller to put away his pop gun."

Lutz demurred with a slight bob of his head.

"Perhaps later, when I'm sure we're going in the right direction."

Pascoe seemed set to argue the point when van der Heyden laid a restraining hand on his arm.

"We've got to get out of here, Jonathan. Any minute now Benghazi could send out a general alert."

Pascoe accepted the wisdom of this. Besides, Lutz wasn't going to harm Hanna. Neither was he going to be allowed to make threats with impunity.

"You'd better watch your back, friend," said Pascoe, "because I might just take it into my head to break it."

The Catalina had been locked on to the Apapa radio beacon for the last five minutes. O'Keefe had descended to 2,000 feet and was watching his instruments when Caradoc screamed: *"Look. . . ."*

O'Keefe's reaction was the instinctive one of a fighter pilot. Fearing an airborne collision he threw the flying boat into a sideslip and winced as they yawed rudderless to starboard.

"What the fuck. . . ."

"Ten o'clock high," yelled Caradoc.

O'Keefe levelled up and tossed a quick glance to port. Several thousand feet above him, climbing rapidly and heading west, was a Sunderland—*the* Sunderland, it had to be. Benutti shouted from aft that he could see it too.

The fuel gauge was in the lower segment. About 300 miles left in the tanks, two hours flying time. But a Sunderland had the legs of a Catalina and the gap could not be closed. They would end up powerless in the Atlantic.

Bastard!

Forty minutes after landing, Flight Lieutenant Saunders was under close arrest and being interrogated by O'Keefe and Benutti in the presence of the base commander and two other officers. Caradoc and Greta had stayed with the Catalina, the NCO to supervise the aircraft's refuelling.

It had taken no time at all to establish who had authorized the gasoline bowser for Able Sugar Nine, and Saunders was now looking extremely frightened. Needless to say, he was more than willing to tell O'Keefe and Benutti all he knew.

"Boxes?" demanded the American. "What sort of boxes?"

"About so big, sir," stammered Saunders.

He made a shape with his hands.

"Wooden with rope handles at either end. Very heavy. I think I know what was in them."

"Go on."

"Bullion, sir. I think they contained gold."

O'Keefe looked at Benutti. It was all making a little more sense now, the reason a giant aircraft was needed.

"How heavy?" he asked Saunders. "How heavy and how many boxes?"

"We're wasting time. . . ."

"Shut up, Joe," said O'Keefe pleasantly. "How heavy and how many?" he repeated.

"About a hundred and fifty, two hundred. But I've no idea how heavy. I wasn't allowed to touch them."

"Make a guess. Could one man carry a single box or did it take two?"

"Sometimes one, sometimes two."

"Sixty or so pounds then," opined O'Keefe. "And multiply that by one-fifty or two hundred. . . ."

Benutti got the drift.

"Between eight and ten thousand pounds, four or five tons."

"Nearer four, which is going to reduce their air speed quite considerably."

"Pascoe let something, slip," offered Saunders, who could see what remained of his life being governed by warders. "He said that by daybreak they would be well on their way to Cape Town."

"Cape Town?" yelped Benutti.

"Another double shuffle," said O'Keefe. "Can we confirm that radar heading as 240, sir?" he asked the CO.

"We can."

"It has to be Brazil," said O'Keefe.

Before leaving the office he asked the CO for two things. First, that Ascension Island radar be requested to log all aircraft on a 240 heading; second, that he and Benutti be allowed to borrow a couple of Thompson submachine guns and a dozen spare magazines.

Outside, he said to Benutti, "Okay, we're an hour adrift, let's say ninety minutes by the time we're airborne. But the differential in aircraft performance doesn't matter any longer. The bullion or whatever the hell they've got aboard has taken care of that. What's more they've got a long way to go. Jonathan will be trying to conserve fuel so he'll keep his air speed down to 160 or so."

"And we've got 180 and no worry about gas."

"A bit more than that. If we chuck out everything we don't need, I can squeeze an extra 10 mph out of the engines. My mental arithmetic's a bit rusty, but providing the air frame can stand up to it, we should be on top of them within eight hours."

Twenty

They were flying at an altitude of 5,000 feet and were west of the Guinea Basin when Lutz reappeared on the flight deck.

"Watch your pockets," said Pascoe.

"Where are we?" asked the German.

Van der Heyden told him.

"Show me on the chart."

The South African spread it open on the navigation table and pointed with a pair of dividers

"About there."

"Excellent. Time to change course, I think."

"No, the heading's fine for Recife."

"I didn't say we were going to Brazil, van der Heyden. You assumed it."

"Oh Christ," groaned Pascoe, "more bloody games. He thinks this is a bus. Where's it to be this time, Lutz? Mexico? New York? How about Croydon? We can do a round trip plus five nights hotel for a gold brick."

"Your humour does you credit, Pascoe, but our destination is St Helena."

"Ignore him, Peter. Maybe he'll go away."

"St Helena," repeated Lutz.

It took a moment for Pascoe to realize the German was being serious.

"You're off your head. There's nothing there."

"Oh yes there is."

"Not for us. Go back to sleep, Lutz. I'll give you a call when we start getting samba music over the radio."

Lutz took it all in his stride.

"We shall all get along a lot better, Pascoe, if you do as you're told. I have no wish to harm Fräulein Baumann, but her continuing good health rests in your hands. Believe me, I am not a capricious person; our eventual destination was decided many years ago. Now we're airborne I'm willing to tell you where it is, but while we're arguing we're heading further west. So, a course for St Helena, if you please."

Pascoe looked up at van der Heyden.

"We've got to assume he knows what he's talking about," said the South African.

"Carver?"

From the engineer's berth Kane said, "We might as well listen. We don't have the fuel to dog-leg backwards and forwards."

Pascoe thought for a moment.

"All right," he said to van der Heyden, "give me a course for St Helena then take over the right-hand seat. It's about time Herr Lutz and I had a little chat."

Van der Heyden consulted the chart.

"Fly 160. I'll work out a more exact heading later."

Pascoe put the Sunderland into a sweeping bank to port. When he straightened up on 160 and van der Heyden was seated, he stood up and faced Lutz.

"All right, we're going to St Helena and I'm waiting to hear why. By the time we get there we'll have used up two-thirds of our fuel. The remaining third won't get us to South America or anywhere else. You'd better have something up your sleeve apart from freckles or we'll be on the island until the authorities pick us up. It's a British island, in case you've forgotten, and the US Air Force has a base just up the road on Ascension."

"Hardly that close," said Lutz calmly. "Ascension is 700 miles away."

"Two hours in the air for a fast fighter."

"I doubt if anyone will radio for fighters. We shall be landing at or about dusk in Manatee Bay and anchoring off Speery Island, which is little more than a small uninhabited rock half a mile from the mainland. No one will see us."

"And what they can't see neither can I." Pascoe made a gesture of disgust. "You're right, we'll be over St Helena around dusk and I don't know the channels. This is a bloody big aircraft and it needs a lot of room to land. If I hit anything we'll cartwheel to Africa."

"There's nothing to hit in Manatee Bay. You continue to underestimate me, Pascoe. As I said a moment ago, this is not caprice. St Helena was selected as the penultimate staging-post before the war. I'd have told you that at the beginning except doubtless you would have wasted time by raising objections. As you are now. There are occasions when it's better to act first and think afterwards."

"It may work like that in your army but I wouldn't call it much of a recommendation. In any case. . . ." Pascoe suddenly realized what Lutz had just said. "Wait a minute . . . What do you mean *penultimate* staging-post?"

"Our final destination is Argentina."

"*Argentina!* How the hell do you expect to get to Argentina with no gas in the tanks?"

"By U-boat."

It took a second or two to sink in, but eventually Pascoe said, "You'd better explain. I'm starting not to like the sound of this."

Lutz collected his thoughts. They had to be told—most of it.

"We've had an agent on St Helena since well before the war. In Germany we call them moles, though I understand Allied Intelligence refers to them as sleepers. He is an accepted member of that very small community and has not been required to act as a spy, use his radio, or jeopardize his cover in any manner. His one function was to wait until contacted, which I did before leaving Munich.

"There are several U-boats still operating out of friendly ports in Argentina, U-boats that did not surface when Germany surrendered and which your Intelligence people doubtless think were sent to the bottom.

"At a signal from my agent one of them will be despatched to rendezvous with us somewhere in mid-Atlantic. The coordinates are still to be decided. Naturally they could not be given earlier as the U-boat had no idea when we would arrive."

"Why mid-Atlantic?" asked Kane suspiciously. "If you've got a U-boat on tap, why doesn't it come all the way to St Helena?"

"Because that would be too dangerous. The rendezvous will be several hundred miles out to sea, somewhere away from the regular shipping lanes, where the transfer of the bullion can be accomplished at our leisure. If we are unfortunate enough to be seen when we land in Manatee Bay, a flying boat bearing RAF roundels will not cause much excitement. The same can hardly be said for a U-boat."

"You're out of your mind, Lutz," said Pascoe, "if you think we're going aboard a U-boat. There are easier ways of committing suicide."

"There will be no need for you to come aboard. The U-boat will be carrying aviation gasoline, enough to take you as far as Cape Horn if necessary."

"And what proof do we have of that?"

"None, I'm afraid. But as I see it neither do you have a choice."

"I've got all the choices. You're the one who's short of options. You're forgetting that I'm the only one who can fly this ship."

"And you're forgetting about Fräulein Baumann."

"No, I'm not."

Pascoe had had enough; Lutz was walking all over them.

"There's not one chance in fifty you'll harm her. If you do, I put this aircraft nose down into the Atlantic."

"I wonder if that's true."

"Don't wonder. You'll only get one shot at it and it'll be your last."

Lutz shrugged.

"I've no wish to play poker with you for such stakes, but if we don't rendezvous with the U-boat, what happens to us is a matter of total indifference to me. I take it you have a compromise?"

"That I do. We'll fly you to St Helena and I'll put the Sunderland safely on the deck. We'll contact the U-boat via your agent and arrange a time and place for the rendezvous. But if the sub isn't carrying aviation fuel, you're a dead man."

"Hold it," said van der Heyden over his shoulder. "We won't know one way or the other until it's too late."

"Oh yes we damn well will. After we make the rendezvous Lutz stays aboard the Sunderland. And he continues to stay aboard until we're refuelled."

"That's an absurd suggestion," protested the German.

"Not to me. Stowed aft are a couple of inflatable dinghies. We'll transfer the bullion and three-quarters of the diamonds to the U-boat while we're refuelling. When that exercise is complete, I'll taxi the flying boat some two miles away. At that point you'll be put into the Atlantic in a dinghy and we'll head for wherever takes our fancy. But if there's any non-sense from the U-boat, if the skipper tries to palm us off with low-grade gas or sink us, you can kiss Argentina goodbye. Take it or leave it, Lutz. If you don't like the idea you'd better say so now. But bear this in mind: to my way of thinking the only reason you'd turn me down is because you're planning some kind of doublecross. Either the sub's not carrying fuel or you intend to gyp us out of our share. I'll give you ten seconds. After that, I'm heading for Brazil."

Lutz didn't hesitate. He had not reached the rank of SS Colonel by fighting hopeless battles against determined opponents. Besides, anything could happen at the rendezvous.

"I agree," he said. "Perhaps you'll call me when we're in sight of St Helena. You're going to need some help setting down."

Pascoe stood at the head of the ladder until the German had descended it and disappeared aft. He was a cool one, Lutz.

"One for our side," he grinned at Kane. "Maybe I should take up poker as a recreation."

"I still don't trust him," said the Australian. "If you ask me the U-boat's no more carrying gas than I'm a ballerina."

Van der Heyden thought the German was telling the truth.

"Lutz is a belt and braces man. He'd make sure that sub was carrying fuel in case he had to get airborne in a hurry. Mind you, that's not to say he's going to let us walk off with a million quid in diamonds. We'd better not dump the bastard overboard until we're out of range of the U-boat's guns. This is a big ship. It would be hard to miss."

* * *

Several hours later, on the flight deck of the Catalina Mike O'Keefe was thinking along the same lines: that Ascension Island should have picked up the Sunderland before now. According to his readings the Catalina had flown 1,300 miles, which meant, at an average speed of 160 mph, that the Sunderland had covered 1,350, give or take a few. They were still too far behind to expect a sighting, but Ascension radar must have seen a blip.

"Try 'em again, Jim."

Via his own headphones O'Keefe heard Caradoc give the PBY's call sign and ask for strength of signal. A moment later an American voice said they were coming in loud and clear.

"Any sign of an unidentified ship on the 240 heading?" asked Caradoc.

"Nothing at all. Everything we've seen we've accounted for."

"Roger, Ascension. Out."

"I don't get it," said O'Keefe. "They can't have gone anywhere else. There's nowhere else to go."

"So what happens next?"

O'Keefe tapped the fuel gauge.

"What happens next is that we need topping up. Call Ascension again, Jim. Tell them we're coming down and that I'd appreciate the Radar Officer standing by."

While Caradoc stayed behind to see to the refuelling, O'Keefe, Benutti and Greta were taken by jeep to the main complex of the USAAF base.

The Radar Officer was in his mid-twenties and from Michigan. He introduced himself as Captain Anderson and looked at Greta appreciatively.

"The RAF flying co-educational these days?"

He was a little less flip when he realized she was German, but he was too well trained to ask questions.

Inside his office he gave them seats and poured each a cup of coffee from a fresh pot on his desk.

"Okay, gentlemen, I'm familiar with the problem and

under orders to give you all the help I can. Which isn't much."

He picked up the radar log.

"This is up to date as of 16:30 hours today. Everything heading west on a course anywhere near 240 has been marked with an asterisk and ticked when identified. As you can see, we've had no strays."

He passed the log to O'Keefe, who ran his eyes down it.

"Isn't it unusual to be able to identify every aircraft?" asked Benutti. "I mean, don't you sometimes get radio malfunctions?"

"We do," admitted Anderson, "though it doesn't happen all that often. I understand you're not a flier, Major?"

"You understand right, though I reckon I've done enough in the last twenty-four hours to qualify for some kind of award."

Anderson smiled politely.

"Then if you're not a flier, Major, you won't understand the seriousness of a malfunctioning radio. To a pilot it's like losing a lung. He can't tell us where he is and any problems he might have, and we can't advise him on weather conditions, navigational hazards, and so on. I've known pilots who'd rather lose an engine than their wireless. In any case, if you're suggesting that we might have overlooked something on 240 because we couldn't raise them by radio-telephone, that hasn't happened. Take a look for yourself."

O'Keefe passed the log to Benutti.

"I don't get it. The Sunderland would have had to damn near overfly Ascension en route to Brazil. You wouldn't need radar. A good pair of binoculars and a keen eye would have done the trick."

"Isn't it possible you've made a mistake?" asked Anderson. "I haven't been told why I'm to co-operate and I'm not trying to make waves, but have you got definite proof the Sunderland was heading for Brazil?"

O'Keefe shook his head.

"Not definite proof, an educated guess. I don't think I'm violating the Official Secrets Act when I tell you that the people we're after are Nazis and that the safest place for the remnants of the Third Reich is South America. Add to that the fact that they took off from West Africa flying 240 and I don't see where else they could have gone. A Sunderland will do 3,000 miles on full tanks. From Apapa to north-east Brazil is roughly that distance. They don't have the fuel for stooging around."

"It could have been a bluff, 240," said Anderson.

O'Keefe had already considered this, especially as Jonathan had used the same tactic at Benghazi.

"No," he said, "they weren't expecting to be followed. As far as they're concerned there's no one on their tail."

Benutti glanced up from the log.

"What are these two items here?" he asked Anderson. "Top of the page and four down. They're both marked UI, which I presume means unidentified."

Anderson frowned at the entries.

"Yeah, you're right, Major. They're both logged as unidentified but neither was flying 240. The top one seems to have come on the screen from the south-east heading north-west. Whichever way you look at it that one couldn't have come from Apapa. The other one. . . ." He shrugged, puzzled. "Well, yes, this does appear to be flying an eccentric course."

"How so?" asked O'Keefe.

"It was first logged at the extreme range of the tube heading 245," answered Anderson. "Then it suddenly veered off on 160."

"It's not marked with an asterisk," Benutti accused, "and 245, for my money, is as close as dammit for an unidentified ship."

Anderson shifted uncomfortably.

"I guess the operator didn't bother because of the change of course." He scratched his head. "But Christ, it's a damn funny way to fly, dog-legging about the Atlantic like that. What's more it's not going to get him anywhere except maybe St Helena, where there's no airstrip anyway."

O'Keefe and Benutti looked at one another.

"Let's see a map," said O'Keefe.

It became obvious immediately. 160 led nowhere but St Helena, and St Helena was only accessible by flying boat.

"It was my fault," said O'Keefe, mentally kicking himself. "I was so convinced they were going to Brazil that I didn't even consider anywhere else. But it still doesn't make any sense. They'll have flown 2,000 miles by the time they get there and that doesn't leave them enough gas to get anywhere unless they tank up. . . ."

It hit them both simultaneously but Benutti got it out first.

"*A U-boat!* They're going to rendezvous with a bloody U-boat!"

It had to be. They were going to rendezvous with something anyway, and Germany had no surface vessels left in the South Atlantic.

"How soon can you get us clearance for take-off?" O'Keefe asked Anderson.

"Any time you're ready, but I wouldn't advise it. Take a peek outside."

It was about thirty minutes off dusk and St Helena was four hours away in a Catalina.

Benutti let rip an oath of frustration, cursing that they'd lost them. O'Keefe wasn't so sure.

"When will the Sunderland get to St Helena?"

Anderson checked the radar log for the time of the course change to 160.

"How fast would it be flying?"

"About 230 mph."

"Then they'll be setting down about now."

"And Lutz still has to contact the U-boat."

O'Keefe was thinking out loud.

"It could be submerged a few miles off the island but that doesn't seem likely. What does is that they've got to go searching for it or it for them, maybe a bit of both. Either way they're not going to try it in darkness, not with limited fuel. What time's sunrise in this part of the world?"

"5.53," answered Anderson. "There's also a three-quarters moon for most of the night."

"Then that settles it," said O'Keefe. "We can assume that they won't take off before dawn but we can't guarantee it. And if we lose them this time we've lost them for good. We've got to get there at least an hour before sunrise, preferably ninety minutes."

"And circle?" asked Anderson.

"And put down."

"That's asking the impossible."

"Maybe not. Do you have anyone on the base who can brief me on the waters around St Helena? I'll need currents, tides, hazards, perhaps a guess where something as big as a Sunderland would land."

"Half a dozen pilots, but I can answer those questions myself. If you want a flat stretch of water with no obstructions, Manatee Bay in the south is the best if not the only place."

"Good. You can show me on the map later. In the meantime, I'd like your engineers to rig me up a couple of extra searchlights on the Catalina like so."

O'Keefe sketched his requirements on the desk blotter.

"They're to converge thirty feet above the deck."

Anderson studied the drawing.

"No problem, but haven't I seen something like this before?"

"Probably. Wing Commander Guy Gibson used the same technique on the Dams Raid in 1943, to release the Barnes Wallis bombs precisely sixty feet above the water."

"And you're going to use it to set the Catalina down?"

"That's the theory."

Benutti picked up the blotter.

"Let's hope it's a bloody sight more than that."

They had spotted the tiny speck that was St Helena fifteen minutes ago. It was a fair piece of navigation by any standards, for the island was barely nine miles long by six wide, one-third the size of the Isle of Wight. As dusk closed in it would have taken no more than a minor course error to have missed it completely and the next stop was Tristan da Cunha, 1,500 miles further south.

Although Lutz had visited the island only once before, in 1937, he had done his homework thoroughly before leaving

Germany and remembered enough of the terrain to be able to draw Pascoe a rough map.

The capital and only town was Jamestown, named after King James II, on the north-west coast. There and in the Longwood area, to the east, were concentrated most of the island's 4,000-odd souls. There was very little south of Longwood, a few tiny hamlets and isolated homesteads.

The main navigational hazards were in the centre: Mount Actaeon and Diana's Peak, 2,685 and 2,700 feet respectively. Manatee Bay lay to the south, midway between Man and Horse Cliffs and Speery Island. The coast of West Africa was 1,200 miles east and that of South America roughly twice that distance west. It was little wonder that the British had dumped Napoleon Bonaparte here after his defeat at Waterloo. St Helena was no Elba. This time the Little Corporal would not escape.

In spite of earlier misgivings Pascoe found that Lutz had given him an accurate picture of Manatee Bay. After wave-hopping once up and down to ensure that there was no driftwood or any other obstructions in his landing path, he put the Sunderland on the water. Ten minutes later they were anchored in the lee of Speery Island.

As it grew dark it was possible to see that St Helena appeared as dead as the far side of the moon. There were one or two lights down coast, but that was all.

It took a few minutes' debate to decide who was to go ashore and who was to stay with the flying boat, but eventually just Hanna and her father were left behind, guarded by Scheringer.

Van der Heyden had the last word. While inflating the dinghy he said, "We're going to look bloody sick if your agent's done a bunk."

Twenty-one

A small two-storey house loomed up out of the darkness. The ground-floor curtains or blinds were drawn, but through a v-shaped chink lights could be seen.

Once ashore, Lutz, aided by torches carried by Mueller and himself, had led the party half a mile down coast to a point where a narrow path ran upwards through a fissure in the cliffs. Here they were 600 feet high, and at the head of the path stood the agent's house. His cover was that of a former chemist who had sold his business in Scotland before the war and migrated to St Helena to get away from it all. He spoke perfect English and his sleeper name was Macdonald. He had indeed lived in Edinburgh for a time and was trained as a chemist. His funds, however, came from Bureau IV, the Gestapo, of the RSHA, the Reich Central Security Office.

"Wait here," said Lutz. "If he sees all six of us at once he may panic."

"If he can see anything at all he's got the eyes of a damned cat," muttered van der Heyden to no one in particular.

Lutz walked forward and knocked on the front door. After a moment it opened and a flood of light spilled out, illuminating both Lutz and the man in the doorway. They held a short conversation before Lutz turned and beckoned.

There were two rooms on the ground floor, one serving as a kitchen and dining-room, the other as a sitting-room. The former was heated by a large wood-burning stove.

Macdonald turned out to be a shrunken, bespectacled individual of indeterminate years, though at a guess he was in his late fifties. He licked his lips nervously when he saw the RAF uniforms, but he said nothing. Neither did Lutz make any introductions. What Macdonald didn't know couldn't hurt any of them.

"Where's the radio?" asked Lutz in English.

"Upstairs," answered Macdonald.

"And the aerial?"

"Upstairs also, back in its crate."

"How long will it take to erect?"

Macdonald shrugged his narrow shoulders.

"Working in the dark, perhaps a couple of hours."

"So long?"

"It's cumbersome. It's not very big, but it's unwieldy."

"What about the tuning?"

"That should be easy enough. Fortunately we are in a good position here. Nevertheless, it will take time."

"Then we'd better get started."

Aboard the Sunderland, Scheringer was dozing near the for'ard hatch. Further aft in the galley, Hanna and her father were each sipping a mug of hot chocolate. For the first time in as long as either of them could remember, they were free to talk without being overheard.

"I don't think they intend letting us go alive," said Hanna, keeping her voice down. She could still feel Mueller's gun pressing against her temple.

"Sooner or later Lutz will try to kill us all."

Her father was feeling his years. The pace of the last few days was taking its toll. He was regretting ever becoming involved with Lutz. He should have gone to the British in Tripoli and turned Lutz in. At least Hanna would be safe.

"We must trust Jonathan and his friends."

"They have one eye on the gold, the other on Lutz. They can't be everywhere at once."

"Agreed, but there's nothing we can do about it."

"Perhaps not."

Baumann looked at his daughter over the rim of his mug. "Only perhaps . . . ?"

Hanna put a finger to her lips and got to her feet. She

fumbled in a cupboard beneath the sink and produced something wrapped in a towel.

"What is it?"

She showed him the Very pistol, fully loaded.

"I found it soon after we left Benghazi. I know what it is because I've seen them before."

Baumann touched her hand gently.

"You must be careful, Hanna."

"I will."

It was after midnight before the aerial was rigged. The radio was an Afu, acronym from the word *Agentenfunk* or agent radio. It was a hand-keyed Morse apparatus the size of a suitcase, tuned by quartz to a single, pre-set frequency and powered by a 10-watt battery. The tuning was not always accurate and had a tendency to drift, especially after lengthy storage.

Macdonald, too, was a little rusty after so many years inactivity, but he could still send and receive at twenty-five words a minute. To begin with he sent a series of Vs, the warm-up operation which flexes the sender's wrist and allows the receiver to tune in.

"Just send my name twice," said Lutz.

He and Macdonald were alone in the latter's bedroom. The radio had no headphones; any answer would be relayed through the speaker. It took three attempts but finally they heard it. To Lutz it meant nothing, but Macdonald grunted with satisfaction.

"Strength four," he said. "They're standing by."

Lutz chose his words carefully.

"Tell them I'm on St Helena with the cargo and that I need a rescue craft within twelve hours. The range of my aircraft is 1,000 miles maximum."

Macdonald tapped out the message and translated the reply into clear. "They're asking us to wait."

Lutz waited. On a table he had spread out a chart of the South Atlantic.

Five minutes elapsed before the speaker burst into life again.

"Figures," said Macdonald unnecessarily, and began writing.

When the operator at the other end finished Macdonald tapped his own key and read from the scratch pad.

"They can pick you up at noon or thereabouts at coordinates Longitude 17° 15′ West, Latitude 18° 15′ South."

Lutz consulted the chart. Very roughly—Pascoe could work out the precise location later—the position given was 600 miles south-west of St Helena.

Perfect.

"Signal that that is acceptable. Tell them to be on the surface for a final visual. You'd better also tell them that we'll be arriving in a Sunderland carrying RAF markings."

Macdonald sent the signal and jotted down the response. Without batting an eyelid he said, "They're glad you told them. The last time the skipper of the rendezvous craft saw a Sunderland it was bombing him."

The speaker crackled again. Macdonald looked less happy when he read out this message.

"They're asking for someone to remain on watch in case there's a last-minute hitch."

"Can you do that?"

"Yes—but the aerial must be dismantled before dawn."

"It will be."

Downstairs Lutz showed the three fliers the chart.

"Noon," said Pascoe. "Noon will mean taking off after daybreak, say 08:30. Flight time will be about three hours, but we haven't got the fuel to stay airborne if the U-boat's late. We're bound to be seen," he added.

"It doesn't matter," said Lutz. "At least, there's nothing we can do about it. We'll stay here the night and return to the Sunderland at dawn."

At 00:25 O'Keefe pulled back on the control column and the Catalina was airborne. The night was clear and according to the almanac the moon was due to rise in thirty-five minutes, setting at 06:45 hours. It was to be three-quarters full and would be an invaluable aid to navigation. E.t.a. St Helena, 04:25.

Somewhere in the small hours Pascoe got up from his sleeping berth near the stove to relieve himself. There were no indoor water closet facilities and he could not find the outdoor cubicle. He did what was necessary well away from the house.

Overhead there hung a bomber's moon, though why the RAF and the Luftwaffe had ever called it that was beyond him. Certainly it was as bright as a winter afternoon. Over to his left he could see the Sunderland moored in the lee of Speery Island. But what was sauce for the goose was sauce for the gander. The bomber could see the target but the night fighter could see the bomber.

Still, all that was over now. This time tomorrow he, van der Heyden and Kane, Hanna and old man Baumann, would be making for pastures new.

At 04:21 according to the cabin clock, Caradoc saw the 2,700 feet of Diana's Peak exactly where it should be, ten miles off the port beam, bathed in moonlight. He tapped O'Keefe on the shoulder, but O'Keefe had already seen the mountain. He grinned at Caradoc and gave him the thumbs-up sign.

The original plan was to fly round the island once in an anti-clockwise direction at 4,000 feet, but this proved unnecessary. As the Catalina overflew Manatee Bay from the west, Caradoc pointed downwards. The huge bulk of the Sunderland, moored in the lee of a rock they knew to be Speery Island, was unmistakable.

"Tell the others," said O'Keefe, fighting back his excitement. "Tell them we've found her and we're going down."

Awake by the front door of the house, Fischer heard the plane go over but paid no attention to it. His function, Lutz had told him in private, was to ensure that Pascoe didn't get ambitious during the dark hours and make for the Sunderland.

It was flying low, he noted, but what of it? There was nowhere an aircraft could land on St Helena.

O'Keefe had made a long sweep to starboard and was again approaching Manatee Bay from the west. Five miles out at 500 feet he switched on the fuselage searchlights. He had tested them on Ascension, made a couple of practice landings there, and they had worked perfectly. He had put the Catalina on the water with hardly a jolt even without the help of the moon.

Four miles out at 300 feet he gave the aircraft a little starboard rudder to keep him well away from the coastal cliffs. "Man and Horse", he remembered they were called, so named because a rider and his mount once fell into the sea there.

Two miles out and with the altimeter reading 200 feet, O'Keefe reluctantly dragged his eyes away from the instrument and concentrated on the slowly converging searchlights. It was his intention to land at the western extremity of the bay and taxi to a point where the Catalina would be out of sight of the Sunderland behind a headland, about 1,000 yards from Speery Island.

In the co-pilot's seat there was little Caradoc could do to help. Further aft, braced against the bulkhead, Benutti and Greta could do even less.

O'Keefe gave the searchlights his undivided attention, willing them to converge. The moonlit sea was rushing past the fuselage at a terrifying rate of knots and Speery Island looming larger by the second. He risked a quick glance at his air speed indicator. It was perched on stalling and they were still in excess of thirty feet above the bay. Beside him Caradoc had his fists clenched without knowing it.

Feet, fractions of feet, inches, centimetres. With a sluggishness that was agonizing the searchlights met.

Reacting instantly, O'Keefe pushed the control column forward. A moment later spray lashed the canopy and they were down, decelerating rapidly. A slight bump, a lurch, an unprogrammed swing to port swiftly corrected, and they were on the sea.

O'Keefe throttled back and flicked on the taxi-ing lights. If anyone was aboard the Sunderland, surely to God they would have heard the Catalina land.

Scheringer had but thought it was part of his dream. Images of aeroplanes were a regular feature of his sleeping hours nowadays.

Lying awake on her bunk Hanna, too, thought she had caught the sound of motors, but finally she put it down to wishful thinking.

In the house they had heard nothing.

With all switches off and the Catalina secure behind the headland, O'Keefe and Caradoc went aft to where Benutti and Greta were waiting.

"I kept telling myself," cracked the American, "that if it worked on the Möhne and Eder dams, it would work here. But there were moments when I had my doubts."

"You should have been up the sharp end," said O'Keefe. "Do you reckon they heard us?"

Benutti said he didn't.

"Or we'd have been getting some flak by now. As I remember it, the Sunderland's fully armed with nine people aboard. That's more than enough to man each machine with a few over."

"Don't think I've forgotten," muttered O'Keefe. "Two Thompsons aren't going to be a lot of use if we're spotted. We're going to have to move like lightning, the pair of us."

Benutti's expression revealed his puzzlement.

"The pair of us . . . ?"

But Greta understood.

"You're not leaving me behind."

"And what about me?" asked Caradoc.

"We can't leave the Catalina unmanned," explained O'Keefe. "That would be asking for trouble. Someone has to stay at the controls, and that means you, Jim. Do you think you can handle it?"

Caradoc nodded.

"I think so. I've followed every move you've made since Benghazi. I think I could take her up and put her down again if necessary. But I don't see why you have to board the Sunderland. Why don't we just sit tight and make it clear that we'll blow it out of the water if it makes a move?"

"Because that way it's a Mexican stand-off," answered Benutti. "Lutz is not going to wait around while we radio Ascension for assistance. He'll try to get out and then we're involved in a firefight."

"Right," said O'Keefe, "though we may not be able to avoid that. In any case," he said to Caradoc, "as soon as it's daylight I want you to taxi round the headland and take up a position opposite the Sunderland. Whether we're back or not, if she makes any attempt to unstick that's your cue to open up. You use the Catalina as a mobile gun platform and make sure the Sunderland does not take off. Have you got that?"

Caradoc looked uncomfortable.

"Even if you're still aboard?"

"That's what I said. If we're not back or we haven't made you some kind of signal, we'll probably be dead. If we're alive the Sunderland's not going anywhere. You've got to promise me you'll do it, Jim. I know it's a hell of a responsibility, but Lutz mustn't get away."

Caradoc knew it was futile to argue. Reluctantly he said he would do whatever was necessary.

"Thanks," said O'Keefe. He slapped Caradoc on the shoulder, "Don't worry about it, nothing's going to happen to us."

"I don't think the man's read the small print," said Benutti.

"Stay behind if you like. I can always take Greta."

"You're taking Greta anyway," said the German girl.

She glared at O'Keefe belligerently.

Benutti put his two cents in.

"I don't want to sound callous or make out I'm taking sides, but she has a right, Mike. She might also be our ace in the hole. Lutz is going to be side-swiped when he sees her and those couple of seconds may be the difference between coming out covered in glory or coming out covered in manure. It's nine to two against. We're going to need all the help we can get."

"Goddammit," snapped O'Keefe, "this is a conspiracy. She'll be in the way. She'll be unarmed and a bloody liability."

"I won't." Greta's voice was totally without emotion. "I will neither be in the way nor a liability, and I'm owed this. You were happy enough to accept my help when you needed it. You'll have to take it now when you don't. I'm coming with you and there's nothing you can do to stop me."

O'Keefe counted to ten before shaking his head. It was her life.

"Please yourself," he said, "but don't expect preferential treatment. If you stop a bullet that's your hard luck."

"Don't sugar it," said Benutti, "give it to her straight."

Fifteen minutes later the dinghy was in the water, O'Keefe on the port paddle, Benutti on the starboard. Caradoc watched them leave before going up to the flight deck.

Two hundred yards away from the massive bulk of the Sunderland, O'Keefe peered into the darkness for any sign of life. There was none.

The flying boat's bows were facing east. Jonathan had evidently landed from the west, using the length of Manatee Bay, as O'Keefe had done in the Catalina.

One hundred yards. . . .

Fifty. . . .

Ten. . . .

Then the dinghy was alongside the huge port float.

O'Keefe held his breath as he sculled towards the for'ard hatch. It was closed.

He would have to take a chance here. If everyone was aboard who should be, opening the hatch without preamble was asking for trouble. If he announced his presence, that would alert the occupants. It was no choice at all, but the odds were marginally in favour of the second alternative.

He signalled his intentions to Benutti before hammering on the bulkhead.

"Come on," he roared in German, "open the bloody hatch!"

On the inside Scheringer awoke with a start, wondering

where all the noise was coming from. Then it registered: Lutz was back.

He swung open the hatch and found himself staring into the muzzle of O'Keefe's Thompson.

Ten minutes later, with dawn less than three-quarters of an hour off, O'Keefe knew the whole story of what had transpired since Lutz landed in Tripoli. The Baumanns were more than eager to talk.

O'Keefe brushed aside Herr Baumann's questions. Both he and his daughter may have changed the colour of their coats now but in the beginning they had sided with Lutz, however reluctantly.

"Where did they go and when will they be back?" he asked Hanna.

She said she didn't know but that Scheringer did.

The former SS Hauptsturmfuehrer was being covered by Greta with Benutti's Thompson. She was holding it in a manner which suggested she knew where the trigger was. The American was aft, examining the bullion boxes.

"You just wouldn't believe the stuff they've got stashed here," he called. "You could mount a revolution with it."

"Don't get greedy, Joe. It doesn't belong to us."

Benutti came for'ard.

"Well, that's a thought, you know, isn't it? Why shouldn't it belong to us?"

Now that Scheringer was well and truly covered by Greta and showed little sign of fight anyway, O'Keefe had grounded his Thompson. Benutti picked it up, casually.

"I mean," he went on, "what's to stop us taxi-ing over to the Catalina, transferring the loot, and heading out? To hell with Lutz, to hell with Pascoe. There's enough back there to keep us in luxury for the rest of our lives."

O'Keefe stared at him.

"You must be out of your mind."

"Fortunately I'm not." Benutti swung the Thompson up in

an easy arc until the muzzle was pointed at O'Keefe's midriff. "Neither is Greta."

"I haven't been risking my neck just for Lutz, Mike," said the German girl. "No man is worth that much hate."

Twenty-two

Something seemed to have happened to O'Keefe's vocal cords.

"I don't believe it," he managed to croak.

"You will, Mike, you will," said Benutti. "Do you know how to use a tommy gun?" he asked Greta.

"Not really, but I suppose if I point it and pull the trigger something will happen."

"Good girl. For a start you can go and point it at the dinghy we came across in. I don't want Lutz seeing it when he gets back. If I can't persuade O'Keefe here to fly us out, we're going to need Pascoe. Hurry it up."

Greta went for'ard. A moment later those in the galley heard a short burst of gunfire. Then Greta reappeared.

"It's gone."

"Good. Any sign of life out there?"

"Not yet."

Benutti waved his own Thompson at O'Keefe and Scheringer, motioning them to join Hanna and her father on the far side of the galley.

"And don't try anything, Mike. I don't want to shoot you, but I will if you give me cause."

O'Keefe's head was still spinning.

"When did the two of you plan all this?"

"From the beginning," answered Benutti. "As the fräulein said a moment ago, hatred is not a good enough reason to chase a man halfway across the world."

O'Keefe didn't understand.

"From what beginning? You didn't know the bullion existed until Apapa."

"Wrong, Mike. Tell him."

"I've known about it for several years," said Greta. "Oh, I didn't know how much or where, but when you're as close to someone as I was to Lutz there aren't many mysteries left. A whispered conversation here, a telephone call there. A scribbled note left on a desk. I knew there was a fortune hidden away, but I expected to share in it. I didn't know Lutz was going to leave me in Germany."

Greta's eyes glittered with loathing. She might not be willing to admit it, but there was more in this for her than the money.

Benutti took up the story.

"Greta came to see me the night she was attacked in Munich. She slept at our headquarters, remember? She told me the whole story, chapter and verse. It sounded wild, but what had I got to lose? Lutz was wanted for war crimes. If we caught up with him before he reached the loot, I'd be bumped up to bird colonel. If it was afterwards, Major Joseph Benutti, US 7th Army, would drop quietly out of sight and spend the rest of his young life drinking champagne. I wanted to let you in on the deal, but Greta vetoed the idea on the grounds that you were too straight. I guess she was right, huh?"

It all fell into place for O'Keefe. Benutti's change of attitude in Munich, his insistence that they kept after Lutz themselves; Greta refusing to be left behind.

"You won't get away with it," he said. "You can't fly this aircraft and even if you persuade Jonathan to do so, you haven't got enough fuel to reach the mainland. There's also the small matter of Jim Caradoc. If you try to take off, he'll blow you to bits."

"Not with you aboard."

"You don't know Caradoc. He'll do what I told him to."

"We'll see. Anyway, that's the least of my worries. Top of the list for the moment is to prepare a welcoming committee for Lutz. Unless you want to change your mind and taxi over to the Catalina?"

"Go to hell."

"Please yourself, but you're making it harder on everyone."

Benutti turned to Scheringer and broke into German.

"Right, Fritz, I'm going to ask you once and once only what Lutz's plans are. If I don't think you're telling me the truth I'm going to shoot off your left kneecap. Then your right kneecap. So start talking."

Scheringer's English was good enough to have followed most of the dialogue between Benutti and O'Keefe. He didn't think the American was bluffing.

He told Benutti about Macdonald and how a rendezvous was being arranged with a U-boat.

"What about Pascoe and the others? Do they go aboard the U-boat as well?"

"No. They will be given their share and the Sunderland refuelled in mid-ocean. Then we shall go our separate ways."

Benutti snorted with disbelief.

"Are you trying to tell me that Lutz is going to let the RAF walk off with a percentage of the loot?"

"He may have no choice. Pascoe is a clever man. In any case, a fifth of our cache will hardly affect the SS one way or the other."

"How's that again? The SS? Maybe you're out of touch, friend, but the war's over. There isn't an SS any more."

"Perhaps not now, but there will be. The Lagos cache is one of many. It will be used to form the foundation of our Movement in Argentina."

"Then one day the Fourth Reich, right? Jesus Christ, you guys never learn, do you. But it makes my job easier."

Benutti smiled cynically at O'Keefe.

"I knew there'd be a bright side to this if I looked hard enough. By relieving Lutz of the booty we'll be making the world safer for democracy. What do you say, eh, Mike? Let's take the money and run."

"It's starting to get light," warned Greta.

"Okay. Keep your eyes on the shoreline. Let me know if you see anything."

Benutti focused his attention on Hanna.

"Now if I heard you correctly earlier, you're Pascoe's girl."

Hanna admitted she was.

"Well, that's just fine. It was starting to bother me how I'o convince him to fly us out of here, but now there's no problem."

"Jonathan won't do anything with a gun pointed at his head," said O'Keefe. "You don't know him."

"It's not at *his* head I'll be pointing it."

"You still don't stand a chance."

O'Keefe made one last effort to reason with Benutti. In a little while Lutz and the others would be back. It would be too late then.

"For God's sake forget it, Joe," he pleaded. "Do that and we'll pretend it never happened. We can put Lutz and his cronies in the bag as we originally intended, and that's an end to it. Look how the odds are stacked against you if you can't see it any other way. Apart from Caradoc there's Lutz himself. You've got no guarantees he'll go along with anything you suggest and there are a lot more of them than there are of you and Greta. Finally there's me. I'm not going to sit back while you screw everything up. You're going to have to deal with me sooner or later and I don't think you've got the backbone to shoot me in cold blood."

"Maybe not," said Benutti, "but let's take those points one by one. Caradoc I can't do anything about. He may open fire, he may not. But this is a lot of aircraft you keep telling me. It outguns the Catalina six ways from Sunday. If it comes to a firefight, we're in with a chance.

"Then there's you. I'm at a bit of a loss to know what to do with you, but I guess you come along for the ride. I'll dump you somewhere in South America. By the time you get in touch with anyone who counts, I'll be long gone.

"Lastly there's Lutz and his merry band of pilgrims. The way I see it Lutz is the only one I need. He knows where the U-boat is and can handle the refuelling. Maybe I'll let him take some of the loot as compensation. I don't know yet. I'll have to play it by ear. But the other krauts aren't wanted on voyage. They're dead, which is something else I'm doing for democracy, saving it the cost of a trial and a hangman."

Scheringer had followed every word of this and protested loudly.

"So you understand English, do you," said Benutti. "Well, that's unfortunate, but maybe I'll include you among the survivors if you behave yourself. Can you think of anything I haven't covered?" he asked O'Keefe. "Apart from the RAF, I mean. I don't think I'll get much flak from them, not when I up whatever their original share was."

"There's something happening on shore," called Greta urgently.

Benutti checked the time. It was 5:46, seven minutes off sunrise.

"Any sign of the Catalina?"

"No."

"Right. Then keep these four covered. If they bat an eyelid or cough without permission, pull that trigger."

"Where will you be?"

"In the for'ard hatch. Pay no attention to what's going on up front, no matter what you hear. Your job's to watch this bunch. Got it?"

Greta nodded. She was pale and tense but there was no disputing the determined set of her jaw.

Benutti disappeared for'ard. O'Keefe made a slight movement but stopped when Greta swung the Thompson in his direction.

"Don't doubt me, Mike. I'll do it."

Mueller and Fischer were at the oars. When the dinghy was a hundred yards from Speery Island, the stillness of the dawn was shattered by the sound of aircraft engines. Seconds later the Catalina poked its nose round the headland.

Lutz knew he had not imagined machine gun fire a little while ago.

"Faster!" he screamed.

Caradoc feathered the props. Through his binoculars he could see the two oarsmen straining at their paddles. It occurred to him that he could wipe out the occupants of the dinghy with a couple of bursts. The range was only 800 yards.

He realized that his hand was hovering over the firing button and slowly he removed it. It was a worrying situation, not knowing what was going on in the Sunderland, but he was not in the business of shooting unarmed men. Not when three of them were in RAF uniform.

Tight against the bulkhead Benutti waited until the dinghy was a dozen feet from the Sunderland before putting the tommy gun through the hatch and firing a short burst in the air.

The effect was electrifying. Where a moment earlier he had been listening to muffled curses in English and German, now there was total silence as the baffled occupants of the dinghy tried to work out the meaning of this new threat.

Benutti didn't give them a chance to gather their wits about them.

"I'm going to say this just once," he shouted in English. "There are six of you out there and I want to see six handguns go into the water right now. If any one of you tries to be a hero, I'm going to lower my sights a few feet."

They couldn't see him, he was sure of that, but he could see them. He counted the splashes. Five. The blonde man—obviously Lutz—was the last to comply.

Six.

"You're to come aboard in the following order," he told them. "Lutz, Pascoe, van der Heyden, Kane. The other two Germans will bring up the rear. Start now. I'm giving you ten seconds. If I don't see any action I'll assume you're planning something."

"We'd better do as he says," muttered van der Heyden.

Fischer was not so sure. He didn't like the piece about the other two Germans bringing up the rear.

"We could rush him. . . ." he began, but Lutz shut him up with a gesture.

"Don't be a fool. He's got a machine gun and we can only go through the hatch one at a time."

"And we don't know how many of them there are," added Pascoe.

"Your ten seconds are up."

"We're coming aboard," called Lutz.

Benutti stood back from the hatch and Lutz scrambled through.

"Get over there, facing the bulkhead. Any funny business and you'll be shaking hands with your Fuehrer in that big bunker in the sky."

At intervals of a few seconds Pascoe, van der Heyden and Kane climbed inside.

Benutti stepped into the hatch as Mueller was about to take his turn.

"Sorry, gentlemen, but we're full up."

The Thompson Benutti was carrying was the M1928 version and held a 50-round drum of .45 calibre ammo firing at a cyclic rate of 800 rpm or approximately thirteen rounds per second. Benutti squeezed the trigger for 1.5 seconds.

The gun bucked in his hands. Of the twenty rounds fired only six struck their intended targets, but they were enough. Both Mueller and Fischer were dead before they hit the water.

Benutti swung the barrel in an arc to cover the four men against the bulkhead.

"Get moving," he said. "Head for the galley. Two of you have got a couple of old friends back there."

Thirty seconds later Lutz knew he was in the middle of a nightmare, that the girl holding a second submachine gun could not possibly be Greta Hoegel.

"Welcome aboard our South American flight, Herr Standartenfuehrer," she said.

There was a temptation to put a bullet in him, but she knew she had to keep her anger under lock and key until Lutz's usefulness was at an end.

Not so O'Keefe. Lutz was first into the galley and O'Keefe recognized him instantly in spite of the intervening years. This was the bastard who had murdered sixteen airmen in cold blood, as well as the Benghazi guard. God knows how many other deaths he had chalked up against his name.

Not caring that he might get killed in the attempt, O'Keefe launched himself at the German, bellowing like a madman.

At the back of the Indian file Benutti could see what was going on but could do nothing about it.

"Don't shoot!" he shouted. If Greta let fly within the narrow confines of the galley, she would almost certainly hit Lutz as well as O'Keefe.

The girl took the only other option open to her. She reversed her grip on the tommy gun and hit O'Keefe across the back of the skull with the butt. He went down without a whimper.

Benutti saw his advantage slipping away, but fortunately for him Pascoe, Kane and van der Heyden were too shocked to do much more than gape.

He pushed past them and stood alongside Greta.

"All right," he said, "let's all calm down before someone gets really hurt."

Lutz struggled to his feet, clutching his throat.

"Is that man insane?"

"Not exactly," answered Benutti. "Just trying to even the score for something you did to him a long time ago."

"I've never seen him before in my life."

Benutti looked at Jonathan.

"Are you Pascoe?"

"Yes."

"Then maybe you've got a better memory for faces than Lutz."

O'Keefe had fallen face downwards. Benutti turned him over with his foot.

"Jesus Christ," said Pascoe.

Five minutes later on the flight deck, Benutti was dictating terms to Lutz. The three fliers were locked in the for'ard starboard lavatory, where Pascoe, considerably shaken, was explaining who O'Keefe was. Greta remained in the galley, watching over the others. She had strict instructions to keep well away from O'Keefe when he came round.

Benutti had not bothered to inform Lutz how he and Greta came to be aboard the Sunderland. He was concerned only with the immediate situation and the urgency of it.

"The way I read it is this. You've got an aeroplane, a pilot, a fortune in gold and diamonds, and a refuelling rendezvous with a U-boat. I've got you. We could spend a few hours arguing with each other or trying to outfox each other, but we haven't got the time.

"We can't hang around here. This bloody aircraft is too conspicuous and maybe Ascension will send a couple of fighters to take a look-see before long. Then there's the Catalina. The pilot has instructions to sink us if we move. He may decide to do so anyway if he doesn't hear from O'Keefe. So, we make a deal."

"What sort of deal?"

"The sort that gives half the booty to the Fourth Reich and half to the combined forces of the RAF and the US 7th Army, namely me."

"Half is an insane fraction. The original agreement was a fifth."

Benutti sighed heavily.

"This is precisely what we haven't got time to argue about or there's going to be nothing to share. The original contract is null and void. *Kaput.* You're at the wrong end of a submachine gun and your bargaining powers are zilch."

"Perhaps more than you think. This aircraft doesn't have enough fuel to make a landfall. Your only hope is the U-boat and I control that."

Benutti was prepared for this response.

"There's always the Catalina. If we can't do business I'll have a quiet word with the RAF and see if we can figure out a method of boarding her. It will be risky, but that won't concern you. Or Scheringer. You'll both be dead."

Remembering Mueller and Fischer, Lutz didn't think the American was bluffing. For the moment he would have to agree terms.

"It seems I have no choice but to accept your offer. Two things bother me, however. The first is Fräulein Hoegel."

"Leave her to me. Sure she'd like to kill you—so would I in her place. But the stakes being what they are, she's not going to rock the boat."

That made sense.

"What about the man who attacked me?" asked Lutz. "I meant what I said. I don't know him."

"His name's O'Keefe and you met some time in 1938. The details aren't important. What is is that you had sixteen of his fellow fliers executed after a raid on Augsburg in 1942. He's also Pascoe's half-brother, but the rest of the story will have to wait. He won't trouble you, I'll see to that."

Benutti squinted across at the Catalina. It hadn't moved, but Caradoc must by now be a very worried man.

"We'd better get the RAF up here."

Pascoe, van der Heyden and Kane listened to what had been decided. As far as they were concerned very little had changed. If anything they were in a better position now. But there were a lot of questions Pascoe wanted answering. He insisted on talking to O'Keefe.

"Alone."

"Forget it," said Benutti. "I'm not having the only two guys who can fly this crate putting their heads together."

"Then you'd better send out for sandwiches because you're not going anywhere."

Benutti reminded him that Greta still had a gun on Hanna.

"You and Lutz have been putting your heads together, haven't you?" sneered Pascoe. "But I'm tired of that record. It's been played too often. You may have Hanna but you've also got a noon rendezvous with a U-boat. It's a three-hour flight assuming perfect conditions, and if we don't unstick by 09:00 we're not going to make it. I don't see the U-boat hanging around if we're not there. Apart from that," he added, "the Catalina's making a move."

Via the binoculars Caradoc had seen Mueller and Fischer buy it and had assumed, for a moment, that O'Keefe and Benutti had taken over. But when nothing else happened he had to think again.

If it came to the crunch he doubted he could fire on the Sunderland, regardless of his promise. If it showed signs of trying to take off, it stood to reason that O'Keefe, Benutti and

Greta were either dead or incapacitated. But therein lay the problem; dead was one thing, incapacitated another.

Perhaps they needed help, a show of strength. Perhaps they were expecting him to use his initiative.

He turned over the motors.

"He's switched off," said van der Heyden.

The distance between the aircraft had closed to 600 yards.

Benutti didn't know whether Caradoc would carry out his orders or not, but he couldn't afford to take chances. The sooner they were out of here the better.

"All right," he said to Pascoe, "I'll give you five minutes with O'Keefe. In the galley. The Baumanns stay with you. I'll be watching you from the for'ard hatch. If I see anything I don't like I'll start shooting. Is that clear?"

"Quite clear."

O'Keefe was semi-conscious when they reached him. Hanna was bathing the back of his head with a damp towel.

Benutti ordered Scheringer up to the flight deck and told Greta to join him by the hatch.

Pascoe knelt beside his half-brother but addressed his question to Hanna.

"How is he?"

"He's all right. He'll have a nasty headache for a couple of days, but I don't think anything's broken." She looked at Pascoe curiously. "Who is he, Jonathan?"

"A relative. It's a long story I'll tell you some day. Can you hear me?" he asked O'Keefe.

O'Keefe struggled to a sitting position. He fingered his skull and winced.

"Somebody's playing a symphony in my head, but apart from that I'm okay."

He screwed up his eyes and focused.

"Jonathan," he said formally. "It's been a long time. Just how the hell did you manage to get mixed up in something like this?"

"I'd need a week to give you the preamble. More to the point, where do you fit in and why did you attack Lutz?"

"I wouldn't know where to begin. Where is he, Lutz?"

"On the flight deck. Who's in the Catalina?"

"A good pilot."

"As good as you?"

"Not quite, but good enough."

Pascoe helped him to his feet. O'Keefe leaned against the sink until the dizziness went. For'ard he could just make out Greta and Benutti.

"I take it you're acting under duress?" he said to Pascoe.

"Mostly greed, I'm afraid. You've got the engineering business. I thought I'd try to come out of the war with a bit more than citations."

"You chose a tough way of going about it, ferrying war criminals out of the danger zone. The guard at Benghazi died, incidentally. Wilberforce was lucky, but Lutz tried to kill them both."

Pascoe was shocked.

"I didn't know that."

"I rather hoped you didn't."

"Not that it matters now," added Pascoe. "And before you start asking me to be noble, remember that it's hard to break the habit of a lifetime and that Lutz has Hanna hanging over my head. You too, for that matter."

"Tell him to go to hell. He's a murderer, Jonathan. Never mind about us. Refuse to take off and we'll put them all in the net."

"You've got two minutes," called Benutti.

"What about me?" asked Pascoe. "And van der Heyden and Kane? It's a big net. We'll be in it too."

"We can work something out."

"That's not possible, Mike. Besides, I've grown quite accustomed to the idea of being rich."

"You're not going to live to spend the money, you know that. Neither Lutz nor Benutti is interested in sharing. Sooner or later one of them is going to try a doublecross and we'll all end up in the crossfire. If you don't care about me or yourself, think about Fräulein Baumann and her father."

"You don't have to concern yourself about me," said

Baumann. "My stupidity has already caused too many problems."

Pascoe thought it over. O'Keefe was right. Before long there was going to be shooting and it would suit his purpose to have Hanna and her father clear of the firing line. Mike too. But he wasn't quitting. He, van der Heyden and Kane had come too far to back out now, penniless. Besides, there was nothing to go back for, not with a murder charge hanging over him.

"I don't think our friends would wear the idea of an unco-operative pilot," he said. "They'd start carving their initials on you and Hanna. On the other hand, if we can somehow get off their aircraft. . . ."

"We? You'd come with us?" asked O'Keefe.

"Yes," lied Pascoe. "But there's no way off. They've got the Tommy guns and we've got nothing."

"We have," murmured Hanna. "Please don't look at me, but I have a flare pistol under the sink."

"One minute," said Benutti.

"Give me the pistol," said O'Keefe.

"That's crazy, Mike." Pascoe put his hand on his half-brother's arm. "You won't get anywhere near them. They'll shoot us down like rats."

"It's the only chance we'll have. Make it quick," O'Keefe said to Hanna.

Hanna dropped the towel with which she'd been bathing O'Keefe's skull. When she bent down to pick it up, she opened the cupboard beneath the sink, took out the Very pistol and wrapped it in the cloth. She passed the whole bundle to O'Keefe.

"You'll never make it," hissed Pascoe.

"Jonathan's right," said Baumann. "We need a diversion."

Hanna looked at him, puzzled. He returned her nervous smile with a confident one of his own. What he was about to do he should have done a long time ago. It was mostly his fault they were in this predicament, his foolishness.

"Time's up," called Benutti.

Baumann moved with remarkable speed for his age. He was out of the galley and into the wardroom, running for the hatch and shouting something in German, before anyone realized what he was doing.

Then pandemonium broke loose.

Hanna screamed, *"Papa!"*

Benutti yelled, "Get back or I shoot!"

O'Keefe was the first to understand the old man's action.

"He's giving us a chance! Follow him up! Watch out for the Thompsons!"

With O'Keefe in the lead brandishing the flare pistol they raced after Baumann. Hanna came next, Pascoe at the back.

Baumann was within a few feet of Benutti when the American let rip, a short burst. O'Keefe saw what was going to happen and ducked in behind a bulkhead, pulling Hanna with him. Pascoe hit the deck.

Three of Benutti's bullets caught Baumann in the right shoulder, spinning him round like a top and slamming him to the floor. Next to Benutti Greta was transfixed.

O'Keefe didn't hesitate when the shooting stopped. He put his head round the bulkhead and fired the Very pistol.

Burning brilliantly enough to temporarily blind anyone foolish enough to look, the flare travelled half a dozen yards and hit Greta Hoegel in the face, setting fire to her skin and hair. Her screams of agony echoed and re-echoed throughout the ship.

And O'Keefe was still moving, making for the hatch, dragging Hanna with him. Benutti had his hands over his eyes, shielding them from the terrible glare and the choking smoke.

O'Keefe and Hanna might have made it if the girl hadn't wrenched herself free to run across to her father.

There was no time to grab her. There was only time to see that Jonathan was still on the floor and Benutti beginning to focus.

Then O'Keefe jumped.

When he hit the water he dived under the Sunderland's keel and came up aft and on the far side. For a split second he thought of trying to swim over to the Catalina, but he quickly decided against it. The safest place for the moment was the sea.

Aboard the flying boat Benutti was regaining control. He kicked the flare out of the hatch and squinted through the smoke. Pascoe was getting to his feet. Baumann was bleeding copiously but apparently still alive. Hanna was bending over him, keening softly.

Greta Hoegel was beyond help. Whether it was due to shock or wounds would never be established, but she was dead. She would not have wanted it any other way. Her face, still blistering and burning in places, was beyond recognition. Benutti felt a surge of nausea as he heaved her through the hatch.

He pointed the Thompson at Pascoe.

"You've got five seconds to get up to the flight deck and get us airborne before I make *Gruyère* of your girl friend."

Pascoe saw that he meant it. Christ, what a mess. But O'Keefe had got out safely by the looks of it.

"What about the Catalina?"

"Fuck the Catalina. Get moving."

Pascoe went up the ladder to the flight deck.

Benutti crossed over to the hatch, to close it. Some freakish current was carrying Greta's body away from St Helena. Poor bitch, he thought.

Still in the water and on the far side of Speery Island, O'Keefe heard the Sunderland's port and starboard outers open up. A few seconds later it started to taxi.

He looked across the bay, waiting for the Catalina to commence firing. But nothing happened.

"For the love of Christ shoot, man, shoot," he urged out loud.

But aboard the Catalina Caradoc had seen two bodies spill through the hatch, one alive and swimming, one obviously dead. Even using the binoculars he could not make out the identity of the figure clinging to the island. It might not be O'Keefe and he couldn't bring himself to punch the firing button if there was a chance that O'Keefe was still aboard the Sunderland.

One thing was quite clear, however: the Catalina was a

sitting target if he stayed where he was. He had to get out, get airborne.

O'Keefe knew nothing of Caradoc's reasoning. Almost weeping with frustration all he saw was the Sunderland taking off like a gigantic bird, followed seconds later by the Catalina.

Then he was alone.

Twenty-three

Once the Sunderland was airborne and he saw that the Catalina was not giving chase, Benutti held a hasty conference on the flight deck. He had no doubts about Caradoc's strategy. It would be once round the island then down to pick up his friend.

There were no prizes for guessing what O'Keefe would do, either. The Catalina might be outgunned, but O'Keefe was fighting mad.

To be on the safe side the order was given to man the Sunderland's Brownings.

Protesting loudly, Scheringer was dispatched to the rear, to act as tail-end charlie. Lutz took the nose berth. Van der Heyden would have to act as co-pilot and engineer in order to free Kane for the starboard midships gun platform. Benutti took the port midships position, from where he could also keep an eye on Hanna, who was kneeling beside her father.

Helped by Kane, she had half dragged, half carried him to the aftermost sleeping compartment and there strapped him to a bunk. Using Kane's bowie knife she had cut away his shirt and patched up his shoulder wounds as best she could. She feared one of the bullets had hit a lung. They were all still inside and he was in a bad way, drifting between consciousness and coma.

Benutti had made it quite clear that permitting Hanna to

stay with her father was a privilege that would only hold good as long as she behaved herself. One false move and he would finish the job he had started. He also warned Pascoe to keep his mind where it belonged, on making the noon rendezvous with the U-boat. If they didn't keep it he could kiss goodbye to Hanna.

Less than five minutes after unsticking, with the Sunderland now the size of a seagull but its course plotted, Caradoc brought the Catalina in low from the west, keeping well clear of Man and Horse Cliffs. His take-off had been far from copybook and his landing wasn't a great deal better, but he managed to achieve touchdown without breaking anything.

Once on the water he taxied across to Speery Island, where he was relieved to see that the figure clinging to the rock was O'Keefe.

He could not risk bringing the flying boat closer than 100 feet because of the wingspan, and O'Keefe had to swim for it. When he scrambled aboard through the hatch he was in a towering rage.

"I thought I told you to open fire on the Sunderland if it looked like taking off," he spluttered.

Caradoc knew he was in for it.

"Well, I wasn't sure. . . ."

O'Keefe interrupted him.

"You're not paid to be unsure, you're paid to carry out orders. You could have crippled the bastard where it lay, instead of which we've now got to chase it. It's armed like a Panzer division and we've got a slingshot. Now that may appeal to you but it doesn't do much for me."

"Look, I'm sorry. When it came down to it I just couldn't do it."

It took an effort but O'Keefe brought his anger under control. Caradoc's only crime, after all, was a reluctance to accidentally kill a friend. Besides, they were wasting precious minutes.

"All right," he said, "the damage is done now. Dig me out some dry clothes and I'll explain what went on over there."

While changing, O'Keefe told Caradoc how Benutti and

264

Greta had turned the tables on him and how he had killed the girl with a Very pistol. The recollection made him shudder.

Fully dressed, he skipped the pre-flight check and taxied into the wind. Caradoc would look after the navigation.

Climbing to 8,000 feet and heading south-west, he continued to brief Caradoc.

"Unless anything else happened after I jumped overboard there are six able-bodied men in the Sunderland, plus a girl. Benutti shot and killed two of Lutz's people and I think the old man bought it while I was making my break. But six is all they need. We can assume that Jonathan's at the helm and probably van der Heyden in the right-hand seat, doubling as flight engineer. That leaves Lutz, Benutti, Kane and the fourth German to man the gun platforms." He grimaced. "It's not going to be easy. The Luftwaffe didn't nickname the Sunderland the Flying Porcupine for nothing. Even without the pilot's forward-firing guns, it's still got enough spikes to take care of a Ju 88, let alone us."

O'Keefe sensed Caradoc's uneasiness and glanced across at him.

"Forget it, Jim. It's done and that's an end to it. And before you ask, yes, I did see Lutz and got whacked over the head for my pains. I also spoke to Jonathan. He's in this because he wants to be, by the way."

"What's he likely to do when we catch up?"

"I don't know. Benutti will have a gun to Hanna Baumann's head among other things, so he'll probably fight. It's either them or us. He has no other options."

"And what about you?" asked Caradoc. "What are your options?"

"Hobson's. If I can't force the Sunderland down I'll have to shoot it down. Assuming I'm capable."

"With Jonathan aboard?"

"With Lutz and Benutti also aboard. What else can I do—let them go? We began this because Lutz killed sixteen of our friends. That hasn't changed. Benutti doublecrossed us so that puts him on the list. But much more than that the loot they've got aboard is for Lutz and his SS cronies to begin the Fourth Reich, or at least allow the surviving members of the

Third Reich to live out their remaining days in comfort. I can't let that happen, Jonathan or no Jonathan."

"Perhaps you won't have to. What's wrong with just shadowing the Sunderland and calling up assistance from a surface vessel when it makes rendezvous with the U-boat?"

"It won't work, Jim. There'd have to be a ship within a couple of hours' steaming distance and I don't reckon we're going to be that lucky. The minute Lutz and Benutti realized we were not going to attack, they'd carry on transferring the bullion and refuelling. Besides, this is my buck and I'm not going to pass it."

O'Keefe took the Catalina up to 10,000 feet, all the while scanning the sky up front and below for some sign of the Sunderland.

"Sooner or later," he said grimly, "we're going to have to get close enough to mix it and pull the trigger. Those are our options, short of calling the whole thing off and making for Ascension."

Caradoc took in the implications of the words "we" and "our". In this modified Catalina the pilot controlled only one forward-firing gun. The others were mounted in the midships blisters, port and starboard.

"You'd better give me some idea of what your tactics are going to be," he said.

O'Keefe nodded his appreciation. Caradoc had a wife and two children waiting for him in England.

"In the first place, a cakewalk it's not going to be, because Jonathan's an excellent pilot," he said. "If I were in his shoes I'd take the Sunderland down to a couple of hundred feet. The only place it's unprotected is its belly and he'll want to make sure nothing gets underneath him. I don't want to fly at him head-on because in those sort of attacks it's usually the pilot who buys it, and I don't want to kill him if I can avoid it. I want to cripple his aircraft, yes, force him down—but not kill him. Neither is a beam attack a bright idea. We're faced with one of the heavy .50s going in and the other one coming out, and flying straight and level to give you a crack from one of the blisters is just a waste of ammo."

O'Keefe peered through the canopy. If he was right in his

estimation that Jonathan would sacrifice height for safety, his airspeed would be down to less than that of the Catalina. He should have a sighting within a few minutes.

"Which leaves a tail-end attack the only alternative," he went on. "If we can knock out the rear gunner on our first pass, we have a chance. We also have two other advantages which have only just occurred to me.

"Number one is that a Sunderland normally carries a crew of thirteen, any of whom can handle a gun in an emergency. But if my arithmetic's correct, they're utilizing all their manpower right now. If we kill a gunner, they can't replace him.

"Number two. With the exception of Jonathan, who has to fly the aircraft, only van der Heyden and Kane have any experience of aerial warfare. So the odds against us aren't as black as they might appear at first sight."

He grinned across at Caradoc with a cheerfulness he was far from feeling.

"You know, for the first time in a long while I've got an idea this might turn out all right."

"We'll soon find out," said Caradoc sombrely, pointing through the canopy.

About two miles ahead, flying at less than 300 feet, the huge white shape of the Sunderland stood out in stark contrast against the dark ocean.

"Get back to the blisters, Jim. The sun's behind us. We've got nothing to lose by trying to jump them."

O'Keefe pushed forward the yoke and put the Catalina into a steep dive.

In the rear gunner's berth Scheringer saw it first.

"Flugboot!" he shouted over the intercom.

Without waiting for orders he opened fire.

On the flight deck Pascoe held the Sunderland steady. He had neither the height nor the aircraft for stunt flying, and in any case his function from now on was to give his gunners a stable platform from which to shoot.

He knew instinctively that his half-brother was at the

controls of the Catalina, and smiled wryly. It was a bizarre state of affairs, but one way or another they'd soon find out who was the superior flier.

O'Keefe kept coming. His experience told him that the rear gunner was an amateur. Considering the range, the .303 ammo could do him little harm.

At 1,000 yards his thumb reached for the firing button. He would get just one chance at the tail-end charlie and he didn't want to waste it.

The Sunderland was poodling along at 160 mph; the Catalina narrowing the gap some 10 mph faster. It gave O'Keefe an odd feeling, attacking an RAF aircraft.

"I'm going to overshoot the bank to starboard as soon as I've blasted the bastard at the back," he announced calmly to Caradoc over the intercom. "See if you can do something to curb the enthusiasm of the starboard midships gunner on the way through."

Thirty feet behind the flight deck, Caradoc gave O'Keefe a Roger and moved across to the port blister.

Even though Scheringer was no air gunner and the .303 ammo no match for the Catalina's heavier .50s, at 800 yards and closing at 82 yards per second, O'Keefe concluded he was near enough and pressed the firing button.

Lumps of fabric flew off the tailplane. He just had time to see the Perspex canopy covering the rear gun turret shatter before dragging back on the control column and stamping on the right rudder.

Below him the Sunderland seemed terrifyingly close and massive, and then it disappeared from his eyeline. As it did so Caradoc opened up with the port .50.

Aboard the Sunderland everyone heard Scheringer's terrible screams as he died, but these were soon overlaid by the chatter of the starboard Browning as Kane returned Caradoc's fire.

But O'Keefe was already into a long sweeping climb to starboard, and he did not straighten up until he was again behind the Sunderland, where suddenly everyone was talking at once.

In the nose Lutz was demanding to know what had happened. Pascoe told him to shut up and keep his eyes peeled.

On the port gun platform Benutti had seen nothing more than a brief shadow of the Catalina as it swept overhead. But the catwalk was filled with the smell of cordite and the clatter of spent shells, and he heard several of Caradoc's bullets strike the upper fuselage.

"Did you hit him?" he called over his shoulder.

"Close but no cigar," said Kane.

Pascoe had to call for order.

"I want the intercom kept clear for essential traffic."

In spite of the grotesqueness of their predicament, second nature took over and he asked for a damage and casualty report. Away from the flight deck only Kane had enough experience of air warfare to be able to answer.

"We're okay midships, but I reckon the rear gunner bought it. Do you want me to go back and check?"

"Hold it a minute, Carver," said Pascoe. To van der Heyden he added, "If Scheringer's had it and O'Keefe does that again, he can cut us to ribbons."

The intercom was still active and Benutti came on the air.

"This is some hillbilly family you two belong to. What do you do when you really get mad at each other?"

"Shut up, Yank," said Pascoe. "Just see to your gun."

He switched off the intercom.

Van der Heyden asked, "Can't we outrun him?"

"We've got a date with a U-boat, remember. Anyway, not without getting some height."

"Then get some."

"Not possible. I've got a rate of climb of 1,200 feet per minute and it would mean exposing my belly. That's Mike O'Keefe out there. He'd blast us out of the sky in thirty seconds."

Van der Heyden looked at him curiously.

"That sounds like a citation."

"Maybe."

Pascoe thumbed the intercom.

"Carver, you'd better take over the rear gun. I can't have

my tail exposed. Benutti, you'll have to move between the port and starboard guns."

"I'll also walk on the water for fifty cents. You've got a spare man on the flight deck."

"And what if something happens to me? We're 300 feet above the Atlantic. If I get hit and there's no one to take over within seconds, you'll be doing a bloody sight more than walk on the water. You'll be gargling it. Get going, Carver. Let me know when you're there."

Two miles aft O'Keefe studied the Sunderland's flying attitude. He hadn't hit anything vital, that was for sure, if you didn't count the rear gunner.

"I'm going to try something else," he called through to Caradoc. "I'm going to come in from the back as before, but pull away to starboard at 1,000 yards. That'll give you a chance to have a crack at the tail. I think I got the rear gunner on the first pass, but they may have replaced him. Okay?"

"Roger," answered Caradoc.

On his way through to the rear turret Kane passed Hanna. She looked up at him unseeingly. It was pretty obvious the old man was dying.

Scheringer was a mess, blood and bone tissue everywhere. He had been hit in the upper torso and neck. The guns appeared undamaged. To make sure, Kane tested them. They worked.

He dragged Scheringer out of the turret and wiped his hands on the German's clothes. Glancing up through the shattered Perspex he saw the Catalina circling for height.

The intercom was also in one piece.

"Okay, Jonathan, I'm back here," said Kane. "The German got the chop, but the guns are fine. By the look of it the Catalina's going to try the same trick again. Maybe he thinks we don't have a tail-end charlie any more."

"Don't you believe it," said Pascoe. "It's just that he's trying to figure out whether I've made the replacement from port or starboard midships. Any indication which way he's likely to break off after the pass?"

"Not a thing."

"Then I'll make a guess and say he'll do the opposite of his first pass and break to port. Benutti, you listen to this too. Kane will count off the range and let me know when the Catalina's at 800 yards. I'll then make a shallow bank to port. If he goes that way you should have a clear shot at him. Got it?"

"I hear you," said Benutti.

"Did you get all that, Carver?"

"Loud and clear."

"Then count it off for me."

From the co-pilot's seat van der Heyden said, "You seem to be taking this all very calmly, planning O'Keefe's death."

"I'll tell you something, Peter. In the first place I don't have any choice. In the second place, with an inexperienced crew it's going to take a lot more than planning to put O'Keefe down. About the best I can hope for is to damage his aircraft so badly that he'll have to make for Ascension."

"Here he comes," called Kane.

The moment Kane opened up, when the Catalina was 1,200 yards off, O'Keefe knew he was dealing with a different quality of gunner on this occasion and that to continue the attack would be suicidal. The tail-end charlie hardly had to take aim; all he needed to do was wait for the Catalina to run into his shells.

"This guy's a bit too good, Jim," he said urgently. "I'm disengaging right now."

He started to give the Catalina some left rudder. As he did so he saw the Sunderland's starboard wing-tip go up as Pascoe put the flying boat into a left-hand bank.

He was not to know it, but as he was speaking to Caradoc Kane had shouted, *"800 yards, Jonathan!"*

O'Keefe had survived the fighter war because of uncannily fast reactions. They didn't fail him now. In the time it takes to blink he had made several calculations. The first was that the Sunderland's starboard wing was now some 350 feet above the Atlantic. Unconsciously, Jonathan had taken the flying boat up a few feet prior to his left-hand manoeuvre, to give him a good safety margin between the ocean and his port wing. The second was remembering that the Catalina's tailfin was only twenty feet high.

There was a bloody big gap separating ocean and Sunderland, and he intended using it.

"I'm going underneath, Jim. Hammer the fuselage as we go through."

Carver Kane couldn't believe his eyes. One minute the Catalina was flying straight at him; the next it had lost 100 feet and was flying below his guns.

The last words he uttered were, "The bastard's gone mad. . . ."

When O'Keefe made his decision only eight seconds separated the two aircraft. Caradoc was already in the port blister, and as the monstrous shape of the flying boat filled his sights, he thumbed the firing button and held it down, raking Pascoe's aeroplane from end to end.

At a range of only a few score feet, he couldn't miss.

Thirty-six H.E. shells hit the Sunderland. Thirty-one of them passed harmlessly through both lower and upper skins of the fuselage. Of the remaining five, one slammed into the galley water-tank, smashing it, one ricochetted off the starboard gun mounting and finally spent itself within inches of Benutti's head, and one penetrated as far as the flight deck, exploding against the navigation table. The other two killed Carver Kane, entering his lungs at an angle of 45 degrees. Long before his heart stopped beating, the Catalina was under the Sunderland and breaking off to starboard, gaining height and distance every second.

In the nose turret Lutz saw it go. But because Pascoe was already committed to the port manoeuvre, the German had no chance to bring his guns to bear.

Pascoe and van der Heyden also saw the Catalina disappear. But it seemed to happen simultaneously with Kane's shout of "The bastard's gone mad. . . ." —and the navigation table being hit.

All in all the attack was over in ten seconds.

"I don't believe it," said van der Heyden, then Pascoe was calling on him for help in dragging back the yoke.

"Damage report," demanded Pascoe when he had the aircraft under control. "Carver, can you hear me?"

Benutti came on the intercom, his voice unsteady.

"I think the rear gunner bought the farm. It's like a big dog and pony show back there, a hell of a lot of smoke."

"Check it," snapped Pascoe. "On second thoughts, stay where you are. It'll have to be you, Peter," he said to van der Heyden. "Benutti won't know what to look for."

"Can you handle the ship?"

"Yes—but make it quick. He's chopping us to bits up here. Check on Hanna at the same time."

Van der Heyden hesitated.

"Maybe we should ditch. If Kane's dead that only leaves Lutz and Benutti on the guns."

"Don't be a bloody fool, Peter. Lutz killed the guard in Benghazi, remember? They won't even grant us the privilege of a firing squad. We'll all hang if they take us alive, the Baumanns too, maybe. Hurry it up now."

Alone on the flight deck Pascoe went over his instruments. Everything seemed okay.

He reset his course, though how long he could hold it he had no idea.

Fuel was no problem. The whole action up to now had taken less than five minutes. But they couldn't hold off O'Keefe until they reached the rendezvous. They had to put him down somehow.

Christ, flying *under* the Sunderland at damn near zero feet. And in a Catalina. Who the hell would have thought it conceivable?"

"Flying Officer Pascoe . . . ?" It was Lutz's voice.

"Yes? What the hell's your problem?"

"I feel that my usefulness at this end is nil. If I understand the situation correctly we've lost Kane and Scheringer. It might be better if I manned one of the midships guns."

Pascoe had to hand it to him, the bastard was still as cool as ice.

"You stay where you are. It would take O'Keefe about five seconds to see we didn't have a nose gunner and then he'd attack head-on."

"And risk killing you—in view of your relationship?"

"And risk killing me—in spite of our relationship. He has an old-fashioned sense of what's right and what's wrong, something you wouldn't understand. He'd rather kill me himself than see me dangle at the end of a rope. You shouldn't have murdered the guard, Lutz. Perhaps then we'd have stood a chance."

"Perhaps. I trust you are watching the other aircraft, incidentally."

"I am."

The Catalina had completed its turn and was standing several thousand yards off to starboard, presumably checking the Sunderland for damage.

Twenty-four

They were relatively unscathed. Some of the rear gunner's shells had torn the fabric on the port wing, but that was no problem.

"I think you shook them up a bit, Jim," said O'Keefe, "but that's one hell of a tough aeroplane."

"You bloody well shook me up a bit too," retorted Caradoc. "It went over me like a bat. This isn't a fighter, you know. I swear to God the main spar bent when you came out from under."

"We're still in one piece."

"For the moment. What's the next move?"

"I dunno. You must have clobbered something, but she's still flying."

"I hope you're not planning the same stunt again."

"No. Jonathan's brought her down to a couple of hundred feet. I don't think I fancy that. There's no one on the starboard gun, though. At least, I didn't see any flashes when I peeled off. I wonder which berths Lutz and Benutti are occupying?"

"Why don't you call them up and find out?"

"If I had any idea which frequency their radio's tuned to, I would. I'd like to know what's going on in Jonathan's head. Surely to Christ he can see it's hopeless."

"You said it yourself, his options are limited. All he can do is see it through to the end. Even if we knock out all his gunners, he can't surrender. It's him or us, there's no alternative."

"I could still let him go. I don't mean allow him to make the rendezvous because that would mean Lutz and Benutti getting off too. But if I can put him in the Atlantic and he survives the impact, I could maybe fly him somewhere. He's not a murderer, Jim. Lutz did the killing."

At the other end of the intercom Caradoc stared gloomily out of the port blister at the scudding waves.

"Jim?"

"You're making up the rules as you go along, Mike. Some of Lutz's cronies will be saying the same thing when the tribunals start, that they killed no one, it was somebody else."

O'Keefe sighed.

"Aye, you're right."

Scheringer was dead, Kane was dead. The rear gun turret would need the services of an armourer before it functioned again, and the intercom was out of action. But there was no damage to the rudder or the elevators as far as van der Heyden could tell.

On his way back to the flight deck he stopped by Hanna. She had cut away her father's bandages in order to repad the wounds, but it was obvious he had only moments left.

The girl was crying. She looked up at van der Heyden, silently imploring him to help. He wanted to say something, but it was too late for all that.

She felt her father's grip tighten on her hand. His eyelids flickered and she thought he was trying to say something.

"Yes, Papa."

She bent closer.

It sounded like "Hanna" but it could have been "Helga", her mother's name. It was, in any case, all he said before he died.

Surprisingly, the tears went then. She had cried herself arid. She unlocked his fingers from her hand and brushed the hair from her face. As she did so her eyes alighted on Kane's knife, lying on the bunk. She picked it up.

The American had shot and killed her father, a helpless old man.

Very slowly she got to her feet.

Taking the right-hand seat and getting the feel of the flying boat's attitude once again, van der Heyden made his damage and casualty report to Pascoe, one eye nervously on the Catalina. It had sheered off to starboard and was gaining altitude. Either O'Keefe was going home or he was preparing for another attack.

"Kane's dead and the rear turret's on the fritz. Other than that, we can still fly."

"How's Hanna?"

"She's unhurt. Her father's dying, though."

"Christ."

"He can perform miracles; we can't. You'd better start coming up with a few answers, Jonathan. Any more passes like that last one and we've had it."

"Answers, the man asks for," muttered Pascoe. "We're low on fuel, we've got a noon rendezvous with a U-boat, and our rear guns are out of action. In an aircraft designed to carry thirteen men we've got four, two of whom are needed on the flight deck. And to top it off, in case you need icing, we have one of World War II's fighter aces prowling off the starboard beam. I tell you something, Peter. . . ."

Pascoe stopped in mid-breath.

"That's it, for Christ's sake."

"That's what?"

"Did you ever read any military history?" Van der Heyden

said he had not. "Well, it was Marshal Foch who said something like: My centre is giving way, my right is in retreat. Situation excellent, I shall attack."

"You're out of your mind," said van der Heyden.

"Not a bit of it. We're sitting here like an Aunt Sally letting him shoot lumps off us, choose his time and quarter. It's the only thing to do."

He flicked on the intercom.

"Benutti, Lutz—listen to me. If you take a look over to starboard you'll see the Catalina gaining height. It's not doing that because my half-brother likes sunshine. He's going to have another go at us and we may not survive this one. So I'm going up there to join him. He's not flying a Spitfire so he's got the same manoeuvrability problems we have."

Over the intercom Lutz announced that he thoroughly approved. Benutti was not so sure.

"He'll fly under us again."

"No he won't. I'm going to do something that makes sure he doesn't. O'Keefe isn't an idiot. He knows I'm short of gunners and you can bet your life he made a mental note that he wasn't fired on from the starboard beam on his last pass. I'm therefore going to fake putting him on the port quarter. He'll assume I'm doing this to give my nose and port midships gunners a crack at him, and with any luck he'll attack from starboard where he thinks he's safe. Except he won't be because you, Benutti, will have changed gun platforms. Have you got that, Benutti? I want you to cross the catwalk to the starboard gun but hold your fire until he's on top of us. This is about your last chance. If you don't get him he'll get us. If you want to go somewhere you can spend that bullion, you'd better make sure you're on target. Do I hear a Roger to that?"

"You hear a Roger," said Benutti, who had not seen, and still did not see, Hanna Baumann at the foot of the ladder which led up to the midships gun positions.

Caradoc pressed the intercom switch.

"They're up to something, Mike."

O'Keefe had already spotted the Sunderland climbing. It

was all Jonathan had left, of course, to come up and meet him.

He glanced at his altimeter, 6,000 feet. The Sunderland's ceiling was close on 18,000 and the Catalina's less than 15,000. Not that Jonathan would play it that way, expose his underbelly. It was to be horns to horns combat. Well, so be it.

"He's trying to put us on his port beam," called Caradoc.

"It figures," said O'Keefe. "Their starboard gun's unmanned."

"What do you want me to do?"

"Are you still in the port blister?"

"Yes."

"Then change sides. We'll go in at his starboard beam to give me a crack with the nose gun. Then I'll peel off to port and let you have a go."

"Roger."

"He's falling for it," said van der Heyden. "Easy now, don't make it too obvious."

"Let me do the driving, Peter. Can you see him, Benutti?"

"I've got him."

"He's still got 3,000 feet on us. When you see his nose go down, that's when it'll all start happening."

"Roger," said Benutti, not taking his eyes off the Catalina.

So hard was he concentrating that he did not see that Hanna had gained the catwalk, Kane's bowie knife in her right hand.

O'Keefe leaned on the yoke, doing mental arithmetic calculations as he did so.

Distance from the Sunderland, two and a bit miles. Height advantage, 2,500 feet. Airspeed, 170 mph. Thirty seconds to contact.

The airframe began to shudder as the speed indicator touched 175.

Twenty seconds to contact. O'Keefe's thumb moved to cover the firing button.

Fifteen seconds. . . .

At 1,000 yards, a heartbeat before the Sunderland's starboard gun opened up, O'Keefe saw hunched on the gun platform the unmistakable silhouette of a man and realized that Jonathan had outfoxed him.

"Shit," he muttered, and threw the Catalina into a sideslip.

But he was too late. Even as the aircraft yawed to port there was a terrible rattle and a series of explosions as a dozen or more .50 calibre HE shells thudded into the fuselage. O'Keefe was unhurt, but in his nostrils was the smell of oil and gasoline.

"We're hit, Jim. . . ."

Then suddenly, inexplicably, the Sunderland stopped firing. *"I hit him!"* yelled Benutti, *"I got the bastard!"*

He became aware of Hanna standing behind him on the catwalk and had enough time to turn and register fear before she buried Kane's knife in his chest.

Hanna Baumann was not a strong girl, but murderous loathing gave her strength. When Benutti fell, blood spouting from his wound, she withdrew the knife and struck him time and time again, not stopping until she was sure he was dead.

Then she threw the knife on to the catwalk and made her way towards the flight deck.

"How bad is it?" called Caradoc.

O'Keefe had stabilized the Catalina at 2,000 feet and was busily checking the instruments. Oil pressure was down and he was losing gas.

"I think the starboard fuel pump's had it and the wireless isn't looking too healthy."

"How long have we got?"

"Hard to tell until I can figure out how fast we're losing fuel. It could be ten minutes, it could be an hour."

"But we won't make Ascension."

"Right."

"What are you going to do?"

There was really no choice, thought O'Keefe. "I'm going after the Sunderland."

"Where the hell are you, Benutti?" Pascoe was saying.

"He's dead."

Pascoe swivelled in his seat. Neither he nor van der Heyden had heard Hanna climb the ladder to the flight deck, but there she stood, her eyes wild, her hands and clothes covered in blood. A jury would have found her not totally sane if asked to give a verdict.

"I killed him," she said.

"You bloody fool," snarled van der Heyden.

"Shut up, Peter, and give me a situation report on the Catalina. Are you all right?" Pascoe asked Hanna.

She was shaking and seemed on the verge of hysteria, but she managed to answer, "Yes."

"Sit over there." Pascoe pointed to the navigator's berth. "Do you understand me? Sit there and don't move."

She nodded and sat down, resting on her elbows, her head on her bloodied hands.

"He's coming at us again," said Lutz over the intercom.

"Christ," swore van der Heyden, "doesn't he ever give up."

Trailing smoke and gasoline vapour, the Catalina had climbed to 5,000 feet, putting it at the same altitude as the Sunderland. It was about three miles directly ahead and turning.

"He's going to come at us straight on," said van der Heyden.

"Did you hear that, Lutz," demanded Pascoe.

The German's voice was still incredibly calm.

"I heard it. He's doing precisely what we want, is he not? Mine are the only guns remaining and he's flying into them."

Van der Heyden had a frightening thought.

"Maybe he means to ram us. If he's going down, maybe he means to take us with him. Can we get some height?"

"Too late."

The two aircraft were approaching each other at a combined speed in excess of 300 mph. The flying time that separated them was thirty-five seconds.

At the controls of the Catalina O'Keefe reckoned this to be his last chance. If he failed to make the kill on his first pass, that was the end of it. He was now losing fuel at an alarming rate and Jonathan would not be slow to spot it. Once he did, he would take the Sunderland up to its ceiling, out of reach of the crippled Catalina.

But there was no way he was going to down the other flying boat with a beam or belly attack. It had just been proved that Short Brothers had built the Mark V to last. And if he couldn't destroy the aircraft, he had to destroy the pilot.

Ten seconds passed. The gap closed to 4,000 yards.

Hunched over his guns, Lutz was content to wait. There was more at stake here than his own life. There was everything the Third Reich had stood for.

Twenty seconds. . . .

"The bugger *is* going to ram us!" shouted van der Heyden. *"Break off, Jonathan, break off!"*

Twenty-five seconds. . . . 1500 yards. . . .

Van der Heyden was sweating.

"You'll kill us, Pascoe! *Break off!"*

"It's a trick, you stupid bastard! He wants me to destabilize the nose gunner!"

But van der Heyden was not listening. Before Pascoe could stop him, the South African had pushed the yoke on his side of the dual controls to port and stamped on the left rudder.

The huge aircraft slid to the left just as Lutz opened fire at 900 yards.

O'Keefe saw the nose gunner's ammunition wasting itself on his starboard quarter as he thumbed his own firing mechanism and held the burst for three seconds, atomizing the nose turret and the Perspex canopy covering the Sunderland's flight deck. Then with the gigantic shape of the other flying boat filling his vision, he dragged back on the Catalina's control column and felt a dull thump as the underside of his fuselage scraped the top of the Sunderland.

But he was still flying and he'd hit his target.

"She's going down!" shouted Caradoc.

* * *

Aboard the Sunderland there was the smell of death.

Pascoe knew he had been hit. There was blood on his tunic and in his mouth, and a terrible pain in his chest. Lungs, he thought laconically.

Glancing to his right he saw that van der Heyden was dead, very little left of his face. Behind him Hanna appeared unhurt, although she was sobbing with terror.

He tried calling Lutz, but there was no response. He had no way of knowing that the former SS colonel was also dead, killed a fraction of a second before van der Heyden when two of the Catalina's .50 shells removed most of his head.

Pascoe estimated that he had a minute or two of life remaining at most. Already his eyes were misting. There was little wrong, it seemed, with the aircraft, but he was in no condition to fly it anywhere.

Except maybe down.

The Catalina was crippled, he knew that. It had been leaking fuel a few seconds before his half-brother had opened fire. O'Keefe's only chance for survival—and Hanna's too— was to board the Sunderland. He hoped his half-brother would have the wit to see that.

"He's flying her down," said O'Keefe.

Several thousand feet below, Pascoe had put the Sunderland into a shallow dive. In no respect was the flying boat out of control.

O'Keefe tapped the fuel gauge. He had, perhaps, thirty minutes left before he crash-landed into the Atlantic. Chances of rescue were remote and Christ only knew what effect that bump with the Sunderland had had on the underside of the fuselage. Even if he could put the Catalina on the ocean, it might sink within minutes.

He'd won the battle and lost the war.

Unless. . . .

He understood then. Jonathan had seen the vapour trail from the leaking fuel tanks and was handing him a survival kit, always assuming the Sunderland could do the opposite of what it was now doing, and take off.

He pressed the intercom switch.

"Jim, I've got a lousy job for you. . . ."

The ocean was rushing up to meet him. Pascoe could feel the blood pumping out of his chest wounds

He could hardly see, certainly not enough to read the altimeter or the airspeed indicator. It would have to be luck and remembered skill.

300 feet.

Jesus, it was a bloody great brute of a thing, the Sunderland. He should have stuck to Lancasters.

150 feet.

Come on, you great fucking pig, he snarled silently at the flying boat. You must have half a million miles on the clock. Let's see if you've learned anything.

100 feet. . . .

Pascoe coughed blood. He could see nothing now, only feel, use his instincts.

Come on, come on. . . .

80 feet. . . . 50 feet. . . .

Spray splashing on his face through the ruptured canopy. He must be there. . . . Must be. . . .

As the Sunderland touched down, Pascoe's last act before dying was to switch off the engines.

Behind him, Hanna crouched against the bulkhead, sobbing quietly.

Caradoc stood in the open hatch of the Catalina, parachute harness on, looking down at the forbidding Atlantic 1,500 feet below. He remembered the last time he bailed out—over the North Sea—and how O'Keefe had waited with his wife and two children until word came that he was safe. He remembered also his vow that he would never jump again.

But there was nothing else for it. Disabled as it was, only O'Keefe could fly the Catalina. If he, Caradoc, found the Sunderland airworthy, he would fire a green flare; if not, a red flare. If a red, O'Keefe would use his remaining fuel hunting for a ship. But the likelihood of finding one was remote. The Atlantic was a big place and O'Keefe would die in it.

He waggled the Catalina's wings, the signal to jump. Caradoc took a deep breath and went.

The parachute open, O'Keefe saw Caradoc land in the ocean a couple of hundred feet from the Sunderland. The NCO slipped the quick-release and started swimming.

O'Keefe hoped it wouldn't take all day to check the Sunderland out. He was already having trouble maintaining an altitude of 1,500 feet. The starboard gunner had evidently damaged more than the wireless and the fuel pump.

Five minutes passed. Then ten. O'Keefe refused to think about Jonathan, whether or not he was still alive. All that, recriminations of whatever, would come later. He had the rest of his life to debate moral issues.

At the end of fifteen minutes he saw a figure appear in the for'ard hatch. A moment later a flare fireball appeared off the Catalina's starboard quarter.

It was green.

There was no need for O'Keefe to jump. Flying exclusively on the port engine, he put the Catalina down within easy swimming distance of the Sunderland and scrambled overboard as water began filling the cockpit.

Epilogue

There were ampoules of morphine in the medicine chest. It wasn't the best sedative in the world, but Hanna Baumann needed sleep. They put her on a bunk in the wardroom and strapped her in. Possibly she would have to stand trial, but O'Keefe doubted it.

The Sunderland was flyable, but there were two problems, fuel and weight. O'Keefe estimated their position as 800 miles due south of Ascension, and that was roughly the gas the flying boat had in her tanks.

He wasted no time in deciding that the dead should be buried at sea. All got the same treatment, Lutz and Benutti included. The canopies of the drogue 'chutes and the personnel 'chutes provided the shrouds, and gold bars the sinkers. It was somehow a fitting epitaph.

Neither did the question of excess weight cause him more than a moment's hesitation. The bullion had already cost enough lives, and it was tossed overboard. The diamonds would be returned to their rightful owners somewhere along the line.

He was not in the least surprised when the Sunderland responded to his inexpert touch by taking off at the first time of asking. As the Luftwaffe had found out to its cost, the Flying Porcupine was a tough aeroplane.

Five hours later on Ascension Island, the afternoon coffee of Captain Anderson, USAAF, was interrupted when a very youthful enlisted man rushed into his office.

"Captain, a seaplane the size of an apartment block has just come in, carrying British markings. There's nothing in the book to say we're expecting anything like that."

"Probably a stray," said Anderson.

Bestsellers from Popular Library

DENVER
by John Dunning   04711 $3.50

A novel about newspaper reporter Tom Hastings and an organized group of faceless killers in the highest levels of Colorado government.

THE HARMONETICS INVESTIGATION
by Gladys M. Heldman   04720 $3.50

A novel about a strange cult, its charismatic leader, and a team of investigative reporters.

CALAIS
by Kathleen Winsor   04703 $3.95

A novel about the fabulous screen star Arlette, by the author of *Forever Amber*.

FALLING ANGEL
by William Hjortsberg   04698 $3.25

"A terrific book. I've never read anything like it."—*Stephen King*

NEW FROM POPULAR LIBRARY